LARONYA TEAGUE

Social Work: The

Carolyn Black

Chronicles

II

I will lift up mine eyes to the hills from whence cometh my help, ALL MY HELP

COMETH FROM THE LORD!

Copyright © 2016 by Iteaguepublishing
Laronya Teague

ISBN-13: 978-0692766071

Editors: Pamela McNeil
Crystal Harris
Cover Photo taken by: RA Jeffers Photography

Trust in the Lord with All thine heart. Lean not to thine own understanding. In all ways acknowledge Him and He shall direct thy path.

-Proverbs 3:5-6

Mine eyes are ever towards the Lord, for He shall pluck my feet out of the net.

Psalm 25:15

Then shalt thou call and the Lord shall answer. Thou shalt cry and He shall say, HERE I AM.

Isaiah 58:9

"If you believe in God, one thing's for sho', if you ain't aim to high, THEN YOU AIM TO LOW!"

-J Cole

Dedication

This dedication is near and dear to my heart for it is for those who have etched a trinket of themselves into the tapestry known as Laronya Teague.
I would like to dedicate this book to:

Gone but never forgotten...

Blanch and James Teague

Alfred Teague

Laney Teague

Arvin Boston

Rick Little

Vic Mayberry

Aunt Ann

Kent Flowers

Willie Mae Perry

Jenny Haney

And

Raleigh Bryant

To those still here:

My Parents: Janice and Steve Gilliam, I LOVE YOU!!!!
The Best Family on the planet: The Teague/Bostons, The Gilliams, The Clodfelters and my Uncle Roger
My two best friends: Chance and Shina

Last but NOT Least:

My beloved Alma Matas

Winston-Salem State University

And

NC A&T State University

Thanks for all the love and life lessons...

Special shout out to everyone who purchased Social Work: The Carolyn Black Chronicles Part 1. **THANKS FOR YOUR SUPPORT**!!!!!

Scenario: The Cycle

What happened to the Man?
His mind full of flashbacks, His life full of setbacks
So what occurred back then?
A father who didn't bother, mama screwing Tom, Deena
and Roger
And Roger's creeping in
Late nights in the bedroom that the Son was sleeping in
And mom's not listening
She ignores all the signs and the tears her Son's
crying
Inside the man's dying
He's confused and abused, doing His best to try 'N
To make sense of Himself
Don't know which way to go
Is this right or is this wrong
And the girls intimidate
Cuz His secrets paralyze Him and He's clothed all in
his shame
And He's filled with such self-hate
Doesn't want to, feels He has to, find comfort in His
pain
So He lets the pain feel good
But He hides it inside Him, does what He thinks He
should
Now a mask is on His face
A woman stands beside Him, a man is behind Him
Now He's on the down low
With a gun to His head; Scenario
This is my story
This is my song
This is my story
This is my song

What happened to the Girl?
Mama viewed Her as a homie and not her little girl
Mama kept Her dad away
He loved Her and not mama; mama's pride outweighed the gain
Mama prepared Her for the streets
In love with the fast cars and the shiny gold on their teeth
And as She began to grow
Mama was accusing cuz she was losing all of her youthful glow
Mama decided She had to go
That's my man, I love him but his eyes took off Her clothes
So She got stuck in white hands
In a foster home, two parent home, her new family had a plan
To meet all their demands
Foster mama wanted the money, foster father smiling funny
And he crept into Her room
Had his way with Her each and every night and She became pregnant soon
So She went back to the streets
She laid with him; she laid with her, to get back on Her feet
And Her son began crying
And She knew why but couldn't choose so to herself She started lying
Because the rent was due
No need for love, just fast cash cause Roger promised to
Scenario
This is my story
This is my song
This is my story
This is my song

What happened to the boy?
Life full of privileges, His desires He was given
So why was there no joy?
His daddy full of chastise, his mom placated and pacified
So His daddy washed off his hands
Turned Him over to mama to make Him into a man
So mama pushed out His chest
Taught Him He was higher and beneath Him was the rest
He became the king of their hill
She gave Him this and mama gave Him that
But to her He turned His back
Compassion He did lack
And He went to school to dictate but all they did was laugh
Because they saw inside His chest
A heart of a coward with money inflated stalwart
His hill came crumbling down
So He learned to prey on the weak ones to reinstate his crown
Then He became a man
No respect from the respected ones so He came up with a plan
To go out to the streets
And throw around His money to those whose minds were weak
He found the perfect match
She was down and had nothing so he lured her with his cash
He made her think that she had won
So she proudly introduced him, Hey Roger meet my son
Scenario
This is my story
This is my song
This is my story
This is my song

Laronya Teague

7

Case#: 32580 The Claw In My Back

Josh:

Dad, hi. It's Josh. Sorry to be messaging you after all this time but can you come get me?

No response.

Josh:

Mom keeps hitting me and I don't want to live here anymore...
Please dad...

Rodney Long:

Where are you?

Josh:

We are in NC. Our address is 8400 Polk St. Ellendale, NC 28687

Rodney Long:

OMW

Josh:

Oh and dad, can you please promise not to hurt mom when you get here?

No response.

Josh:

Dad?

No response.

Josh:

Dad? Are you still there?

Knock. Knock. Knock.

"Who in the hell is this at my door at…" 34 year old Carriann McCoy reached over and looked at her clock. "4:00 in the morning?"

Knock. Knock. Knock.

She got up and headed towards the door but something stopped her. She didn't know if it was instinct, God, or just plain silliness, but she returned to her room and retrieved her gun from her nightstand. She then crept towards the door and looked out the peephole. However, whoever it was had their finger covering it, blocking her ability to see. Her heart began pumping as she quietly cocked her gun and laid her ear against the door.

Knock. Knock. Knock.

Startled by the knocks, she jumped back.

"I ain't opening that damn door," she whispered to herself just as a cold chill dashed down her spine. Her hands began to shake and she almost dropped the gun.

"Oh my God, what if he found me again?"

Knock. Knock. Knock.

She stood there, frozen, not knowing what to do.

"Mama who's at the door?" Carriann almost jumped out of her skin as she turned and saw her 13-year-old son Josh standing behind her.

"Shhhhhhh! Be quiet! I don't know who it is." She whispered.

"Why do you have your gun?" He whispered back but a little louder than she felt was necessary.

"Shut up I said!" She said as quietly as possible through gritted teeth.

KNOCK. KNOCK. KNOCK. KNOCK. KNOCK.

This time the knocks were louder and more intense.

"Josh, go call 9-1-1." She whispered.

"For what? What I'm s'pose to say?" He asked, clueless. Carriann wanted to punch him in his throat.

"Just tell them somebody's banging on our door and won't announce who they are," she replied impatiently, almost breaking her whisper.

Josh sucked his teeth. "Mama that's stupid. They not gonna come for that."

She sat her gun down on a side table and slapped him upside his head.

"Do what I said!"

BANG. BANG. BANG. BANG. BANG.

The knocks became loud bangs. She quickly reached back over and grabbed her gun.

"Who is it?" She yelled.

Silence.

"Well I'll tell you one damn thang; you'll not get your ass in here unless you say who you are," she yelled at the door. "Now I done called the police so you can act stupid if you wanna." The knocks grew silent. Then suddenly she heard a "Tap, Tap, Tap, Tap" coming from her living room window. She spun around and saw a tall dark shadow lurking behind her thin curtains. Her heart almost jumped out her chest but she knew she had to do something.

"Fuck this," Carriann said and fired a warning shot through the window close enough to scare whoever it was but far away enough not to hit him. The person jumped away from the window just as Josh came running back into the living room.

"Mama! Is it daddy?" He asked as his little body trembled.

"I don't know. Get down on the floor and stay there!" she yelled as she pivoted in a circle with her gun aimed, unsure where the perpetrator would go next. She was scared to death but she had to protect herself and her son in case it was her dangerously abusive husband, Rodney, who'd stalked her across three states. After eluding him in Fosterberg County for the past three years, she was finally beginning to feel safe. Nevertheless, she had made it a point to learn how to fire a gun because she'd made up in her mind that NC was her last stop and she wasn't running any further.

Suddenly she heard glass shattering from her bedroom and then from Josh's room as the person, more than likely her estranged husband, began taunting and terrorizing them.

"The Lord is my Shepherd, I shall not want. He maketh me to lie down in green pastures…" She quoted as glass from the bathroom window shattered.

"He leadeth me beside still waters, He restoreth my soul. He leadeth me down the path of righteousness for His name's sake…." The kitchen window burst and glass flew everywhere.

She aimed her gun. "Yea though I walk through the valley of the shadow of death, I will fear no evil for Thou art with me…"

BOOM! CRACK!

The front door flew open and its frame cracked like a toothpick. In front of her stood her 6 ft. 5, 275 pound estranged husband Rodney, holding a machete, smiling wickedly. Her anxiety kicked into high gear and the sight of him frightened her so intensely that she couldn't move.

"Bitch, I told you I'd find you. You'll never get away from me." He sounded like a monster or more like Satan with a seething, bone-chilling voice. "I came for my son."

"Mama I'm going to call the police!" The faint sound of Josh's voice broke through her fear and unfroze her stance. She wanted to slap him shitless for not calling the police earlier as she had directed him to do. However, there was no time for that now.

"Son, if you move near that phone, I'll chop you and your mama up into small pieces. Matter of fact, I think we're all going to die today as a family anyway."

"Call the police Josh!" Carriann screamed. Rodney could see the fear all over Carriann and it pleased him. Her hands were shaking and unsteady even though she was the one with the gun. He began walking towards her. She began backing up.

"Yeah, bitch. Thought you was gonna get away from me, huh?"

"Rodney please leave us alone." Carriann begged in a voice as unsteady as her hand. Rodney took another step forward. She took another step backwards. Her heartbeat increased and her breaths became shorter. Rodney took another step towards her; the evil smile on his demonic face became more malicious. Carriann took another step back and hit the side of the couch, which caused her to fall to the ground and involuntarily fire the gun. The bullet grazed the side of Rodney's face, which turned his smugness into rage. He lifted the machete into the air and charged at Carriann. She knew she no longer had a choice. Her hands suddenly became steady and her target became clear. She fired several shots, emptying her gun on Rodney. He staggered forward and dropped right on top of her.

"I'll see you in hell bitch but first, I'll see you every night in your dreams. You'll never get rid of me." Rodney whispered in Carriann's ear with his last breath.

"Mama! Mama!" Josh screamed as he ran over to Carriann.

"HELP ME! GET HIM OFF ME! GET HIM OFF OF ME!" she screamed to the top of lungs as the two of them struggled to push Rodney's heavy body off her. She scrambled to her feet and the two of them ran outside to wait for the police. Carriann welcomed the fresh air although her hands continued shaking uncontrollably. Her adrenaline was still pumping and her legs threatened to collapse underneath her. The gun remained in her hand as she continued looking back towards the door. Although she'd seen Rodney's dead body lying on the floor, his final words still haunted her and she waited for him to come running outside to finish her off.

"I'm sorry mama. I'm so sorry. This is all my fault," Josh cried breaking her trance.

"Josh what are you talking about baby? This ain't your fault." She pulled him close to her and wrapped her arms around him.

"Yes it is mama. Please don't hurt me."

"Josh, this is not your fault."

"Yes it is mama. You kept hitting on me so I found daddy on social media and asked him to come get me because he loves me and he would never hit me like you do."

Carriann released Josh and pushed him in front of her so she could look him square in his eyes. Her body, which was already experiencing a full spectrum of instability, fear, and anxiety, began to make room for rage as she stood looking at her child, trying to process what he'd just said to her.

"YOU DID WHAT?" Carriann heard her voice shift to the same voice she'd heard coming from Rodney.

"God help me! Please mama I'm sorry." Josh said as he slowly began backing up, away from his mother. Carriann's face morphed from that of concern and compassion into one of an ominous intent as she began taking slow steps towards her son. He wanted to run but his fight or flight system betrayed him and cemented his feet to the ground. Urine began to stream down his legs.

Blinded by the emotional gamut swinging back and forth inside of her body, Carriann lost her sense of time and space. Her rationality went on vacation as the flashbacks of Rodney *and* Josh's mental and physical abuse played before her eyes. Propelled by rage, anxiety and the pursuit of liberty, she pounced on Josh and cracked the side of his head with her gun. He dropped to the ground effortlessly. And her hands, which were no longer in her control, became iron clamps as she wrapped them around Josh's thin neck and began choking the life out of him. Although her petite son was the recipient of her emotional breakdown, all Carriann saw was Rodney...and she needed him to die once and for all.

"Die, Rodney. Die!" She whispered as she glared into his eyes.

Unable to respond, Josh was at his mother's mercy. His last thoughts before darkness overtook him were, "She's really gonna kill me this time. I shoulda listened to her and called the police."

Carolyn Black

"Val, girl what are you wearing to the Mayor's Ball?" I asked, referring to the first Annual Mayor's Appreciation Charity Ball whereby the new Mayor was throwing a big upscale party paying homage to all the county employees from the sanitation workers to the county managers. The invitation stated that all we had to pay was twenty-five dollars for dinner and dancing whereas everyone else who wasn't a county employee could attend by invitation only if they were willing to pay the three hundred dollar cover charge. The main thing that caught my eye, however, was the "what happens here, stays here" tagline, which meant we could let our hair down and party without judgement. Hell, I stopped reading the invitation after that.

"Girl, I don't know. I'm going to call your girl Janice and get her to hook me up," she replied while slinging her freshly done hair. I shook my head and laughed. I knew Val had something to prove especially since her husband Maurice, who she'd left after his affair, was the Mayor's best friend, which meant he would definitely be at the Mayor's Ball as well. I figured she was going to go all out so she could "let him see what he was missing." However, although she was trying to be hard, I knew she missed him and wanted him back.

"Why? What are you wearing?" she asked me.

"I have no clue. What's the theme again?" I asked.

"Well, according to the invitation it's an 80's/90's theme. But that's kinda weird because the style of dress was so different for each era. I actually hated the 90's fashion." Val responded shaking her head shiftlessly.

Not being able to resist, I replied through giggles, "Um well, I can't tell you hated the 90's because you just stopped wearing those ugly chunk heel shoes and baby doll dresses a few months ago." Val looked at me and rolled her eyes with a smile because she knew I was telling the truth. Janice had changed Val's fashion sense so drastically that the heifa had forgot who she was. Now *she* was the one walking around like she was the shit and the heifa was unapologetic about it too. I admired her but at the same time I was worried that Janice and I had created a monster.

"Hey Carolyn, you have a call on line 1," Mario said as he stuck his head into Val's office.

"Ok. Thanks," I responded as I jumped up awkwardly and walked past him without making eye contact. I had been completely avoiding him since the night we slept together. I felt dirty and ashamed and I didn't know how to interact with him. I knew we couldn't go back to being the old Carolyn and Mario because he had seen me naked and danced inside of my Juicy. I also knew that a relationship with him was out of the question so I bowed out like a coward. After giving him the cold shoulder for about a month, he finally got the hint and left me alone. Now he only spoke with me and interacted with me within the realm of our jobs. We no longer sat together, hung out together, or frequented Jar Bar together like we used to. Not to mention I didn't have anybody to clown Jenetta with because Val was the supervisor and she wouldn't cross that line.

I hated the way things were between Mario and me. I was pissed with myself because I should have controlled myself but instead I allowed my vulnerability to put our friendship at stake. Now I had nothing. I sighed and picked up the phone in my office.

"Fosterberg County Department of Social Services, this is Carolyn Black."

"Hi Ms. Black, this is Officer Marlon Steele and we have a mother in custody who shot and killed her husband and then physically assaulted her thirteen year old son and put him in the hospital. He's at Fosterberg Memorial, room 242 and thank God the neighbors came outside or she would have killed him too.

She's so out of it Ms. Black that she doesn't even remember what happened."

"Oh Lord! Thank you Officer Steele. I'm on my way," I replied as I gathered my briefcase and headed to the county jail. I decided that since the boy was safely in the hospital I would go and talk to his mom first so I could find out where her head was.

When I arrived at the jail, I showed them my badge and briefed with Officer Steele. He led me into a small room where a fragile looking woman sat solemnly at a table waiting for me. She was very petite with beautiful, milky white skin, small beady; bloodshot eyes and a cute little button nose. Her shoulder length, jet-black hair was thin and greasy and her leg shook uncontrollably. In front of her sat a cup of coffee, a pack of cigarettes and an ashtray full of cigarette butts.

"Ms. McCoy? Hi, I'm Carolyn Black with Fosterberg County Department of Social Services," I said as I extended my hand to her. She accepted my hand and gave me a weak smile.

"Hello, Ms. Black. I suppose if you're here then I must be in a lot of trouble. Is my son ok?" She asked.

"Well I haven't been to see him yet because I wanted to talk to you first. I'm here to find out what happened. So I guess I'll start by asking you how you got here."

She sighed and lit up a cigarette. She took a long drawl and then began talking.

"Ms. Black, if I wasn't sitting here in this jail right now, I would think that I was having a nightmare. And I still keep pinching myself just to make sure that I'm not asleep."

"Well Ms. McCoy, I can assure you that I'm real and that this is not a dream. Start at the beginning and tell me what you remember," I replied.

She sighed again and took another pull. "Well Ms. Black, I'm originally from Omaha, Nebraska. I've been here in North Carolina for three years. I came here to get away from my husband, Rodney. I met the son of a bitch when I was seventeen years old. We got married as soon as I turned eighteen so I could get the hell away from my family and well, he started beating me and treating me like his slave about three months after we got married. I thought that he would lighten up after I had my son Josh but it just got worse because he hated the fact that my son loved me." She took another drawl on the cigarette as her leg continued to shake. "So then, when Josh was old enough, Rodney started teaching him to hit me too and wasn't a damn thing I could do about it." Her chin began to quiver as she put the cigarette out and lit another one. "It was terrible, Ms. Black. Rodney would call me a bitch and then Josh would call me a bitch. Rodney would hit me and then Josh would hit me and I'd just sit there and take it. Rodney loved it. Matter of fact, I think it made the sick bastard get a hard on," she said and stared off into space for a second. Then she continued.

"My family wasn't any help because my daddy still beats my momma to this day and my brothers, hell they beat their wives too. My sister is somewhere strung out on drugs so I couldn't call her...and I learned my lesson about calling the police on Rodney because as soon as he'd get out of jail, he'd beat me bout to my death. Anyway, so when Josh was around eight or nine years old, the school called and told me that he was hitting on the girls at school and calling them stuff like bitches and whores. I told Rodney about it and he gave my son a high five." She took a puff. "Then I started thinking about my life and my childhood. I didn't want my baby growing up being no woman beater, so I packed my baby up one night and I moved to Kentucky with a girl I met one day when I was in the hospital after Rodney broke two of my ribs. We stayed there for about 6 months and I finally started getting Josh on the right track. Then one day, out of the blue, the girl called me and told me that Rodney was at the diner she worked at asking questions. So, I packed us up and fled to West Virginia with one of her cousins who helped me get into a battered women's shelter. We lived there for about 4 months and somehow Rodney used Josh's social security number and found out where he was going to school. But once again, God was with me because it just so happened that I'd kept Josh out of school that day and Rodney couldn't find the shelter since it was deep back in the mountains. They made me leave anyway because my cover was blown and they knew he wouldn't stop 'til he found me so they set me up at a spot in Tennessee. I got smart and changed our last names and social security numbers in hopes that he wouldn't find us. But in my urgency to get away from him, I forgot that half of his family was from Tennessee and Josh ended up going to school with several of Rodney's cousins' kids. So when Josh came home one day and told me that 'Uncle Bryan said to tell you hey' I almost died. The people at the shelter worked it out for me to move to North Carolina and here is where I've been for the past three years. I finally thought I was safe and then Rodney showed up again at about 4:00 this morning. He busted out all my windows and kicked in my door...and all I remember..." Her breathing increased and her chest began rising and falling. Tears welled up in her eyes and her hands began shaking as she took another drawl on the cigarette. "All I remember is him having a machete." Her voice became shaky as the tears fell.

"Every time I close my eyes Ms. Black, I see that blade coming at me and that's the last thing I remember. I don't recall nothing else except waking up here and them telling me that I killed Rodney and I almost killed my son." She started rocking and gasping for air. Sweat beaded up on her forehead and the cigarette fell from her mouth into the ashtray. I could see that she was in the beginning stages of having a panic attack, so I jumped into action.

"Ms. McCoy, look at me. Look at me. You are a strong woman. You're a survivor and you made it through all those things. Now take a deep breath and tell me what color my shirt is."

Inhale, exhale. "What?"

"Tell me what color my shirt is," I repeated.

"Red," she gasped.

"Ok." I grabbed her hands and held them gently.

"Squeeze my hands as firmly as you can," I directed. She obliged.

"Ok, now take a deep breath, count to five in your head and exhale." She did as I told her.

"Ok, let's do that again except this time I want you say 'I'm alive' after you exhale." She followed directions and I continued working with her until she calmed down. She finally began sobbing which was what she needed to do in order to let it all out.

"I'm just so tired Ms. Black...tired from being beat down all my life and tired from running. I'm tired of being afraid and I'm tired of being unhappy," she said sadly, as she relit her cigarette.

"Ms. McCoy, you don't have to be afraid anymore," I assured her. "Rodney can't hurt you anymore." She wiped her nose on her arm and finished smoking her cigarette.

"Do you know what would make you hurt your son?"

"No ma'am I don't. He's all I got."

"Have you ever hurt him before?" I asked.

"Well, I tan his hide every now and then if he gets too sassy or does something bad in school but I ain't never hurt him."

"Does he still hit you and call you names?"

"Well..." She lit another cigarette. "It's been getting a lot better since I been busting his butt, but it took me a long time to teach him that it wasn't right for him to be hitting his mama."

"What do you use when you 'bust his butt'?" I asked.

"Nothing really, mostly my hand." Carriann replied.

"Where do you hit him at?"

"Well, since he's a teenager, I mostly pop him upside his head or punch him in his chest. I used to pop his butt but he's too old for that now."

"Ok Ms. McCoy, thank you for talking to me because I know that was hard for you. I'm going to talk with the officer about some things and I will be back to see you either later on today or tomorrow, ok?"

"Yes ma'am," she replied. I got up and walked out. As soon as the door closed behind me and I was out of her sight, I leaned up against the wall and took a couple deep breaths myself. "Good Lord. Jesus. These cases are crazy." I mumbled to myself as I shook my head. When I finally got myself together, I went to talk with Officer Steele.

"Officer Steele, is what she saying about her husband true?" I asked as I inquired about what Ms. McCoy had told me.

"Yes ma'am I'm afraid so. We called Omaha and they verified the police reports. We also called the woman she was living with in Kentucky and she verified Ms. McCoy's story too, plus when we gathered the evidence from the crime scene, everything she said was true. We ain't gonna charge her for the death of her husband, but we just can't understand why she attacked her kid like that. She pistol-whipped him and the neighbors said that it took three of them to pry her hands loose from his neck. And he's a tiny little thing but apparently, he's a fighter because he's still here with us. " I shook my head in disbelief and gave Officer Steele a few numbers so that he could get a counselor in with Ms. McCoy as soon as possible. Then I headed to the hospital to check on her son, Josh.

"Right this way Ms. Black," the nurse said as she led me to Josh's room. "Honey, that child is lucky to be alive. He has a concussion and his mother almost strangled him to death. Wait 'til you see the big gash on his head not to mention the dark purple imprints on his neck," she continued and opened the door leading into Josh's room. When I walked in, I saw a small framed, fragile looking teenage boy lying in bed asleep. The dark purple handprints on his neck and the large bandage on the side of his head confirmed what the nurse and Officer Steele had told me. I inhaled and then exhaled slowly. *Here we go.* I thought to myself.

Even in his sleep, I could see the torment and sadness on his face. I wanted to cry so bad for him. I wanted to rock him in my arms and tell him everything was going to be ok. My heart felt heavy because he was so small and helpless. I just couldn't understand what had possessed Ms. McCoy, a battered woman herself, to act so savagely towards her own son and being that Ms. McCoy had no recollection of what had happened I knew my answers would have to come from Josh.

"Josh? Wake up honey. You have a visitor," the nurse said as she shook him gently. Startled, he jerked straight up in the bed and looked around nervously as if someone was after him.

"Baby, its ok. No one's gonna hurt you. This is Carolyn Black and she's a social worker with Fosterberg County Department of Social Services. She needs to talk to you about what happened last night, ok?"

"Ok," he whispered hoarsely. "But can you stay in here with us?" he asked pitifully.

"Yes baby, I'll stay in here with you." the nurse replied and glanced at me.

"Hi Josh. How are you feeling?" I asked, wishing I had a better conversation starter.

"I'm ok. Where's my mama?"

"Well, she's still in jail for what she did to you," I replied. He scowled as if he was confused.

"Jail? What do you mean she's in jail?" he asked.

It was my turn to be confused so I returned his scowl.

"Honey, she put you in the hospital. She almost killed you. Yes, she's in jail."

He looked at me intently for a few seconds and then he looked over at the nurse who shook her head, confirming my statement. His mouth flew open and his breathing increased rapidly.

"No! No! I didn't want her to go to jail. I..." deep breath, deep breath. "I..." deep breath, deep breath. "I just, I just wanted her to stop hitting me."

"Josh, honey calm down, it's going to be ok." The nurse said, trying to comfort him.

"No! I want my mama! I want my mama!" He began screaming and trying to get out of the bed. I stood there, not knowing what to do. I didn't know whether to restrain him or hug him. Luckily, the nurse was on top of her game. She firmly cradled him in her arms and started rocking him until he calmed down. His shrieks turned to sniffles and he finally started talking.

"This is all my fault. I knew I shouldn't have contacted daddy on social media but mama...she, she kept hitting me all the time. And, and it started happening a lot and her hits got harder. Then, she started drinking and calling me daddy's name when she got drunk."

"Wait? What do you mean you contacted your dad on social media?" I asked.

"Well, daddy used to beat her real bad and he made me hit her too. I didn't want to, but I was scared he'd beat me if I didn't and I knew he wouldn't let mama hit me back, so I took the easy way out. I guess I shoulda just let him beat me too..."He became silent and dropped his head.

"Josh, please, keep going," I coaxed. He sighed and continued.

"Anyway, when we finally got away from him, I thought everything was going to be ok. I was still hitting her and cussing her though because I was so used to it but since daddy wasn't around no more she started hitting and cussing me back...but it was like she hit me with a vengeance though. Eventually I stopped hitting her and cussing her because I didn't want her to hit me no more, but she kept on anyway." He started getting emotional again, but I needed him to remain focused.

"Ok Josh, I know this is difficult but you have to keep it together so you can tell me what happened this morning. And I apologize but I also have to take pictures, ok?" I said as I retrieved my Polaroid camera from my briefcase. He shook his head and continued.

"Well she punched me in my chest yesterday morning real hard. See?" He pulled up his gown and showed us a large bruise on his bony, little chest. Glad that I could cover up my reaction with the camera, I snapped a picture.

"And I just couldn't take it no more. So when I got to school, I got on the computer and looked my dad up. When I found him, I messaged him our address and told him to come get me. I didn't think he was going to get here that fast and I told him not to hurt mama when he got here..." I wanted to take my hand and smack my forehead. *No wonder she lost it and choked him.* I thought to myself, although I remained silent as he continued.

"Anyway, when he got here, he started banging on the door and acting crazy. He busted out all the windows and kicked in the door. And when he came in, he had his hunting machete. He told me and mama that we were all going to die and he charged at mama and she started shooting him. He fell on top of her and I had to help her get him off. When we got outside, I told her that I had messaged him and told him where we was so he could come get me. I kept telling her I was sorry but she lost it and hit me on my head with the butt of her gun. I blacked out and woke up here."

I was completely stunned. I didn't even know how to respond. I couldn't believe that this child could even sit here and regurgitate the things that he'd just told me. I was thankful that I got to him when I did because I knew that once he really processed what had happened, he was probably going to shut down.

"Josh, I really appreciate you telling me the truth. You are a very brave young man. And you can't blame yourself for this, ok. This is not your fault."

"Yes it is. If I wouldn't have called daddy, he wouldn't be dead and mama wouldn't be in jail."

"Baby, you did what you thought you had to do. Your mama will be ok and your daddy can't hurt you or your mama anymore, ok?" the nurse chimed in. He sniffled.

"When can I see my mama?" he asked.

"I don't know Josh. I don't know," I answered. And I really didn't know. I wasn't sure as to what type of charges the police were going to bring against Ms. McCoy but because of the injuries Josh had sustained I figured they were probably going to charge her with felony child abuse. Nevertheless, as I looked from his head to his neck, regardless of the charges we were still going to have to take Josh into custody.

My first step was to call Val so I stepped out into the hallway and briefed her on what was going on. She was just as in shock as I was.

"Does he have any family or anyone he can stay with?" Val asked.

"I really don't think so Val because they were on the run and based on the way Ms. McCoy described her family, none of them are fit. I guess you need to go ahead and start calling some of our foster parents. He's probably going to get released tomorrow or the next day, so we gotta move quickly," I replied just as a pretty, young woman with a striking resemblance to Ms. McCoy walked briskly towards Josh's room.

"Ok. I'm on it. I'll call you back," Val said and hung up. I dropped my phone in my purse and followed the woman into Josh's room.

"Josh! Oh, Josh! Are you ok?" the young woman asked as she rushed over towards Josh and gently wrapped her arms around him.

"A'nt Renee?"

"Yes baby it's me. What happened? What happened to you?" She cried, as she lightly rubbed her fingers over his head and neck.

"Nothing. I'm ok. I'm just glad you're here. I haven't seen you since I was like seven years old. How did you know I was here?"

"Well, I been living in Greensboro ever since I left Omaha. I had no clue you and your mom were living less than an hour away until something told me to call your grandma today. She told me that Carriann called her and said that y'all were in North Carolina, Rodney was dead and you were here in the hospital. But never mind that Josh, just tell me what happened to you. Did Rodney's sorry ass do this?"

"No A'nt Renee...Mama did it after she killed daddy...but she didn't mean to." he said softly. Her eyes bulged out of her head and her mouth dropped.

"Oh my God. Oh my God. Oh baby. Lord, Jesus, help us," she said and began hugging him again. As I watched the exchange between the two of them, my wheels started churning. If this was the strung out sister Ms. McCoy had been talking about, she didn't look like she was still on drugs, which meant she could be a possible placement. I immediately introduced myself.

"Um ma'am, my name is Carolyn Black and I work for the Fosterberg County Department of Social Services." I handed her a tissue as she looked up at me, somewhat reluctantly and defensively.

"Hi. My name is Renee, Renee Mastersen. I'm Carriann's baby sister. So uh, what's going on? Are you going to take my nephew away from his mother or something?"

I sighed. "Um, Miss Mastersen, let's step outside and talk for a second please."

"Yeah, sure. Of course," she said and followed me out. Once we were out in the hallway I wanted to test her little bit and see if she would volunteer to take Josh before I asked her.

"Well, I didn't want to say anything to Josh yet but yes, most likely we're going to have to place him in foster care for a while until we can conduct a full investigation. However, I can't give you all the details just yet until I talk with my supervisor and your sister," I said and waited for her response. She stood there silently for a moment and then the tears started again.

"I need to see my sister, please."

Miss Mastersen followed me to the county jail where they were holding Ms. McCoy. I contacted Val on the way there and let her know what was going on. I told her not to get her hopes up though because I wasn't sure if the sister would be willing to take Josh. Once we arrived at the jail, Miss Mastersen and I waited for the officer to take us to the visitation area. When he finally came to get us, he led us back to the small room I'd met Ms. McCoy in earlier that day. When he opened the door and the two sisters saw each other, I thought they were going to tackle one another.

"Carriann?"

"Renee!" Ms. McCoy jumped up from her chair and ran over to her sister. "Oh God, Renee! Sister! Oh Lord, sister I missed you so bad. I'm so glad to see ya. You look so good!" Ms. McCoy wailed as the two of them squeezed each other tightly. A tear snuck down my cheek before I even realized it. The love they had for each other was palpable, which made me think about my sisters and how the disgust they had for me was just as palpable. A pang of envy and hurt boomeranged through my heart. I just couldn't understand why these two sisters could love each other so much when mine hated me. Things weren't as bad as they were before my mom's surgery but once my mom started getting better; they began distancing themselves from me again. I would have given anything to have my sisters love me like the two women standing before me loved each other.

When Ms. McCoy and Miss Mastersen released their embrace, they sat down and started talking. I just stood there silently and let them talk.

"What are you doing here, Renee? Granted I'm happy as hell you're here, but how? Where did you come from?" Ms. McCoy asked as she and Renee continued holding each other's hand.

"I had to get the hell away from Omaha or y'all woulda found *me* dead somewhere. I was drugging and prostituting and all kinds of crazy shit. Hell, you know! Anyway, you remember my friend Thandie from high school?"

"Yeah." Ms. McCoy replied.

"Well, she got a job in Greensboro and convinced me to come with her. And I couldn't tell y'all I was leaving because I knew y'all woulda tried to stop me. And after I saw the way our dear brother, Woodie, beat the hell out of Tracy, I knew I couldn't be around our family no more. I really hated leaving you though, especially with Rodney's crazy ass. Anyway, so when I called mama this morning to check on her, she told me you were here. What the hell happened?"

"I honestly can't remember, Nay. All I know is that I'm in a shit load of trouble." She released her sister's hand and lit a cigarette. She put her hand on her head and started crying.

"Nay, I put my own child in the hospital and I was so out of it, I don't even know how or why."

"Don't cry sissy. We're gonna get through this together. God sent me to Greensboro to get cleaned up for a reason. He knew you was gonna end up here needing my help," Miss Mastersen replied as she soothed her sister. "Listen, she told me..." Miss Mastersen looked over at me and pointed, "social services is gonna have to take Josh into custody for a while until we can get things sorted out. So I wanted to see if you'd rather for him to come live with me, so he won't have to go into foster care."

Ms. McCoy took another pull on her cigarette. "What'd I do to him? How bad is it?"

Not wanting to answer, Miss Mastersen looked back at me and I finally broke my silence.

"Well Ms. McCoy, according to the police, your neighbors and Josh's injuries, you hit him across the head with the butt of your gun and you almost choked him to death. He also has a large bruise on his chest from where he says you punched him."

She swallowed hard and licked her lips. I saw her chest begin to rise and fall again.

"No way. No way." She shook her head. "There's no way I would have done that to my own child. I don't believe you." Ms. McCoy looked at her sister for solace but Miss Mastersen's solemn look confirmed my statements. Ms. McCoy looked back up at me as she continued shaking her head in disbelief.

"Are you seriously telling me that I hit my son with a gun and choked him?"

"Yes ma'am, I am," I replied.

"Oh God, no, no. I don't believe you. Y'all are bullshitting me! Ain't no way in hell I'd do that! Renee, are you doing this shit so you can take my son away from me?"

Miss Mastersen scowled. "Are you crazy? Listen to yourself. Why would I do something like that?"

"I don't know! I don't know! This doesn't make sense." She took a pull on her cigarette. "I, I just don't believe I would do something like that."

I reached into my briefcase, pulled out the pictures and laid them on the table in front of her.

As she looked from one picture to the next, all the color drained from her already pale face.

"Oh Jesus, no." She began sobbing. "Oh God. Oh Lord. I'll never get my baby back. Oh God nooooo!" Miss Mastersen wrapped her arms around her sister and laid Ms. McCoy's head on her shoulder. She gently began stroking Ms. McCoy's hair.

"Shhhhh. It's going to be ok sissy. I'm here. I'm here."

"Did...did he say what happened?" Ms. McCoy asked as she lifted her head.

I sighed. "Well Ms. McCoy, he said that he was the reason your husband found you. He said you've been hitting him a lot, especially when you're drinking. And he said he was tired of you beating on him so he sent his dad a message on social media and told him where you guys lived so your husband could come and get him. He said after you shot your husband, he told you how your husband had found you guys and then you hit him with a gun and started choking him." I answered her frankly. She closed her eyes, took a long draw from her cigarette and shook her head again.

"That little shit! It's all starting to come back to me now. Yeah, he's right. I don't remember hitting him or choking him, but I do remember him telling me that. I just lost it because I couldn't believe he would do that after all Rodney has done to us or should I say to me. I guess I understand though because Rodney never hurt Josh. The son of a bitch was too busy teaching Josh how to hurt me…,"she said angrily as she smashed her cigarette butt into the ashtray and lit another one. After taking a long pull, she continued. "And he's right about me hitting him too…you know, I thought I got our family's crab claw out of my back when I left at eighteen and married Rodney. He was older, came from a rich family and I thought he really loved me. Then I became my mama, an abused wife. So when I finally left Rodney I thought 'hell yeah, *now* I'm free from the claw' but look at me. The damn thing's still there and just as deeply embedded as it was before, because now I've become my daddy and Rodney; a damn abuser who beats her own kid." Her leg shook as she continued smoking her cigarette. She was silent for a while before she began speaking again. I could tell she was in deep thought. She blew out a stream of smoke and resumed talking.

"Ms. Black, I don't wanna be like this no more. I need help. I thought I could do it by myself but I can't. My boy is all I got in this world and I don't want that crab claw going in his back. I don't wanna pass my family's fucked up pathology to him and I'm not one of those kind of parents who will fight to hold onto their kids to save face and maintain some damn pride. I'd much rather let him go so he can have a chance…so if it's ok with you, I'd like for him to go live with my sister. At least that way he'll be with somebody who I know loves him *and* me while I'm getting myself together…but I do want my baby back though, eventually." She looked at me with pleading eyes.

"We'll cross that bridge a little later on down the line Ms. McCoy but first things first. I'll need to do a safety assessment and a home inspection with Miss Mastersen in order to make sure that her home environment is safe and conducive to raising a child. We'll also have to do a background check and a drug test as well."

"Sure, when do you want to get started?" Miss Mastersen asked.

"Well, let me step out and call my supervisor. If she says it's ok to move forward, we'll need to schedule a Team Decision

Making meeting. Under the circumstances, we'll try to conduct it here so that Ms. McCoy can be involved. We'll do all the paperwork, schedule a home assessment and if everything comes out ok then we'll move forward with Josh coming home with you." I replied.

"Ok. Let's do it." Ms. McCoy replied. So I stepped out and called Val. She approved it and informed me that she would meet me at the jail with all the necessary documents. I then contacted one of my colleagues in Greensboro who owed me a favor. She agreed to do an immediate home investigation later on that afternoon upon Miss Mastersen's return home.

After Val arrived, we did all the initial paperwork and got the ball rolling. We informed Miss Mastersen and Ms. McCoy that as soon as the home investigation and background check cleared, we would be able to move forward. They both agreed and the three of us headed out to complete the final portions of the investigation. At the end of the day, I was so glad to see five o'clock that I clicked my heels. I couldn't wait to get home and smoke a blunt. I was tired but at the same time, I was grateful that things seemed to be working out well for Ms. McCoy and Josh.

On my way home, I decided to go check on my mom who was recovering tremendously. When I got there, I saw my dad's car in the driveway and I began wondering what he was doing home so early because he usually worked until at least seven or eight o'clock at night. I automatically began to panic, thinking something had gone wrong with my mom. I slammed the car in park and jetted to the front door. I took out my keys, unlocked the door and quickly entered the house. All the lights were out and I didn't hear anything. I walked all around the downstairs area trying to find my mom and dad but I didn't see them. I ran and looked in the back yard and no one was there. My heart was pounding and tears began welling up in my eyes. Thoughts like, "What if my dad had to call the ambulance? What if my mom had another heart attack?" kept rolling through my mind as I began climbing the stairs two at a time towards my parent's room. Panicked, I slung their bedroom door open and almost had my own heart attack because my mom was on top of my dad, riding him like a bull, as his hands grasped her hips and his mouth covered her breast. Their favorite Marvin Gaye song, *Distant Lover,* was playing in the background and they were so into in their lovemaking that they didn't even notice me, so I quickly backed up and closed the door.

"Wow...that was disgusting. I officially want to gouge my eyes out," I said silently to myself as I crept back down the stairs. I was glad that my mom was ok, but I definitely made a mental note to knock on their door from then on. I got back into my car, but I wasn't quite ready to go home yet. So I made a stop by my Cousin Brandon's house so I could smoke a blunt and tell him about what I had just walked into.

I knocked on the door and let myself in as I usually did when I went to his house. The smell of weed and the words of Young Jeezy met me at the door. I walked through the kitchen and into the living room and stopped dead in my tracks because there was Brandon...and I be damn if he wasn't also getting his freak on with some bald headed looking chick on the couch. I stood there for a minute trying not to laugh because unlike my parents, this was more entertaining. In fact, the way Brandon was pounding the girl; giving her the best he had, was funny as hell. He was sweating, panting, and yelling out, "Whose is it? Whose is it?" And the baldhead girl was squealing, "Ooo daddy it's yours. It's yours." I almost pissed my pants. But this time instead of leaving, I decided to be a cock blocker because I was feeling some type of way about everybody getting some except me.

"Brandon!" I yelled, startling him. He jumped up, or should I say *out of,* and fell off the couch onto the floor.

"Damn Carolyn! What the hell is wrong with you?" He yelled, trying to cover himself up with a couch pillow while the baldhead girl scrambled around trying to retrieve her clothes.

"Who is she Brandon? That better not be one of your bitches." she squealed as she almost tripped trying to pull her panties up. I was laughing so hard at them that I had to bend over just to keep from falling myself.

"No, this is my no-knocking ass, cock blocking ass cousin who don't know how to pick up a phone and call before she come barging up in a brother's crib."

"Shut up Brandon, I don't ever call before I come over here," I replied with a giggle.

"Well damnit, your ass betta start. Shit! Now I got blue balls. I was just about to bust a nut! Nah fuck that, you know what, Camella, come on, we going to the bathroom and finish. I ain't walking around with no damn blue balls. Carolyn, we'll be right back," he said, obviously pissed and dragged the girl with him into the bathroom revealing his flabby naked ass in the meantime. I almost threw up, but I got another good laugh out of it. I also noticed a half of a blunt lying in the ashtray, so I plopped down on the couch to indulge until I remembered what had just happened on the couch. I jumped up so quickly that I hit my knee on the table.

"Shit!" I yelped, although I never relinquished on reaching for the blunt. I lit it up and let the smoke fill my lungs as I cautiously sat down on the adjoining love seat. In the meantime, I heard the same rendition of, "Whose is it? Whose is it? Ooooo daddy it's yours," coming from the bathroom. I giggled and continued puffing on the blunt. Just as I was starting to feel my body begin to float in the air, Brandon and baldhead Camella came staggering out of the bathroom, all sweaty and disheveled. In my high state, I began to giggle which then turned into a full-blown round of laughter. And Brandon; being high as well, joined in on my laughter as did Camella. When we finally regained our composure, we finished the blunt and I told them the story about mom and dad, which ignited another 30-minute, nonstop round of laughter.

I loved Brandon because he never ceased to make my day. We smoked another blunt, ate some concoction that Camella cooked up and then I decided to head home. I was high and happy, but as soon as I walked through the door, my two constant companions; sadness and loneliness met me there. An old acquaintance who I hadn't seen in a while, horniness, also met me. I was high and not only were my parents getting it on, so was Brandon, which slightly made me feel jealous. I hadn't been dealing with my "toys" anymore since my mother had become privy to my "secret life" because I didn't want to disappoint her. It was cool though because I really didn't have time anyway, especially since taking care of my mom occupied a lot of my time; plus my only two remaining toys, Brad and Dewayne, didn't appeal to me anymore. I just wasn't in the mood. I wanted someone to love me and me only. I wanted someone to come home to everyday just like my parents and my sisters had. The only person that I did have was Val since she wasn't talking to Maurice anymore. I figured that misery loved company and I finally had someone who was just as miserable as me to hang out with.

I sighed, dropped my purse on the counter and headed to the shower. I opened my "toy drawer" and pulled out my waterproof bullet, which had recently become a replacement for my "living toys". I then turned on some slow music and took off my clothes. I got into the shower, leaned up against the wall and let the hot water roll down my naked body. I spread my legs and let my fingers massage my Juicy. My nipples hardened and my body temperature began to rise. I took my bullet and then began pleasing myself. The combination of the hot water running across my already sensitive nipples and the vibration of the bullet in between my legs made me cum hard which alleviated the horniness briefly. However, the sadness and loneliness stayed right beside me. Tears welled up in my eyes but I forced them back. I quickly finished my shower and got out so that I could smoke another blunt, drink a glass of wine and hopefully fall into a deep sleep to numb the pain I was feeling inside.

Ring, Ring, Ring. Startled, my head jerked up off the pillow and I looked around. As I became coherent, my phone rang again.

"Hello?" I whispered.

"Girl, I know your ass ain't in the bed at 9:30! Get up right now and put you on some clothes. That dope band that played last week during amateur night at Jar Bar is performing tonight with a couple other headliners. It's Thursday night and we don't have to go to work tomorrow. I'll be over there to get you in about 20 minutes." *Click.*

I sat there holding the phone, dumbfounded still half sleep. "No this heifa didn't just try to pull rank on me." I laughed to myself as I "obeyed" Val's orders to get up and get dressed. I wanted to wear something comfortable so I put on a long, floor length, maxi skirt with a pair of flats, a tank and a blazer. Val, who promptly arrived 20 minutes later, was wearing a fitted knee length skirt with a polo shirt and a pair of wedges. Val's hair was moving with the wind and mine was in a ponytail with split ends popping out. Val's skin was glowing and radiant while mine looked like an oil field. But I didn't care. I was happy for her because she was finally enjoying herself for once. And I was finally able to take a break from being "pretty" so that I could be Carolyn, whoever that was... Plus, I finally understood how Val had gotten caught up in choosing comfort over beauty for so long, because it was so liberating. I didn't care if I shaved my legs, I didn't spend hours trying to figure out what to wear nor did I spend hundreds of dollars going to the spa for facials and waxing and blah blah blah. Not to mention, since I wasn't dealing with my toys anymore, my money was a little bit tight.

I didn't have to look good at work because Mario and I weren't talking anymore and the families on my caseload didn't give a piss what I looked like because they'd rather not see me anyway. My parents loved me regardless and I figured that if I looked shambled enough, my sisters would be satisfied and no longer have a reason to continue popping the air out of my balloon. And hell, I fit right in around Brandon and my little brother John because apparently none of the heifas they dealt with could have possibly owned a mirror anyway.

My mom getting sick, the drama with Demarcus and the incident with Mario was life altering for me, and it made me realize that I was doing too much. Being with married men had its benefits but I'd grown weary of it. I never expected them to leave their wives for me but seeing how *Demarcus*, out of all of them, had chosen the hood rat over me that night despite the fact that she'd walked in; probably fresh out of jail, looking like she had a family of cardinals flapping around in her head, had opened my eyes. It forced me to grasp the full-blown concept of who I was, a mistress, and what that meant in its entirety. My experiences with Brad and Dewayne had been superficial and I really didn't count my relationship with Jermaine/I mean Avery, because he was an imposter; so in those instances I really didn't feel like a mistress. However, realizing that Demarcus saw *me* as a side chick was a reality check. It left me raw and exposed. My cockiness and sense of entitlement crumbled and the realization of my *true place* literally punched me in the face. Just thinking about it pissed me off all over again because although I was nothing more than a fantasy and a good time to Dewayne and Brad, even they would not have treated me with such disrespect and callousness as Demarcus had.

"Carolyn, did you hear me?" I snapped back into reality and turned from the car window to look at Val who was driving.

"Huh, what did you say?"

"Girl, oh my gosh! I been sitting here trying to tell you about how Maurice all of the sudden stopped blowing my phone up. You think he has somebody else?"

"Girl how am I supposed to know? Maybe he's just catching the hint that you don't wanna be with him anymore." I said knowing that she was dying to fix her marriage. A look of panic crossed her face and she got quiet. I; not wanting to sit at the bar and hear about Maurice all night, decided to smooth her over.

"Girl, you know Maurice ain't going nowhere. He's just trying to beat you at your own game," I said with a smile. Apparently, it worked because she started smiling again, but it still backfired on me because she continued rumbling off at the mouth about Maurice for the remainder of the car ride to Jar Bar. I rolled my eyes and prepared myself because I knew I was going to be hearing about him the rest of the night whether I liked it or not. But at least she felt like she was back in control though because that would at least allow us to have a fairly decent time.

As Val and I walked into Jar Bar, I laughed to myself. It was funny how the tables had turned; here I was frumpy and here she was fabulous. We made a beeline to the bar just as a young man in his 20's began humming the intro of a song. He was crispy black and he looked malnourished but when he opened his mouth and began singing, his voice was so strong that it paralyzed me.

> Mmmmm, mmmm, mmmhmhmhmmm
> Could it be your nice caramel tone
> Could it be your lips that have me blown
> Could it be your every morning smile
> While we're grinding as if to make a child
> Could it be that busy little mind
> Your cool words that help me to unwind
> What oh what is it about you
> That makes me wanna fight for you
> Make things right for you
> Protect all of you
> Bow down to you
> Girl it's true.....I love you
> Although I'm a hardened man
> A scarred man and broken man
> You've forced me to take your hand
> And for the rest of my life my queen
> Be your man, Be your man

I stood speechless at the bar. The passion that this young man encompassed within his singing made it obvious that he was in love and that he meant every single one of those words to whatever woman he was singing them to. I started to feel emotional because no man had ever professed that type of love to me, except Demarcus and it was now meaningless. A pang of hurt ricocheted throughout my chest but I quickly shook it off and dismissed it. I then promptly ordered a shot of vodka and gulped it down as soon as the bartender sat it down in front of me.

"Come on girl. Let's get a table and order some wings. I'm starving," I said as gulped down another shot of vodka; trying to distract myself.

"Girl, I ain't eating no damn wings this late at night. I been working my ass off in the gym and I be durn if I'm getting ready to mess all that up. I'll have a salad." Val replied, rolling her neck. I smiled and shook my head. This heifa used to be the queen of late night eating but now she was a woman on a mission and that was to make Maurice sweat. Everything she did revolved around her appearance and her vengeance towards making Maurice realize what he was missing. She'd told me about how beautiful the woman was that Maurice had been with at the restaurant that day and since I'd shown her how beautiful *she* could be; she was like a woman possessed.

"Uh Val, I understand that but if you gonna be drinking then you have to eat something that's going to soak up that liquor and salad ain't it honey. You've already had two shots of tequila and I promise you, salad with ranch dressing ain't gonna play nice with the alcohol in your stomach. And damnit, I ain't cleaning up no throw up so either you eat something that's gonna stick to you or don't drink." I said candidly.

She smacked her lips and relented. I knew that ass wasn't gonna give up the booze because although she was a mad woman about her appearance, she was still in mourning and alcohol was her means of coping. I personally prefer weed to alcohol but I digress.

As we sat at the table, taking shots and eating chicken wings I realized that we both were pathetic in our own way. I was broken and tired because of men, while she was going crazy trying to reinvent herself in order to regain a man's attention. Ultimately, we both were just two women trying deal with pain that ran so deep it rumbled in our stomachs. Loving a man and being hurt by one had rocked us to the core in every area of our lives. It'd ignited a makeover; in my case a make under, based off our self-evaluations. Our self-esteem, our appearance, our mood, our overly excessive consumption of alcohol and in my case a little Mary Jane, was currently motivated by our involvement with men. And I hated it. However, like I said, I was actually enjoying the diversion from my past lifestyle, which had previously taken all my energy to maintain. Now, all I was required to do was get up, brush my teeth, put on lotion, throw on some clothes, brush my hair back into a ponytail and leave.

Damn! Val has actually been onto something for all these years. I thought to myself as I looked over at Val whose buzz was causing her eyes to cross. I literally laughed out loud.

"Girl bring your butt on before you end up standing up on one of these tables singing *Bennie and the Jets,*" I said as I stood up and threw some money on the table.

She let out a drunken laugh that was louder than necessary and scooted her chair back awkwardly which resulted in her drunk ass landing on the floor. She jumped up quick, like a crackhead; her glassy, red and widened eyes darted around, trying to make sure no one saw her. Luckily, we were at the back where it was dark and loud because people were still performing...but I saw her, and I laughed my ass off. Tears rolled down my cheeks as the heifa then proceeded to bend over, pick the chair up and stagger out of the bar without as much as a word.

"Her old ass is gonna be sore as hell in the morning," I laughed to myself as I followed her. Right as we neared the door, I felt a tug on my arm. I turned around and it was Jermaine, I mean Avery. I instinctively jerked my arm away from him before I actually realized who he was. Once I did realize who he was, I wanted to swing on him.

"Jermaine, I mean...Avery?" I said with disgust. "Don't be grabbing on me! Have you lost your mind? I should sock your lying ass in the eye."

"Come on, girl. Don't be mad at me. Neither of us knew that we had Zian in common. Besides, you knew what it was between you and me. We was just having sex and that's it. And it sure was some good ass sex might I add." He said seductively and licked his lips.

No this sucka didn't! I thought to myself. "Dude are you serious? I don't even know your real name. By the way, which one is it?" I asked.

"That doesn't matter sweetheart. All that matters is me missing how I used to stroke that fat cat between your legs." He said boldly. I blushed as my Juicy began reminiscing because that "stroke" *had* been good as hell and I bet Zian's crazy ass didn't even know what to do with it. Nevertheless, I had my boundaries and sleeping with a friend's man was one that I didn't cross.

"Dude. Get on up out of my face. Regardless of how good that thang was and I do have to admit that it was good...as hell, Zian was my friend and that shit ain't cool." I replied coolly, although I was getting a kick out of flirting with him. And in actuality, the *only* reason that I wasn't still sleeping with Jermaine, I mean Avery *was* because of Zian. Otherwise, I definitely would still be riding that thang to the break of dawn because his sex really was that good.

"Well, it's your loss sweet heart." He said.

"I'll take that loss. See ya," I said, and walked out confidently.

When Val and I arrived at my house, I made sure she was good to drive and then I jumped into my own car. Since it was only 12:30 and I was wide awake, I decided to go back to my Cousin Brandon's house. I knew he was probably still up and sure enough all the lights were on when I got there. I knocked loudly on the front door this time and let myself in. Brandon and my little brother John were sitting on the couch smoking a blunt.

"Yes! I'm just in time," I said as I plopped down on the couch beside Brandon.

"What up Cee? Where you coming from this time of the night, girl?" Brandon asked.

"I was at Jar Bar with my supervisor." I replied.

"Damn! What'd yo' ass eat? Barbeque ribs with a side of shit? Your breath smells like a dog fart!" Brandon exclaimed covering his nose. Embarrassed, I immediately began blowing my breath into my hand.

"And what's that red shit you have all over the side of your face?"

I jumped up and ran over to the mirror. "Barbeque sauce!" I replied as I vigorously wiped my face with my hand. Brandon and my little brother John immediately started laughing at my expense, which pissed me off. They clowned me for the majority of the night but it wasn't them that I was concerned about because I knew if Brandon smelled my breath and saw the barbeque sauce smeared on the side of my face then so had Jermaine, I mean Avery. I was completely humiliated and the old Carolyn scolded me. "You big dummy! You never let a man catch you slipping!"

I was pissed because I had allowed my new indifferent attitude and embraced comfort to get out of control. Wearing less than fashionable clothes and ponytails was one thing, but being the chick with the dog breath was unacceptable. I initially thought my newfound comfort was liberating but it had taken a humiliating turn. I wasn't pressed about looking glamourous anymore, but as soon as I got home, I immediately put my compact back in my purse and made sure that I had some power punching breath mints on deck.

I paced back and forth, trying my best to figure out how to pick up my face; which I'd left lying on the floor at Jar Bar with Jermaine, I mean Avery. Then the craziest, most idiotic thought in the world popped into my head.

"I can't let him think I fell off, so I'm going to call him over, blow his mind and then put his ass out." My pride was on the line because I presumed that my social gaffes had made a mockery out of me. I never wanted an ex or someone I was dealing with to catch me looking or being anything less than flawless and since that jerkbox had, I had to redeem myself. My fingers involuntarily dialed his number and he answered on the second ring. I told him that I had changed my mind and would like to see him for old time's sake and he told me he would meet me at the Fosterberg Inn in about thirty minutes. I ran and jumped back in the shower, brushed my teeth and put on some "smell goods." Zian crossed my mind briefly, but the need for redemption and good sex pushed her right on out. Plus, her punching me in my face and spitting on me had officially defriended her anyway. The thought of that spit sliding down the side of my face quickly dissipated any hint of guilt I felt.

Just as I was grabbing my keys to leave, my phone rang. It was Jermaine, I mean Avery calling to tell me that he couldn't make it and that he was going to have to take a rain check. My pride and my face, which I had finally began to pick up off the ground, plummeted right back down to the floor and hit it hard. I wanted to ask questions but fear of further reproof stopped me. I accepted and counted it all joy because I figured that he probably spared me from making a dumb mistake anyway. So I climbed in bed, pulled the covers over my head and went to sleep.

Case#: 32581 More Than Thugs

25-year-old Andre Perry pulled up at Chunky Monkey's Daycare Center to pick up his two daughters; 4 year old twins, Mayah and Layah. He sat there frustrated, as he loosened the tie around his neck. He looked at himself in the review mirror trying to figure out what it was about him that said "loser", "thug", or more than anything, "don't hire me." He had been out all day looking for work with little to no prospects. He was sick of watching his eight months pregnant wife, Katina, work her ass off at the local hospital while he brought in little to no income. He had been a big time drug dealer when he and Katina first met but when she gave birth to the twins and he looked into the eyes of those precious baby girls, he vowed that his drug dealing days were over. But that was then and this was now. He'd been out of work for almost a year since his lay off from his construction job. And since the Governor had decreased the amount of time that people could receive unemployment benefits, he was no longer getting an unemployment check. He'd been out looking for work every day since he got laid off and initially he wasn't really worried because he felt like he would be able to find a job, but he didn't.

The family had gotten by off his wife's income and the money he was bringing in from the odd jobs he'd been doing for a local contractor. However, now that the project they'd been working on was over, he began to panic. He didn't know what he was going to do. And it didn't help that when he walked into the daycare to get his girls, he was met by the director who promptly told him that if he didn't pay by the end of the week, the girls couldn't come back. He nodded his head that he understood and went to get his babies who ran and jumped into his arms as soon as they saw him walk through the door. His heart spilled over with joy but his mind remained full of sorrow and frustration.

After he secured the twins in their car seats, he headed to the hospital to pick up his wife. He pulled in front of the hospital and when she saw him, she waddled out painstakingly but smiling, nevertheless. As he watched her, glowing and absolutely beautiful, he thought about how he loved her more than anything and how he wanted to give her the world. He jumped out and went to meet her in order to help her into the car. They embraced and kissed each other deeply. He opened the door for her and helped her in. Once she was in the car, she attempted to bend over so that she could remove her shoes, but her bulging belly prevented her from doing so; therefore, Andre bent over and did it for her. When he removed her shoes, he saw that her feet were red and swollen with blisters on them. He wanted to cry but it was at that pivotal moment that he decided to call his homie Marcus and get back in the game long enough to stack some money so his wife could go out on maternity leave. He knew it wouldn't take him long to make enough money to sustain the family. So while his wife and kids sat waiting in the car, he ran into the grocery store to "get a couple things" but more so to call Marcus. And Marcus, who loved Andre and would do anything for him since Andre had saved his life on more than one occasion, gladly told him to come by the crib later on that day and pick up "his cousin" which they used as a code name for cocaine. Andre felt disgusted for what he was going to have to do but the vision of his pregnant wife's swollen and blistered feet made him feel otherwise. He was a man and he wasn't going to have his wife working and paying the bills while he sat around twiddling his thumbs; waiting for a breakthrough.

Andre drove his wife and daughters to the house to drop them off. Katina asked him where he was going and at first, he didn't want to respond because he knew she would try to deter him. But he wasn't going to lie to her because they had promised each other a long time ago that no matter how bad it hurt, they would never lie to each other. So when he told her that he was going to see Marcus, she immediately dropped her head but she didn't argue with him.   She knew her husband, and by the look in his eyes, she knew that no matter what she said, it wasn't going to change his mind. She squeezed him and kissed him passionately.

"Baby please be careful."

"I will," he said as he got out and opened the door for her and the twins. As he pulled off, he began gritting his teeth because he hated selling drugs; especially since the majority of his family members were on them; including his own parents. He regretted not going to college but it had felt good for him to be able to use his hard earned drug money to pay for Katina to attend Winston-Salem State University and graduate with her degree in nursing. His thoughts began to overwhelm him but he shook them off because there was no time for weakness. He pulled up at the trap house where Marcus handled his drugs and knocked on the door. A tall, muscular man opened the door and immediately recognized Andre. They gave each other dap and he led Andre to the back room. As he followed "the watchman," Andre looked around and saw a small group of about five people sitting around in the living room drinking beer and talking. He nodded at them and continued to where Marcus was bagging up his coke. They also hugged and gave each other dap.

"Damn man, I thought you was out the game forever," Marcus said.

"Shit, me too. But I don't plan to be back in long though. I just need a come up real quick," Andre replied. They talked business and since Marcus was already making so much money and looked at Andre like his brother, he simply gave him a "quarter brick" and told him not to worry about paying him back. Andre thanked him graciously, put the coke down inside his pants and walked out the door; not noticing the group of young boys standing in the kitchen watching him; sizing him up.

Andre returned home to find his wife cooking dinner. He kissed her and gave her "the look" letting her know that he had the product. She shook her head and continued dinner. Once they had eaten, bathed the girls, and put them to bed, Katina prepared a pot of boiling water for her husband. In his drug dealing days, she'd helped him cook crack on many occasions and was a pro at it. Andre walked into the kitchen with "the product" and began preparing it. Katina, who was born and raised in the streets herself, was very street smart and cautious. She knew that her husband had one thing on his mind and that was providing for his family, but on the other hand, she also knew that even when he was a drug dealer, he had a tendency to be naïve at times. Therefore, she wasn't taking any chances, especially with her babies in the house. She went into their bedroom and retrieved her husband's shotgun as well as her own pistol that they kept hidden in a lockbox under their bed. She waddled back into the kitchen, handed her husband his gun, and laid hers on the table. He smiled at her and shook his head.

"Man I love you." He said as he took his gun and laid it down on the kitchen table as well. They both sat down at the table and began making crack. As they were finishing up, Andre grabbed his gun and walked into the pantry to get some plastic sandwich bags. As he was retrieving the bags, he heard Katina screaming.

"Baby! Oh my gosh, Baby...!" Suddenly, Andre heard a loud cracking, "BOOM" sound coming from the back door. As he ran to see what the commotion was, he saw three masked figures running in. Katina immediately picked up her gun and began firing at them since she was sitting at the table facing the back door. She hit two of them, but the third man fired and hit Katina who fell to the ground. Andre, who came from behind, saw Katina hit the ground and lost his mind. He fired his gun and blew the side of the intruder's head off. He made sure the other two were dead and then ran to Katina's side. She was conscious but badly wounded. The shot, which had hit her in the shoulder, just inches away from her heart, had knocked her over onto the floor. She tried to get up but Andre wouldn't allow her to.

"Don't move! You don't know where the bullet is or what damage it did. Stay where you are," Andre said hysterically.

"Andre, you gotta flush the crack before the cops get here. Hurry!" Andre quickly followed her orders. His adrenaline was pumping and his heart was pounding. He quickly gathered the "product" and ran into the bathroom. He flushed the crack down the toilet and stood there impatiently in order to make sure that everything went down; which all of it did with the exception of a small portion.

"Fuck!" He almost yelled out too loudly as he waited for the toilet to fill back up. He knew he didn't have any time to waste and he still had to call 911. Once he made sure the crack was gone, he ran into their bedroom, grabbed a pillow and ran back into the kitchen. He put the pillow under Katina's head and quickly called 911. He then frantically began the tedious task of trying to dispose of any remaining evidence or residue. And although Katina was extremely weak, she continued coaching him. He started out wiping off the table but he saw something moving out of the corner of his eye. He grabbed his gun and quickly pivoted in the direction of the movement but he found that it was his twin girls peeking around the corner. He didn't want them to see their mother or the dead bodies lying on the floor so he picked the girls up, carried them back to their room, and instructed them to stay in bed until he came and got them. He then rushed back into the kitchen to continue cleaning up just as he heard the sirens. He quickly picked up the trashcan and started throwing things away.

"Baby, put our guns on the table. I don't want no shit and put your arms up when they come in. Hurry baby." Katina said weakly. He did as she told him. He tried to wipe the table as best as he could in a haste. He then quickly dropped to his knees beside Katina and threw his hands in the air as the cops and ambulance arrived. When the police came in, he announced who he was, who his wife was, and that his children were in the next room. The first responders automatically loaded Katina up and wheeled her outside to the ambulance.

"Baby, I'm right behind you as soon as I get the girls situated. I love you," Andre said and kissed Katina on her lips.

"I love you too," she whispered.

An officer walked up to Andre and asked him what happened. Andre told the officer that the intruders had kicked in their door and fired at them; therefore, they fired back. The officer asked if he had any enemies or individuals that wanted to harm them and Andre replied that he didn't.

"So, it's very convenient that both you and your wife had guns. Were you expecting them?" The officer asked smugly as his eyes scanned the room.

"No, we weren't expecting them. I don't think they woulda kicked our door in if they thought we were waiting on them." Andre replied, just as smugly.

"Uh, Officer Mackly, can I speak to you for a sec?" Another officer asked from the kitchen.

"Yeah sure," Officer Mackly replied. "I'll be right back Mr. Perry."

"Alright. I'm going in here to check on my girls." Andre said as the officer nodded at him.

"Fine, just don't touch anything, ok?" Officer Mackly replied as Andre glared at him and walked into his girls' room. They were full of questions but he remained silent, only assuring them that everything would be ok. By that time, the place was swarming with cops, forensic teams and detectives. Three bloody dead bodies were laying on the kitchen floor, the house was a disaster and his wife was in the hospital. Andre was very anxious because he wanted to get himself and his girls out of there so he could be with his wife. He felt guilty because all of this was his fault and he didn't know what the outcome was going to be. He felt confident that he had done a fairly decent job of cleaning up all the drugs but when Officer Mackly came into the room holding two big Ziploc bags full of evidence with a smirk on his face, Andre's heart dropped. Most of the things Andre had thrown in the trash including the baggies and some articles used to cook the crack were all in the bags.

Detective Mackly began reading Andre his Maranda Rights as he placed Andre under arrest. One of the female investigators on the scene, who actually knew the Perry's, convinced Detective

Mackly to allow the girls, who were distraught, to ride with their father in the back of the police car while she called CPS.

Carolyn Black

"Carolyn, I love you but your ass needs to get a life. I mean don't get it twisted, I love having you over here but you messing up my game. And by the way your mom talks, you're messing up her game too. What the hell's goin' on with you? You don't go out no more and you walking around here looking like 'Laura Ingle' in them damn hoop skirts and raggedy ponytails. I mean damn! What's the deal?" Brandon asked me after I'd barged in on him again. Luckily, this time he was home alone.

"Damn Brandon! So...what, you don't want me coming over here no more? If it's like that, then I'll just leave," I said grabbing my things; my feelings hurt.

"Chill Shawty. You're always welcome over here, but I'm just not used to this Carolyn. I mean, is all this because of that bum ass dude I knocked out at Buster's?" he asked. I sighed. Yeah, that was part of it, but I just didn't want to admit it to him. My life had been crappy before, but now I felt like I was nearing rock bottom, and Brandon was right. I just didn't care to take pains with myself anymore. I didn't have any men in my life, which had caused me to lose my desire to look good and feel energized. And the reality of it was; I just didn't want to be bothered anymore. Brad and Dewayne had called me several times but I ignored them. And I wasn't really interested in getting involved with anyone else so I figured if I didn't look the part, then I wouldn't get it. I felt ashamed of myself for being depressed because my mom was obviously doing much better, I was back working and for the most part everything was going fairly well in my life. But since I'd allowed men and vanity to become a curse for me...again, I had chosen to fall back for a while. I needed to do some soul searching and focus on myself, and dealing with men was too much of a distraction. The only men that I needed in my life was my dad, Brandon and my little brother John.

And I was going to be up under them for a while whether they liked it or not.

"I mean, I been chilling and taking care of mom dukes, making sure that she's ok that's all," I replied, telling a half-truth. Well actually a fourth of a truth.

And Brandon, knowing me all too well, gave me a "yeah right" look. And just as he was about to continue his lecture, his doorbell rang. He answered it and in walked a sexy little tender roni. My dried up Juicy started to moisten a little. I mean, I was chilling but apparently, *she* wasn't.

"What up B?"

"What up Jarrod? What you looking for?" Brandon asked; referring to his street pharmaceuticals, as he and Jarrod dapped each other up.

"Let me get a dub," Jarrod replied.

"Alright, you can come on in and sit down while I get it ready. This is my cousin Carolyn," Brandon said, introducing me.

"Nice to meet you. Wait, I remember you." Jarrod said, looking me up and down. I took a long look at him also and realized that he did look familiar, but I couldn't place where I'd met him. I prayed to God that he wasn't one of my old clients.

"Uh, you look familiar but I don't know where I remember you from."

"You used to babysit me when I was about eight years old. I'm Betty Harris' son." He replied.

"Oh yeah, I remember you. That was a looooong time ago. How old are you now?"

"I'm 27." He answered.

Damn! I usually didn't like younger dudes but he was fine.

"Dang, you're all grown up now. How's your family doing?" I asked, trying to make small talk.

"They doing good."

"Good." I replied and then there was an awkward silence.

"Listen Carolyn, this is probably going to sound really crazy right now but I had the biggest crush on you as a kid. You probably don't remember this, but I never will forget that time when you came home from college and we were at church for the annual Christmas program. You had on a red and white sweater dress and I remember starring at you the whole time imaging that you were Mrs. Claus and I was Santa," he chuckled. I blushed and shook my head awkwardly. I really didn't know how to respond.

"I hope you don't take this the wrong way, but I still think that you're beautiful and I would love to take you out sometime," he continued boldly. I could feel my face turning red. I then became self-conscious, wondering if I had food in my teeth, bad breath or a booger in my nose.

"Uh thanks, but I'm almost 35 years old. You're a little too young for me. Plus, I did used to babysit you. That would be kinda weird," I replied, bashfully, with a nervous laugh. I couldn't believe this young boy had me sweating like a schoolgirl.

"Carolyn, I'm not a kid anymore. I'm a grown man. I graduated from North Carolina Central with a criminal justice degree and I'm pursuing my master's. I have a job, my own car and my own crib. Age ain't nothing but a number baby. I can give you anything...and more than a man in his 30's can give you," he concluded but seductively.

Cornball. I rolled my eyes; nevertheless, my Juicy started throbbing because I knew the young'uns aimed to please in bed. My face was probably blood red and once again, I was speechless.

Ring. Ring. Ring. It was my work phone. *Thank you Jesus.* I said to myself as I fumbled around in my pocket to get it; almost dropping it as I pulled it out.

"Excuse me I gotta take this," I said as I got up clumsily and walked closer to the door.

"Fosterberg CPS, this is Carolyn speaking."

"Carolyn, this is Valerie. Listen, I know you're not on call but Mario is sick so I need you to meet me at the county jail ASAP. Girl, we have a mess going on here. Some intruders shot a pregnant woman who's in the hospital and although I don't know why, the police arrested her husband. Now he's in jail and the couple's twin daughters have nowhere to go. So, how quickly can you get here?" She asked.

"I'm on my way," I said, thankful for the distraction. I began gathering my things just as Brandon came out holding a twenty sack of chronic for Jarrod.

"Brandon, I'll holler at you later. Thank God I didn't smoke that blunt with you because I just got called in on a case," I said, heading to the door. "It's been good seeing you Jarrod."

"Likewise Carolyn. Hopefully this won't be the last time," He said with a boyish but mischievous smile.

I ignored him and hauled ass getting out of there. My old self was telling me to slide him my number so I could at least have an occasional bed buddy, but my new, insecure self was saying to me "what's the use?"

I got into my car and headed over to the county jail. When I arrived, Val was standing beside her car anticipating my arrival.

"Hey Carolyn. How's it going?" Val asked.

"I'm good. What's going on?"

"Well we have a 25 year old dad and 24 year old mom with twin daughters. According to the police report, three men broke into the family's home and shot the mom who is now in the hospital."

"Good gosh! That's terrible. But what's that have to do with us? Why are we involved and why is dad in jail?"

"Well, allegedly mom and dad were cooking crack when the men broke in because the cops found cocaine residue in a pot in the kitchen. They are thinking that the intruders attempted to rob them. The issue for us is the parents have no family the twins can stay with since dad's in jail. Then we have to consider child endangerment if they are dealing drugs in the home and putting the children in harm's way."

"Oh dag. That sucks. The poor mama probably got caught in the crossfire," I said shaking my head.

"Well, hold on now. Don't underestimate the wife because she's the one who shot the first two men and killed them. Dad only killed the third one after he shot the wife. Shoot, that heifa is a gansta boo, honey," Val said. I laughed.

"Ok so what's the plan?" I asked.

"Well, mom is going to be in the hospital for a while because unfortunately she is in serious condition; especially with her being pregnant. And since dad is in jail I'm guessing that we are going to have to put the twins in an emergency placement until we figure out what's going on."

"Where are the twins now?" I asked.

"They are actually here in a holding cell with their dad."

"What?!" I asked baffled.

"I know right. But because they didn't have anywhere to take the girls, they allowed them to ride over in the police car with their dad and sit with him in his cell until we got here," she replied.

"Wow, that was uh, very considerate of them."

"Yep. But we have a problem." She said ominously. I rolled my eyes and sighed.

"What?"

"None of our emergency foster care placements are answering the phone and the girls are only 4 years old, so they can't stay at any of the level 2 placements or emergency shelters for teens. So....uh....I don't know what we're going to do."

"*No* family?" I asked.

"Well, that's why the officers called us. I hope that they at least have a family friend or a neighbor that they will feel safe leaving the girls with. You know; a kinship placement."

"Ok," I said hoping and praying that we would come up with somebody.

"Otherwise, I guess they'll be staying with you," she said and laughed with a little too much seriousness in her eyes for me.

"And that's going to be a big Oh Hell No! I ain't on call tonight honey, you are. I'm just here as a side kick," I said also laughing while also returning her serious look but with a little more intensity.

"We'll deal with that later. So anyway, *let's get it started, oooohoooh, oooohoooh!*" She rapped mimicking the MC Hammer song. I just shook my head and kept walking.

But you hated the late 80's/90's era... I laughed to myself.

We entered into the county jail, showed them our badges and informed them why we were there. The officers discussed the charges with us and informed us of how serious things were. They informed us that the children appeared to be unharmed but that they were in the home when the incident occurred. They also informed us that the father; Andre Perry, had been very cooperative and concerned about the welfare of his babies.

"He doesn't appear to be a knucklehead but then you can't always judge a book by its cover," one of the officers said as he led us to the secluded area with a large holding cell divided into two sections by bars. On one side, I saw two small girls lying on a cot, wrapped up in blankets, asleep. The cot sat directly against the bars, which separated the two cells. On the other side of the bars was a handsome young man who was pacing back and forth. He appeared to be devastated and I could tell that he'd been crying because dried tears stretched from underneath his eyes down under his chin.

"Hi, Mr. Perry. My name is Valerie Whitman and this is Carolyn Black. We work for Fosterberg County Department of Social Services."

He stopped pacing and looked over at us. His eyes then went directly to his twins who were sleeping peacefully and what little bit of life he had remaining in his face drained completely away. However, he only shook his head, snorted and resumed pacing without saying a word. Val waited a few more seconds and then she continued.

"Um, Mr. Perry, we uh came here to discuss the welfare of your twin girls." She said and paused again momentarily. He continued pacing.

"Mr. Perry I apologize for having to be so blunt at such a bad time but you know, with you being in jail and your wife being in the hospital, we really need to know if you have somewhere you'd like for us to take your children because, um, obviously they can't stay here." He continued pacing but I noticed a change in his breathing, which was getting deeper. Val glanced over at me and I looked back at her feeling just as helpless.

"Mr. Perry...?" Val said gently as possible. "Mr. Perry please. I know we are probably the last people that you want to see right now but it's late and we can't leave these girls here. Do you have any family members or close friends who the children can stay with until we complete our investigation or at least until you get out of jail?"

I saw him squeeze his eyes closed and take a deep breath, but his mouth never opened.

"Mr. Perry," I said patiently. "Hi, my name is Carolyn Black." I stuck my hand through the bars hoping he would come to shake it, which he didn't.

"Um, you just gonna leave me hanging?" I asked wittily with my hand still extended. Baffled by my statement, he gave me a confused look. He, however, still left me "hanging." So I continued.

"Mr. Perry you have to be a good person for the police to have let your babies stay here in the cell beside you. So let's sit down and come up with a solution together. And if you want, I can arrange for the detective to let you and I talk in a less restrictive area and Val can stay here and watch the girls since they're asleep." I flashed a wicked smile and side eye at Val. She tried to kick me discreetly but she did it so clumsily that he noticed. Plus, it hurt so I'm sure I grimaced although I recovered quickly. I was worried that he wasn't going to take us seriously and shut down even further. However, our "wittiness" seemed to work in our favor because I saw something that remotely resembled a smile, cross his face, so I kept going.

"Uh, Mr. Perry, my arm's kinda getting a little tired over here. Please come shake my hand before it falls off."

He relented and walked over to me. He more so gave me a low high five than a handshake but I accepted it.

"Thank you Mr. Perry. So have you gotten any news about your wife?" I asked. The almost pleasant look that had been on his face began to vanish. I began to panic because once again I was afraid that I'd lost him; however, once again things worked in my favor. He finally started talking. He told us about how he'd been struggling and that he wasn't a drug dealer. He also talked how much he loved his wife and he cried when he talked about how neither of them had family. He couldn't go into detail about the case but he made it a point to keep telling us that he wasn't a drug dealer. And after about an hour of hearing his life story, Val kicked me again but she was definitely more discreet *and* precise than she had been previously. She announced that she was stepping out to make a few phone calls and I knew that it was time for me to get homeboy to start wrapping it up.

"Everything I do, I do for my wife and my babies, Ms. Black. They are all I have and I would never do anything to hurt them. I swear."

"I believe you Mr. Perry, but in the meantime, we still have to have somewhere for your babies to stay. Your wife is in the hospital and you're here so we have to get them to a safe place. You don't know anybody? A friend, a coworker, a cousin, a nurse, a doctor or somebody?" I asked.

He sat and thought intently for a moment.

"Nah man. I really can't think of nobody. This is a question my wife would be better at answering," he replied quietly as his head dropped.

"Well Mr. Perry, right now it's just me and you. I'm doing everything possible to keep the girls with someone they know. There has got to be somebody; otherwise we're going to have to place them in foster care." *Or at Val's.* I thought to myself.

Desperate, I opened my brief case and pulled out a piece of paper. I used a technique I learned in graduate school called an "ECOMAP" which identified people from within the family, community and/or whoever else was somehow linked to the family. We started out with family and then we looked at co-workers, past baby sitters, associates, daycare workers and everyone else he knew. It was still slim trimmings until Mr. Perry had an epiphany.

"Hey, what about Cinda Graves, the investigator who convinced the police to let the twins come with me? She's black and the twins know her because they play with her daughter at the daycare and we've taken them to some play dates at her house. Katina, my wife, knows her pretty good because when Cinda's dad was in the hospital, Katina was his nurse. Shit, Katina pretty much nursed him back to health. And Cinda and Katina have actually hung out a couple times, plus she's the Po Po, so I would feel safe letting them go home with her for a few days until I get out of here or my wife gets out of the hospital; whichever one comes first." He babbled.

"Cinda Graves." I said as I wrote her name down.

"Ok you keep thinking about it and I'm going to check and see if I can get in touch with Ms. Graves," I replied, as I jumped up and headed towards the exit before he could get started talking again. Hell, I was tired and ready to take my ass home.

They buzzed me out just as Val was walking back in.

"So, any luck?" I asked. She sighed.

"Nope. Ms. Betty is out of town, Ms. Jordon hasn't completed her recertification classes yet, and Ms. Beverly is full until tomorrow evening. We might have to look into the next county over. Or one of us may have to seriously take them home for the night until Ms. Beverly's house comes open."

I rolled my eyes and completely dismissed her. It wasn't no way in hell I was taking no kids to my weed-scented house.

"Well, he asked me to check on a Cinda Graves. She's actually the investigator who called us. He said she knows the family pretty well because their kids go to the same daycare and his wife was her father's nurse when he was in the hospital, so she might work out for us."

"Well don't get your hopes up if she's assigned to the case. She can't have his kids in her house while she's investigating him for drug charges and murder," Val said sarcastically.

"Well, I guess your ass best be heading to the grocery store so you can get some food to feed those babies with then," I replied just as sarcastically because she was starting to piss me off being a freaking "Debbie Downer." *What happened to MC Hammer?* I thought to myself as I walked over to the officer working behind a large glass window. I asked for Ms. Graves' information and he informed me that she was actually in the building, so he paged her for me.

Val leaned against the wall silently with a smirk on her face. I wanted to slap her to sleep.

"Ms. Black? Hi. I'm Detective Cinda Graves. How may I help you?" a young African American female officer asked me as she extended her hand to me.

"Hi Detective Graves. As you know, I work for CPS. This is my supervisor Valerie Whitman." They shook hands and greeted each other.

"Detective Graves, I understand that you know the Perry's pretty well correct?" I asked.

"Uh, yes. I know them fairly well. Why, what's this about?" She inquired.

"Well Detective Graves as you may know, the Perry's don't have any family members that can keep the girls tonight. And as you also know, I can't leave them here. All of our foster care placements are unavailable for the night and we would prefer to have the children with someone they are familiar with. So, when we were asking Mr. Perry if he knew of anybody that fit into that category, since they don't have any family members available, he mentioned you. Would you be willing to take care of the girls until we can get one of our beds open, which hopefully will be sometime tomorrow evening?" I asked as professionally as I could, while trying to mask my desperation and desire to get down on my knees and beg. She responded with a look of confusion and reluctance.

"Detective Graves we will understand if you can't take the girls since it may be a conflict of interest due to you being an investigator on the case and I know that we are asking a lot but our options are very limited right now." Val said, sounding as if she was more so trying to sabotage the plan versus endorse it. This time, I wanted to kick her. *Wasn't she the one who mentioned the kinship placement crap in the first place?* I was so mad, I literally wanted to bark in her face like I was pit-bull, but I kept my cool.

"Well uh, they actually took me off the case anyway because of the conflict of interest. And they really are good people. My family loves Katina because she was so good to my father when he was in the hospital and my daughter loves the twins, so I would be glad to help in any way I can," she replied humbly. I smiled, unbeknownst to Detective Graves, mischievously and cut my eyes at Val. And when Detective Graves wasn't looking, I discreetly added a wink. Val then discreetly shot me a bird, but she gave in and smiled back.

"Ok, so I will go with Detective Graves and make all the arrangements and check the home. And Ms. Black, you can stay here with Mr. Perry and the twins," she said and bounced a smug look my way, which she quickly morphed into a professional one. I bounced a "touché" look back at her and we parted ways.

The Next Morning

"What's up man? Andre." Andre said as he extended his hand to a young Hispanic man who was sitting alone eating breakfast.

"Que pasa? Luis." He accepted Andre's hand and they gave each other dap.

"So what you up in here for man?" Andre asked. Luis looked at Andre quietly before answering.

"It doesn't even matter man." Luis answered frankly. "What about you?"

Andre sighed. "All I can say is a dream deferred homie." Andre replied in seemingly higher spirits because he was grateful that Marcus was coming to bail him out.

"And what dream is that?" Luis asked which surprised Andre because no one had ever asked him about his dreams before except his wife. He was stumped for a second because he didn't know whether to spill his guts like he wanted to or try to be cool and make it seem as if it wasn't a big deal. However, since he didn't know the man, he chose to spill his guts because he figured that with all he'd been through in the last year, hell within the last 24 hours, he had nothing to lose.

"Well, since I was a kid I always liked to build things. I would use blocks, rocks, boxes, paper, anything! Anything I could get my hands on that I could put together and stack. I started working in construction a few years ago and I fell in love with it. So, to answer your question, my dream is to own my own construction company but my focus right now is finding a way to provide for my family. I was laid off a year ago and I been doing odd jobs here and there, but I can't get nothing stable. I have two little twin girls and a son on the way. My wife, my wife Katina…" He began getting choked up, but he cleared his throat and continued.

"My wife Katina has been holding the family together and that shit makes me feel like a chump. I mean, I'm grateful that God blessed her with a good job but it's my job to provide. Man she shouldn't…she shouldn't have to be suffering because of me. I gotta do something man." Andre's eyes met Luis'. Andre's eyes were full of desperation *and* determination but Luis' eyes were unreadable. Neither of them spoke until Luis broke the silence.

"So you're the man that the police let keep his little girls in the cell?"

Andre smiled in spite of himself and nodded his head. "Yeah man, that would be me."

"You know, it is funny that you would mention that you are into construction because my papá who owns a very well-known construction company in Virginia just got hired by this young pastor to build some megachurch on the outskirts of this county. It is at least six months of guaranteed work, but you have to get there today by 1:30 p.m., so make sure you get there. It will be my papá, Mr. Garcia, and my older brothers."

Andre's heart began to pound. He looked up at the clock. It read 10:15 a.m.

"Do you think he will hire me if he finds out I've been in jail?" Andre asked anxiously.

"Are you crazy man? Look where we are meeting. My papá is good at reading people and he looks at the heart. After that, all he cares about is if you work hard and don't steal from him. Just tell him that his son Bama Jama sent you. "

"Bama Jama?" Andre asked, intrigued by the incongruence of the name. Luis ignored him and continued without answering the question.

"Are you familiar with Maricott?"

"Yes, it's about 30 minutes from here."

"Ok. You have to be at the Maricott Inn today by 1:30. And will you do me a favor? Will you tell my papá that the heart attack wasn't his fault and that Mi Belleza Eva and I send our love? And Andre, 'siempre estaré contigo,' tell my dad that too. Ok?"

"Ok." Andre replied although he was confused and skeptical, but excited and hopeful all at the same time. He didn't want to ask any more questions, but there was one in particular that he couldn't refrain from asking.

"Uh how do you say that Spanish phrase again?"

Carolyn Black

Beep. Beep. Beep. My alarm began blaring. I hit the snooze button and rolled back over. I was still tired from the night before since I'd gotten home so late after dealing with the Perry's. Nevertheless, I forced myself out of bed, got into the shower and let the hot water wake me up. When I got out, I dried off and walked back into my bedroom. I lathered up with lotion and Vaseline and then headed to the closet to find something to wear. I chose a pair of khaki pants and a white blouse. I got dressed, brushed my hair up into a ponytail and prepared to head out. As I was walking towards the door, on instinct, I made sure to stop and look in the living room mirror before I left out. As I was checking for nose and eye boogers, I caught a good glimpse of myself. My face was all pale and bland looking and my eyes had lost their sparkle. And to top that off, a big red pimple was in the initial stages of protruding from my chin. Tears welled up in my eyes, but I fought them back. I picked the mirror up and slammed it on the floor, causing glass to fly everywhere.

"I don't care! I don't care! I don't care!" I chanted to myself in an attempt to *convince* myself that I really didn't care.

When I arrived at work and walked into Val's office, I felt ashamed and self-conscious. She wore a pale yellow Polo shirt and a nicely fitted gray pencil skirt. Her hair bounced and swayed with any movement that she made with her head. She wore lip-gloss and eyeliner and flower patterned sandals that matched her shirt. The hussy even had freshly arched eyebrows. And there I stood, wrinkled and raggedy. *I don't care, I don't care, I don't care*. I chanted again in my head, although in actuality, I did care. I felt like the ugly girl in the crew and I had nobody to blame but myself. However, I chalked it up and pressed forward...until Val tried to play me.

"Dang girl, you look like hell. Did you roll out of bed and come straight to work?" she said with a giggle that I perceived to be a little bit condescending. It kinda pissed me off, but I let it go.

"Girl, I'm tired. I ain't worried about trying to be cute."

"Hmmph. You sho' ain't lying about that. Ooo and girl, I have some bomb stuff that I ordered offline a few months ago, that will dry that pimple up on your chin. I'll give you some," she continued, ditzy as a doorknob but with some apparent cheekiness. I tried to bite my tongue but C. Black just wouldn't let me because although I may have compromised my appearance, my dignity was still somewhat intact.

"Val, are you really trying to clown me? I mean really, *you* of all people. Please don't forget that it was *I* who introduced *you* to Janice, honey, and helped *you* look the way *you* look now. Otherwise, you'd still be walking around here looking like somebody's great aun'tee circa 1993. Girl bye." And I said it with a straight no chaser mean mug. She peered at me momentarily and I stared right back at her with a "what's up?" look in my eye. Val and I loved each other but we weren't shy about bumping heads. Our supervisor/supervisee relationship boundaries were clear when it came to work related things, but they were wide open at times when it came to getting personal. Val's mouth had always been slick and my tolerance for disrespect had always been minimal which caused us to have head on collisions from time to time. When she saw I wasn't playing, she rolled her eyes and walked over to her desk.

"Why you being so sensitive? I was just joking around."

"And I was simply responding to your 'joking around.' Now what's up with the Perry family?" I stated bluntly. "And by the way, give me some of that pimple cream."

She cut her eyes at me and picked up the Perry's file. "Let the grueling process begin."

We made some phone calls, did some research and checked in with Detective Graves regarding the girls. We talked back and forth with the police and began collecting data so we could get the investigation wrapped up as soon as possible. We then visited the mother who was finally awake and talking. She was a cute brown-skinned girl with glowing skin and long dreadlocks with blonde tips. She asked a lot of questions but she wasn't combative. Being a nurse, she understood the process and she was willing to cooperate. And her love for her husband Andre was palpable. She lit up when she talked about him and how good of a man he was. She was so proud of him for having chosen Detective Graves as a temporary placement for the twins and she held herself together, although no matter how hard she tried, she couldn't stop the tears from falling. Shortly into the investigation, the door barged open and Mr. Perry strode in.

"Andre!" Mrs. Perry exclaimed, as she tried to sit up and extend her arms to him. He ran over and embraced her as gently but as firmly as he could without hurting her. He kissed her all over her face while continuously saying, "I'm so sorry baby. I'm so sorry." He then laid his head on her belly.

"How's my son doing?"

"Dre he's fine and so am I. How'd you get out?" she asked excitedly.

"Marcus hired some big time lawyer and they got me out." He answered. He then turned to us and nodded. "Mrs. Whitman, Ms. Black."

We both said hello and he turned back to his wife.

"Baby listen, I don't know if they told you but Cinda has the girls, so they're ok. I'm going to Marcus' crib so I can take a shower and change clothes. Then I have to make a run, ok?" She studied him for a second not wanting to question him but after everything that had happened, she just couldn't help herself.

"Uh, Dre; can I speak to you alone please?" Mrs. Perry asked still trying to sit up.

"No Katina, I don't have time for questions. Don't worry everything's going to be ok. You just focus on getting our babies back home. I'll be back here as soon as possible." He kissed her on her forehead and disappeared as quickly as he came in.

She looked at us; unsure as to what to say. I could tell she wanted to break down, but she asked to see her girls instead.

"Well Mrs. Perry as we were saying before Mr. Perry walked in…" Val began as the door opened; interrupting her again. A forty something white female with short curly black hair and wide hips walked in wearing scrubs. I saw Val rolling her eyes out of the corner of my eye.

"Thelma. Hi." Mrs. Perry said, appearing to be somewhat nervous.

"Katina are you ok? Dr. Moretz told me you were a patient when I got here this morning so I thought I'd better come and see you. How are you?" she asked as she walked over and grabbed Mrs. Perry's hands. She turned and acknowledged us. "Ladies."

We nodded.

"I'm fine thanks." Katina replied.

"Well listen, since I'm here I wanted to talk to you about your plans regarding whether or not you are planning on going out on short term disability or if you're planning on returning to work and using some sick time when you're released from the hospital." As I listened to the exchange, I figured that this lady had to be her supervisor and I also thought about how weird it must be for Katina to be a patient at the very hospital that she worked at.

"Well I don't have any sick time or vacation days left that I can use because what little bit I had left, I was saving for when I go out on maternity leave so I can still get a check until my short term disability kicks in. But, I guess I will have to use it to cover my stay here because I was planning to work up until I don't feel comfortable enough to work anymore."

"Katina you've been severely injured and you're over 8 months pregnant. As a nurse, your supervisor and your friend I really think that it's best that once you're released from the hospital, you go ahead and go out on short term disability."

"But Thelma, I've already told you I don't have the sick time to do that. I will be ok. Andre is having a hard time finding a job and we need the money right now."

"Katina, I know all that. That's why I got with a few of the girls and we're going to give you our sick time. Mine starts over next month and I haven't used much of it anyway so I have plenty to share. Margo, Rachel and Eddy are going to chip in with me and all that together should at least give you three weeks. I've already gotten it approved with Dr. Pedenon and Peggy so it's all set. When you get out of here you're not allowed to return until 6 weeks after that precious baby boy is born, you hear me?" Thelma said with a large and proud smile. Katina sat silently with her mouth open. I saw her eyes watering up.

"That's the best thing that anyone has done for me in a long time. Thank you so much Thelma."

"It's our pleasure Katina. You're such a beautiful person and we just want to repay you. And you should see all the stuff that some of your old patients brought when they found out you were in here. We have it all in the other room. I'll have Randy to roll you in there when you feel up to it."

Katina sniffed and squeezed the woman's hand. "Thank you, Thelma."

Once Thelma walked out of the room, Katina allowed herself to break down and cry but this time they were tears of joy. Val and I looked at each other and then we excused ourselves out into the hall. As we reflected on all the acts of kindness that people; even the police, were bestowing upon this young couple, we concluded that they had to be good people. But we just didn't know what type of parents they were yet. Our goal was never to split families up, but more importantly, to keep them together so we decided to go out on a limb and arrange for the twins to come and spend some time with their mother at the hospital. Once the girls arrived, of course, we had them checked out and as we expected, everything came back clear.

Mr. Perry

Andre pulled in at the Maricott Inn and parked Marcus' black Caprice that sat on twenty-two inch rims. Any other time he would have been embarrassed by coming to an interview in a car like that, but his desperation and gratitude trumped his embarrassment. He was grateful that his friend had gotten him out jail, gave him something to wear to the interview, and then blessed him with a way to get there. He looked in the review mirror, straightened his tie nervously and looked at the clock, which read 1:10. He took a deep breath and began praying.

"God, I come to you humble and naked because I don't have any pride anymore. All I have left is a drop of hope and you. Lord, please forgive me for putting my family in harm's way, but God I didn't know what else to do. Please let me get my family back and Lord please provide a way for me to take care of them. Thanks. Amen." He took another deep breath and got out of the car. He walked into the shabby little inn and greeted the receptionist at the front desk.

"Good afternoon, Miss. I am here to meet with a Mr. Garcia regarding a construction job. I'm a little bit early, but I wanted to make sure I got here on time."

"Uh, I'm sorry sir. I don't understand. I know who Mr. Garcia is but he didn't tell me anything about hosting any interviews."

"Well, I don't know if it's anything formal but I was just told to be here by 1:30 to meet with Mr. Garcia and his sons." Andre replied trying not to panic.

"Well I'm sorry sir. I can't help you."

"Ma'am listen, it was one of Mr. Garcia's sons that actually told me to come here today. I *have* to see Mr. Garcia today ma'am. It's my last chance. I need this job." Andre plead. The receptionist stared at Andre; examining him. Seeing the desperation in his eyes moved her and she felt his pain.

"O.k. Mr...?"

"Perry, Andre Perry."

"O.k. Mr. Perry. You can wait over there." She pointed towards a shabby little couch positioned in front of a large bay window. Andre sat nervously, shaking his leg as he waited. He had no clue what Mr. Garcia looked like and he started to get up to ask the receptionist. However, at 1:30 on the dot, a small group of men, one who appeared to be much older than the others, walked in. Assuming that these were the men he was looking for; Andre ran up to them like a man possessed and started asking for a Mr. Garcia who owned a construction company. They all stopped and looked at him like he was crazy.

"Who's asking?" one of the younger looking men asked defensively.

"My name is Andre Perry. I was told that you all were looking for some construction workers to work on the megachurch contract."

"Well, somebody told you wrong. Now excuse us we have work to do." the young man who apparently was the spokesperson for the group said. They all then turned and began walking away, dismissing Andre as if he were a leper. Andre stood there with his balls in his hands, feeling defeated. He wanted to cry and get on his knees and beg but his manhood wouldn't allow him. He chalked it up and turned to leave. And just as he was passing the receptionist's desk he heard the lyrics, "She's a bad Mama Jama" coming from a small radio. Luis' words ricocheted in his mind and he quickly turned around and ran back towards the men who were standing in front of the elevator. The men appeared to become agitated with Andre and looked at him as if he was a menace.

"Wait, please. Bama Jama sent me. He told me to be here at 1:30 so that I could talk to his father Mr. Garcia." The men grew silent and began looking at each other suspiciously. The elevator door opened, but no one moved. The older man in the group stepped forward and walked straight over to Andre. He was so close that Andre could see the gray hairs poking out of the old man's nose.

"What did you say?" he asked. Andre swallowed what seemed to be a golf ball in his throat.

"Uh, I said that Bama Jama sent me. Are you Mr. Garcia?" Andre asked calmly. And although he was shaking and nervous, he maintained eye contact with the man he presumed to be Mr. Garcia.

"I am Mr. Garcia, but I want to know who told you that name? No one knows that name outside of us men standing here now."

"Your son Luis told me. I...uh, I was in jail with him this morning and as we were talking, I told him about how much I love working in construction and how I haven't been able to find a job and he told me to be here today at 1:30. And he said to tell you Bama Jama sent me." Andre replied, but Mr. Garcia wasn't buying it. He jerked Andre up by his suit and slammed him against the wall. The other men gathered around them.

"You lie! That is impossible. There is no way my son Luis was in jail this morning!"

Afraid and angry all in one, Andre began regurgitating the conversation he'd had with Luis earlier that morning verbatim. And he made sure to give them a thorough description of what Luis looked like.

"...and he told me to tell you that the heart attack wasn't your fault and that him and someone named Mi Belleza Eva send their love. Oh yeah and he said..." Andre slowly and cautiously reached into his lapel and pulled out a piece of paper by which he had written down the phrase that Luis had told him to say.

"Forgive me if I say this wrong because I don't speak Spanish but he also said, 'Siempre...estaré...contigo.'"

When he finished reading, he looked back at Mr. Garcia whose face had gone from defensiveness to disbelief. He slowly released his grip on Andre and to Andre's surprise; Mr. Garcia laid his head on Andre's shoulder and began sobbing. The other men, whom Andre assumed to be Luis' brothers, all put their hand on Mr.

Garcia's back and joined him in crying. Andre was completely confused out of his mind, but he said nothing. He didn't know what they were crying about but he recognized pain because he was familiar with it himself. He also wrapped his arm around Mr. Garcia and put his hand on Mr. Garcia's back.   Once Mr. Garcia got himself together, he grabbed Andre's hand.

"Come; follow me into the conference room so we can talk," he said as he lead Andre and the other men into a small conference room.

"Have a seat." Mr. Garcia urged. Andre obliged. He was thankful that his suit was black because he was sweating profusely.

"Mr. Perry, I do not understand any of this. It is impossible that you could have been in jail with my son today but it is even more impossible for you to know the things that you have said to me without actually having talked to my son."

"So you didn't know he was in jail? I told him that I didn't want to tell you that part because I was afraid that you wouldn't hire me. But I don't understand. He told me not to worry. He said you read people well and look at their heart. He said that as long as I work hard and don't steal from you, that's all you care about. And Mr. Garcia, I'm a hard worker and I've never stolen anything from anybody. I just need a chance, sir. I have twin girls and a wife who is eight months pregnant that I have to provide for. This is my last chance and if it wasn't for Luis telling me about this opportunity, I wouldn't be here. I guess since you're his dad and he sent me, he figured you'd be more willing to listen."

Mr. Garcia studied Andre, as did the other men. Their eyes never deviating from Andre's throughout the conversation. They looked for truth; they searched for deception but they found nothing more than sincerity. Mr. Garcia took a deep breath and closed his eyes, digesting what Andre was saying to him.

"Well, you would be right about that." Mr. Garcia said and paused. He smiled a weak smile. "Luis always knew how to get my attention...even in death..." Mr. Garcia said emotionally. Andre wrinkled his brow, unsure if he'd heard Mr. Garcia correctly.

"Ex-Excuse me?"

"Mr. Perry, my little brother Luis died from a heart attack two weeks ago today at a jail in Virginia. He had had a little too much to drink and the police pulled him over and took him to jail so he could sober up. He called my dad to come and get him but we were meeting with the preacher about building the megachurch and my dad missed Luis' phone call. He died a few hours later." The "spokesman" said.

Mr. Garcia let out a loud sob. "And I blamed myself until now."

Andre sat frozen, his eyes wide. The hairs on his arms stood up. He finally understood why Mr. Garcia had acted so viciously towards him earlier.

"Uh, Mr. Garcia, this must be some type of a mistake. We must not be talking about the same person. I saw this man with my own two eyes. There's no way he could have been dead. I'm sorry for the confusion." Andre replied as he stood up to leave.

"Mr. Perry, Mi Belleza Eva is my wife. She died five years ago. And Bama Jama is a puppet that I made for Luis when he was four. He loved it so much that we started calling *him* Bama Jama. And me and my sons were meeting the preacher here today so we could tell him that we decided not to take on the megachurch project. He is supposed to be here at 2:30. No one knew about this meeting except for the preacher and us. And we got here today at 1:30 because my son Hector..." He turned and looked at one of the men. "Wrote the wrong time down. So Mr. Perry, this by no means is a mistake...it is God." Andre sat there quietly for a while so that he could process what was going on. He believed in God but the situation seemed too unreal, in fact, it seemed and sounded crazy. He looked around, to make sure he wasn't being "punked" or something similar, but then *why would someone waste their time in punking someone as common and unknown as him*. No matter how he tried to twist and turn things, he eventually concluded that Mr. Garcia had to be right but it was still unbelievable to him. He knew God was real and worked in mysterious ways but a ghost? A spirit? Or maybe it was an angel who'd come down disguised as Luis in order to not only bring about a pivotal point in Andre's life but to also set Mr. Garcia free of his guilt. At that very moment, Andre finally realized and accepted that no one could explain God or define Him, nor could they explain His ways. He accepted that God could do whatever He wanted, however He wanted and He showed Himself in a way that Andre could have never fathomed. A way, Andre concluded, that would ensure that Andre and the Garcia's knew without a shadow of a doubt that it was in fact God and nothing or no one else that had bestowed a miracle upon them. Andre felt shaken but in a positive manner and he knew that he *could* never doubt God again.

When Andre was finally able to talk, he asked Mr. Garcia, "So what does 'siempre...estaré...contigo' mean?"

"It means, it means...I will always be with you," Mr. Garcia replied. Andre tried to hold it together but he dropped his head and wept.

Carolyn Black

Val and I sat chit chatting as we "monitored" Mrs. Perry with her cute little twin girls.

"Carolyn, I'm so horny I don't know what to do with myself. I want to have sex so bad. You think I could call Maurice for a quickie and then send him home?" Val asked very seriously. I laughed.

"Girl, you are crazy."

"Uh no, I'm serious." She leaned in. "Girl I've started..." Her voiced dropped to a whisper. "Touching myself down there and it feels so good. But it makes me want the real thing even more. Before long, I'm gonna be humping the bed post."

This broad didn't crack a smile, which let me know it was time for me to introduce her to the infamous silver bullet.

"Well sister, I think it's time for you and me to take a trip to the toy store."

"The toy store?"

"The sex toy store, girl. Goodness gracious."

"Ohhhh ok. Yeah. That's exactly what I need. When we going?"

I laughed. "We can go when we get off if you want to," I replied. Hell, I needed to restock my own "toy drawer" myself. I'd worn my bullet out.

"It's a date," she said all too happily. I shook my head. *Wow.* I thought to myself.

Shortly thereafter, Mr. Perry walked in wearing a black suit. When he saw the twins sitting on the bed with their mother, he rushed over to them. He squeezed them both and covered them with kisses just as he had their mother. And it seemed as if they were just as happy to see him. I noticed Mrs. Perry examining him with her eyes from head to toe.

"So how'd the run go Dre?" Mrs. Perry asked.

"Let's just say I met God today."

"What?" Mrs. Perry asked confused.

"Nothing," he smiled. "I got a job KaKa and I start next week!"

"Oh my gosh, baby! Really? Where?" Mrs. Perry screamed.

"With Garcia and Son's Construction Company. They just closed a deal to construct a megachurch on the outskirts of town and they appointed me as the team lead." A smile spread across Mrs. Perry's face. She nodded her head and they gave each other a pound.

"Well, I have some good news too. When I get out of the hospital, which will probably be by the end of the week, I won't have to come back to work until after the baby is born. Thelma and some of the girls donated their sick time to me so that I will have some income coming in until my short term disability kicks in." Mr. Perry leaned in and their foreheads touched. They looked into each other's eyes and then kissed.

"I love you baby. Everything's going to be alright." Andre said.

After Detective Graves came and picked the twins up, we offered Mr. Perry a room at one of our boarding houses. He refused because he wanted to stay at the hospital with Mrs. Perry. We decided to reserve the room anyway because we didn't know when the police would allow them back into their house since it was still a crime scene. We also gave them a few vouchers to get clothes and toiletries for themselves and the twins.

"So how long are our girls going to be with Cinda?" Mr. Perry asked as he stroked his wife's hair as she laid on his chest.

"Well, a lot of it is going to depend on the police investigation but probably no more than a few weeks to a month while we are conducting our investigation. We can't knowingly allow your children to reside in a home where drugs are possibly being manufactured and distributed, especially if people are breaking in your house. That could have really gone bad if the girls had been around." Val answered gently but candidly.

"Yeah, I know." Mr. Perry replied.

"We have up to fifteen months to work with you all as a family and monitor things, but to be frank; I really don't think it will be that long."

"I know how things look, but I love my family and everything I do, I do it for them. We will cooperate with you guys because I have no doubt that we will get our girls back," Andre replied.

"Ok, great." I said and went over and shook their hands. "We will meet again tomorrow morning to discuss visitation and reunification. We will also do a needs assessment to see what services need to be set in place for you all."

"Alright," they replied.

As we walked to the car, I yawned. I couldn't wait to get home to the phatty waiting on me in my ashtray.

"Val, I really think they're good people. They may dibble and dabble in the drug game but I really don't think we'll have any more problems after this. I think they've probably learned their lesson. And if they are having financial problems, then we can help them with that. I feel good about this one. What about you? What'd you think about their demeanor?" I asked Val because most of the "street pharmacists", that I knew were really good people and loved their kids but a lot of them were in survival mode, trying to make some paper. Then, there were those like Brandon who were good people with no intentions on harming anybody but they were like the 7-11; always open with anything you needed. However, in Brandon's case, I know he wouldn't keep his kids and his product in the same house.

"Uh Carolyn, I'm off the clock. I don't give a damn about their demeanor. Are we riding in your car, my car, or are we driving separately?"

"Driving where?" I asked, confused.

"To the sex store! I wasn't playing," she snapped and I couldn't help but to laugh.

"Calm down. You acting like a fiend."

"Well everybody doesn't have multiple choices like you."

"Actually I don't. Me and Demarcus fell out and I really don't want to be bothered with the other ones. I'm kinda just chilling."

"So, you never get horny?"

"Heck yeah! But I have quite a few Bob's that I call on when I'm in desperate need."

"Bob's? What? What are you talking about?" She asked inquisitively.

"Come on. I'll show you."

After we went to "Mama's Toy Store" on the sketchy side of town and bought Val a Bob aka a battery operated boyfriend, we decided to go home, freshen up and then meet at Jar Bar later.

When I got home, I decided to take a shower with my new toy, Black Bob. He was long and black with ticklers on the end. I was so excited. I couldn't wait to get my clothes off and get into the shower. About thirty minutes later, I got out feeling light, airy, and refreshed. I skipped into my bedroom and slathered lotion all over my body. I put on matching underwear for the first time in 3 months and floated into the back of my closet were I'd hidden my "C. Black" clothes. I selected a red, strapless one-piece jumper and gold sandals. And although I didn't deter from wearing my ponytail, I did at least put on some cute, dangly earrings and a little bit of eye shadow. After I was dressed, I reluctantly checked my reflection in the mirror and was pleasantly surprised. I put on a little bit of tinted lip-gloss and as I walked to the door, I felt the sway began to resume in my hips.

Val and I met in the Jar Bar parking lot and when she got out of the car, she also looked refreshed and a bit cross eyed, might I add. She was all smiles and giddy.

I laughed. "Well, I see you must have introduced yourself to Bob before you came." She laughed too. "Girl, I sure did and I think I'm in love. Why didn't I know about this earlier?" she asked.

"I don't know but you better use those things sparingly or else you'll be hooked."

"Well honey by the way Bob the Builder had my walls shaking, it's too late. I'm already hooked. Uh, can you say, Maurice who?" she said and snapped her finger. I shook my head again. She always had me shaking my head.

"Come on Crazy! Let's go celebrate." I replied. So we headed in and went straight to the bar. The first round of tequila shots was on me.

"To multiple orgasms!" I toasted. Val burst into laughter but she toasted me, and seriously at that.

"I'll toast to that one," a deep voice said behind me. I turned and there stood my present nemesis; Jermaine, I mean Avery.

"And by the way, you look stunning Ms. Black," he said. I was speechless. I had no comeback nor did I want to flirt with him especially in front of Val. She would kill me if she found out that I'd actually called that fool a few weeks ago especially with all the drama that had occurred between Zian and me.

"Thanks," I replied quickly and uncomfortably.

"Can I buy you ladies a drink?" he asked as he undressed me with his eyes.

"Uh no thanks I'm good," I said awkwardly and quickly turned back around to where I met Val's constipated looking face. I rolled my eyes but once he'd walked off, she began drilling me.

"I know good and damn well you ain't still messing around with that raggedy ass piece of shit."

"What are you talking about? Hell no, I ain't messing with that liar. I guess since he keeps running into us he thinks that he and I have an amicable relationship, but he's sadly mistaken."

"Well, I hope you wouldn't go there, especially since Zian was your co-worker *and* your friend. Plus that man is married Carolyn and sleeping with a married man is messed up," she said with a little hint of judgement in her voice.

"Val, chill ok. I got this."

"Ok, whatever." And there was an awkward silence between us. I knew she was still feeling raw because of the situation between her and Maurice, but I'd be damn if she was going to project that onto me. I took another shot just as a very cute white man got on stage. And when he started singing, I had to do a double take because that man COULD SANG! And the song he was singing was dope as hell. I actually couldn't believe that he, a white man, was singing it. Shit, I smiled and starting bobbing my head.

> You're different every time you come into the room
> Caramel, chocolate, peach, colored hues
> OOOOO black woman, look, look at you
> You turn me on so much, mmmmh I love you
> Ooooo black woman, mmmmm, black woman
>
> Curly hair, wavy hair, straight hair
> You other women should beware
> Black woman when you walk by, all I can do is stare
> OOOOO black woman, look, look, look, look, look at you
> Ooooo black woman, mmmmm black woman, I love you
>
> I hear your strong, deep mind
> Your feisty words that draw the line
> Black woman I ain't afraid of you
> Oooo black woman, mmmmm black woman, I love you
> I said, I love you

As I was vibing to the song and thinking about how the singer might be in bed, my phone chirped. It was a text from Jermaine, I mean Avery. I want to put my face in between your legs. That red jumpsuit is sexy as hell. Let me take you home with me tonight.

Well Damn. I smirked as a giggle slipped from my lips. I typed back: I'm not doing this with you dude. Jermaine...opps, I mean Avery.

He replied: You don't have to do nothing because I will do everything. Come on. Let me make you scream.

I tried to be hard, but my Juicy was letting me down. I looked at Val who was smiling and enjoying the song. I didn't want to let her down because I knew she was right. At one point and time, Zian and I had been friends and Jermaine, I mean Avery was probably still married to her. But then again, on the other hand, Jermaine, I mean Avery and I had been messing around for quite some time before I found out that he was marrying Zian *and* that his name was Avery. He and I had never had anything beyond a sexual relationship, so I didn't even identify myself as his mistress. We had strictly been bed buddies and the thought of him dropping some of that good sex on me from time to time was starting to appeal to me again. And my pride, not my compassion, was calling the shots. So it was up to my pride as to how I would proceed. Would I leave him hanging like a sick puppy or would I get my rocks off, kick him out and never see him again as a means of getting my revenge? My pride *and my Juicy* chose the latter so I texted him back: I don't think you're capable of making me scream anymore. I'm over it, igniting a game of flirtation and verbal foreplay.

He replied: Oh really. Well get rid of Oscar the Grouch and meet me in the bathroom in five minutes so I can show you.

My Juicy began to swell as the excitement of having an orgasm in a public place with a man who I knew could put it down, began to entice and tantalize me. I turned and looked towards the bathroom and our eyes met. He was standing there leaning up against the wall near the entrance. He slowly, seductively licked his lips. An electric current from my Juicy raised me up out of my chair.

"Val, my stomach is bubbling a little bit. I need to go to the ladies' room. I'll be right back." I said and walked off before she could respond.

Game on.

My sashay involuntarily guided me into the bathroom where he was standing with his shirt in his hand. We said nothing. He pulled me into the stall and laid his shirt on the top part of the toilet. He unzipped my jumper and let it fall down to my ankles. He picked me up, sat me on top of his shirt, straddled the toilet seat, put my legs across his shoulder and commenced to making a meal out of my Juicy. And it felt so good, cosmic to be exact. He took me to Mars and once I was able to return to earth, he redressed me, wiped his face and walked out of the bathroom without as much as one word. I remained in the stall because my body was still firing off rockets. I had to get myself together. I was angry with myself because I had opened up Pandora's Box, but instead of feeling guilt and shame, I wanted more. And he knew that he'd trapped me.

The rest of the night was a blur. Val babbled on about this and that, but all I could think about was how, an hour later, my Juicy was still popping. I wanted him in between my legs so badly that all I could do was gyrate my hips to appease my Juicy. But I damn sure wasn't going to call him or respond to our bathroom rendezvous because I didn't want him to know he had me fiending for him.

"Girl, what the hell is wrong with you? That must have been some shit you took in there because you been all spacy ever since."

"Girl, nothing. I'm good. Come on let's take another shot." That was so I could take the edge off and get her off my back. So we went back to the bar. I ordered another shot of tequila and so did she. We downed them and ordered one more. And just as my Juicy was finally starting to calm herself down, Val went to the bathroom and Jermaine, I mean Avery, took the opportunity to come over and continue teasing me. He stood right beside me, his body brushing against mine, and ordered a drink. He remained silent although he slid me a note and walked towards the door. The note read, "I'll be at the Fosterberg Inn, Room 301 if you want to see what else I have planned for you." My Juicy went crazy. I looked up as he was gazing at me from the door. He winked at me, then turned and walked out. By the time Val returned from the bathroom, I had my shit together ready to go.

"Dang Carolyn, you are such a party pooper. At least take one more shot with me."

Damn it! My Juicy's gravitational pull towards Jermaine, I mean Avery, began rushing me. I downed the shot too quickly and almost choked. Tequila spilled out of the corners of my mouth and rolled down my chin. I quickly wiped my mouth, gave Val a swift hug, and left her standing there with her mouth open.

I tried to drive slowly so that I didn't seem desperate, but I really wanted a piece of that meat. When I arrived at the Fosterberg Inn, Room 301, I had no reservations regarding what I was about to do. When Jermaine, I mean Avery, opened the door, he was completely naked and although my battery operated friend "Black Bob" hung low, it was of no comparison to what was hanging in front of me. My insides yearned for a thrust that came attached to the body of a man.

He pulled me inside and unzipped my jumper. My nipples hardened. He took off my panties and half bra and threw them to the side. He took my hair down and let it fall on my shoulders. He then stood back and admired my naked body. He walked up on me and used his body to push me up against the wall. He cupped my boob and put it in his mouth. And with his other hand, he slid it down into my Juicy. All I could do was lay my head back and let him have his way. He licked my body from head to toe. Then he picked me up, wrapped my legs around his waist and sexed me all over the room, everywhere except the bed. And the next thing I know, I was screaming...

When I got home that night, my body was satisfied but my soul was troubled. I lit a blunt, took off the red jumper and put it back in its place in the back of my closet. As I stood looking at that forbidden section of my closet, puffing on my blunt, I vowed to stay away from it because apparently it took me back to C. Black circa a few months ago when I did more and thought less. I couldn't believe that I'd just slept with Jermaine, I mean Avery's, lying ass. Then I thought about how happy my Juicy was, so I changed my mind and instead of labeling that section in my closet as "stay away" I decided to name it "break in case of an emergency."

C. Black was making her comeback.

Case#: 32582 The Mayor's Ball

After an hour long sex fest with Jermaine, I mean Avery; I drove home feeling so good. Since we'd reconnected, it seemed as if we couldn't get enough of each other and we fell right back into our usual "don't ask, don't tell" routine. All we shared was pure, unadulterated mind-blowing sex...and I loved it. There were no feelings, no expectations, minimal dialogue and no hiding. With the current state that my life was in, hell, I was unable to withstand any other type of relationship anyway. I didn't need all the extra bullshit but my Juicy made it apparent that she needed sex...and I obliged her.

When I arrived home, I took a shower and began getting ready for the Mayor's Ball. After I was dressed, I gave myself one final look in the mirror and gave my damn self a high five. I was looking good and the smile on my face was infinite. Val and I had met up with Janice and told her what we needed in order to be the two baddest chicks in the place at the Mayor's Ball. And just like always, she came through. My hot pink one shouldered dress with the huge bow on the shoulder was going to shut it down. My 80's style makeup was just right and I wore my hair smoothed over to one side with the loose hair flowing wild and free. I did a quick Shug Avery "shimmy" and headed to my car so I could go and pick up Val.

I pulled up in front of her house and blew the horn. I pulled my sun visor down and continued to admire myself. I touched up my lipstick and put the visor back up. Just as I was leaning back into my seat, I happened to catch a glimpse of Val as she stepped out the door. My mouth dropped to the ground and all my confidence about being *THE* hottest chick at the ball went straight out the window. Val stepped out the front door wearing a very form fitting silver dress with large ruffles at the bottom. She wore neon pink lipstick and shiny silver eye shadow. Her beautiful long hair was pulled back into a neon pink, rhinestone encrusted banana clip and she rocked thick, wispy long bangs that hit right below the arch of her eyebrow, which put even more emphasis on her beautiful brown eyes and makeup. She looked beautiful but I could tell by the way she walked that she wasn't quite confident in herself. She walked self-consciously with her shoulders hunched over and since she was still learning how to walk in heels, she slid a couple times before she finally made it to the car.

"Hey girl, what's up?

"Hey Val," I replied.

"Wow, you look pretty," Val said as she plopped into her seat. I didn't even respond because when I was able to see her up close and personal, she looked even more beautiful. I stared at her for a second before I responded.

"Thanks Val, but honey, you are the show stopper right now. You look absolutely stunning. Hell, I'm a little bit jealous," I said playfully. She blushed and dropped her head bashfully.

"You really think so?" she asked, sheepishly.

"Yes I really think so," I replied genuinely.

"Awww thanks. Your girl Janice is the truth honey. Now, let's go party!" She squealed as her confidence began to dominate her shyness.

We pulled up at the extravagant Belleclaire Hotel and handed the keys to the valet guy. When we stepped into the ballroom, it was as if time stopped. We walked slowly, but with so much pizazz that we overpowered the room. I was so proud of Val because it was as if she was another woman. She held her head high and walked with confidence and a *fierce* (finger snap) sashay. And even though I had made a "grand entrance" on many occasions, hell most occasions, this time felt different for me because I was starting to feel like Carolyn Badass Black again. Nevertheless, because I'd done it so many times before, I fell back and let Val shine. I knew she was on a mission and that was to show Maurice what he was missing. I giggled to myself because I knew Maurice was going to piss his pants when he saw her and I was 100% sure that her "get back" plan was going to work.

And as soon as Maurice; who was standing by the bar talking to Mayor Bostain, saw me and Val walking towards them, he noticeably stopped midsentence and lost his ability to speak as well as his will to move his eyes off Val. She attempted to keep walking passed them but I made it a point to make a beeline over to where they were because Val was in training and I was teaching her to put her foot down. What was the use of her looking all beautiful and shit if she wasn't going to flaunt it and make Maurice eat dirt? I knew she wasn't going to talk to him because she was still trying to be hard so I figured that if she ignored him and flirted around a little bit; nothing major, it would drive Maurice insane and he would come crawling back to her. I knew she wasn't going to be disrespectful and get out of line with it but although Maurice was a good guy, I knew how bad it felt to get hurt by a man; therefore, I understood her trying to make him sweat some.

"Hey, Mayor Bostain," I said somewhat seductively as I reached out to shake his hand, which he took and kissed.

"You can call me Terrance." he replied with a clever smile. I threw my Tyra Banks "smize" at him and turned to Maurice.

"Hey Maurice," I said smiling warmly, giving him a side hug.

"Hey Carolyn," he said to me although he was still looking at Val. I laughed to myself. *Hook, line and sinker, she's got him.*

"Hi Valerie," Mayor Bostain greeted Val, although he barely took his eyes off *me.*

"Hello Mayor Bostain," Valerie said, still refusing to even look at Maurice, much less acknowledge him, although I noticed the goose bumps on her arms as she snuck peaks at him out of the corner of her eye. I knew that she missed him just as much as he missed her plus, Maurice was a nice looking man. He rocked a pair of tailored MC Hammer tuxedo pants with a matching jacket. He wore big square eyeglasses and a white collared shirt with a thick gold link chain laying on his chest.

"You ladies look beautiful," Mayor Bostain said, giving me a carnal look.

"Thanks, you don't look too bad yourself," I said firing back. A chill went down the back of my spine and I shivered. Then my body began to heat up. *Hell yea, Carolyn Black, come on back girl.* I thought to myself because if the mayor wanted to play games, I was the right one to play with. Valerie mumbled a bashful "thanks" and grabbed my hand as we walked off and prepared to have a "meeting in the ladies' room." As soon as we walked through the bathroom door, Valerie's poised exterior broke down.

"Oh my gosh Carolyn. I really got to him. My heart is beating 1,000 miles a minute. I'm shaking. This is going to sound so inappropriate, but I got such a rush out of making him salivate like that. I'm going to torture him until the end of the night and then I'm going to take him home and punish him. Oh my gosh Carolyn, I'm so wet down there," she rattled mindlessly as she paced back and forth in front of the mirror with the most serious face I'd ever seen in my life. She was actually baffled and surprised that she could be a sexy, exotic woman who commanded attention with her body and not just her brains. She loved the fact that Maurice desired her and it turned her on. She knew that she didn't want to be a sex kitten every day, but the look that Maurice had given her shook her up and I knew she was a changed woman. I was trying so hard not to laugh because the heifa was actually talking to herself, seriously contemplating and assessing the last five minutes of events that had occurred between her and Maurice. I turned and faced the mirror in an attempt to busy myself with tidying up my makeup so that I wouldn't start laughing in her face.

"No, seriously Carolyn, my body is on fire right now. Touch me, feel my arm," she said as she flung her arm towards me.

"Uh Val, I love you and everything but you do know that's the same reason Candy got her ass beat, right? I ain't with that funny shit," I said as I giggled and put my forefinger on her arm, which really was hot.

"You feel it?" she asked, still not cracking a smile. At that point, I lost it. I laughed so hard that tears rolled down my cheeks.

"Carolyn, this is really not funny. I am soaking wet down there and I have on a thong so I'm scared that if I go around him, I'm going to have an orgasm. Seriously, and I have to hold out until the end of the night. I can't let him get to me. I'm controlling this."

"Girl, whatever. I'm willing to bet you that you won't make it to the end of the night before you cave in."

Loving a challenge, Val straightened up and shook my hand. "I bet you I won't say anything to him tonight but...I am going to punish him tomorrow," she said deviously.

"So, you're saying that you're going to go all night long without saying one word to him, nothing?" I asked.

"Yep. That's exactly what I said," Val replied. I chuckled.

"I bet you one hundred dollars you won't make it till the end of the night." I challenged her and held my hand out.

"I bet you I will." She took my hand and shook it; sealing the deal.

"Ok. No exceptions either and I don't won't no shit out of you. I want my money."

"No, I want *my* money, in fresh twenty dollar bills," she said looking at me seriously.

"We'll see."

"Ok, whatever," she replied as she walked over to the mirror to touch up her hair and makeup.

"Damn, who knew I could look so good? Let's go drink and party!" she said, snapping her fingers. I laughed and followed her out of the bathroom. We peeked around the door in order to make sure that Maurice wasn't at the bar and once we saw that the coast was clear, we went over and ordered drinks. I ordered a Grey Goose and pineapple and she ordered a Long Island Ice Tea. As I was digging inside my clutch to get the money, I heard a deep voice from behind me.

"Now Carolyn Black, do you think I'm going to let you and my sister pay for those drinks?" Startled, I turned around and saw Mayor Bostain standing there looking delicious with his sandy brown skin, low cut, dark brown hair and hazel eyes. And by the looks of his outfit, it was apparent that he had collaborated with Maurice on the MC Hammer theme because he wore a replica of the suit that MC Hammer wore on the cover of his *Two Legit to Quit* album.

I smiled, snapped my clutch shut and said, "I guess not." He laughed at my candidness and said something out of earshot to the bartender. He turned back to me and with a mischievous look, he said, "Enjoy your night."

"Thanks Mayor Bostain, I mean, Terrance," I said, batting my eyes.

"You're welcome." He paused and then leaned in with his mouth against my ear. I could smell his cologne.

"Save me a dance," he whispered.

"Sure," I replied seductively, although his breath was a little tart. He turned and walked off. I giggled to myself. I was enjoying playing this game with Mayor Bostain because I was bored and tired of being a loser, lame-o. I knew he probably wanted to have sex with me and even though I really wasn't feeling it, I still planned to have some fun with him.

"Let's make a toast," Val said once the bartender had given us our drinks.

I giggled. "To what?" I asked.

"To driving these men wild and making them get down on their knees and beg," she replied, so out of character. I laughed and raised my cup.

"Here, here! I'll toast to that," I said, obliging her nevertheless. We toasted and chugged down our drinks.

"Let's get another," Val said. "I'm ready to party."

"I'm down. Let's do this," I said and turned to order another drink. And as I prepared to pay, the bartender informed me that Mayor Bostain had started a tab for us; therefore, we could drink whatever we wanted all night long. Val and I high fived.

"Let the party begin," Val said as we clinked glasses again and then headed to our assigned table. I was a little disappointed that our table was in the very, very front because for starters, I've never liked sitting in the front and since the drinks were free, I wanted to be closer to the bar. But I chalked it up and sat down. The table was decorated beautifully with an assortment of candles, black and gold plates and a colorful wildflower arrangement. A server dressed in all black came up to me and Val and asked us what we would like to drink. Assuming that she was talking about the usual choice of water or tea, I jokingly said, "a Sex on the Beach." And the server replied, "ok," turned to Val and said, "for you ma'am?" Val and I looked at each other bewildered.

"Uh... I'll have a Long Island Iced Tea, but first, how much are they?" Val asked, cautiously.

"Drinks are free all night at this table ma'am. Everyone at the ball gets two complimentary glasses of wine if they choose but for this table you can have whatever you like, all night long." The server replied and walked off. Val and I looked at each other again.

"Girl, are you sure we're at the right table?" I whispered. She picked up the seating card and checked it.

"Yeah, it says MB with the gold star on it," she replied.

"Ok. Well screw it. But we can't get too drunk because we'll be acting crazy and Maurice will definitely have you in the bathroom stall before the stroke of 12:00," I said and giggled.

"Whatever girl. I know you don't believe me but I'm going to win this bet," she replied confidently, as the server sat our drinks down.

"I wonder what they're serving, I'm starving." I said as my stomach growled. I could smell the aroma of food in the air, but I couldn't pick up on what it was. Shortly thereafter, the waiters began bringing out salads and more people began making their way to their tables. One by one, each chair at our large 20-seat table became occupied. But Val and I, who were feeling somewhat tipsy, were so busy laughing and scheming that we didn't even notice until the waiters sat our salads in front of us. Val's greedy butt immediately picked up her fork and slathered her salad with ranch dressing. I, knowing the consequences and repercussions of mixing alcohol and ranch dressing, immediately intervened. I knew that this "new Val" thought she could drink, but *I* knew that she couldn't, so I had to keep my eye on her. I wanted her to get tipsy enough to let loose but not to where she would lose all her faculties. And I definitely didn't want the heifa somewhere throwing up.

"Val now look, I know you're trying to be cool and woo Maurice so I'm warning you, you better not eat that salad with that ranch dressing on it. I told you that before. Your ass is gonna be somewhere throwing up and that means no get back for you and Maurice tonight. Plus, I really don't feel like taking care of your ass. I might try to get lucky myself tonight." I laughed even though I was serious. Jermaine, I mean Avery had put it on me earlier but his sex was retractable so I had no problem going back.

"Well, what am I supposed to eat then? I need something on my stomach." She whined. I reached over to a breadbasket sitting on the table and handed her a roll.

"Here eat this bread. It will soak it up a little bit and then once we eat, we can drink some more later," I said. She took the roll and gobbled it down, as did I. They actually were very good and they were warm, which made them taste even better.

"You better hope they're serving some type of chicken," I said as I looked up and saw Maurice walking in our direction. Panicked, I tried to warn Val.

"Maurice is coming!" I whispered as loudly as I could.

"What?" Val asked.

"MAURICE IS COMING. He's right behind you," I said as quickly as I could but I was too late. Maurice and Mayor Bostain walked up right as Val turned around to look. She jumped and quickly turned back around.

"Ladies are you enjoying yourselves?" Maurice asked as he sat down on the other side of Val while Mayor Bostain took his seat on the other side of me. Val nudged me in my ribs so hard that it almost took my breath away. She turned towards me; making it a point to turn her back to Maurice, gave me an "Oh my gosh" look and then quickly gathered herself. I, trying to recover from the blow to my ribs, had an epiphany. Now I understood why all the drinks were free; we were at the Mayor's table, which came with all kinds of different perks. Since Maurice and Mayor Bostain were best friends, of course Maurice would sit at the Mayor's table and it was apparent that he had something to do with us sitting there as well. I was impressed. I had to give it to Maurice. He was playing hardball. I hoped that Val was on her "A" game because by the way Maurice was playing his cards; she was going to be paying me that hundred dollars. And I laughed to myself because knowing Val; she probably didn't even realize what was going on. She was very intelligent but she was missing a few links when it came to common sense.

I couldn't believe I was sitting at the Mayor's table. And by the way Mayor Bostain was dropping lines in my ear, I felt like I was his date, although he hadn't formally asked me. I put my big Vanna White smile on and pretended to be interested because it made me feel powerful. Out of all the women here, I was the one sitting at the Mayor's table, *with* the Mayor. But all that came crumbling down when I saw Jenetta and Mario walking in together, *as a couple.* I almost died and probably poked a hole through Val's leg when I saw them walking towards *our* table together laughing and Jenetta had her arm wrapped around Mario's. Val and I looked at each other in shock. Maurice stood up and gave Mario dap as he introduced Mario *and* Jenetta to Mayor Bostain. Mayor Bostain greeted them and then bent over and whispered in my ear.

"I'll be right back gorgeous. Don't go anywhere."

"Ok." I replied, almost throwing up from the stench of his alcohol mixed with cow manure breath. I saw Mario looking at me as he pulled out Jenetta's chair for her. When he saw me look at him, he quickly looked away.

I felt a pang of confidence because that look meant that there was still a possibility that he still felt something for me. I smiled to myself and decided to play along with his game, but it felt weird because it was Mario. I knew that things were different between us since our night of passion and I took the blame for it, but I didn't realize that things were that bad. Especially to the point that we weren't speaking and somehow in the midst of our estrangement, he was forming an alliance or by the looks of things, an intimate relationship; something he used to have with me, with Jenetta. Jenetta of all people. As often as we'd sat around and clowned her, I couldn't believe that he was actually walking around with this heifa on his arm. And although I hated to admit it, she looked pretty, and of course Mario looked stunning and they even looked cute together.

I didn't want them to think I even remotely cared about their relationship, so I used my drink as a distraction. I grabbed my Sex on the Beach, threw my head back and gulped the final remains of it down. And just as my head came back down, facing the middle of the table, my eyes met Brad's. I almost choked on my drink. *What the hell is he doing here?* I asked myself. Then I remembered that we were at the Mayor's table and of course, Fosterberg County's most wealthy citizens would be sitting there. And we, Val's team of social workers, were really only at that table because of Maurice and his elusive plot to get Val back.

"Val, will you come with me to the bathroom?" I asked, giving her the "we *need* to go to the bathroom look."

"Yea, I'll go with you," she said gratefully, desperately wanting to get away from Maurice who was unsuccessfully trying to engage Val in conversation. When we arrived in the bathroom, we both released a sigh of relief. I made sure no one else was in there and when we saw that it was all clear, the floodgates reopened.

"Carolyn, oh my gosh. I feel like I'm in the twilight zone. Can you believe that we are sitting at the Mayor's table, with me sitting right beside Maurice? And he smells so good. He thinks he's slick, but I got this. I know what he's trying to do and it ain't gonna work. And what's up with Jenetta and Mario? Girl are they a couple? I thought he hated her. This ball is already starting off crazy, but the music is on point though," she gibbered jabbed, snapping her fingers.

"Well, I'm sure you're enjoying it being that the 90's was your favorite era. And yeah, Maurice is smooth for sitting us at the Mayor's table. I have to give him credit for that one. Plus, we can drink freely all night from the bar as well as our table, girl that money is getting closer and closer to my hand," I laughed. She scowled at me and rolled her eyes.

"Whatever, that doesn't impress me. He had sex with another woman, Carolyn. And even if we were together, we would probably still be sitting at the Mayor's table anyway because they are best friends. He better come harder than that if he wants me back," she said rolling her eyes and neck.

"Have you forgiven him?" I asked.

She became silent for a minute and began to think.

"I don't know yet Carolyn. I love him so much that my bones ache, but the thought of him being with another woman sends this piercing sharp pain through my heart. I miss him terribly and I want him to come home. I just don't know if I can ever trust him again," she replied as her head dropped down.

"Val, Maurice is different. He really loves you. I wasn't going to tell you this because I didn't want to get involved, but he called me one night and begged me to help him get you back. I told him just like I told you that I didn't want to be involved. But he told me to give him 2 minutes to tell me what happened and before I could answer, he started talking. He told me that he didn't have sex with that woman. He said that he met her at a party at his homeboy's house and they just started talking and then flirting. And then he said they decided to meet for lunch and it just happened to be the day that you were out walking. So, God sent you out on that walk for a purpose and that was to save your marriage." I said and shrugged my shoulders. She looked at me but remained silent, so I continued.

"And I believe him, Val. Anyway, you think you have problems, let me run mine down to you. On top of the fact that we are sitting at the Mayor's Table; with me sitting beside a very flirtatious *and* hot breath Mayor Bostain, I not only have to deal with Mario and Jenetta, which is making me want to vomit; girl how about Brad is at our table *and* he's with his wife. So how bout I'm sitting at the same table with two men that I've already had sex with and one that *wants* me to have sex with him! Both of the men I've slept with have dates and I'm here alone pretending to be with

Mayor Bostain; which by the way, I must admit is working in my favor so far because it keeps me from looking like a total loser. But I'm sorry, Mayor Bostain is cute and all, but he's too corny to be so cocky, his breath is ferocious and my Juicy hasn't gotten juicy, so it looks like I'll be going home alone tonight anyway," I ranted, feeling as if my dilemma was exciting, juicy and captivating. I expected a dramatic response but Val, who had been half listening, not only gave me a delayed response but a somewhat lackluster one in my opinion.

"Brad's at our table? Where's he sitting? How does he look?" she asked, leaning in.

"I'll show you when we get back. He's gorgeous," I admitted.

"Well, come on let's go," she sighed and began trudging towards the door. But then she stopped suddenly and pivoted towards me.

"Wait, wait, wait, you haven't had sex with Mayor Bostain and you've obviously slept with Brad, so does that mean that you slept with Mario?" she inquired with her eyebrows raised.

I closed my eyes and dropped my head, realizing that I hadn't told Val about me and Mario because once again I had had an inappropriate interaction with a coworker. In my buzzed state of mind, I'd let my guard down and forgot that she was my supervisor because here lately we'd been hanging like friends. I wanted to kick my own self up the butt, but I had let the cat out of the bag and now it was too late to pull it back in. I was sure that Val was aware of how things had changed between Mario and me especially since we weren't talking at all now, but she and I really never had time to talk about it because she was too wrapped up in her own drama. There was no turning back now so I looked her in her eye and admitted it.

"Yes," I replied. I didn't know whether she was going to play supervisor and rip me a new butt hole or be a squealing girlfriend who had just learned some juicy gossip. Thankfully, it was mostly the latter.

"I knew it! I knew it! I knew something was up between you and Mario. So that's why you guys aren't talking and that's why he's with Jenetta. But Carolyn, I'm warning you, keep that crap at home. I'm not replacing any more social workers on your account, especially not a young black male. Now I love you, but you'll have to go before he will," she said candidly, assuming her supervisory role. "But...I still wanna know details," she giggled. I snorted and threw my head back.

"Well, that was a bipolar statement," I replied rolling my eyes. "I'll tell you about all that later when it's just me and you. Now come on. I at least want to enjoy my dinner since everything else is going array tonight. And listen; do not tell Maurice that I told you what he said because I said that I wasn't getting in it."

"I'm not going to say anything," she replied as she reached for the door handle. She turned back and looked at me.

"Carolyn, you're not going to win this bet. I know you told me that crap to soften me up, but it's not going to work," she said, snapping her finger. I giggled.

"Even I am not that conniving. I'm being honest. Maurice is really a good guy and he loves you," I said as a pang of envy and hurt ricocheted across my chest. "Who knows if he would have gone through with it, but like I said, you stopped it before it even got a chance to go there."

She looked at me, desperately trying to find truth in what I was saying. Her eyes became misty and tears threatened to drop from her eyes.

"Carolyn, I believe that he loves me, I just don't know if I believe that he didn't sleep with that woman. And the way they were sitting and kissing that day..."Her voice trailed off. She shook her head and continued.

"I just don't know if I can trust him Carolyn and that hurts so bad."

"I know Val and what Maurice did was very inappropriate. The flirting, that incident; all off it. However, I still believe him when he said he didn't sleep with her."

"But he probably would have had I not seen him that day," she argued, but I wasn't backing down either because I knew her and Maurice were made for each other.

"Val, I know Maurice and honey, another woman could never take him away from you however, a man's physical needs can be overpowering. And although he may love you to death, there's something about…" I started singing the hook from a Jay Z song. *"The power of the P-U-S-S-Y.* And Maurice is a very handsome and cool dude and women are attracted to that. Maurice is a good man but he's also human and sometimes innocence becomes tainted, one thing leads to another and boom you have an infidelity on your hands. Val, I'm going to keep it real with you, you're being stubborn and I understand your hurt and anger, but honey you better hold on tight to that man or someone else will. And by the way, is Jenetta going to get the 'You better leave that crap at home' talk since she's obviously dating Mario; her coworker?" I asked jokingly, but seriously at the same time because I was actually very perturbed by the whole Mario/Jenetta situation and I was tired of being the only one getting chastised because of the collisions between my job and my personal life. Plus, I missed Mario and I didn't want to share him with another woman, especially Jenetta.

Val rolled her eyes. "Whatever girl. Come on let's go."

We both turned and checked our appearance in the mirror one more time and walked out just in time to see the servers carrying large, covered platters to the tables. We made our way towards our table with our stomachs growling in anticipation of what would be on the menu. However, when we arrived at our table, there was nothing there but the salads we'd left there earlier. We looked at each other; confused because several people at our table as well as other tables were already eating. Luckily, Maurice and Mayor Bostain were near the stage talking to the DJ, which was a relief for both of us because we weren't ready to deal with them yet. I peeped in the direction of where Brad was sitting and noted that he wasn't at his seat either. Jenetta and Mario were engulfed in conversation and didn't seem to notice us, which was ok with me. Feeling relieved, Val and I both sat down in our seats as two servers immediately approached us carrying two large silver platters.

"Mrs. Whitman this is your platter," the server said as she sat the platter down and removed the lid. Valerie looked up at her, baffled that the server knew her name. She then looked at her food and her mouth dropped.

"What is it?" I asked. She started laughing and shaking her head.

"Ma'am, this is your platter," another server said and sat my food down in front of me.

"Thank you," I replied. Still perplexed by Valerie's response, I said, "What in the world are you laughing at?"

"That dude really thinks he's slick. This is the exact same meal that Maurice prepared for me on the day he asked me to marry him. He must have had this specially ordered just for me because I'm sure no one else has 'Four Cheese Lasagna Hamburger Helper' smothered in parmesan cheese with creamed spinach and corn on the cob. I can't believe he remembered," she said and glanced in his direction, while attempting to be discreet. But Maurice's eyes were already on her and when their eyes met, he didn't flinch. Val, on the other hand, quickly jerked back around in my direction. I could see her chest going up and down as she tried to calm herself.

"Hamburger Helper?" I laughed.

"Girl, we was po'," she said, also laughing. "And the dude really thought he was doing something too. But it really was cute though and it was good as hell too. He has some kind of 'secret sauce,' as he says, that he puts in everything he cooks. I don't know what it is, but I have yet to be disappointed." She smiled reminiscing as she bit into her food. I shook my head and began stuffing roasted lamb, red potatoes and green beans into my mouth. The food was delicious and I savored each bite.

"Oh my gosh Carolyn. This dude cooked this himself. I can taste the secret sauce!" Val said.

"Hello Ms. Black." A deep voice said from behind me, taking my attention off Val. I jumped, almost choking on my food. Chills shot down my spine and my body shivered because I recognized Brad's arrogant but sexy ass voice anywhere. I grabbed my napkin and wiped my mouth as I quickly swallowed my food. Hoping that I didn't have food in my teeth and smeared makeup, I straightened my back, began batting my eyes and turned around to find Brad *and* his wife standing there. I froze and I know the initial look on my face was probably priceless but I quickly recovered. I regained my composure and morphed into my "business associate" mode. I was a little rusty but all my years of being a mistress had prepared me to handle myself in situations like this, and although I hadn't talked to Brad in a while, I loved how our relationship was. It was wild and exciting and I loved Brad's arrogance and fearlessness. He would never cower away in sticky situations like Dewayne and Demarcus had. Here he was, boldly standing in front of me, his other woman, with his wife by his side and engaging in conversation with me. I laughed to myself. I had had sex with this man on a private jet over the middle of the Red Sea and had had my Juicy eaten relentlessly in the back of a taxicab in Jamaica so I was obliged to play along.

"Mr. Martinelli. How are you? I apologize that you caught me right in the middle of large bite of food," I replied with a giggle, as I reached out my hand.

He kissed it as his thumb caressed the back of my hand.

"Well, it is dinner time. I would like for you to meet…Sophia. Sophia this is Carolyn Black, a colleague from the "Helping Hands" charity that I sponsor."

"Hello, Mrs. Martinelli. Nice to meet you," I said, greeting her.

"Oh no, this isn't Mrs. Martinelli." Brad corrected me, "She's my assistant." Which meant that he was screwing her. I became pissed and *slightly* jealous because how dare he bring another woman *besides* me or his wife to a function. And although the heifa didn't look anything like Brad's type because she was a blonde; I had to admit she was gorgeous. She was petite, but she was curvy. She had beautiful light brown eyes and she wore a tight gray tube dress with black booties. She wore her long blonde hair big and teased with lots of hair spray and her make-up was composed of electric blue eye shadow and hot pink lipstick. Brad, who was pushing hot over the Richter scale, was dressed like Jason Priestly with his hair slicked back, ripped jeans, and a flannel shirt that he wore open with a white V-neck t-shirt underneath.

"Ms. Black," *Sophia* replied with a nod; also sizing me up as if she knew that I was no more his colleague than she was his assistant. And Brad stood there silently undressing me with his eyes; enjoying the little *exchange* that was going on between Sophia and me.

Asshole! But I fought to play it cool. Brad knew exactly what he was doing and I wasn't going to let him win. I'm sure he knew me better than that.

Val cleared her throat several times signaling me to include her in this "ring of fire." Thankful for my nosy supervisor, I introduced her.

"Uh, Mr. Martinelli...Sophia..." I said coolly, although I wanted to completely disregard that whore, "I would like to introduce you to Valerie Whitman, my supervisor."

"Hello," they said, greeting each other.

"Well enjoy your meal," Brad said giving me a discreet wink just as Maurice and Mayor Bostain were returning to their seats.

"Bradley Martinelli! What's up buddy?" Mayor Bostain said as he and Brad shook hands and embraced. He shot me a look as if he was inquiring as to how I knew Brad. But I just smiled and ignored his look.

"Mayor Bostain. How's it going?"

"Hey, you can't touch this!" Mayor Bostain said laughing and twirling in a circle, mocking MC Hammer. I rolled my eyes to myself. *This dude is the cornball of the year*. But then out of nowhere Mayor Bostain leaned in and whispered, "You sure are beautiful. Don't forget to save me a dance tonight?" in my ear. Ecstatic that Mayor Bostain was right on cue, I nodded and smiled seductively; not taking my eyes off Brad whose competitive nature was now being challenged. I wasn't necessarily interested in Mayor Bostain because he was lame but his company in front of my adversaries was very much welcomed. And because he was the

Mayor, he had to entertain his guests so that kept me from having to *entertain* him. I had planned to come to the ball and be low key but it didn't look like that was going to happen. I peeked over at Mario in order to see if he also had noticed me and Mayor Bostain, but him and Jenetta were still talking and appeared to be in their own world. I was disgusted but I refused to allow them or Brad and his "assistant" to ruin my night.

"Well, enjoy your meal and make sure y'all take advantage of all the free alcohol that the guests at this table are privy to," Mayor Bostain said as Brad and *Sophia* returned to their seats. A server approached Mayor Bostain and asked him if he was ready to eat and he replied that he was.

Dinner was going by fairly smooth. I politely pretended to be interested as Mayor Bostain rattled off corny stories and unfunny jokes but the shit with Mario and Jenetta was really getting to me. At first, I really thought that he was doing what he was doing to get back at me but as I watched them out of the corner of my eye, I noticed his smile and the glow in his eyes. He liked her. I wanted to kick myself because there was no doubt in my mind that if he and I were still talking, he would be *my* date, especially to something like this.

During the intervals when Mayor Bostain's breath became too unbearable, I tried to talk to Val, but Maurice had her on lock. I noticed his hand on her thigh and when she saw that I noticed it, she tried to move it, but Maurice's grip was latched securely to her leg. I smiled wickedly and started singing "Money, money, money, mon-ey...Mon-ey," the hook to "For the Love of Money" by the O'Jays. She gave me a side look and flared her nose, but Maurice's hand didn't move. I felt Brad watching me but I ignored him. The thrill of it all was starting to diminish because I really didn't care about him at that point and I knew it was killing him. I didn't have the desire to sleep with Brad anymore and with the exception of him bringing that hussy with him, he really wasn't getting too much of a rise out of me.

"Well, it's time for me to do my thing. Don't forget about that dance later on tonight," Mayor Bostain said as he got up and made his way to the podium. Val, Maurice and I ordered a round of drinks and began taking shots as Mayor Bostain addressed the guests.

"Lastly, I'd like to thank everyone for coming. You all look hot in your late 80's, 90's attire. Make sure you go get your photos taken at the back of the room because this is definitely going to be a night to remember," he laughed. I rolled my eyes. "The servers are coming around with your choice of vodka, tequila, cognac or champagne. We are going to take a shot because the elegance ends now and the real party is about to begin. We are going to dance our asses off and drinks are on the house for the next hour. Now, I want everybody to know that at this party, you can let loose and have fun. That's the reason why I didn't allow cell phones and had you all to sign a privacy agreement. This is a place where you can feel comfortable to be yourself. You can drink all you want and dance any kind of way you want. This is a no judgement zone. So everybody raise your glasses..." Val and I, along with everyone else, raised our shots. "And let's shot it out to what happens at the Mayor's Ball, stay's at the Mayor's Ball." Everybody took their shots and then a simultaneous ripple of gasps spread throughout the room in response to the liquor shooting down our throats.

"Wooo!" Mayor Bostain shuddered. "Alright, now I need all my frat brothers to meet me up front. Waiters, y'all serve another round of drinks." Mayor Bostain said as several men, including Maurice, gathered into a formation at the front of the room. Mayor Bostain nodded at the DJ who began playing, "Turn This Mutha Out" by MC Hammer. The men began "stepping" and dancing an obviously choreographed routine. They were awesome and Mayor Bostain's flawless and fluid movements rather intrigued me. Maybe he wasn't such a cornball after all and his ploy for getting the crowd hyped up was definitely working. I turned to tell Val my thoughts about Mayor Bostain but she was too busy faltering under Maurice's spell. His eyes remained on her the entire time he was dancing.

"Come on, let's go to the bathroom and freshen up," she said, grabbing my hands and dragging me to the bathroom.

"Dag Val, I wanted to watch their dance until the end," I whined. Mayor Bostain and the alcohol I'd been drinking was starting to make me hot.

"Girl, I need to retreat for a second. Plus, I want to rinse my mouth out and check my makeup."

I sighed and rolled my eyes. I followed her into the bathroom where we touched up our makeup and chit chatted about everything that was going on.

Brad sent me a text stating, "I wanna bite that beautiful round ass of yours." And I texted him back, "I bet you do." He responded, "I do, so when can we make it happen?" I replied, "I'm sure your ASSISTANT or should I say my STAND-IN, Sophia, would be obliged to let you bite her ass." And he responded, "Jealous?" I texted back. "Nah, bored." He replied, "LOL, I miss your ornery ass Carolyn. Come spend the night with me so I can make all your WET dreams come true."

I texted back. "Already occupied for the night. Going to have to take a RAIN check."

He replied, "well said, but I AM GOING TO HOLD YOU TO IT." I laughed but didn't respond. Val and I rejoined the party whereby the dance floor was now packed and everybody was jamming to "Get into the Groove" by Madonna. Val and I returned to our seats and ordered drinks just as the DJ began making an announcement.

"I would like to take this time to slow it down a little bit. I have this young man right here who has something he wants to say to a special lady in his life." Val and I rattled on about this and that but she stopped midsentence when she heard, "Hi everybody my name is Maurice Whitman." She jerked around and so did I.

"I did something really bad that caused my beautiful wife to leave me. Well, I want her back and I have something that I want to say to her. DJ…"Maurice said, as the music for "I Want to Be Your Man" by Roger and Zapp began to play.

Maurice mouthed the words *"Hey Lady, let me tell you why, I can't liiiiiiive my life without you"* and began walking towards Val, serenading her; seducing her with his eyes. She grabbed my hand

and held her breath. She tried to be tough but Maurice was relentless. He grabbed her hand and stood her up. He pulled her close to him. His face was very close to her face as he serenaded her, while also slow grinding with her. I saw a bead of sweat roll down her back and I laughed to myself. And when the words, *"Cause what I've got to say, is sealed with a kiss and a wedding ring"* blasted through the speakers, he dropped to his knee and pulled out a one carat diamond ring encompassed by small red rubies. I saw a tear drop from Val's eyes, and at that point, I knew it was a wrap because that Benjamin Franklin was mine.

She extended a shaky hand and allowed him to put the ring on her finger. He stood up and they embraced tightly, holding onto each other for dear life. Everyone around them began to clap but they didn't hear because they were too wrapped up in each other. They continued moving slowly to the rhythm of the song; no one else in the world except them. Maurice's hand glided firmly but lovingly up and down Val's back.

Other people also began dancing. I sat smiling, genuinely happy for Val, who was swaying, with her eyes closed but I was also a little sad. The scene from *The Color Purple* where Shug Avery makes up with her father in the church and Celie is standing with the stomach virus face flashed in my mind. I knew my partner was gone and that female companionship that we'd shared was going to be minimal. I wasn't a hater, so I shook it off and resumed smiling. My smile however quickly turned to a frown when I noticed Mario and Jenetta slow dragging in my peripheral view. I didn't want to turn and look but my neck moved involuntarily in their direction just as Jenetta happened to look at me.

"Fuck!" I almost said out loud. Her mouth curled into a sinister smile and *she* winked at me. On impulse, I shot her a bird and mouthed, "Fuck you" because I hoped the trick didn't think she was getting to me. Yeah I was pissed about her and Mario and it was definitely a blow to my ego but the fact that I've never liked her gave me some leverage. I didn't like her ass yesterday, I didn't like her ass today and I sure as hell wasn't gonna like her ass tomorrow. So I had no problem with giving her the middle finger seven days a week if necessary regardless of who she was screwing. I rolled my eyes and turned right to where Brad and *Sophia* were dancing to a now playing "Please Don't Go" by New Kids on the Block.

"Shit!" I mumbled and quickly turned to my drink before they also noticed me looking at them. *This is some bull crap!* I thought to myself. And although I already had a drink, I walked over to the bar as a diversion. I sat down and ordered myself another drink. Depression was on my heels but I was fighting it with every ounce of strength that I had. I couldn't blame anyone but myself for my troubles because I had created them and it was I, who was going to have to fix things. I sighed and downed my shot of tequila.

"Hey Carolyn." I swung my head around and saw Mario standing there, looking great. I had a flashback of the passionate night we shared.

"Hey Mario," I said coolly. I looked for Jenetta but she wasn't with him. He turned towards the bartender and ordered a drink.

"So where's Jenetta?" I asked.

"That's none of your business. I didn't come over here to engage in conversation with you. You happened to be at the same bar so I was being cordial by speaking. Otherwise we have nothing to talk about," he stated bluntly...and it stung.

"Come on Mario; after all we've been through...how can you say we have nothing to talk about?" I pleaded.

"That's the same thing I've been thinking for the past few months. But obviously I was wrong and right now sweetheart so are you." He turned, picked up his drinks and started to walk away.

"Ok you're right. After that night happened, I got scared and I just didn't know what to do, so I avoided you. I apologize but come on, really Mario? I get it, you're mad at me and all, but Jenetta? I mean that's kinda scraping the bottom of the barrel isn't it?"

He stopped, pivoted and walked straight up to me; only inches away. His face changed into an angry scowl that actually kind of scared me and took me off guard.

"Let me tell you something, not long after our...tryst, I was in the bottom of the barrel because my mother passed away and Jenetta was right there with me; scraping. So yeah, it might be crazy but it is what it is. She was there. Where were you? And by the looks of things..."He paused and looked me up and down, "You're right there at the bottom with us but at least we're working our way out while you're still *scraping* around looking for scraps," he said as he turned and walked off. I stood there, speechless...stunned. I felt tears coming so I quickly scrambled to the bathroom. I ran into the stall and gulped for air. I inhaled and exhaled. I threw my head back and forced the tears to stay in my eyes. My heart literally felt pain and my chest felt as if it was going to cave in. I kept taking deep breathes until I got myself together. When I was finally able to walk out of the stall, I checked my appearance in the mirror and of course my face was red but it was slowly regaining its beautiful hues. I touched up my makeup and headed to the bar to get one more drink to calm my nerves and regain my buzz. I knew that tonight was definitely going to be a night that I went home and smoked a blunt. I laughed because with all the craziness I had going on, the song "I Got a Story to Tell" by Biggy flashed through my mind. The sad part was that I didn't have anyone to call and tell it to. I shook off the urge to cry again and began bobbing to the music. "Jump Around" by House of Pain was playing and everybody else looked like they were having fun and I didn't want to be left out. I straightened up and strutted to the dance floor where I saw Val and Maurice jumping around, laughing and having fun. I joined them and thankfully, they welcomed me into their circle, which also made me want to cry, but I shook that off as well. Out of nowhere, Mayor Bostain appeared.

"Carolyn Black, I've been looking for you, I thought you'd left. You promised me a dance and I want it," he said, smiling from ear to ear. I gave in and laughed. He was handsome in his MC Hammer attire, plus he could dance and I guess someone must have alerted him that his breath smelled like dragon balls because I didn't smell it anymore. I took his hands and we also began "jumping around." And as time progressed and more and more hits were played, I found myself laughing and actually having a good time with Mayor Bostain. The four of us went to the bar so that we could cool down and "refuel." I was already tipsy and so was Val, but nevertheless the music and the fun kept us going, so we kept drinking. By the end of the night, I was so drunk that I could barely see straight. Val passed out so Maurice threw her over his shoulder and carried her to the car. I staggered towards my car with every intention of driving myself home but Mayor Bostain's car drove up beside me and the back window rolled down.

"Carolyn Black, now I know you are not going to try to drive home. You're at the Mayor's Ball for goodness sake and I am responsible for making sure that everybody gets home safely," he slurred. "Now get your fine ass in this car and let me take you home." I started to object, but then my very limited amount of rationality kicked in and I decided that getting a ride home from Mayor Bostain was a better idea. As I was staggering to the other side of the car, I saw Mario and Jenetta leaned up against Mario's car; kissing. He had his hand up her dress and it looked like they probably weren't going to make it far beyond the backseat of the car once they got in. I stopped because I was drunk and I just couldn't take my eyes of them. Once they parted, Mario looked over at me and I turned too quickly, which caused me to stumble and fall onto the Mayor's car. Embarrassed as hell, I quickly regained my footing and opened the car door. I also felt ashamed because Mario saw me getting into the car with Mayor Bostain and I was sure that he assumed the worse. But something in me clicked and I no longer cared.

I slid in, onto the plush leather seats and inside a wolf was waiting. One who had been trying to dress in sheep's clothing for a very long time. One who thrived in the comfort and familiarity of excitement and risk taking. One who salivated in anticipation of devouring their prey. That wolf was me...

Case#: 38583 Satasha and Malasia

16 year old Satasha Carter pulled up in front of her best friend, Malasia Talley's house and blew the horn. As she waited for Malasia, she put the final touches on the blunt she was rolling and licked it to secure it from unraveling. Malasia ran out of the house and jumped in the car.

"What's up girl?" She asked, hugging her best friend, excited to see her.

"What up! Girl, what took you so long? I got this good loud and I'm ready to smoke it," Satasha said as she held up her freshly rolled blunt and grinned mischievously.

"Well fire that shit up then girl. Shoot, I couldn't wait for you to get here. Grandma been getting on my nerves so bad today and then my crackhead mama came by trying to get money from me because she knew I got my SSI check so we been arguing like cats and dogs. Honey, after the day I've had please believe I need that blunt." Malasia said, leaning her head back against the seat. Just as she was about to close her eyes and reflect on her day, she heard some whimpering coming from the back seat. She jerked her head around and saw that Satasha's three-month-old daughter, Mariah, was sitting in the backseat.

"Girl, get the lighter out of the dashboard so we can fire this bitch up," Satasha said as she sniffed the blunt from top to bottom.

"Uh Satasha...it's almost one o'clock in the morning. Why do you have Mariah out this time of night? Aaaand we can't smoke this blunt with her in the back seat. Don't you think the smoke from the marijuana is bad for her?" Malasia asked looking at her friend as if she'd lost her mind.

"Girl, a little bit of smoke ain't gonna hurt her. We can crack the window, plus it might put her little ass to sleep," Satasha said with a giggle.

"Hell nah! Just drop her off with your mom," Malasia replied. Satasha then returned Malasia's "are you crazy" look and said, "Now you know my mama is just as bad, if not worse than yours and although I may not be the best mama in the world, I be damn if I leave my baby with my mama's ass so she can leave her in the house by herself. You remember the *last* time I left her with my mama...she laid in shit all night. Now, look in the dashboard and hand me the damn lighter!"

"Satasha, I really don't think this is a good idea. I mean we can smoke tomorrow or something. I just don't feel comfortable smoking weed with the baby in the car and then driving around high with her in the back seat. Anything could happen and I can deal with me getting hurt because it's my choice to smoke and ride high, but she's a baby and she can't protect herself."

"Girl, stop tripping. Ain't nothing gonna happen. Now, you can get your ass out if you want to and I'll go smoke by myself, that's up to you, but I'm gonna smoke regardless," Satasha said annoyed, reaching over Malasia to get the lighter out of the dashboard. Malasia took a deep breath and briefly contemplated. She thought about going back into the house with her nagging, alcoholic grandmother and crackhead mama who were still awake and then she thought about missing out on the fire weed Satasha had that would help her erase her day.

"Fuck it," she thought to herself because she knew that at least if she went along, she could keep her eye on the baby since Satasha was so wild and irresponsible.

"Go ahead girl," Malasia said reluctantly.

"Hell yeah! That's what I'm talking about," Satasha said as she popped a mixed CD into the CD player and put it on number 5. Just as her favorite song in the world, *Itchin'* by Future, began to play, Satasha took a long toke on the blunt, put the car in first gear and pulled off. She passed the blunt to Malasia who also took a long pull. As Malasia let the smoke fill her lungs, she laid her head back, closed her eyes and began to bob her head as her troubles slowly began to melt away.

Satasha turned the music down. "Ooo girl, I know what we can do since you so paranoid about us smoking in the car with the baby. We can hit it a couple of times, put it out, and then go to Pee Wee's house and smoke. I can lay her down on his bed until she falls asleep," Satasha exclaimed as if she'd solved the world hunger epidemic.

"Do you think Pee Wee is up this late?" Malasia asked.

"Uh, yeah. Pee Wee hustles so he's always up," Satasha replied.

"Ok cool. I'm down." Malasia said feeling relieved. However, her relief dissipated as soon as they pulled up in front of Pee Wee's house and she realized that there was a party going on. Several cars lined the curb, loud music was playing and several people, scattered throughout the yard, stood around talking and getting messed up.

"Dag. Well there goes that plan," Malasia said quietly, as she shook her head.

"Bullshit! We going in here and have some fun. I told you we can lay her down on Pee Wee's bed," Satasha replied.

"Satasha have you lost your mind? Are you crazy? This ain't no place for no baby. All those people standing around drinking and getting high. Plus, how you gonna look walking up in there carrying a baby?" Malasia asked, disgusted with her best friend. Satasha grew silent as the weed buzz she was feeling made her think deeply about what Malasia was saying.

"Damn girl. You're right. I'll probably look ghetto as hell going up in a party with a baby. I got an idea. Listen; we can just leave her in the car, lock the doors and crack the windows. And I'll just keep coming out here checking on her."

"Hell nah, Satasha. That's stupid as hell. We ain't doing that shit. You know what, take me home and I'll just keep her."

"Why you being a party pooper, Malasia? She's my baby and you don't tell me what the fuck to do with her. Ain't nothing gonna happen to her. Now get out of the fucking car and let's go party." Satasha said as she opened the door.

"Did you hear what the fuck I said? I said take me home. I'm not going in no damn party and leaving this baby in the car. What the hell is wrong with you? You don't even smoke crack like our mamas do and you still a bad mama. I don't understand. That shit is wrong Satasha! She's a baby. You can't leave her in the car. What if she wakes up while you in the house? What if somebody kidnaps her? I mean damn, anything can happen." Malasia snapped.

"Malasia, you getting on my nerves and you killing my high," Satasha said as she reached for the blunt and lit it back up. She took a long, deep pull; turned around and blew the smoke in the baby's face.

"Now she won't wake up. Satisfied?" Satasha asked sarcastically and got out of the car. Malasia sat dumbfounded with her anger welling up inside of her as her mind flashed back to all the heinous and irresponsible things that her own mother had done to her. She just didn't understand how any mother could put drugs or anything else for that matter, before their child. And Satasha, who'd been her best friend since they were in 1st grade, knew firsthand what it was like to have an unfit mother and here she was doing the same thing to her own innocent baby. Malasia's breathing intensified and tears began to roll down her face. Unable to control her rage, she jumped out of the car and grabbed Satasha by the back of her head. She began pounding her any and everywhere that her fists would land. Satasha, who quickly gained her footing, fought Malasia as if she was a stranger in the streets. Both girls; blinded by rage, fought mercilessly; blow for blow as the people standing outside took out their camera phones and began recording the incident instead of trying to break it up.

"World Star Hip Hop!" One young man yelled out.

"5-0!" Another person yelled, alerting everyone that the police was coming. Everyone outside took off running. Satasha and Malasia, however, were fighting so hard that they heard nothing and saw no one except the flashbacks in their heads. It wasn't until the police pulled them apart that their past pains re-entered the file cabinets of their minds and the present resumed. The police also found the baby girl sitting in the back seat of the smoke filled car. They arrested the two girls, took them to jail and called CPS.

Carolyn Black

I rolled over, glanced at Mayor Bostain who was snoring lightly, and wanted to throw up. I knew that my having sex with him was a drunken pity lay because I had been so upset about Mario and Jenetta...and Brad and Sofia and to be honest, Val and Maurice. But the way Mayor Bostain had sweated all over me and gang banged me like I was a prostitute had me pissed off. Not to mention that I didn't even cum so the whole thing was a waste of time. And to top it all off, I felt amateur like some Carolyn Black, circa 2002 shit when I was still "letting" men run over me. I was angry at myself because I didn't have any money, shoes, clothes, jewelry much less an orgasm to show for my time. Hell, I didn't even have my car, which was usually a no no for me. I had learned the hard way that no matter where I went when a man was involved, I would always drive my own shit or have access to my own shit so I could bounce whenever I needed to. I sighed heavily and looked at the ceiling. I didn't know what I was supposed to do anymore. Was it time for me to give up being a mistress and/or a woman who was uninhibited when it came to feeding her sexual needs? Or was I in an intermission and the Mayor was just a bad experience, a causality of war along the way? Since Jermaine, I mean Avery and I had started back having sex, the fire within me was slowly starting to reignite. I was beginning to feel powerful again and desirable. And Mayor Bostain had initially fueled my power trip, but this poor excuse of a lay made me realize that I was rusty and needed to regain my footing. With my eyes wide open and my buzz nonexistent, I could see things clearly and the cornball that Maurice had initially introduced me to was the same cornball who'd arrogantly given me the worst sex I'd ever experienced in my life. I wanted to kick myself, but I ended up kicking him instead. He didn't move. Therefore, I started shaking him so he could get his ass up and take me to my car.

"Terrance, Terrance. Wake up," I said, shaking him, although he still didn't budge.

"Terrance," I said a little louder as my shake became a little more forceful. He stirred but still didn't open his eyes, which annoyed me.

"Terrance. Wake up!" I said louder. He finally rolled over and groaned.

"Wussup baby?" He asked groggily as he put his hand on my thigh, making me gag.

"I'm ready to go home. Get up so you can take me back to my car please," I said calmly.

"Baby you can stay until the morning. I'm still a little bit tipsy and I don't feel like driving."

I bit my bottom lip in an attempt to keep myself from flipping on him because I felt my blood beginning to boil.

"Terrance," I said with my final attempt at being cordial. "I am ready to go home now. I'm on call this weekend.   Now get up please and take me to my car. I would call a cab but you live out in the boondocks and ain't no cabs coming out this far. So I'm asking you nicely to get up and please take me to my car."

"Look, I'm tired, I'm sleepy and I'm still drunk. I ain't going no damn where. Hell you better be glad I'm even offering your ass the opportunity to stay. Most of the time when I bring bitches up here, I screw em' and put em' out without caring whether they get home or not. Now, I ain't gonna do *you* like that because Maurice is my boy and you his girl. So you best to lay your ass back down and chill until I get ready to take you. Hell, matter of fact, why don't you put this fat dick in your mouth and suck me back to sleep since you interrupted my slumber," he said as he jerked the covers over himself and rolled back over. I sat dumbfounded. *Did this dude really just come at me like that? This cornball ass punk with the "Rough Side of the Mountain" breath? Oh Hell nah!* Then I realized he probably did think I was a loose booty because his corny ass was

Social Work: The Carolyn Black Chronicles II

actually going to take me home when I got into the car with him, but I'd come onto him since I was so pissed off and *vulnerable*.

I rolled my eyes at my damn self. *Dummy! What did you expect? Now this sucka probably thinks he's the shit.* Nevertheless, I wasn't gonna let his ass talk to me like that and regardless if he did think I was a loose booty, he was taking my ass to my car whether he liked it or not.

"Terrance! Get your ass up and take me to my car now or I'm going to get your keys and take myself. It's up to you."

He rolled over and looked at me like I was stupid. "If I'd known you were going to be this much trouble, I would have left your chicken head ass on the curb where I found you. Now I told you..." I punched him dead in his mouth. He sat up to counterattack, but I hit him with a two piece, one to the nose and one to the side of his chin and laid him out cold. I jumped up, put my clothes on and looked around for his car keys. Once I found them, I got into his car; a brand new Mercedes Benz and drove to the venue to get into my own. When I arrived, I started to beat his car to pieces but he *was* the Mayor and I didn't want to go to jail. So opting to relieve my overfilled bladder instead, I commenced to peeing everywhere I could inside his Benz. Once I emptied my bladder, I opened the door, got in my car and headed home. On the drive to my house, I felt liberated because even though he got a free ride into Juicy Land and had tried to make me feel like a slut, I still had the pleasure of beating his ass and pissing in his car.

As soon as I walked in my house, I headed straight to the shower. Unexpectedly, the tears that I'd dared to exist came anyway. Yeah I felt tough but I also felt embarrassed and although I didn't want to admit it, I really did feel like a groupie. But more than anything, I'd responded impulsively by sleeping with him because my ego was under attack and I needed a way to protect myself. However, I ended up making a bad choice and in turn I shitted myself. I should have just brought my black ass home but I decided not to sweat it because it was a lesson learned.

110

I started putting my pajamas on and immediately cocked an attitude because my work phone started ringing. It was almost 2:00 a.m.

"Fosterberg County DSS, this is Carolyn Black speaking," I answered, trying to hide my disgust.

"Hello Ms. Black. This is Officer JD Collins and I have a baby down here at the police station. We were doing our routine patrol and as we were riding through Sandy Farms, we saw two teenage girls fighting in the middle of the street and when we broke them up, we noticed that there was a baby in the car. And the car was so cloudy with marijuana smoke that I almost caught a buzz myself, so I figured that we'd better give you guys a call."

"Thanks Officer Collins. I'm on my way," I replied and hung up the phone. I dressed quickly, got myself together mentally and dragged myself over to the police station. When I arrived, I found Officer Collins who led me into a small conference room where two teenage girls sat across from each other; handcuffed. A small baby girl in a car seat was sleeping beside one of them. As I walked over to introduce myself, I noticed their disheveled hair and clothes, as well as their war wounds. *Oh hell, what's this shit going to be about?* I asked myself.

"Hello, young ladies. My name is Carolyn Black and I work for Fosterberg County Department of Social Services. Which one of you is the mother of the child?" I asked politely, but neither one of them spoke. I sighed because I knew it was going to be a long night. I waited before I spoke again.

"Listen, its 2:30 in the morning. I don't have time to play games with you girls. Based off the information that I gathered from Officer Collins and the fact that I don't have anyone to speak for the baby, I can take her into custody and be done with it. I know you guys are probably looking at me as the big bad Social Worker but contrary to popular belief, I really am here to help. So what's it going to be because I'm not asking anymore? Now, which one of you is the mother of this child?" I asked more sternly. Both girls remained mute.

"Ok. Have it your way," I replied as I walked towards the sleeping baby.

"I'm her mama," the girl sitting across from the baby replied sarcastically, as she sucked her teeth and rolled her eyes making me want to slap the taste out of her mouth.

"Ok. And what is your name young lady?"

"*Sa-tasha*," She replied with major attitude.

"And what's your name?" I asked, directing the question towards the other girl.

"Malasia," she replied more respectfully.

"Ok. Thank you. Now, please tell me what's going on. Why do you all have this baby out this late at night?"

"It's really none of your business. She's my child and I'll do whatever the fuck I want to with her," the mother replied with her chest stuck out. I had forgotten how disrespectful teenage girls could be and my hand began itching to smack some sense into her.

"Satasha, right?"

"Yeah that would be me," she replied, rolling her neck.

I ignored her ignorance and proceeded. "How old are you?" I asked as three women walked into the room; all loud and extra ghetto, might I add.

"What the hell is going on here Satasha? I got a call from the po-lice about your bad ass being in jail because you out fighting in the streets with the baby in the car. You such a stupid ass little bitch." One of the women yelled as she pointed her finger in the young girl's face. Her hair was sticking up all over her head, she had dried slobber all over the side of her face and she wore high water pajamas with ran over house shoes. Satasha dropped her head and didn't respond.

"Well, Malasia's ass ain't no better. No wonder y'all two heifas are best friends because both of y'all dumb as hell," one of the other women, who looked just as rough, said to the other young girl.

"Look mama, I don't wanna hear that shit right now." The girl replied calmly.

"Who the hell you talking to like that?" the remaining woman, who looked to be in her fifties, asked as she walked over to Malasia and slapped her like I had wanted to slap the baby's mother, Satasha. Malasia jumped up to retaliate but the handcuffs stopped her. I quickly went over and got in between them. Officer Collins also walked in to provide me with some assistance.

"And who the fuck is dis mutt bitch?" Satasha's mother asked, referring to me.

Mutt? I hadn't heard that one in a long time and it stung a little. And my fingers that were once tingling for Satasha were now tingling for these ghetto ass witches in front of me.

"My name is Carolyn Black and I am a CPS worker. Now, if you and these other two ladies can put your ignorance to the side, we can try to get to the bottom of this mess. Otherwise, if you wanna continue being ghetto and grimy, I can get ghetto right with you. So what's up, let's do this." I snapped without thinking. *Thank God Val isn't here.* I thought to myself but I was serious as hell. I regretted having to go there because I was already walking the line at work; however, I knew that if I didn't check Boonsheika and the Ghetto Girls on the spot, their vicious disrespect towards the girls *and me* was going to be relentless. So I stood my ground, looking them straight in their eyes and waited. Officer Collins' eyes bulged out of his head, as did everyone else's. I guess no one expected that from a social worker who looked like me, a mutt.

"Well excuuuuse me, Ms. CPS worker. I didn't know you could talk to people like that." "Boonsheika" replied.

"Well, I don't know why you thought that you could talk to *me* like that. Now let's get back to the reason why we're all here. So please have a seat so that we can get this over with." I waited for them to sit down and then I continued. "Again, my name is Carolyn Black and I work for Fosterberg County DSS. Let's start out by going around the room and introducing ourselves to each other so that everyone here knows who everyone is." I said more calmly.

"Well, my name is Jackie Carter and I am Satasha Carter's mother and the baby, Mariah Carter's grandmother." Boonsheika replied.

"And I'm Diyanetta Talley and I'm Malasia's mama." Ghetto Girl Number One replied.

"And I'm Joyce Leverette Jones; Malasia's grandmother," Ole G' Ghetto Girl Number Two replied.

"Ok, so let's get started. How old are these girls and why do they have an infant out at 2:00 in the morning? That's my first question," I asked cordially already knowing the answer. I tried not to judge people, but my years of experience had put me up on game and most of the time I was able to recognize drug addicts and poor excuses for parents. And these hood rats were the exact make and model of both. Therefore, I understood exactly why these girls were out so late. However, I was willing to hear what Boonsheika and the Ghetto Girls had to say.

"Well, I don't know why this little dumb shit is out with her baby this late at night. She don't listen to a damn thing I say and she's fast as hell which is why her little hot ass has a baby at 16," Boonsheika replied. Satasha remained silent with her head down.

"Well, Ms. Talley, why is Malasia out this late at night?" I asked Ghetto Girl One.

"Who knows? Didn't you hear Jackie say they do what they want to? Malasia is rebellious as hell and I've had problems out of her since she was a small child."

"Whatever," Malasia mumbled. "When were you ever sober enough to notice my problems? I been with grandma my whole life and God knows that's been a train wreck, so who are you to talk?"

"Don't back talk me bitch. Grandma already hit you in your mouth; don't make me do it again."

"I dare you. Your days of beating on me and shitting on me are over. I wish you would put your hands on me." Malasia said, looking her mother stone cold in the eye.

"Um ladies, we're getting off track. If we don't get to the bottom of this, we're going to be here all night. So, what I'm going to do is talk to everyone separately and then we will make a decision as to what to do with the baby."

"What you mean 'what to do with the baby'? She's going home with me. I don't give a damn what you do with Satasha because her little ass needs to be locked up. It might teach her some sense, but my grandbaby is going home with me."

"And what you gonna do with her? Sell her to the highest bidder so you can get some crack?" Satasha asked, finally breaking her silence.

"You know what? I'm sick of your mouth. I'm bout to beat yo' ass," Boonsheika said as she stood up with her fist balled up, ready to sock Satasha. But I caught her arm mid swing and slammed her onto the table as *professionally* as I could mind you, with a sprinkle of what I really wanted to do to her. I held her down by her neck so she couldn't move.

"Officer Collins, please escort these ladies out of here while I talk to these girls who appear to be more mature than the adults," I said sarcastically.

"Come on ladies. You all can wait in the other room," he said as I cautiously let Boonsheika up and walked her; with my hand still holding the back of her neck, to the door. Once the Ghetto Girls were gone, I shut the door and sat down with the girls. I also had Officer Collins to take them out of their cuffs.

"Ok girls. Please talk to me and tell me what's going on. Its late and we need to get the baby somewhere warm and safe," I said gently, realizing that I was dealing with too very hurt and battered young girls.

"I ain't got shit to say to you lady," Malasia said as tears rolled down her face.

"Me either," Satasha replied.

"Listen, I'm only here to help you…"

"Help us? Help us? Bitch please. We don't need your help now. Where the fuck was you when that crackhead bitch was leaving me home alone with no food or heat? Where was you when we was sleeping in cars? Where was you when my mama was selling my clothes *and* me for crack? Where was you when Malasia's mama was leaving her with any and everybody while she was out getting high? Where was you when her alcoholic grandmother was beating her with extension cords and feeding her pork and beans while everybody else was eating fried chicken?

Where was you when her grandmother's men were beating her and touching on her tits? Huh? Where was you then? Man get the fuck outta here. Ain't nobody been here for us but us. We all we got. The only thing our crackhead mamas did right was be best friends so me and Malasia could meet and take care of each other!" Satasha yelled through tears. I didn't say anything initially, as her words soaked in. I just let her cry and get it out. My heart ached for them but at the end of the day, I still had to do my job.

"Do either of you have a dad involved? I asked.

"My mama kept me from my dad. I didn't even know he existed until he died and I started getting a SSI check, which my mom tries to steal every chance she gets. Ms. Black, you just don't understand what we been through. We've sold our bodies just to get clothes and shoes for school. We've had to steal to eat. We've had to nurse our mothers back to health after they got some bad crack, but here *we* are in jail; sitting in front of a social worker when all Satasha wanted to do was make sure that her baby was with her. Listen, I agree that Satasha needs help with the baby because she does put her in some dangerous and unhealthy situations but that's because that's all she knows Ms. Black. That's all both of us know," Malasia said softly.

"You guys don't have any other family members that you can stay with?" I asked.

"No." They said in unison.

"Well, what about the baby's father?" I asked. Satasha exhaled and began shaking her leg. She was silent for a while, and then the silent tears turned into a loud and piercing sob. Malasia got up and put her arms around her.

"She doesn't know who the father is because she was gang raped by some tricks we met at a hotel who we thought we were just stripping for," Malasia replied. I wanted to drop my head but I had to remain professional.

"Girls, I really am sorry that you went through all that. This is why it's important that people call us in these types of situations. So many times cases like yours go unreported and if we don't know what's going on then there's nothing we can do about it. In the meantime, now that we do know, I can help you now. Satasha, the first thing that I have to do is take the baby to the hospital for an examination to ensure that she's ok. You all exposed her to a significant amount of second hand marijuana smoke. I don't know how harmful that may be for her, or if it's harmful at all, but that's what has to happen right now. Secondly, um, we have to figure out where to go from here as far as getting a safe environment for you guys *and* the baby. I need to step out and talk with your mothers and I will need to consult with my supervisor as well, so you guys stay put and I will send Officer Collins in here to bring you all something to eat and drink. Where is the baby's diaper bag just in case she needs to be fed and changed?" I asked.

"It's in the car at my friend Pee Wee's house," Satasha replied.

"Ok. Well, I don't know if you guys are going to be charged for the fight and for having marijuana in the car, but Satasha you may be charged with misdemeanor child endangerment because you all were smoking weed and driving around with the baby in the car." They both sucked their teeth but remained silent. I walked out and went to go get Officer Collins. After he took over with the girls, I went in to meet with Boonsheika and the Ghetto Girls who had no genuine concern for the girls' wellbeing at all. They, in fact, told me that they wanted to have the girls locked up and out of their homes because they were "tired of dealing with their bullshit."

"Well I'm sorry. Those girls belong to you and it's your responsibility to take care of them. Now, this case will probably go into treatment status because the girls are 16 and for the most part can look out for themselves. However, you will be under the watchful eye of DSS for 6-15 months based on the need. The other option is for us to have them placed at St. Mary's which is a shelter for homeless and parenting teens," I replied.

"Well, let them go there then." Boonsheika said indifferently.

"Well that's fine but if they do go there, please believe that you are still responsible for them, which means that any government assistance you are receiving on their behalf will go to

St. Mary's and you all will be required to pay child support until they are 18." I responded with my head cocked to the side knowing good and well that those trifling hussies would think twice before they let their "meal tickets" go.

"Uh, well, I ain't paying no damn child support and my mama needs her food stamps since she disabled and can't work. So, well, I guess Malasia can stay. And uh, Jackie, I guess Satasha can stay with us too since you don't want her," Ghetto Girl One said with modesty faker than the weave she wore in her head.

"Hell no bitch, you just trying to get more food stamps and you know it'll be a lot more if the baby comes. I got mine, you just worry bout taking care of yours." Boonsheika replied.

"Uh huh," I said rolling my eyes not caring if they saw. "Well, I have to take the baby to the hospital to get her checked out. I will release the girls into Officer Collins care for now because I don't know if they are going to have to spend the night in jail or not. Once the baby is released from the hospital, she will be placed in a temporary placement until we figure out what to do next."

"Oh, hell nah. You ain't putting my grandbaby in no foster care. You crazy as hell," Boonsheika said, getting up out of her seat. I was two seconds away from slapping her ass but I continued maintaining my professionalism.

"Ms. Carter, I suggest you sit down. Where were you when your sixteen-year-old daughter was out driving *your grandbaby* around, smoking weed in the car? Now, I wish I could send her home with one of you guys, but I can't until the home environment is deemed safe and suitable for her to live in ok?" I said as politely as my thinning tolerance would allow.

"Whatever," Boonsheika replied as she sat that ass down.

Yeah, that's what I thought. I said to myself as I walked out. I checked back in with the girls to alert them to what was going on.

"Satasha, what kind of formula does the baby drink so that I can let them know at the hospital?" I asked.

"Well, she drinks Enfamil, but I ain't had none so I been giving her regular milk," She replied. This time I didn't restrain my head from dropping. *What the hell?* I thought to myself. I sighed loudly and replied, "Honey, you can't give a baby regular milk. It will make her sick. She's too little to be drinking that. Lord have mercy," I said as I picked the baby up and took her to my car. I strapped her in and drove her to the hospital. And just as I was checking her in, my personal cell phone began ringing. I didn't answer because I was preoccupied with the baby, but I was curious as to who the hell was calling me at almost four a.m. on my regular cell phone, especially when it kept ringing back to back. Luckily, I had it on vibrate so I wouldn't distract the doctor, but as soon as I got the opportunity to check it, I saw that it was Val who had been calling me. Figuring someone had called her about the case I was working, I quickly called her back. She answered on the first ring.

"Carolyn, what the hell is wrong with you?"

Confused, I asked, "Huh? What are you talking about Val?"

"Girl, are you crazy? You jumped on the Mayor and then stole his car? What in the world is going on? What happened? Where are you?" She demanded. Hearing her regurgitate the events that occurred between me and Mayor Bostain actually made me laugh because now that it was over, the shit was funny.

"Val, it's a long story, but I'm actually glad you called because I'm at the hospital with an infant. I got a call at about 2:30 this morning."

"What?! Fix it Jesus," she replied with a sigh. "What happened and ain't you still drunk?"

"No honey, I left my buzz at the Mayor's house. And by the way, his car is at the venue. Make sure you let him know I left him a gift in the front seat."

"She said his car is at the venue and she left him a gift in the front seat," I heard Val say followed by an "ok" from a deep voice in the background.

"Oh shit. Is that Maurice?" I asked giggling.

"Shut up, Carolyn. Now tell me what's going on with this case." I snickered and began briefing her about the girls, the baby and my adversaries, Boonsheika and The Ghetto Girls.

"Well, I'm going to call and tell Officer Collins to take them straight to St. Mary's once they are released. Then that way they will be out of that environment and Satasha can be monitored with the baby and put through parenting classes," Val said.

"Well, I think that's the logical answer but my concern is that because those girls have been raised by the streets and in the streets, I don't think they will stay at St. Mary's."

"Ok, so you think we should let them go home? What about the baby?" She asked.

"See that's the tricky part. That girl is a complete replica of her mother when it comes to caring for that baby. Plus, you have to factor in the point that the baby is a product of rape, therefore her motherly bond is somewhat compromised and I don't think that any amount of parenting classes is going to change that. When I told her that I was taking the baby to the hospital, she didn't even flinch. I don't think she wants that baby."

"But Carolyn, we can't send them home to their environments and then put the baby in foster care with strangers when she has parents. We have to think about the future of this baby. You and I both know that babies that young need their mother."

"Val, I am thinking about the future. That girl has no parental bond with that child and I know that eventually that baby is going to fall under the radar just like those girls have and it's going to create a vicious cycle. I'm not going to let that happen. I feel like we should get the girls in Intensive In Home counseling for 3-6 months and mandate that their guardians participate and get in substance abuse treatment. Hell, all we gotta do with them hood rats is use food stamps and government benefits as leverage. Shit, they'll walk the chalk line for that, honey. Then that way we can keep our eyes on them and protect the girls at the same time. We can make sure that they are attending school regularly and help them get jobs because personally, I think they are set in their ways. Well, I take that back, because if Malasia was the parent then I would be down with the St. Mary's idea. She has more of a bond with the child than the mother does plus, she has some sense. But the problem is that she's going to ride with her BFF regardless of what we say or do, so I really think we should have the baby placed and allow supervised visits so that we can monitor them more closely."

"Carolyn, listen, I'm still buzzing and I'm exhausted. We'll talk about this later on today. In the meantime, go ahead and take the baby to Ms. Jones' house until we can schedule a TDM."

"Ok, cool, and uh tell Maurice I said hi. Oh yeah, and make sure you bring me my Benjamin Franklin too!" I said laughing.

"Whatever! Speaking of that, what the hell happened with you and Terrance?"

"Girl he tried to play me. I was ready to go home and he came at me sideways so I put the paws on him and took his car. But I left it parked at the venue and the keys are under the seat."

"Oh my gosh Carolyn! And what was this 'gift' you left him? I hope your crazy ass didn't do nothing that's going to get you put in jail."

"Nah, I didn't break any laws, let's just say I uh, relieved myself." I grunted with a giggle. Val sighed.

"Carolyn Black, what am I going to do with you?"

"Not a damn thang," I said and hung up the phone.

Monday Morning

Val and I argued vehemently over how to handle the case of Boonsheika and the Ghetto Girls and their offspring. I stood by my suggestion of putting the case in treatment status because I knew those girls; especially Satasha, was not going to last at St. Mary's. I felt that they would do better in their natural environment as long as we could put services in place for them. I figured we could work with them and eventually transition them into a more appropriate placement as time progressed. However, Val overruled me and had the two girls as well as the baby placed at St. Mary's.

"Damnit Val! You have Maurice's cock on the brain and its clouding your judgment," I barked at her.

"Don't you speak to me like that in this professional environment Carolyn Black! I'm the supervisor and I know what I'm doing. I don't want to hear anything else about it. Are we clear?"

"Yessum missus. We's clear," I said sarcastically. She gave me a sharp look, which let me know that I'd better chill out, so I vacated the premises and went to sit in my car so I could calm down. My phone began ringing and when I looked to see who it was, I saw that it was a private number calling so I didn't answer. However, when the call came through for the third time in a row, I began to panic; thinking it was someone calling about my mom.

"Hello?"

"Bitch, you think you gonna sucker punch me, steal my car, piss all in it and get away with it?"

"Who the hell is this? Oh wait; the inside of my ear is on fire so this must be none other than dog breath Terrance Bostain right?" I snorted with chuckle.

"Fuck you, you dusty butt, dry as a desert, tragic mulatto! You're going to pay for this shit! If I'd known that I was gonna be running my meat through a patch of sandpaper I wouldn't have wasted my time."

"Terrance, *your meat* doesn't stick out far enough to be running through anything and how was I supposed to get wet when you're breath evaporated the moisture from my body. Honey, I don't even count what we did as sex anyway. It was more like a nightmare."

"Oh, it was sex alright; it was just the worst sex *ever*. Hell I assumed it would be good cause you look like you have a couple of miles on you and they say experience is the best teacher."

"Well, honey if that's the case, it's apparent that you ain't had no experience *or* mouthwash. But I learned my lesson though; no more pity sex for me; especially from cornballs with stank ass breath."

"Trick, you came onto me. Remember that. I mean I understand because *I am* the mayor and all, but who knew you was gonna act like a low class hood rat and piss in my car. I mean, who does that?"

"Well, your wack ass tried to disrespect me like I was a groupie. All you had to do was take me to my car and we could have charged the bad, I mean TERRIBLE, sex to the game. However, you wanted to be an asshole, so that's why you got your ass beat!"

Silence.

"So, you wanna hook up and try it again?" he asked.

"Uh, hell no," I replied sarcastically.

"Well, I promise you that if there is a next time, I'll make it worth your while."

"I doubt it because your penis will always be small and your breath will always be bad, so I'll pass."

Silence.

Then I heard him giggling which turned into full-blown laughter. "Carolyn, although you've officially become another notch on my belt, you are crazy as hell and quick on your toes! I love it! We don't have to have sex anymore...unless you want to... but you're cool, so we can let bygones be bygones"

I started laughing too and shook my head. "Sure Bad Breath Bostain."

Later on that day, I went by my Cousin Brandon's house and hung out with him and my little brother John.

"So what you gonna do for your birthday next week Carolyn?" my little brother John asked me as we passed around a blunt.

"Damn, I been going through so much stuff, I forgot about my own birthday. Hell, I don't know what I'm going to do. Probably nothing but the same thing we doing right now," I replied.

"Damn Carolyn. I wanna know what happened to my sister. You lame as hell. You used to be turnt up and now you all old acting and shit. And don't tell me that it's because of mommy because Brandon told me how you walked in on her and daddy getting their groove on. How you gonna let your parents be more exciting than you?" My little brother John asked with his head cocked to the side.

"Shut up John! Just because I ain't ghetto fabulous like your ass don't mean I'm lame. And how you know I ain't getting it in?" I snapped.

"Hell look at you. Looking like a damn librarian."

"I told her ass the same thing," Brandon chimed in. I shot both of them the middle finger.

"And how would you know what a librarian looks like John, you can barely even read," I cracked

"Whatever. Your old ass is turning 35 next week and I don't care what your boring ass says, we turning up for your birthday. Matter of fact, we gonna party John Black style. I'm personally gonna throw you a party myself," my little brother John said, rubbing his hands together. I looked at him and smacked my lips.

"Boy bye! Ain't no way in hell I'm attending anything thrown 'John Black' style. Hell, the last time I was at a party with your ass, your prissy ass sister Sylvia got into a fight with one of your hood rats. Ain't no way in the world you gonna have me somewhere where I have to duck and dodge bullets," I replied with a laugh.

"Whatchu' mean? I don't be throwing no ghetto parties like that."

Brandon and I looked at each other and we both started laughing.

"Dude are you serious? Do you remember your high school graduation party that ended with shots fired and the police getting called? Do you remember the shit that happened on your 21st birthday? Hell, does your ass remember your 30th birthday party a few months ago where people was fighting over a spades game and that girl got hit in the head with a liquor bottle? And you couldn't do shit about it because we had to carry your drunk ass to the car because you was passed out. Hell nah, you ain't throwing no party. You can help me plan it but I be damn if I get shot up over your hood ass," Brandon replied in between giggles.

"Whatever. I bet y'all's black asses had fun though didn't you?"

"Off course we did John," I said, pulling his head to my chest and rocking him, being facetious.

"Get off of me," he said and jerked away from me.

"Anyway, speaking of the hood, let's go to Busters. This blunt got me wanting to bob my head and eat some fish," Brandon said excitedly.

"Hell yeah. I'm down with that," my little brother John replied.

"Uh Brandon. You do remember what happened the last time you and I went to Buster's right? I mean, hell, we probably can't even go back up in there," I said.

This time Brandon smacked his lips. "See, there you go being lame as hell. They don't give a damn about us fighting and shit as long as we don't tear nothing up or kill nobody. All they care about is our money. So get yo' ass up and let's go have some fun...Black style baby!" I laughed and took a few more tokes off the blunt because I knew he was right.

"Alright let's go," I replied as I got up and grabbed my purse. Maybe I was looking lame on the outside, but it sure didn't have anything to do with me not getting sex because Jermaine, I mean Avery, had been blowing my back out.

One Week Later

Ring. Ring. Ring.

I wasn't sure if something was actually ringing or if I was hearing the throbbing pain ricocheting back and forth inside my head.

Ring. Ring. Ring.

With my head plastered to the bed, I blindly reached over and fidgeted around on my nightstand for the phone. My head was pounding so hard that I didn't even want to open my eyes.

"Hello?" I whispered groggily in a deep raspy voice.

"Get your ass up girl! It's your birthday." Val squealed into my ear, which made my pounding head hurt worse.

"Val, please....honey; you're talking too loud."

"Girl what are you talking about? Screw that. Get your old ass up. I'll be over there in two hours to pick you up. I'm taking you for a mani, pedi day at the spa. And then I'm taking you to get your hair done because I'm sick to death of that damn ponytail," she said, still screaming.

"Damn Val, call me back later. I love you and everything but I'm not getting up this early," I replied, getting annoyed.

"Uh, Carolyn, it's one o'clock in the afternoon. I'm guessing by the sound of your voice that you must have had a long night last night."

"1:00?!" I sat straight up in bed and opened my eyes, which I immediately regretted. The light from the sun turned the pound in my head into the digging of a jackhammer, which quickly made me lay my ass right back down.

"Yes, honey. It's one o'clock. Now get your ass ready. Our appointment is at three thirty. You gotta be fly for the humdinger that your cousin Brandon has planned for you tonight."

"Damn it's my birthday. Why can't I just sleep all day until time to go to the party?" I whined.

"Because you can't. Now get up! I'll be there shortly. Smooches," she replied, still louder than I needed her to be, and hung up.

I sighed because I wanted nothing more than to lay in bed and sleep the day away. Me, Brandon, my little brother John and surprisingly my sisters, had all gotten together last night and had a pre-birthday party celebration whereby we smoked about 5 blunts and polished off three fifths of Patron. I was paying dearly for it, but being hungover was not the only thing that was keeping me in bed. I was depressed. Here I was, 35 years old with no husband, no children and no life. I didn't even have my tricks anymore with the exception of Jermaine, I mean Avery's broke ass, who wanted to do nothing more than bang my brains out; which was starting to get boring because I was starting to miss my variety pack of "toys".

How, at 35, did I get here? I thought to myself sadly, as my head continued pounding. I wanted to cry so badly, but I heard the spirit of the old Carolyn Black begin to whisper in my ear.

Bitch, get your crybaby ass up. You're alive, you have a job, you have a badass crib, your parents and family are ok and you don't have a sorry ass piece of a man that you have to answer to. And on top of that, your ass is 35 years old and you can put even the hottest 25 year old to shame. Not get your ass up and celebrate your birthday."

"You damn right!" I said out loud to myself. I jerked up again like an idiot and my throbbing head punched me in the face and knocked me right back onto my pillow. Once I got the pounding under control, I slowly raised up and got out of bed. I went straight into the kitchen and took a Goody's powder. Then I held my nose and gulped down a V8, which my favorite uncle had taught me to drink a long time ago to ward off hangovers. I then lifted my hands and looked up. "God I thank you for letting me see another year. *And* I'm still fine as hell." I giggled. "Ooo, Sorry, sorry. I didn't mean to cuss God. You know what I meant," I said and then headed towards the shower. Once I was done, I went over to my closet to figure out what I was going to put on. I mean it was my 35th birthday after all and I did want to look fly as hell so I went to the back of my closet where my "break in case of an emergency" clothes were on standby, waiting to be worn again. I picked out an army green romper, which I paired with gold sandals and accessories. And just as I was brushing my wild mane into a messy bun on top of my head, my doorbell rang. I looked at the clock and it was exactly 3:00 on the dot.

Damn Val. I laughed to myself as I headed towards the door and opened it. There she stood, wearing a pretty yellow sundress. She actually looked really cute.

"Shit, Val. You must have damn near wrecked your car trying to get here on time."

"Girl, shut up and give me a hug." She laughed. We embraced.

"Happy Birthday girl. I know you've been going through a lot lately but tonight, you and I are going to party like rock stars. Maurice already said he was going to drive for us so we don't have to worry about having a DD."

"Maurice huh? Mmmmhmmmm...yeah. You know your ass owes me 100.00 dollars speaking of that right?" I laughed.

"Whatever. As much money as I'm about to spend on your old ass you better shut up about some damn hundred dollars. Come on let's go."

"Ok, we can go but don't try to change the subject. I want my hundred dollars and I want all the details," I replied with a wicked laugh.

"Well, I don't kiss and tell but let's just say that lingerie paired with my 'banana' lesson most definitely has paid off." She snapped her finger feistily and walked towards the car. All I could do was laugh.

After Val and I had pampered ourselves, we went shopping. My hair looked absolutely gorgeous all blown out and flowy and my skin had the shimmering glow that it was used to having. I felt refreshed and I couldn't wait to pick out a sexy ass dress that said, "Today is my 35th birthday and I'm still the shit." After I found my "I'm the shit" dress, Val and I decided to go ahead to the Mac counter and get our makeup done since the party would be starting soon anyway. Once we were done, Val dropped me off at home and told me that as soon as she was done getting dressed; her and Maurice would be by to pick me up. I knew we were going to be late, but it was ok because it was my birthday and I planned to make a grand entrance.

Brandon had reserved one of his parent's upscale restaurants for my party and had it decorated from top to bottom with red and silver décor. He had hired a Jamaican band and one of the hottest DJ's in NC, who just happened to be one of his loyal customers, to do the music. When Val, Maurice and I walked in, heads turned, mouths dropped and women grabbed their men. The party was packed. People were dancing, drinking and eating the deliciously prepared American, Dominican and Italian entrées (my favorite might I add). I was impressed because Brandon had outdone himself. I was so glad that he had taken over and not my knucklehead brother. But, then I noticed that the gold tooth bandits and hood rats; who had been given a strict "no drama" warning, were scattered throughout the party alerting me that my little brother John had had some say so in the party planning.

The Reggae band was so hot that I almost regretted having worn the 5-inch heels that I had on. Luckily, I had a pair of slippers tucked inside of my medium size clutch that I could slide on as the night progressed.   As Val and I worked the crowd and made our way to the dance floor, I saw Brandon heading towards me.

"Happy birthday Cuz!" He said as he picked me up and squeezed me.

"Damn Brandon, you outdid yourself. This party is off the chain. And I can't believe you remembered how much I love Italian food," I replied with a huge smile on my face.

"Girl, you know I got you. And your whole family is here. Including your parents, my parents, all of our cousins and your sisters."

"Where are they? I saw some of our cousins but not our parents," I replied.

"Well, they all back there in the "old people" section. They didn't wanna listen to our style of music, plus they knew we were gonna be getting tore up so they wanted us to be able to party without being concerned about disrespecting 'em. Come on, follow me."

I didn't know where he was leading me, but I obliged. We went back into one of the small private dining areas and there sat my parents, aunts, uncles and older family members. My grandparents were even there which made me want to cry. I rushed over and began hugging everybody. They all greeted me warmly and gave me lots of hugs, kisses *and* birthday money.

"Happy Birthday Curly," my dad said as he hugged me and kissed me on the cheek.

"Thanks dad," I replied.

"Now come over here and have a seat. We ain't gonna keep you from your party too long but we brought you back here because we all just wanted you to know how much we love you and we wanted to give you some gifts," my dad said.

My mom chimed in, "And I will never forget how you took such good care of me when I was sick. Now granted it's time for you to leave me the hell alone cause me and your daddy are getting

our groove back, but nevertheless I love you and I appreciate you."
We all shared a laugh, especially me, Brandon and my little brother
John because we knew that they actually *were* getting their groove
back.

My dad then led me to a table, which held three gifts, a
medium size box, an envelope and a small box. I immediately
opened the medium sized box first because I figured the bigger the
box, the better the gift. When I opened it, I squealed because it
was a vintage Louis Vuitton purse along with a pair of gold Louis
Vuitton earrings. Then, I opened up the envelope. Inside was a two-
week itinerary for a tour of Italy that concluded with a three-day
stay in Venice. I screamed and jumped up and down with so much
excitement that my boobs almost popped out of my dress. Going to
Italy had been a dream of mine since my teenage years. I was so
happy that I started doing the Cabbage Patch. My family laughed
and shook their heads because they all knew I was crazy.

Lastly, I reached for the small box. My heart began to pound
because I wondered what more they could give me. As I tore the
gold wrapping paper off, my paternal grandmother joined me.

"This one is from me," she said with her thick Spanish accent
and squeezed my hand.

I opened it and inside was a pair of pearl earrings and a
matching necklace.

"Oooo Grammy, their beautiful," I gasped as I fingered the
pearls.

"These pearls were passed down to me from mi abuelita
who received them from her abuelita. They are over 100 years old.
I was going to give them to you on your wedding day but since God
only knows when you are going to get married, I figured your 35th
birthday would be the perfect time to give them to you." She
looked me in my eyes with seriousness as she continued holding
onto my hand.

"Treasure them Curly because they are priceless and
antique. They are very precious to me. And one day you will be
able to give them to your own daughter. I love you baby girl and

happy birthday," Grammy said with a smile of pride on her face. I hugged her tightly and thanked her as I teared up.

"Aww, I love you too Grammy." We embraced and shared a moment.

"Ok. Welp, now that that's over, let's go in here and get wasted! There's a party going on," my little brother John said, interrupting our sentimental moment.

"Yeah all this sentimental shi..." Brandon began as my grandmother gave him the evil eye. "Sorry Grammy, I meant to say won't you come on in here and do the stanky leg with me." He corrected himself jokingly as he draped his arm around my grandmother's shoulder and kissed her on the cheek. She rolled her eyes at him.

"Get on outta here Brandon before I get a switch after your ass," Grammy said and put her hands on her hips. All of our mouths dropped then we all started laughing. I forgot how feisty my grandma was but I totally understood where we all got it from.

After I thanked everybody once again and handed my gifts to my dad for safekeeping, we all rejoined the party. Everybody was dancing and having fun; including the "old heads" in our family. Brandon actually got grandma to do the stanky leg after all, and my parents might as well have been having sex on the dancefloor by the way they were bumping and grinding. I was dancing with my little brother John when Brandon came and pulled us to the side.

"Listen, let's go smoke this phatty real quick."

"I'm down," I replied. So we met up with my sisters and headed to a "smoke spot" that Brandon had designated in a tiny office at the very back of the restaurant. In route, I heard someone call Brandon's name. We all stopped and turned around. There stood Jarrod looking like 1.5 million dollars.

"What's up Jarrod?" Brandon said as they gave each other dap.

"Ain't nothing. Sorry I'm late. I just got off from work," he replied while focusing in on me...giving me a savage look that made my body get hot.

"You good man. We were just about to go smoke a blunt if you wanna join us."

"That's wussup. I'll match you a blunt." He then walked over to me. "Happy birthday Carolyn. You look beautiful." I immediately began to blush which threw me off because he was a kid and how in the hell was I letting a 12 year old; as I often referred to the young'uns, get to me.

"Thanks," I replied bashfully as I quickly turned and followed Brandon. I did however make sure to sashay a little harder because I knew my ass looked magnificent in my dress and I felt like a little bit of teasing wasn't going to hurt anything...so I thought.

We all smoked and laughed in the tiny little room. One blunt ended up being three and the entire time we were smoking, Jarrod never took his eyes off me. No matter how hard I tried to focus on everybody else, my eyes continued to find their way back to him. My nipples became hard and my Juicy became moist. *This little boy is trying to seduce me...and it's working.* I thought to myself.

"Come on y'all, we gotta go back to the party before people start noticing that we're missing. Plus, we gotta take some shots," my little brother John said as he walked towards the door.

"Yeah, let's go!" I replied as I got up to follow him. I tried to walk past Jarrod quickly but he gently grabbed my arm and whispered in my ear, "Save me a dance." His warm breath on my ear mixed with the euphoric feeling the weed was giving me almost made me bust a nut right then and there, but my sister Sylvia saved the day.

"Carolyn, come here. I want to talk to you for a sec," she said. Although I was somewhat concerned about what she had to say, I gladly accepted. Olivia looked a little pretentious about separating from her minion, but she continued walking ahead with everyone else.

"Listen, Carolyn. I just want you to know that I really, really love you. I know I've been a bitch to you most of your life and I'm genuinely sorry from the bottom of my heart. These past few months that I've actually spent being around you has shown me how cool you really are. Hell, you're actually cooler than Olivia's stuck up ass," she said with a giggle and continued. "But anyway, I'm not trying to get all sentimental on you but I just wanted you to know how much you mean to me and hopefully we can start hanging out more. I hate that we've wasted all this time, but I really want to start getting to know you better. You're my little sister and I want to have a relationship with you. Can you forgive me for the way I've treated you?" She asked with a look of genuine remorse in her eyes.

"Of course I forgive you. I appreciate that and I really love you too." We hugged each other tightly but it seemed as if she didn't want to let me go. When we finally did release each other, we both were crying. We wiped our faces; laughing at ourselves and walked hand in hand back to the party, which was still going strong. The difference, however, was Jarrod. Everywhere I went, I felt his eyes on me. Even Val noticed and asked me who he was. I told her that he was one of Brandon's friends, but as the night progressed, I knew things between us was going to go further and evolve into him becoming one of *my* friends.

As we all took a brief intermission from dancing, we headed to the bar to take some shots. Jarrod walked towards the bathroom and when the coast was clear, I pulled Brandon to the side.

"Brandon, what's up with your boy? He's been on me all night and his little ass is cute as hell. If he keeps on messing with me, I'm gonna give him something to make him go home and suck his thumb," I said with a laugh, although I was serious as hell.

Brandon smirked. "Cee, Jarrod's cool as hell. I mean he's a young'un so you can't be falling all in love with him and shit, but it wouldn't hurt to get them pipes cleaned out so you can stop walking around here looking like an old maid. Go on and get with him. He's alright."

Damn Brandon. I thought to myself. I was hoping that he was gonna cuss me out and tell me to leave Jarrod alone, but when he gave me his blessing instead, *I knew good and well* it was gonna go down tonight between me and Jarrod. However, since I was riding home with Val and Maurice after the party, I figured I could use that as my escape. But that plan got shot all to hell when Val walked up to me and the crew later on that night and announced that she was "going home because she felt nauseated, since she'd eaten a couple pieces of cake and drank a lot of liquor."

"Damn Val. You know better than to eat cake and drink vodka girl. I'm not ready to go yet; it's only 12:30," I whined as I got up to begin gathering my things.

"Girl, you know good and well we'll get you home." Brandon slurred.

"Well, I shall not be getting in the car with your drunk ass. In fact I hope that chicken head you been hanging with all night is going to drive *you*," I replied, laughing.

"Sis, you can ride with me and Olivia. I'll take you home," Sylvia said as she looked at Brandon and shook her head.

"Girl, but you live in the total opposite direction from me. That's way out of your way."

"Shhh, it's not a big deal. Now that's the end of it. We will take you home," she concluded, shutting me down.

"Humph, feisty!" I laughed and snapped my finger.

"Well good because, I'm about to throw up right now," Val said as she took off running towards the bathroom with Maurice trailing behind her, which made us all burst into laughter. We all took a few shots and made our way back to the smoke room so we could smoke another blunt. As we passed the blunt around, I brought up the story about how Sylvia had beat the shit out of my little brother John's girlfriend at Sylvia's birthday cookout.

"That hoe wasn't my girlfriend...but she sho' had that snatch though," My little brother John said, spellbound.

"Oh man, that shit was funny as hell. You beat that girl's ass," Olivia said in between bouts of laughter.

"What was her name?" I asked, as I hit the blunt.

"Hell, I don't remember. Oh wait, Tina, her name was Tina," my little brother John replied. "Tina with the big tits." He laid his head back and closed his eyes; reminiscing I suppose. I rolled my eyes.

"Damn man. I hate I missed that shit. I would have loved to have seen Sylvia's debutante ass dropping them paws on somebody." Brandon laughed.

"Well, I might be *a debutante* or whatever, but I have a stiletto on one foot and a tennis shoe on the other. And at any given time I will kick that stiletto off and beat that ass if I have to," Sylvia replied, rolling her neck. We laughed but we knew she was telling the truth. Hell, all of us had a small bit of cray cray in us, which meant we were all down to fight if necessary.

We finished the blunt and headed back towards the party. As we walked onto the dancefloor, the DJ began playing a slow jam and before I knew it, Jarrod and I were slow grinding. He took his fingers, ran them down the bare part of my back, and then wrapped his arms firmly around my waist.

"Carolyn, can I take you home tonight? I promise I'll make sure you get there safely," he whispered in my ear seductively.

"Um, it's ok. My sister is going to take me," I replied coyly, as fire shot throughout my body.

"Carolyn, stop fighting me. I know you want me just as much as I want you. And I promise I'll make it worth your while."

"Jarrod, you're too young for me. I used to babysit you for God's sake. I'd feel like a child molester." He released me and looked me in my eyes. He moved in as closely to me as he could causing our bodies to press against each other. Then, he kissed me. Brandon, who was dancing beside of us with his chicken head, gave me a wicked smile and started nodding his head. I shot him a bird, unbeknownst to Jarrod.

"Um Jarrod, you can, uh, drop me off but that's it...ok." I said, trying to be firm knowing good and well what was going to happen once we got to my house.

"I can handle that. Shall we go now?" he asked.

"Um, uh yeah we can go now. The party will be over soon anyway," my mouth said involuntarily, under the full control of my Juicy and not me.

"Ok. Let's go," he said as he grabbed my hand and walked me towards the exit.

"Wait, I have to tell my sisters."

"Ok. I'll meet you out front."

"Ok," I replied bashfully and walked over to where my sisters were sitting.

"Hey Sylvia, I found another ride home so you don't have to go to the trouble of taking me all the way across town," I said. They both looked at me with smirks and raised eyebrows.

"Yeah heifa, I bet you do have a ride home. I saw how that little boy has been all over you all night." Olivia said. I blushed and began to feel ashamed because here I was again, with some random man while they were both married and with families. I dropped my head.

"Girl, what you looking like that for? The days of us chastising you and making you feel like shit because you're not married are over. Honey, I envy you. You can do whatever the hell you want to do, when you want to do it. Girl bye, marriage ain't all it's cracked up to be. Shit, if I knew then what I know now, I woulda waited a little while," Sylvia snorted.

"Not me, I love being married but what you do is your business honey," Olivia replied with just a hint of sarcasm.

"Don't mind her boring ass," Sylvia giggled. I smiled and felt relieved that they no longer looked at me like I was a hoe. Of course, they didn't know about my being a mistress but just having the approval of my two big sisters for once in my life made me feel good inside. I began to feel emotional again because I couldn't believe that my sisters and I were actually becoming *sisters*.

"Well, with that being said, I have a young buck waiting to be rocked to sleep so I'll see you girls later," I said as I winked my eye and turned to leave.

"Carolyn." Sylvia ran up to me and wrapped her arms around me, which caught me off guard. "I love you little sister and I'm so proud of you. Now, go give it to him Black style!" she said and slapped me on the ass. I gave her a high five and met the young'un who was waiting for me outside. I got in the car and I immediately became aroused. He was so damn fine with his light brown eyes, close cut fade, and sandy brown skin.

"Ready?" he asked, smiling.

"Are you ready?" I replied confidently although I was nervous as hell. He chuckled and nodded his head.

When we arrived at my house, we smoked another blunt as we talked and began the casual dance of small talk, which we knew would eventually lead to the bedroom. He really was cool as hell and if he were older, he would be the kind of man that I would really be interested in. He actually kind of reminded me of...Demarcus. After we finished smoking, he reached into his pocket and pulled out a small box.

"Here, I got this for you for your birthday."

"Jarrod, you didn't have to do that....but, since you did, I guess I'll take it. What it is?" I said jokingly, starting to get more comfortable.

"Open it and see," he replied. So I obliged and was amazed to see that he'd gotten me a pair of gold, doorknocker earrings with "C. Black" written in the middle. They actually made me want to cry because they resonated with me at a point and time in my life when I was feeling so lost and unlike myself. Looking at them gave me a boost of confidence and reminded me of who I actually was. *Young'un, your ass is in trouble,* was what I really wanted to say but I gave a more modest response.

"Oh my gosh, Jarrod, I love them! Thank you so much."

"You're welcome," he said proudly. "Now I have one more thing I'd like to give you," he said.

"What's that?" I asked.

"Well as I was driving down the highway yesterday, they started playing this song and it made me think about you." He pulled out his phone and began playing, "Let's Chill" by Guy.

"Can I have this dance?" he asked as he got up and extended his hand to me.

"You sure can," I replied, impressed because most guys in their twenties had no idea about that song, nor how to use it.

Satasha and Malasia

"Girl, hurry up! We gotta get out of here before the cops get here and catch us," Satasha said as she rushed Malasia to leave St. Mary's Home for Teen Girls.

"Satasha, so you just gonna leave the baby?" Malasia asked bewildered.

"Yes! She'll just slow us down. Plus...." Satasha's voice dropped. "Plus, she'll probably be better off without me anyway...now come let's go."

Malasia looked back at the baby and their room; contemplating if she should follow Satasha who was standing by the door, tapping her foot, waiting impatiently. Although Malasia had a sickening feeling in her stomach, she squeezed her eyes closed and exhaled. She then reluctantly grabbed her things, and ran out with Satasha. As soon as they opened the door, the alarm went off. They quickly jumped into Satasha's car and sped off.

Carolyn Black

The young'un and I barely made it through the song before we were kissing and touching and tearing each other's clothes off. He picked me up; which turned me on to the max, carried me into my bedroom and laid me down on the bed. I began panting and my Juicy was soaking wet. He took his pointer finger and starting from the middle of my breasts, he slid his finger all the way down over my stomach and abdomen, into my Juicy. He played with her and teased her. Then he began tasting her. I arched my back on impulse and grabbed onto the sides of the bed. He then climbed on top of me, put my breast in his mouth and introduced his man to my Juicy. The young'un was turning me out...and I let him, as I felt my body getting ready to explode.

Satasha and Malasia

"Satasha, slow down! You're going like 80 miles an hour in a residential area!" Malasia yelled.

"Shut up, Malasia! We have to get to I-40 before the police catch up to us! We're almost there. Chill out! I got this."

"Satasha! OH MY GOD! The light is red! STOP!"

But it was too late. Satasha ran the light and smashed into an oncoming car.

Carolyn Black

"Oooooooo Jarrooooooood!" I screamed as I came...hard. And it felt so good. But as soon as we were done, and I opened my eyes and looked into the young'un's face, I got slapped by the hand of shame. Once again, I felt like a whore, a prostitute who'd given away her body for a pair of gold earrings.

Damn you, new Carolyn! I hate you and I hope you die! I wanted to yell.

Satasha and Malasia

Satasha opened her eyes and tried to look around, dazed. Her head was pounding and blood covered her hands. She painstakingly turned towards Malasia who was knocked out cold with blood pouring down the side of her face. Satasha's air bag had deployed and the windshield was shattered. It took a few seconds for her to really register what was going on and when everything became clear, she lost it.

"Malasia! Malasia! Wake up. Oh my God! Wake up!" But Malasia didn't move. Satasha reached over and shook Malasia, but she still didn't stir. Her adrenaline was pumping and her heart was pounding in her ears. She looked herself over more thoroughly and found that with the exception of some deep cuts and a throbbing head, she was ok. She heard the distant sound of sirens and she panicked.

"I love you Malasia. You're all I've ever had and I'm sorry. I'm so sorry. I'll come back for you I promise. Please forgive me." She kissed Malasia on her forehead, jumped out of the car and ran.

Carolyn Black

Bitch if you don't get your whiny ass together! You need somebody else on the team besides Jermaine, I mean Avery's ass, anyway. Plus it didn't work out with Bad Breath Bostain so now you have somebody who not only can give you good sex but he can also give you the companionship you been looking for. Hell, in actuality, you ain't gotta see his ass no more anyway unless you want to. You are in control! He's cute, he's educated, no kids and more than anything...NO WIFE OR GIRLFRIEND! So chill ma! Enjoy yourself and let me take over because you're becoming too much of a damn crybaby! Carolyn Black scolded me.

Jarrod was in the bathroom and I was laying on the bed, fighting back tears until the Carolyn Black in me quickly straightened me out. There wasn't anything wrong with me having a little bit of fun. Plus, I knew I was smart enough not to get all caught up with the young'un. I wasn't going to be one of those cougars who fell in love with a younger man and got my heart ripped out when the inevitable happened.

I got up and headed into the bathroom to take a shower as Jarrod was walking out.

"You trying to go to Waffle House and get something to eat?" He asked. "I have another blunt so I figured we could smoke and then get some breakfast."

"Hell yeah. I'm down. Just let me get in the shower," I said with my confidence back on my shoulders.

"Cool," Jarrod replied as I jumped into the shower.

"Carolyn your cell phone is ringing," Jarrod yelled from outside the door.

"Ok. I'll get it when I get out. It's probably Brandon calling to be nosy," I said with a giggle. As I was lathering up and bathing, I also heard my house phone ring.

"Dag girl, you are blowing up. Your cell is ringing and so is your house phone."

I sucked my teeth. "I know it ain't nobody but Brandon's ass. I'm coming," I replied as I continued taking my sweet time because I had every intention of torturing Brandon and making him wait for all the juicy details. However, when my phone continued ringing I began to get a little concerned because although I knew Brandon was nosy as hell, it wasn't like him to call back to back. My heart began beating fast and I quickened my pace in the shower. The last time my phone rung like that was when my mom was in the hospital and the thoughts of something being wrong with my mother made me begin to panic. I quickly finished my shower and began drying off. Just as I was opening the door, Jarrod was walking towards me, talking on his cell phone. His face told me that something was wrong and immediately my heart dropped.

Case#: 38584 Hawaii

My heart throbbed in my ears as I looked around at my family members scattered throughout the hospital waiting room. Some were hugging each other and crying. Others sat with their head in the hands, shaking their legs. I stood there feeling like I was inside of myself. I could hear everything going on inside of my body: my heartbeat, blood gushing through my veins, synapses firing and the slow sound of my breath, inhaling and exhaling. Everything outside of me sounded like it was being blown through a tube; bouncing back off my ear like an echo. I heard my body moving forward but I wasn't for sure how. My eyes landed on my little brother John as he jumped up and almost clobbered me; popping my ears open to everything going on outside of myself. He gripped me so tightly, I felt like he would break my arms. He buried his face in my chest and sobbed loudly. I tried to reciprocate his embrace but my arms hung; ossified, so I stood there helplessly. And since my ears were now privy to my surroundings, I had no choice but to hear what was being said, hence the hugging, crying and shaking of the legs.

"They say Sylvia died instantly in the crash."

"Well, thank God she didn't suffer."

"What about her kids?"

"Oh my God...why? I just don't understand. Why her?"

"She was such a good person and so beautiful."

My mind flashed back to three hours ago which seemed like a breath that had gotten lost in wind. Nothing made sense because I felt like I was wondering aimlessly around in a dream that I couldn't wake up from. My party felt real, the anomalous hugs and conversations I'd had with my sisters felt real and the great sex that I'd had with Jarrod damn sure felt real, but my mind kept telling me that the shit currently transpiring before my eyes *couldn't* be real. There was no way in the world that everyone had left my party happy and intact only to have things end in the manner they were trying to end in now. So I concluded in my head that Jarrod and I had simply smoked some killer weed and we were now passed out on my bed asleep and I was having a nightmare. I figured that all I had to do was ride the waves of the dream out until it was time for me to wake up and call my sister.

My little brother John loosed his grip, but he didn't let me go. I wrapped my arm around his waist and walked him over to a small couch. I pulled him on my lap like I used to do when he was little and I rocked him. I found myself taking deep breaths, trying not to explode but then I remembered that I was "dreaming." When my little brother John was finally able to sit up, I asked him where Brandon and my parents were.

In between sniffles, he replied, "Mom and dad are back there with Olivia and Brandon went to get Aunt Glenda and Uncle Ronnie." I heard my sister Olivia's scream through the walls. Carl, Sylvia's husband, sat in front of us and cried openly without shame.

"Ok John, get your big butt up," I said as I smiled and kissed him on his cheek. A police officer walked up to us with a solemn look on his face.

"Hello, my name is Officer Patrick Palstinsky. I'm sorry for you all's loss. Uh, who's the spouse?"

"I am," Carl whispered through tears.

"Again, I'm sorry for your loss, Mr. Bervard. Uh, could I speak with you privately sir?" the officer asked.

"No sir. Anything you need to say to me, you can say it in front of our family," he replied weakly.

"Yes sir. Well, I wanted to give you some of the items found at the scene of the accident," he said and handed Carl a bag full of items.

"Sir, what exactly happened?" Carl asked.

"Well two teenage girls went AWOL from St. Mary's Shelter for Homeless Teens and we assume that they were speeding trying to get away when they ran the red light and hit Mrs. Bervard and your sister-in-law going approximately 80 miles per hour."

Carl gasped and broke down, as did my little brother John.

"St. Mary's?" I heard myself say without realizing that I said it.

"Yes ma'am," he replied. "The driver fled the scene and the other young lady succumbed to her injuries as well." He paused. "I just want you to know that an APB has been issued for the driver. We will notify you as soon as an arrest is made and again, I'm sorry for your loss," the officer said and walked off.

Ok dream, you can end anytime you get ready. I thought to myself as the two girls, Satasha and Malasia that Val and I had placed at St. Mary's immediately popped into my head. I sighed and shook my head as I began to pinch myself on the arm. I prayed to God that He would wake me up because the dream was becoming too real. I waited for a unicorn, a fairy or a sun filled beachfront with little red devils running around to pop up so that I could rest easy in the comfort of knowing that I was dreaming. I started to feel like I was going to be sick, so I excused myself and got out of there as quickly as I could. Jarrod, who was hopefully accompanying me in my bed, while also accompanying me in my "dream," walked beside me. I opened the door and a gush of very welcomed cool air rushed my face. I inhaled it with my eyes closed, but when I opened them, I saw Boonsheika and the Ghetto Girls casually walking towards the hospital door chit chatting like they were going into a laundry mat instead of a hospital.

Oh God no! Please Jesus wake me up. Please Jesus wake me up. I pleaded as my heart started pounding.

"I knew those two idiots was gonna do something to kill somebody eventually. It's a damn shame that Satasha didn't die instead of Malasia though. At least she had a little more sense than Satasha did."

"Damn, bitch, why you gotta wish my daughter dead? She's the one with the baby. Hell I guess social services ain't gonna have no choice but to give her to me now. Dummies!"

"Well, at least you can get a check for her. Oh shit, I just thought about something. Now that Malasia's dead, I bet I can still get her SSI check for a month or two before they realize she dead."

"Ain't neither one of y'all heifas worth a damn. I mean, we can't change what happened to em' but shit, hell...y'all can at least act like you care a little bit."

"Whatever mama...On some crazy shit though Jackie, I've always known Malasia was gonna leave us. I just didn't think it was gonna be like this. I actually thought the little bitch might try to go to college or something."

My stomach jerked and I began throwing up right on the ground in front of them.

"Damn, that shit's disgusting!"

"Nasty bitch! Throw up in the trash can!"

"Oh shit, Di. That's that social worker bitch who had Satasha and Malasia put in that home."

"What?! It is her! Bitch this is your fault!" Ghetto Girl One screamed, walking up on me like she wanted to do something, suddenly filled with despair. "You took my baby away from me and look what happened. I'm going to sue your ass, you mutt bitch!"

I was helpless and couldn't respond because my stomach was still deciding if it wanted to regurgitate any further.

"Aye, chill yo." I heard Jarrod say from beside me.

"Who the hell are you?"

"It doesn't matter. I said chill. Go on bout your business before we have a problem out here."

I stood up and wiped my mouth on the sleeve of my shirt. They started laughing.

"Looks like *somebody* had a long night."

"Girl, I ain't mad at ya, I done had plenty of those."

"Shiiiit, we probably have one tonight." They laughed and high fived.

"So, when can I get my granddaughter?" Boonsheika asked. I looked at her like she was crazy but I remained silent.

"I want my granddaughter. Y'all already caused my daughter to kill her best friend and hit the road. Who knows when I'll see her again. Y'all ain't keeping my grandbaby too."

I still didn't respond because I was afraid of what might come out of my mouth. I walked past her and headed towards Jarrod's car.

"Hey! Hey! I know you hear me talking to you! Hey!" Boonsheika yelled behind me but I kept walking. She grabbed my arm and I jerked away from her; prepared to swing. A ball of rage from inside my belly sparked out of my eyes and my look must have been fierce because she cowered away and rejoined the Ghetto Girls. I turned and kept walking. When I arrived at Jarrod's car, I leaned against the hood, which was still warm and involuntarily shook my leg because I knew I wasn't dreaming.

"Um, I don't know if this is the appropriate time to ask this but, do you wanna smoke a blunt?"

I smiled weakly and nodded my head, so we got in the car. He opened up his ashtray and retrieved a half of a blunt. He clicked the lighter and put the blunt to his lips. He lit it and passed it to me. Grateful because an emotional ball was forming in my throat, I took a long pull and laid my head back against the headrest.

"Thanks for looking out for me back there."

"You good....um Carolyn listen, I'm really sorry about..."

"Ssssh." I put my fingers over his lips. I leaned over and kissed him as deeply as I could because I needed to Control/ALT/Delete my mind. He returned my kisses. And assuming that he understood what I was doing or trying to do, he obliged me.

"Put your seat back," he said in between kisses and I did as I was told.

"So you wanna get away, huh? Well, I'm about to blow your mind." he said as he took his hand, which was cold from the cool night air, and slid it down my pants. I shivered. He took his fingers and started playing in my Juicy. He unbuttoned my pants, slid them off, along with my underwear and threw them on the floor. I spread my legs. He leaned over, kissed the top of my bush and licked the rest of the way down to my pleasure zone as I closed my eyes. My spread legs became wings flying me across the ocean to Hawaii. I perched on the rim of a volcano and waited for the eruption. I decided that reality was not an option. I wasn't ready... not yet.

I was still in Hawaii when Jarrod and I walked back through the hospital doors. I was calm because I was floating through the air. I drifted through the maze of doctors and nurses and envisioned them as well as the people sitting in the waiting room as people walking or lying on the beach. My family sat around waiting for the Luau to begin. Brandon and my Aunt Glenda sat beside my little brother John and my Uncle Ronnie. Brandon came straight over to me and wrapped his arms around me. I welcomed his embrace and pretty much fell into it. We held each other for a long time. When we released each other, he gave Jarrod some dap.

"Thanks for looking out fam."

"You know I got you," Jarrod replied.

I hugged my aunt and uncle and sat down beside my little brother John. He laid his head on my shoulder.

"Well, you ready to go see Olivia?" he asked. I wanted to say no because I was afraid to see her. I wasn't sure how to wrap Hawaii around her because being hit by a car going 80 miles per hour made me afraid of how she would look and seeing her would force me to accept some type of reality surrounding the situation. Nevertheless, I knew I had no choice but to go.

"I guess," I replied reluctantly.

"Ok. Let's go."

"Uh, Carolyn you want me to go with you or you want me to go home?" Jarrod asked.

"Come on man. You good. You family," my little brother John answered for me. And I was actually very happy that he did because he'd saved me from having to sound desperate.

As we walked together towards Olivia's room I tried my best to maintain the image of hula dancers dancing on the beach in their grass skirts but the closer we got, the more anxious I became. We turned the corner and my parents were standing in the hallway holding each other. Their embrace was firm and locked. My dad rubbed my mom's hair.

"Hey Ricardo. Hey Willie," My Aunt Glenda said as her and Uncle Ronnie walked over to them. My parents unlocked one side of their embrace to let them in but they never let go of each other. I walked over and waited until they released my aunt and uncle. They pulled me in tight and mama bear/papa bear hugged me. I suddenly wasn't afraid anymore. The need for the sun and sandy beach disappeared temporarily because I felt my parents' strength. Their child had died yet here they stood together, unbreakable. I felt ashamed for my weakness. I balled up any emotions that threatened to shake me and threw them away. If my parents could be strong under the circumstances and maintain their composure then so could I. Plus tears were unnecessary because they weren't going to change anything anyway.

My parents led us into Olivia's room. It was actually very large and as upscale as I'd ever seen a hospital room be. She was lying in bed with both her eyes almost swollen shut. She wore neck and back braces, her right leg was in a cast; elevated in the air by straps, and her right arm was broken. But she didn't look gory, which really helped me maintain my calm. Her husband and kids stood around her talking. We all walked over and joined them. We hugged each other and since I still didn't have the words to say to my sister, I bided time by being last to interact with her. It didn't matter though because when it came my turn I still didn't know what to say. So I kissed her on the top of her head and began rubbing her good hand.

"Hey Olivia," I said meekly.

"Carolyn, is that you?" Olivia asked.

"Yeah. It's me. I'm glad you're ok," I replied.

"I thought it was you. Under the circumstances, I can barely see but you stand out so well with that light bright skin that I'd recognize you anywhere," she said with a scratchy voice.

Wait, was that a blow? I thought to myself but I didn't respond.

"Did you have a good night with your friend?" she asked somewhat condescendingly. Her tone was throwing me off and I couldn't decipher if she was trying to disrespect me or if she was awkwardly trying to make conversation.

"Uh, yeah, I guess," I replied completely confused. She was silent for a moment and then she started talking.

"The entire time we were riding, she kept talking about you. I told her she needed to be paying attention to the road instead of yib yabbing about something that wasn't important, but she wouldn't listen."

Ok, that was a blow. I thought to myself as she continued.

"She bragged about you sleeping with that teenage boy that you brought in here with you and how you were just so free. I told her that she shouldn't mistake liberation with promiscuity. We got into a debate, she took her eyes off the road and now she's dead," she said calmly while still spitting her daggers.

My mouth began drying up because I couldn't believe that she was going *this* far. I expected some mixed emotions but not a full-blown attack. Nevertheless, I remained silent.

"I knew that one day you being a yellow whore would have a lifelong effect on all of us. If you wouldn't have been somewhere, with your nasty white legs in the air, our sister would be alive and I wouldn't be laying in this hospital bed. If we hadn't been debating about you, then she wouldn't have taken her eyes off the road. You're like a curse Carolyn. Everything you touch turns to shit. I tried to tell her it was unnecessary for her to make amends with you but she insisted. Now, look where it got her." She paused. "I would give anything for you to be down in that morgue instead of Sylvia."

"Olivia that's enough!" my mom yelled.

"No mom! Sylvia has kids that need her and a husband and John is your only son. Carolyn doesn't have anything. If we were going to have to sacrifice somebody, why couldn't it have been her?"

I felt like I was being stoned and I stood there and took it because my mind refused to send me a response.

"Come on, Carolyn. We'll walk outside for a second. Apparently, she's done lost her mind," my mom said crossly as she reached for my hand but I didn't take it.

"Yeah mom, take up for her like you and dad always do." Tears rolled from her swollen eyes into her ears. I turned and headed towards the door with my shoulders drooping. But then I started getting mad. I turned around and walked back over to Olivia's bedside.

"You know what Olivia, fuck you!" I turned to my parents, "Sorry, mom and dad." My dad tried to grab my arm, but I jerked away and continued. "Everything you've ever been is because of your dependence on Sylvia. Without her, you ain't shit; *your* life no longer has a purpose. So instead of worrying about me, you better be trying to find your identity. Yeah, I may have done some bad things in my life but I'll wear it because I know who I am; flaws and all." That was a lie, but I continued. "Now that Sylvia's gone, let's see how long you can survive without either leaching on to somebody else or having a complete mental breakdown. And to be real with you, I actually foresee the latter," I clapped back, then turned around and walked out. I heard several people call my name but I just kept walking.

"Bitch," I said to myself. I was so angry but I welcomed it. I needed to feel something and anger was just what the doctor ordered.

On the ride to my house, Jarrod and I rode in silence as I kept thinking about the things Olivia had said. And although I tried to hang onto my anger, it wasn't the mean things Olivia had said to me that was on my mind. I kept imagining Sylvia looking beautiful in her royal blue, ankle length jumpsuit as she was driving, talking about me and how proud she was of something I'd done. Even though Olivia had said it in a snide way to hurt me, it gave me some solace in knowing that I was one of the last things on Sylvia's mind before she died. But it also broke my heart because I was one of the *last* things on her mind, and I would never get to talk to her again. I wouldn't get to high five her and tell her about how good Jarrod's pole was. Nor could I confide in her, my guilt for sleeping with him because of his age. I started getting angry at God because I was pissed at His timing. Why now and not five or six months ago when we hated each other? In hindsight, me and Olivia shared one thing in common and that was, "why did it have to be Sylvia?" Then, I started getting choked up, but I took a deep breath and turned on the radio. I didn't even like the song that was playing but I started singing along anyway.

When we finally arrived at my house, Jarrod walked me to the door. He squeezed me tightly and kissed me on my cheek.

"Well, I guess I better head out. I know you probably need some time to yourself."

No, I really don't. I wanted to say but my pride wouldn't allow me to ask him to stay.

"O.k.," I mumbled.

"Well, I guess I'll see you around. You have my number. Call me anytime if you need me or even if you don't need me."

"Thanks Jarrod," I replied genuinely. He squeezed my hand and walked towards his car. Carolyn Black began scolding me.

"Screw pride! Tell him to stay! You can't be alone tonight."

But I don't want to be a whore; laid up with him when I should be mourning my sister. I argued with her inside my head.

"Sylvia would want you to, Now ASK before he leaves!"

Ok. Ok. You're a pushy ass heifa. I said to myself before realizing that I was really having an argument with myself like I was crazy. I quickly pulled out my phone and called Jarrod's number. His phone started ringing and he stopped to answer it. When he saw that it was me, he turned around and gave me and his phone a strange look, but he humored me and answered. I giggled.

"Hello?"

"You said to call you anytime if I needed you. Well, I uh, need you. Can you stay a little while longer?" I asked choosing to sound needy instead of desperate, since I was feeling both. I saw a smile cross his face.

"Of course I'll stay with you," he replied.

"Ok. Bye." I smiled back and hung up the phone. I wanted to run and jump on him but of course, I couldn't do that...Carolyn Black wouldn't let me. I stood at the door waiting for him, thankful that he didn't reject me. When he arrived where I was standing, I grabbed him by his shirt and pulled him into the house. I shut the door behind us and immediately went and wrapped my arms around him.

"Thank you for staying Jarrod. I'm really going to make it worth your while," I said sincerely because I was honestly very grateful that he was with me. I kissed him passionately, took his hand and led him to my bedroom.

The next morning or should I say; afternoon, my work phone began ringing off the hook. I lifted my head, which was plastered to Jarrod's chest and looked around. The light from the sun hit my eyes and illuminated all of Jarrod's sexiness. The mixture of our intricate sex scents hit my nose and I smiled as I reached over to retrieve my phone.

"Carolyn Black," I answered groggily.

"Carolyn. Oh my Gosh, it's Val. Wake up I need to talk to you." I got out of bed and walked into the living room so that I could have some privacy.

"Val what's up?" I asked.

"Carolyn. Oh Lord. I feel so terrible. You were right about those girls."

"What girls?" I asked, still somewhat sleepy and discombobulated.

"Those girls, Satasha Carter and Malasia Talley." I didn't say anything because my brain was still rebooting, so she continued.

"They ran from St. Mary's last night and had a car accident. Malasia died in the car crash and so did a woman in the other car. Satasha is on the run and no one knows where she's at. I feel so terrible Carolyn. I should have listened to you." As she rambled on my brain finally started working and everything started sinking in. My morning oblivion began wearing off and reality hit me. Waking up on top of Jarrod had allowed me to elongate my denial but Val, being her usual high killing ass, turned what was supposed to be a bad dream back into reality. My body started filling heavy as if my insides weighed too much to stay lodged in place. Emotional distress was moving from my mind to something I could *feel* physically in my chest. Darkness and haze no longer shielded me therefore; I was naked and vulnerable.

I'll fix that though. I thought to myself as I retrieved a half smoked blunt from the ashtray.

"Carolyn, do you hear me? Are you there?"

"Yes, Val I'm here."

"Well, why aren't you saying anything? I know it's killing you to say I told you so," she said sarcastically.

"Well if the shoe fits," I said coldly as I boldly lit my blunt and took a pull.

"Carolyn Black, are you smoking a blunt while you're on the phone with me?" she asked a little too authoritarian for my liking.

"Why does it matter? I'm at home, on my day off. I mean what's up?" I asked annoyed.

"Whatever, Carolyn. Go ahead and get it over with. Go ahead and mock me for making a mistake. Everybody makes mistakes sometimes and that includes you," she snapped.

Oh no she didn't! This heifa really got a lot of nerve right now. I thought as I purposely took another pull on the blunt not only to spite her, but also to keep myself from saying something I might regret.

"Carolyn! This is not a joke. A woman and a teenage girl are dead!"

"I know it's not a joke Val!" I yelled. "The woman who got killed in the other car was Sylvia, my sister, who I just finished partying with for my birthday." As soon as my ears grabbed the words from my mouth, I instantly regretted saying them. They tasted like cow manure coming out and they made the inside of my chest sting, but the blame game offered a welcomed new distraction so I continued without missing a beat. "So pardon me for smoking a blunt after one of the mistakes; this one happening to be yours, resulted in our client killing one of my sisters, ruining my birthday for the rest of my life and increasing the level of hate that my remaining sister feels for me." Silence responded through the phone. My mouth started to get dry so I walked briskly to the kitchen. I opened the refrigerator and retrieved a gallon jug of water. There was no time to waste on getting a glass, so I gulped the water straight from the jug. Val remained silent for a moment. I assume she was processing what I said as I was trying to erase it because I was beginning to feel the pain of reality and I needed to get to Hawaii quickly, so I had to get off the phone.

"Val, look I'm sorry. I have to gg..."

"I'll be over there in 20 minutes," she said and hung up without giving me an opportunity to respond. I sighed and plopped down on the couch. I relit the blunt and let the THC fill my lungs.

"Good morning," a deep voice said from behind, startling me. I jerked around and saw Jarrod walking over to sit beside me. He was wearing boxer briefs and no shirt. His body was nicely ripped and his bulge flapped as he walked. The daylight that had previously been a curse to me was now suddenly starting to take a turn for my good.

"Oh my gosh Jarrod, you scared me," I half said, half whined.

"My bad. I'm sorry," he replied. I passed him the blunt.

"Listen, my supervisor is on her way over here and I'm really sorry but I need you to go." I said frankly.

"Oh ok. Yeah, I understand," he replied unfazed by my candidness. He hit the blunt again and got up to walk off.

"Hey, wait." I stopped him. "Listen, we've got less than ten minutes before you have to be leaving. And seeing that body in the daylight is making my Juicy, juicy." I took my finger, stuck it in my mouth and pulled it out seductively. I spread my legs, took that wet finger and began playing in my Juicy. He didn't say a word but his bulge no longer flapped as he walked over to me. He got on his knees, pulled me to the edge of the couch and five minutes later, I was screaming.

"Ok I'm out," Jarrod said as pulled his shirt over his head and headed towards the front door. I followed him. He leaned in to kiss me, but I turned my head.

"I don't wanna expose you to my morning breath," I said.

He laughed. "It's all good."

"I really appreciate you being here for me. Can I still call you sometimes?" I asked evaluating if I sounded desperate or not.

"Of course. Matter of fact text me later on this evening and I'll take you out for dinner if you're up to it."

"Thanks. I'll keep that in mind. I'll probably have to do the family thing today though so I don't know," I replied.

"Well, you have my number and I have yours. I will call and check on you later. If you fill up to it, we'll kick it."

"Ok. Thanks Jarrod. For everything, really. I don't know how I would have gotten through last night or should I say this morning if you wouldn't have been here."

"You're welcome," he said and left.

"Mmmm, I like him. Maybe there really is something to this whole cougar thing," I said to myself as I walked towards the bathroom to freshen up. But my doorbell was ringing before I could hit the corner. I figured Jarrod had left something so I didn't bother putting on my robe. However, when I opened the door in my tee shirt and panties, there stood Val. She damn near tackled me trying to hug me. As she was squeezing me to death, she kept telling me how sorry she was. I heard her, but I was focused on the fact that I was half-naked, smelling like sex wrapped in weed and I was sure she could smell it. Once she released me, I saw a huge sex stain on the couch that she was getting ready to sit on.

"Wait! Don't sit there. Let me go get my robe," I said as I scurried to my room and put on my housecoat.

"Come on. We can go in the sunroom," I said directing her away from the cum stained couch. We went in the sunroom and sat down. It was a beautiful day outside and the rays from the sun beamed in through the glass.

"Carolyn, you're right...this is all my fault. If I had just listened to you about those girls none of this would have happened," she sobbed. Although I tried my best to be angry at her and continue engaging in the blame game, I found myself comforting her. The situation was messed up altogether. Olivia could blame me for going with Jarrod instead of her and Sylvia driving me home, which I'm one hundred percent sure the heifa didn't want to do anyway. I could blame Val for not following my professional advice; we could blame Boonsheika and the Ghetto Girls for being terrible parents, but regardless, shifting the blame wasn't going to change anything.

"Val, listen, we gotta go by St. Mary's and get Mariah. Miss Partene is one of our best foster parents and I think she will take very good care of her. I feel just as bad as you do about this situation but maybe if we make sure that the baby has a better life, then maybe we can make some kind of sense out of this. I saw the girls' mamas at the hospital and they didn't even care Val. They were talking about money and partying when one of their daughters is dead and the other one is God only knows where. Satasha's mama even had the audacity to tell me she wanted the baby and it took everything in me not to punch that bitch in the face," I said, punching the palm of my hand with my fist, as I began to get angry.

"You're right Carolyn, but I can handle it. You don't have to go."

"Val, just make the arrangements while I'm getting dressed. It won't take me long," I said as I got up and headed towards the shower.

"Ok," she retreated.

After I got dressed, we headed to St. Mary's. When we walked in, Mariah was sitting in a high chair and one of the nuns was feeding her. We briefed with them, packed little Mariah up and took her to Miss Partene's house. I sat in the backseat with her while Val drove. She was a beautiful little girl with smooth, dark velvet skin and big shiny black eyes. She cooed and latched her little fingers around mine as I laughed and played with her. She was such a sweet baby that for a split second, my biological clock began ticking in my ears. I wasn't sure if I wanted to have kids, but even if I did want them, I damn sure didn't have any positive candidates who could be the father. I sighed and kept playing with the baby. She was in a much worse situation than I was being that she had no one. I was thankful that because she was a baby, she had the opportunity to be oblivious to her current state and I planned to make sure that she didn't have to grow up like Satasha and Malasia had. But I wasn't sure if a judge would give us full custody of the baby with Satasha and Boonsheika running around since they were biological family members. I wasn't as worried about Satasha getting custody but more so about Boonsheika because I knew we would have to work our asses off to actually prove that she was unfit. The bitch was street smart and knew exactly how to work the system. All she had to do was "clean herself up" temporarily and make it appear that she was taking care of the baby. And since the state didn't require a caregiver to love a child; and I knew without a shadow of a doubt that Boonsheika didn't give a damn about nothing more than getting Mariah's check, I knew that that poor baby would get no nurturing. However, I found solace in that she would at least be safe with Miss Partene for the next couple of months while we conducted our investigation.

After we transitioned Mariah into Miss Partene's care, we went back to my house. I got out of the car thinking that Val was going to leave and go home, but she didn't. I really didn't want to be bothered because I didn't feel like talking. But I also didn't want to be alone either. So, I was in between a rock and a hard place. What I did want to do was smoke a blunt and have sex or watch a movie or something, anything to keep me in Hawaii.

"So, Carolyn, is there anything you need me to do? Do your parents need anything? What can I do to help?"

"You can tell me about all the sex you and Maurice have been having since y'all been back together," I replied. She looked at me bewildered.

"Look Val, I don't wanna talk about all that other crap right now. I wanna laugh and hear about how you been making Maurice's toes curl. I bet y'all had sex last night didn't you?"

"Well, not last night but we did this morning." She blushed and giggled. I laughed out loud.

As she began discussing how things were going between her and Maurice, Jermaine, I mean Avery texted me: I wanna lick on your titties. I texted back: When and where daddy?" He

replied: Our spot in Boone. I wanna look over the mountains while I'm stroking you. **I started getting excited:** Ok daddy, meet me in an hour, **I replied.**

I rushed Val out the door and freshened up. I rolled a travel blunt and jumped in my car. When I arrived, I met Jermaine, I mean Avery at our discreet little spot in Boone. We had a few drinks at the bar and engaged in some meaningless small talk. As we took a shot of tequila, he pulled out a bottle of prescription pills. He opened it and popped one in his mouth. He downed it with another shot of liquor.

"What's that?" I asked.

"Xanax," he answered.

"Xanax? You have panic attacks or anxiety problems?"

"No. The shit just makes me feel awesome. It's like smoking ten blunts in one setting without having to roll or spray air freshener. They make me feel so calm that I don't give a damn about shit. The sex is out of this world too. Here you wanna try one and make this a night to remember?"

"Uh, um. What's the side effects?"

He laughed. "I just told you. And it's only for tonight Carolyn. It's like taking an aspirin for a headache or something." I didn't have a headache, but my heart was trying to ache. Plus, I had encountered several clients and other people who took Xanax and they were ok, so I figured it was safe.

"Fuck it. Why not? Give me one."

One Week Later

Val gave me the week off for bereavement so that I could be with my family as we planned the services for the funeral. Sylvia's body was so severely damaged that we couldn't have an open casket, therefore we had to go through millions of pictures so that we could find one suitable enough to put beside the casket. Her husband Carl was a wreck, as were her children. Olivia, who was out of the hospital, was inconsolable and my parents were barely hanging in there, which meant that the majority of the funeral planning fell on me. I accepted the task though because I felt that God was giving me one last chance to show my sister how much I loved her. But it was still difficult nonetheless. Thanks to Jermaine, I mean Avery; I had some Xanax to go along with the weed and wine that I was consuming so although I was planning the burial of my sister, who I still hadn't accepted to be dead, I was still in Hawaii floating to the sound of the waves. And at the end of the day when the Xanax began to wear off, Jarrod came by with weed, tequila and passionate sex. And if he wasn't available, Jermaine, I mean Avery was available for the wild sex that was accompanied by more Xanax, weed and liquor.

I floated through the week up until the day of the funeral. Brandon, my little brother John and I smoked about four blunts the morning of. Then, on my way to the church, to make sure everything was together, I popped two Xanax. When I walked into the church and looked around, I was damn proud of myself and I felt that Sylvia would be proud too. She had a beautiful canary yellow casket covered with wild flowers because I knew that yellow was her favorite color and I remembered her loving wild flowers. The family had collectively selected a beautiful picture of her that I had blown up and framed for the service. The programs looked extraordinary with pictures of her and the family as well as some inspirational poems about getting through the death of a loved one. I had selected "Blessed Assurance", "My Soul Has Been Anchored" by Douglass Miller and a few other hymns for the choir to sing and I had included a scripture; Philippians 4:7 on the program as well. The church was empty with the exception of the ushers, pastor and funeral home director, so I felt confident *and* high enough to float over to the casket so I could talk to my sister.

"Sylvia, there are some things that I never got to tell you, so I'm going to tell you now. I always admired you and Olivia when we were growing up. I thought y'all were so cool and beautiful and I was so proud to be your little sister. And...and if I ever did anything to hurt you or whatever I did to make you hate me so much, I'm sorry. I'm so sorry and I would give anything for the chance to make it up to you. Olivia told me that you were proud of me for sleeping with Jarrod. And sister I just have to tell you that mmmmm mmmm mmmmm, that little boy is all that in bed. Anyway, I love you and rest in peace," I said and giggled at my little joke. I felt so jovial that I bent over, popped a kiss on the casket and turned around to leave so that I could rejoin my family at the funeral home. Olivia, who was in an automatic wheelchair, sat parked right behind me, which, would have normally scared the shit out of me, but I was too high to feel anything.

"What the hell?" I said and then quickly covered my mouth realizing that I was in a church. Although she sat in a wheelchair with bruised and black eyes, she still found a way to look down her nose at me and examine me from head to toe. I was so high I didn't even care.

"You really are disgusting. Are you high?"

"Trick I might be," I shot back with a laugh and started walking away.

"Carolyn," she called after me. I stopped and turned around.

"What?"

"She hated you because you were always running around thinking you were better than us with your light bright self. She was ashamed of you because you were a whore and everybody was always coming up to us telling us about how you were spreading that wore out twat all over Fosterberg County. You were always running to your mommy and daddy trying to steal their attention, and then when John came you tried to hog him too. I remember everybody missing the majority of my dance recital because mom and dad had to pick your whiny ass up from granny's house before the snowstorm. It was always Carolyn this and Carolyn that..."As she sat there, walking down memory lane, firing off her snide remarks, I began to realize that *she* hated me and because she hated me, she made sure that Sylvia had hated me as well.

"Olivia, I have never done anything to you or Sylvia. I've never taken your things, I never bad mouthed you and I never told mom and dad about you and Sylvia getting fingered by Teddy Bishop and Rodney Banner every other Sunday at church." I threw that in there just to remind her she wasn't perfect. Surprisingly I was calm, but as more memories flooded my mind, I let the good times roll...and I enjoyed it.

"I never told mom and dad about how you used to steal money from mom's purse to buy cigarettes. And even when you set my room on fire smoking a cigarette, I didn't snitch you out. I didn't tell Aunt Helen that you were the one that backed into her car and I didn't tell Sylvia that I saw *you* giving Carl a blowjob the week before their wedding. Do I need to continue?" I asked humbly with a meek smile. Her mouth dropped to the ground, so I took that as a "yes."

"Ok and I never told them how you used to do evil things to me like telling me to put bubble gum in my hair or telling Sylvia that I had a contagious skin disease that made my skin look different from y'alls. Even when you got me jumped by those Dominican girls for telling them it was me sleeping with one of their boyfriends when it actually was you, I protected you. I did everything in my power to try to make you and Sylvia love me. Not only did I keep your secrets, I washed your clothes, bought you gifts and tried to come to y'all for advice. I used to think that I was Cinderella and y'all were the evil stepsisters, but now I see that it was all you. You made Sylvia hate me because you hate me, you low down piece of trash," I said calmly, with my smile remaining. *Yes Xanax!* I cheered inside my mind and continued.

"What were you afraid of Olivia? Did you think I was going to take Sylvia away from you because that's not the case. I had enough love for both of you and I believe that Sylvia did too. I was so lonely, Olivia. I really didn't have any friends growing up and I needed y'all. I didn't have anybody to talk to about boys and periods and music and fashion and things like that. It hurts so bad to know that I had two older sisters who were right in the next room that I could have shared those things with, but it's like y'all completely quarantined yourselves away from me without even giving me a chance and I want to know why."

She smirked. "I'm not talking about this right now. I'm not in the business of defending myself to anyone...especially you, so this conversation is over," the heifa said, dismissing me. Then she proceeded to roll around in her electronic wheelchair and turn her back on me as if I was nothing. I stood there for a second, watching her roll away, not knowing what to do or say, but Carolyn Black slowly began trying to push through the Xanax cloud. So I caught up with her and put my hand on her shoulder.

"No, Olivia answer me. You brought it up. Just tell me. Please. What did I do to make you hate me?"

She stopped and looked me right in my eyes with a hate that was palpable. "You were born," she said and put her wheelchair in "drive" and continued rolling off. Her words were so cold that a shiver almost went down my spine and I knew she was serious. My birthday party flashed before my eyes, as did the past few months whereby I'd thought that my sisters and I were actually moving towards reconciling. But Olivia's hate for me was rooted and grounded and since Sylvia was no longer present to force a bridging of the gap between me and Olivia, she could now bury me with Sylvia. Thankfully, although I was in a church, standing near the coffin where my dead sister was lying while watching the other one cease to exist, I actually felt nothing. But her callousness had triggered the Carolyn Black in me and a reaction was inevitable.

Beat her up! Who cares if you're in a church? She deserves it and you gotta do it now. Don't lose the moment, floated somewhere from the back of my brain. I could feel the anger wanting to rise up from the pit of my stomach but I could also feel the Xanax beating it back down. Since the Xanax was keeping me from giving her a Carolyn Black beat down, a more serene approach flashed before my eyes as I watched her buzz down the aisle with her back turned to me. The vision pleased me so much that I enacted it. I calmly walked up behind her, took the handles of her wheelchair and flipped her ass over. *Thanks Xanax*. I thought to myself as I half floated, half sashayed out of the church with a smile and a whistle.

Case#: 38585 Love?

I popped two Xanax and washed them down with a bottle of water as I sat in the parking lot of my job, pissed because it was supposed to be my day off. My legs were sore from having sex with Jermaine, I mean Avery earlier that morning and luckily we'd had sex in the shower so all I had to do was grab the soap, wash up and hit it to my job.

I pulled down the sun visor, checked my reflection in the mirror and got out of the car. I walked over to where Val and a group of other social workers were standing in front of a small bus.

"Hey Carolyn," she said and hugged me. I didn't reciprocate her hug, but I still greeted her. She released me awkwardly and handed me a blindfold.

"What's this for?" I asked.

"You'll see," she replied and walked off.

"Ok everybody, put your blindfolds on and then I'm going to lead you on the bus to your seats, understand?" Valerie said loudly so that we all could hear her clearly.

"What the hell?" I grumbled out loud to myself as I looked at her like she was crazy. We; the group of social workers and I, stood outside, on a Friday morning, our day off, waiting to go with Val only God knows where. The only thing we were privy to was what was going on right before us. I didn't understand the secretiveness especially having to wear blindfolds. I heard a lot of sighs and grunts; mine included, but we reluctantly obliged her. I was the last person to put on my blindfold though because I had to make sure that nothing crazy was going on.

"Now, like I said, I am going to lead all of you guys onto the bus and for the entirety of the ride, you are to remain silent. You cannot speak or touch the person sitting beside you until I say so...period. When we arrive at our destination, you all will receive a reward but only if you adhere to my rules. That means no touching, no talking. I'm going to come by and check on everyone to make sure that you aren't peeking and then I will lead you onto the bus."

Although I couldn't see what was going on, I could hear her shuffling people around. When it came my turn, I said nothing, although I wanted to beg for a window seat. Luckily, when I sat down, I didn't feel anyone beside me so I immediately claimed the window seat anyway.

"Ok everybody now remember no touching or talking. I'm going to be walking up and down the aisle monitoring y'all," Val said. I leaned my head and shoulder against the window and got comfortable. I prayed that the trip would be a nice long ride because I wanted to go to sleep. I really didn't care about anything courtesy of the Xanax that was starting to kick in and I really wanted to take advantage of it by catching some Z's.

I heard the bus crank up and felt it rumble. I closed my eyes underneath the blindfold just as I heard the door open and shut back. Sleep crept up on my heels and I could feel myself drifting off. I heard the doors open again just as Val said, "Follow my lead and I will guide you to your seat." The sound of her footsteps got closer and closer to me.

"Ok, you sit right here. Remember, no talking at all." I felt whomever sit down beside me, but I really didn't care. I just snuggled up closer to the window and went to sleep.

"Ok everybody, we're here," Val said gleefully. I jerked straight up and opened my eyes but they met darkness. I almost panicked for a second until Val's voice registered in my brain.

"Remember no talking and do not take your blind folds off until I tell you to." I didn't know how long I'd been asleep but since I was feeling the full effects of the Xanax, I would assume it was at least twenty to forty five minutes. I sighed as pieces of the dream that I was having during my slumber popped into my mind and then quickly dissipated into the Xanax haze. I was grateful because for some reason I remembered it having something to do with my sisters.

"I will come and lead you where you need to go and then I will announce when you all can take off your blindfolds. And once again, no talking, no touching." Val announced, commanding my attention.

I heard her footsteps coming towards me. "Ok, I'm going to put your hand in your partners hand so you can help each other off the bus. Remember, no talking."

That didn't make any sense to me because we were both blindfolded, plus I didn't feel as if I needed to hold anyone's hand anyway, however, I obliged. My partner's hands, which belonged to a man, were very sweaty but I felt him wipe them off on his pants. He retook my hand and we began walking forward. We made it off the bus and Val led us a little ways somewhere where I could feel grass under my feet. Once we were at our designated spot, the person and I didn't release hands because we didn't know if we were allowed to or not. And we couldn't ask because we still weren't allowed to speak, so I had to continue holding hands with Mr. Sweaty Palms.

"Ok everybody. Thanks for your cooperation." Val paused and then began to speak again. "I just want you all to know from the bottom of my heart how much I appreciate you all and everything you do. Y'all work y'all's butts off and today is all about me and the other supervisors showing you guys some appreciation. We have a surprise in store for you. I know that you guys' job is hard and sometimes it seems like there's never a light at the end of the tunnel or a happy ending but I'm here to let you know that all of you guys' blood, sweat and tears does pay off. You can now speak and you may also take off your blindfolds."

"Thank God!" I said as I jerked my hand from Mr. Sweaty Palms. But when I took off my blindfold and my vision became clear I saw Mario standing in front of me. I was speechless as was he. We stood there looking at one another for what seemed like forever and then without saying a word, we smiled at each other and embraced.

"Mario, I'm..."

"Shhhhhhh. The past is the past. Let's just erase it and move on. I missed you Cee. You are my friend and as long as I at least have you as a friend, I'm good."

"Thanks, Mario," I said as we continued embracing. I felt the urge to cry but once again, my new friend Xan Xan wouldn't allow me to feel. After we released each other, I became coherent of our surroundings. We were at a park with several picnic tables and a small stage with a podium and banner that read, "Thank You" on it. There were also several small groups of people standing around holding signs. And as I honed in more closely on the signs and the people, I noticed a group of my old clients holding a sign that said, "Thank you Ms. Black." I was amazed and in shock.

"What in the world is going on?" I asked Mario.

"I have no idea Cee," he said as he shook his head. Many of the other social workers, who were also beginning to recognize what was going on, looked around in shock as well. Val then came by and had us to disperse in the direction of where our clients were standing. As I joined my group of clients, the first face I saw was that of BaLing Haun. She was with her baby boy and his grandparents. I also saw the twin boys, Luke and Lane standing with their new foster parents, the young lady named Angel standing with her foster mother and Tia Barksdale standing beside Rob Sr. who was holding Rob Jr. The Campbells, along with Geraldine were also standing there, holding hands and smiling. Xanax or not, I started getting choked up, especially when they all circled around me, hugged me and simultaneously began saying, "Thank you Ms. Black."

As I was hugging BaLing, I noticed Val standing off to the side with her hands clasped, smiling as tears rolled down her cheeks. I nodded my head at her because I appreciated what she was trying to do. I released BaLing and then hugged everyone else. We then all went to our designated table, sat down and talked. BaLing told me that she'd left her baby, Henry Jr., at the hospital because she had been too traumatized to raise him, therefore she had to "go off the grid" temporarily so that she could get her head together. She told me that she'd began seeing Dr. Weaver; her old therapist again in order to help her cope with the death of her husband, Henry. She said that Henry Jr. still lived with his grandparents while she worked through her issues, but she proudly announced that although he didn't live with her, she was very involved in his life and came by to visit him almost every day. I asked her if she'd ever considered looking for her birth parents and she reported that Dr. Weaver was helping her with that as well.

Luke and Lane looked a lot happier and they weren't as scrawny as they had been when I first met them. Their foster mother told me that they were doing fairly well in school and were making some progress in therapy; however, because they were still very traumatized, she was concerned that they continued to respond to many things based off the trauma that they'd endured. She said that Lane was still wetting the bed and displayed high levels of anxiety, while Luke was more aggressive and angry. We both agreed that those things were to be expected, but overall, getting them away from their mother; who was in jail, was the best thing that ever happened for them. She thanked me for helping the boys to reconnect with their maternal grandparents who gladly took them every other weekend and on the holidays. She told me that the boys were bonding very well with them and the family connection was very beneficial in helping the boys to heal.

"Ok boys; remember what y'all said you wanted to tell Ms. Black? Go ahead," Their foster mother coaxed. Luke and Lane approached me bashfully, but with matching smiles and those beautiful, clear blue eyes. They each handed me a rose; one red, one yellow and said, "Thanks for saving us Ms. Black." I accepted the roses and hugged them.

"Awwww, thanks boys," I said. "I'm glad to see that you're doing ok."

I then began talking with the Campbells. Quincy, Jalisha, their 2 boys and Geraldine all sat together as a family. Geraldine was her regular "shit talking" self and I smiled because I got a kick out of it. She kinda reminded me of how I was probably going to be at her age minus the cigarette parched voice and MuMu dress. They informed me that since Felicity's death, Quincy and Jalisha both had begun going to counseling and Quincy had not laid a hand on Jalisha since then.

"Thank you Ms. Black for being there for us and for coming to the hospital when...when Felicity died. Y'all are some good people and yuns didn't just leave us hanging when we needed y'all the most. Hell, and you'll be proud to know we're all going to the nut doctor so we can get some help dealing with all the hog shit we have going on in our life. We still ain't perfect but we're on our way to recovery," Geraldine said as she shook my hand. "Uh, can I smoke a cigarette out here? All this damn family stuff is making me edgy."

I laughed. "Yes honey, you can smoke a cigarette," I replied.

"So, where is that other girl, uh, uh, what was her name?" Quincy asked.

"Zian?" I asked.

"Yeah, her. Oh wait, there she is right there. She's walking over this way now." I turned around and saw a very pregnant Zian walking over towards where we were standing.

Oh Lord. I sighed because I didn't know if she still had beef. I hadn't seen her since our little dispute over Jermaine, I mean Avery, and the fact that I was fresh off his Johnson a few hours ago didn't help things. I know my ongoing relationship with him should have bothered me, especially since she was pregnant, but it didn't. After the throwing of hands, any friendship is over in my book and not only had Zian hit me, she'd spit on me, so that definitely 86ed our relationship. I would never touch her being that she was pregnant, but I straightened up and got myself together anyway, just in case she tried to sucker punch me again. However, as she waddled closer to where I was standing, her countenance told me that she came in peace.

"Carolyn! Carolyn!" she said as she extended her arms to hug me. I accepted her embrace cautiously.

"Carolyn, I'm so sorry for everything. You were right about Avery. He was a piece of shit and he is such a liar. I don't know how I didn't see it."

I do. I thought to myself as I recalled how gullible and naïve she'd always been; nevertheless, I remained silent.

"We're separated and I filed for divorce. The only good thing that came out of it is this precious baby I'm carrying in my stomach."

"That's nice. So what are you having?"

"A girl. And Carolyn I'm so excited," she squealed.

"Hey Zian!" the Campbells said as they came over to greet her. Glad for the distraction I went over to converse with Rob Sr. and Tia Barksdale. They told me that they'd gotten back together and were planning a wedding. Tia glowed as she showed me her cute little diamond. She told me that she'd been clean since the last time she and I met and she was still in treatment weekly. Rob Sr. reported that he was slowly getting back on his feet and had enrolled in school so that he could get a better job. He kissed Tia and the baby and squeezed them tightly. I could tell how proud he was of his little family. I smiled but a twinge of sadness and envy sparked briefly in my chest as I doted on their love and ride or die relationship. I was happy for them, but I just wasn't happy for me. However, I pushed those thoughts to the side and congratulated them.

I then moved on to Angel so I could get an update on her. She told me that although she was in foster care and her mother was serving time in jail, they kept in touch regularly via letters and phone calls. She told me that her mom had really changed and their relationship was becoming more like a normal mother/daughter relationship. She also told me that she had located her father and he was also stepping up as a parent, although we; CPS, had ruled him out as a safe placement for Angel. I hugged her as well but I feared for her because I didn't know if she could handle her beauty and that coke bottle body she was rocking. I had walked in her shoes and I knew that although she was beautiful, she had a long road of jealousy, insecurities and men with bad intentions to face. I prayed for God to give her strength and a prudent mind.

Seeing the resilience from my old clients moved me. They had dealt with and were still dealing with some very hard times in their lives, yet they were still standing and still fighting. It gave me a little bit of hope for my future because if they could still stand tall with their heads held high then so could I. When it came time to eat, everyone congregated in a designated area whereby we joined the other groups of social workers and their clients. Val did a brief appreciation speech and as the event was ending, she walked up to me and squeezed me.

"Carolyn, how are you?"

"I'm ok Val. I'm cool."

"I know, I know. It's just that you don't talk to me anymore unless its work related and you've become so unapproachable. I know you've been going through hell, but you don't have to do it alone."

"Listen, I don't want to talk about this right now. This is supposed to be a happy day. Please, don't kill it for me."

"I'm not trying to..."She looked at me for a moment. "Carolyn, are you high?" She asked. I sighed, rolled my eyes and dismissed her question.

"Where's Jenetta at?" I asked, hoping that she'd moved to the South Pole.

"Well, I kinda planned this event when I knew that she was going to be on vacation because I really wanted you and Mario to be able to talk and make amends without any distractions."

"Oh. That was thoughtful," I replied blandly. She peered at me.

"Carolyn, please. Please let me help you. You're so trite and emotionless. I haven't seen you crying or mourning and you walk around like you're a zombie or something. Carolyn it's ok to cry..."

"Thanks Dr. Phil," I said, cutting her off as I walked away.

On the bus ride back, I ignored Val and caught up with Mario. That's until he started wanting to talk about my sister. I quickly changed the subject and asked about him and Jenetta. He told me that they'd had a whirlwind relationship but he'd had to cut her off because she'd started getting crazy. I shook my head and smiled. When we arrived back at DSS I honestly felt like he and I were on the mends, but I knew things would still never be the same.

On the way home, Xan Xan started wearing off, but I still felt good. I couldn't wait to get home so I could smoke a blunt, pop a few more Xanax and play "Good Day" by Ice Cube. Today had actually been a good day and I wanted to take advantage of it. So as soon as I walked into my house, I kicked off my shoes, put my purse down and played the song. As it played, I partly walked/danced to my room as I took my clothes off. I put on a pair of old sweat pants and a cami and walked to the kitchen to pour myself a glass of water so I could indulge with my new homie, Xan Xan. Right as I was about to pop Xan Xan in my mouth, my doorbell rang.

"Who in the world is that?" I asked myself as I sat my Xan Xan on the table and walked to the door. I neglected to look through the peephole and jerked it open figuring that it was probably Brandon but instead, standing in front of me was Demarcus.

My mouth dropped and my breathing almost became non-existent.

Damn that Xanax is strong as hell cause I KNOW I must be seeing shit, I thought to myself. But as I continued staring at him, he didn't disappear or morph into somebody else. My heart started pounding and beads of sweat popped up all over my body. My heart and my brain began conversing and my Juicy started putting in her two cents. I didn't know whether to punch him in his face or tear his clothes off. The last time I saw him, he was throwing me across the floor in the name of *Charmanita* right after he'd caressed *my* hands and looked into *my* eyes. I couldn't believe that he had the audacity to come to my house unannounced like everything was ok. My hand brushed against the side of my sweat pants and I realized what I must have looked like, but I didn't give a damn. I couldn't move until I heard him speak, so I waited without saying a word, looking him right in his eyes with the meanest mean mug Xan Xan would let me conjure up.

"What's up? Cat got your tongue?" he asked slyly with a slick smile that pissed me off. *Really dude. That's it; after all you've done to me.* I thought to myself. Although Xan Xan was beginning to make its exit, I still fought to keep my cool. My body parts were in a heated debate and the anger that I was feeling felt good to me, which wasn't good for Demarcus. However, the residue of Xan Xan offered a compromise that I was willing to accept. Instead of knocking his teeth out, I slammed the door in his face, walked over to my stereo and turned my music up. I strode over to where my next dose of Xan Xan was waiting for me with my head held high and gulped them down with some water. I then walked over to my ashtray whereby a nicely rolled blunt was laying and sparked it up. I laid my head back against the wall and let the smoke fill my lungs. *Damn today was a good day.*

The next morning, I woke up to the smell of fried chicken and coffee. I thought I was dreaming so I rolled back over. Then I heard movement coming from inside my kitchen, which made me sit straight up in the bed. I listened in to make sure I wasn't dreaming, but the sounds continued. My heart began pounding and my hands shook as I quickly reached over into my nightstand and pulled out my gun. I jumped out of bed and crept towards the kitchen. The smell of the fried chicken intensified and my stomach began growling.

What the hell is going on? I asked myself. *Who's in my house cooking?* Sweat rolled down my brow as I cocked my gun, leaned flat against the wall and peeked into the kitchen. To my surprise, it was some chubby broad wearing pajamas standing over my stove, frying chicken. I pinched myself because I thought I was tripping. *Damn I gotta leave this Xanax shit alone.* But as I stood there watching her, weird as it was, I knew I wasn't dreaming.

"Who are you and what the hell are you doing in my house?" I asked with my cocked and loaded gun, pointed directly towards her head. I looked around to see if she was alone. I didn't see anyone but a cell phone was laying on the table, as was a bag of weed, a box of cigars for rolling purposes, blunt guts and a freshly rolled blunt. *What the…* I thought to myself. The girl who had raggedy box braids and the words "Blunted Out" tattooed on the side of her neck, dropped the spatula and threw her hands in the air.

"Yo, look I'm just doing what I was told to do." She said.

"Look home girl, I don't know who you are or what your business is but you have about 2 seconds to explain yourself or I'ma start shooting." My heart was pounding and I was scared as hell, but I was also serious as hell.

"Ah girl, sit your wanna be *Set If Off* ass down somewhere," a male voice from behind me said. I spun around on my heels ready to "set if off" for real and there stood my little brother John and my cousin Brandon. I wanted to bust out laughing because I should have known when I saw the hood rat at the stove and the blunt guts on the table that they weren't trailing too far behind.

"What the hell are y'all doing here this early in the morning? And who is this random in *my kitchen* using *my* stuff. Y'all know us Black women don't play that with having another woman in our kitchen."

"Girl bye. I was hoping to get yo' ass back from when you busted in on me and almost gave me blue balls. But by the looks of those bone blocker cotton pajamas you wearing, I guarantee ain't no chance of that. Poor Jarrod must couldn't hang huh?" my cousin Brandon laughed.

"Forget you Brandon," I said as I punched him playfully. "I never get caught slipping." I joked.

"Anyway, damn gurl, where you been at? Yo' ass fell off the face of the earth. I know I told you to get a life, but I didn't tell you to go missing," Brandon said as he grabbed me by my head and pulled me in for a hug. I tensed for a second but his hug felt safe. I prayed that their visit would be swift and unsentimental because in my haste yesterday morning, I'd forgotten to get some extra Xan Xan's from Jermaine, I mean Avery, therefore I only had one left and it usually took two to get me to Hawaii.

"Yeah, we missed you sis. My girl, Mayja'nosha in there can throw down in the kitchen, so I brought her over here to cook us up some breakfast. Then I'm going to take her home and tap dat fat ass, ain't I girl?" my little brother John said as he walked over to whatever her name was and smacked her on her booty. She began smiling and the next thing I know, this dude was sliding his hand down her pajama pants and kissing on her neck.

"Now, damnit come on now! Ain't nobody wanting a side of cat juice with they chicken and waffles. Cut that shit out," Brandon yelled as I felt myself laughing. It shocked me but it felt good. I headed to the bathroom to wash my face and freshen up. When I returned, we smoked the blunt they'd rolled and sat around and talked junk to each other. I was still on edge, but I started calming down some thanks to Mary Jane. Once the food was finished cooking, home girl made everybody a plate, sat out all the condiments and poured everyone a glass of orange juice and a cup of coffee. Of course, she catered to King Tut aka, my little brother John, first. She had a big ole; sloppy ghetto booty that apparently had my little brother John mesmerized because he couldn't keep his hands off her. Every time she walked by, his hand made some type of contact with her butt. I was trying my best to hold onto my "no emotions" stance but the jiggle of her booty and the sleazy smile on my brother's face made it damn near impossible. This dude at one point and time even started rubbing his hands together like she was a tenderized steak. Silent tears were rolling down Brandon's face because we were both seeing the same thing. However, he kept his head down and ate to keep my little brother John from noticing.

"John Daddy, you need anything else baby?" she asked as she flicked her braids from her face, causing one of them to fly across the room and land on the floor. Ladies and gentlemen, that was a wrap for me and Brandon. Brandon, who was biting into his waffle and I, who was sipping on my orange juice, almost had a food calamity. Brandon damn near choked on his waffle and the juice got caught in my throat and shot out of my nose. However, once our airways were clear, it was over. Our faces popped and the laugher erupted.

"What y'all laughing at?" she asked defensively.

"Come on now sweetheart. You know what we laughing at," Brandon replied in between laughs. I couldn't even talk from laughing so hard. The braid was the straw that broke the camel's back, but there was just so much more to it. Yes, I was laughing about the braid...and the jiggling booty but more so because she was a typical John Black chicken head who was going to cook for him, clean for him, be at his beck and call and "love him long time" in the bed. And she looked like she had one of those sloppy wet, wet coochies; just like my little brother John liked it. The only thing missing on this one was gold teeth.

"John Daddy, why you letting your peoples laugh at me?" The "John Daddy" only made me laugh harder which only pissed her off even more. She jumped up from the table and went to retrieve her braid, which gave me and Brandon another panoramic view of her sloppy butt. We howled. My little brother John sat looking clueless for a second because I'm one hundred percent positive that he was *proud* of that broad...although there would be another one next week. He eventually caught on to why we were laughing and he started laughing too.

"I don't know what you laughing at Brandon. You can't say shit with them ex-con hoes you be bringing around," my little brother John cracked, completely disregarding the fact that the chick was standing right there.

"Well, at least they hair don't be flying through the air like snakes on a plane," Brandon replied.

"That's because they don't have none," I chimed in directing my comment towards Brandon. My cheeks were hurting from laughing. And I had to agree with my little brother John because it seemed to me like Brandon walked straight to Hell to retrieve his girls. They were as gully as they came. My little brother John dealt with straight rats whereas Brandon dealt with *crazy* girls who had shot somebody and carried blades in their jaw. On top of bearing a striking resemblance to the physical attributes of my little brother John's type, the only thing that really differentiated them was the "crazy" because my little brother John only liked submissive chicks that kept their mouths closed and their legs open.

"Y'all some disrespectful mutherfuckers! I come up in here, cook y'all food, make y'all plates and y'all turn around and laugh at me and talk shit like I ain't even here. That's fucked up!" the girl yelled, yielding our undivided attention. But we actually only looked over at her because we were annoyed that she'd interrupted our conversation. True indeed, we really were being disrespectful but it wasn't on purpose, nor was it personal towards her. I was just so used to Brandon and my little brother John's routine that most of the time I didn't even take time to remember their chicken head's names or what they looked like...and neither did they. It may sound harsh to say, but she nor the other broads were of any relevance and unfortunately, they got treated as such.

"Mayja'nosha, who the fuck you think you talking to like that? You better ease back," My little brother John said with the straight face and home girl quickly changed her tone.

"I'm sorry John Daddy but I felt like y'all was making fun of me."

"Well, if you had of been minding your business like you were supposed to then you wouldn't be feeling that way. Now go on and sit down until we get ready to go. Nah matter of fact, start cleaning up this mess," my little brother John stated candidly without as much as a blink of his eye. She looked like she wanted to say something but the look in his eyes muted her. She followed orders and began gathering the dishes and clearing the table. I started feeling guilty especially since it was my house, so I got up and started helping her. After we finished cleaning up, we smoked again and they left. I skipped around the house as I began preparing to get in the shower and get dressed. The visit with my two favorite people was just what I needed and it had set the tone for my day. I felt good inside for a change and I wanted to hold onto it as long as I could.

I put on some music and jumped in the shower. But after I got out, I didn't know what to do with myself. I watched some television and smoked on a blunt. However, the solitude was beginning to take its toll on me, so I got up and popped my last Xan Xan. And although I really didn't want to deal with Jermaine, I mean Avery; I didn't have a choice so I called him. We met at a low budget motel, popped a Xan Xan and had sex. He sent me home with a nice supply of pills so I hoped that I wouldn't have to be bothered with him for a while because he was starting to irk me. He had gone from being my "dick in a glass" to my everyday lay and I didn't want that with him. Although his sex was good and he supplied my Xan Xan, I still didn't trust him. When I got home, the night was still young so I got in the tub, soaked my Juicy in apple cider vinegar and called Jarrod.

Sunday Afternoon

"Thanks for stopping by last night Jarrod. You have really been a beacon of light in the midst of all this darkness," I said as I pecked Jarrod on his lips.

"Yeah you're welcome. Listen, I uh, I been thinking about you and me and all the time we've been spending together..."

Oh hell, here we go...

"And I'm really starting to fall for you and I just wanted to know if we can take things to the next level. I don't wanna be your bed buddy anymore. I wanna be your man and I know you're concerned about the age difference, but it's really not that big of a gap. Plus like I said, I'm mature and I can be all the man you need me to be," he said as he kissed me on my neck and shoulder. My heart started racing because I most definitely wasn't interested in being in a relationship with him, but I also didn't want to risk losing him because I needed him as a distraction when I didn't feel like dealing with Jermaine I mean Avery. I didn't know how to respond, but I knew it had to be delicate or else everything was going to blow up in my face.

"Awww, that's sweet Jarrod, but I'm just not ready to be in a relationship yet, baby. We're still getting to know each other. I care a lot about you and I like having you around. You're one of the most intellectual men I've dealt with in a very long time, but let's just play it cool and go with the flow," I said as I ran my fingers across his chest and looked into his eyes. "Matter of fact, come on, let's talk about this in my bedroom," I said seductively and grabbed his hand.

"No! I'm done with that Carolyn. I feel like you're using me for sex and I ain't no damn gigolo. Either you gonna be with me as my woman or we ain't gonna be nothing. Which is it?"

Damn you sound like a bitch right now, was what I wanted to say but I opted to continue pleading my "let's be friends" case instead.

"Jarrod, we've only been seeing each other for about a month. Why you rushing things?" I asked gently.

"Why you dragging your feet? When you wanna be with somebody it doesn't take forever to figure *that* out. Now I know I wanna be with you, but it's apparent that you don't feel the same."

"Come on, Jarrod. You tripping."

"Nah man. Forget this shit. I'm out," he said and slammed the door in my face. I sighed and headed towards my bathroom.

"Welp, another one bites the dust," I said out loud to myself as I got in the shower.

Later on that day, I went to my parent's house; although I would have rather had all my teeth extracted, for Sunday dinner. I made sure to dope myself up with weed and Xan Xan before I stepped one foot into their house. I knew the atmosphere was going to be melancholy so I wanted to be prepared. I got out of my car and walked up on the porch, but as I was opening the door, I heard a chorus of laughter. I walked through the house into the kitchen and half my mother's side of the family was there as well as Brandon, his parents, my parents and my little brother John. I went in and greeted everybody as my eyes darted around the room looking for Olivia.

"Where's Olivia?" I asked, hoping that she was in Istanbul with no plans of ever coming back.

"She wasn't feeling good so she couldn't make it," my mom answered. I wanted to do a cartwheel, but instead a strong feeling of peace coated the inside of my body. As we sat down to pray, I thanked God for giving me a day with my family whereby Olivia's dark cloud didn't rain on my parade. Although my family talked about Sylvia and shed a lot of tears, Xan Xan protected me and I floated through the evening without a glitch.

Case#: 38586
Hattie, Xan Xan & Witch's Brew

"Stop crying ya little pussy and be a big boy."

"But I don't wanna watch this movie, Eddie. It's too scary. The monsters come and chase me in my dreams."

"You dumb shit, they're not real. They ain't coming to get ya. Now get on that couch and watch that damn movie before I beat the hell outta ya."

6-year-old Peter looked at his mother for support but she was too busy wrapping a belt around her arm, waiting for Eddie to stick her with the needle that made her sleep and nod for hours at a time. Peter fought back his tears because he knew that Eddie would beat him if he cried, so he reluctantly went to the couch and sat down. He tried to close his eyes but Eddie slapped him on the back of his head and barked out, "Open ya eyes, ya little pussy. I'm gonna make a man outta ya if it kills me." Helpless, Peter sat there as the images of people getting stabbed and chopped up with knives and machetes flooded across the screen. He thought of his favorite song that his music teacher had taught him and focused on the very top of the TV. He peeked over at his mother who had her head laid back and her eyes closed as Eddie stuck the needle into her arm. A tear slid down Peter's cheek but he quickly wiped it away before Eddie saw him.

"Ya ready to be daddy's whore?" Eddie asked Peter's mom; Patra, who could do nothing more than nod her head as the heroin crept through her veins. Eddie then stood and jerked Patra up by her arm. He laughed loudly. "Yeah, daddy's got something for ya." He then dragged her effortlessly, as if she was a rag doll, towards the bedroom.

"Eddie, no! Please don't hurt my mommy," Peter screamed, fearing that Eddie was going to beat his mother the same way he'd beaten her earlier that week. Her face was just now regaining its normal color from the black, blue and purple hues previously stamped there by Eddie's fist.

"Shut up, ya little bastard!" Eddie dropped Patra on the floor and headed towards Peter with his hand raised. Peter ran and curled up in the corner. Just then, EJ, Peter's infant brother, began crying. Eddie stopped, pivoted and headed towards the room where Peter and the baby slept. Peter, fearing that Eddie would hurt his brother, jumped up bravely and headed towards his brother's cries. However, when Peter reached their room, Eddie was actually rocking the baby, trying to get him to stop crying. Peter calmed himself down and slowly began to breathe normally. Eddie continued to walk around, rocking the baby; however, he wouldn't stop crying.

"Excuse me, Eddie, but he's hungry. He hasn't ate all day."

"Shut up! I don't need ya help, little pussy. Matter of fact get ya ass back in there and finish watching that movie. NOW!" Peter ran back into the living room and jumped on the couch just as the TV screen projected images of a zombie eating the face off a teenage boy. Peter's hands began to shake and sweat poured down his little brow. He wanted so badly to cover his eyes but he knew that Eddie would retaliate. He resumed focusing on the top of the TV and singing the song in his head. However, he could not mute out his little brother's cries. He crept past his mother who was still lying on the floor with her eyes looking nowhere, towards the baby's room and peeked in. Eddie's gentleness was wearing off. He held EJ tighter and rocked him with frustration.

"Shut up, shut the fuck up," he began saying quietly through clenched teeth. Peter ran into the kitchen, grabbed a bottle out of a pile of dirty dishes and washed it the best he could with water. He then looked into the refrigerator to see what he could find to put in his brother's bottle. The only thing he saw was some of Eddie's orange juice that Eddie had forbidden them to drink. However, out of desperation, Peter poured some into the bottle and mixed it with water in hopes that Eddie wouldn't notice such a small amount missing. He ran back to the room where EJ was now screaming at the top of his lungs.

"Here Eddie, he's just hungry and thirsty. Please give him this bottle. He'll stop crying," Peter pleaded. Eddie jerked the bottle out of Peter's hands and mushed him so hard that he fell on the floor and hit his head. Eddie stuck the bottle in the baby's mouth and the baby began gulping the mixture hungrily.

"Get up Pussy. Here, take ya brother until he gets done and put him back to sleep," Eddie instructed. Peter, who was a bit dazed, obeyed because he knew that as long as he had to tend to EJ, he wouldn't have to watch the movie. Eddie handed Peter the baby and picked Patra up off the floor. Peter watched as Eddie slung her across the bed and ripped her clothes off. He then turned her over onto her stomach and pulled down his pants. He took his private parts out, got on top of Patra and then began pounding her mercilessly. Eddie, who noticed Peter watching him, shot Peter a sly smile and winked his eye. Peter quickly scrambled away and continued rocking the baby who had almost finished his bottle.

The baby eventually fell asleep in Peter's arms. Peter kept rocking him and kissed him on his head. And since Peter wasn't tall enough to put the baby in his crib, he laid him down on the dirty and tattered mattress that he slept on. However, as soon as Peter laid the baby down, the screaming and crying resumed. Peter rocked him frantically out of fear that Eddie would come back. But when the baby began throwing up violently, Peter had no choice but to try and wake his mother.

"Eddie, mommy, the baby needs help. He's throwing up. His stomach must be hurting him," Peter said frantically.

"Get the fuck away from here Pussy. Can't ya see me and ya mom are busy. Ya come back in here and I'll kill ya. I'll kill ya mom and that dirty ass bastard of a baby too. Ya understand?" Eddie yelled and threw a shoe at Peter. Peter who was holding the baby, turned quickly in an effort to shield his baby brother from being hit by the shoe which instead hit Peter hard on his back; knocking him over. Peter gripped the baby tightly and held his head in his hands to keep him from getting hurt. Sharp pains shot across his back and through his hands but he shook it off because he knew he had to take care of his brother. He got himself together, walked into the bathroom and grabbed a dirty rag so that he could clean himself and his little brother; who had grown so weary, he could only release short whimpers.

Peter then removed the baby's fully soiled diaper and noticed bruises and scratches on the baby's bottom. Tears rolled down his cheeks as he wrapped a towel around the baby's bottom since he had no more diapers.   The pain in his back began to intensify but instead of feeling the pain, Peter began to feel a game changing fear. He couldn't bear the thought of Eddie beating on EJ or hurting him like he hurt him and his mother. The images of the slasher movies began flashing through his mind. One thing that he learned from watching all those scary movies was that there was always a survivor who killed the bad guy and got away. Peter heard Eddie's loud snore; which meant he was sleep. At that moment, he knew what he had to do. It was time for him to be the hero, the good guy at the end. He gently laid his brother down on a pillow on the floor, went to the table where Eddie's knife was laying and crept into his mother's room where Eddie and his mother were both sleeping. Peter let the images from the movies guide his hand as he stabbed Eddie until his arms were tired. His mother didn't move.

Monday Evening
Carolyn Black

I turned off my computer and began gathering my things. I couldn't wait to get home to a blunt and Xan Xan. I felt kind of guilty for being so excited about taking pills, but taking them meant that I felt nothing, which was necessary for the time being, especially since Jarrod had kicked me to the curb and I really wasn't in the mood to deal with Jermaine, I mean Avery. Seeing Demarcus had messed me up and although I wanted to spit on him, I didn't want him to know I'd been with another man, or should I say men, which pissed me off because I hadn't even heard from him since I slammed the door in his face. I expected him to call or come by begging or pleading, but he didn't. At first, I felt proud of myself for standing my ground but as time passed, I started feeling terrified that he may have actually taken the hint. My phone rung and I grabbed it quickly; hoping it was Demarcus.

"Carolyn Black," I answered breathlessly.

"Hi Ms. Black. This is Officer Leon Petrea and we have a 6 year old and 3 month old here at Fosterberg County Hospital. Uh, it's a very messy and extensive case so I will need to brief you when you get here. I know it's late in the evening but how soon do you think you can get here?" the officer said into the phone.

Shit! Why did I answer the damn phone? I thought to myself.

"Give me 30 minutes and I'll be there," I replied while sighing and rolling my eyes.

"Ok, see you then. I'll be waiting for you at the ER," he said and hung up.

I prayed on the way to the hospital because I didn't know if I was ready to walk through those doors again. I pulled into the parking lot and I began sweating. My heartbeat increased and I felt like my chest was going to cave in. Therefore, I quickly pulled out of the parking lot and headed home. I screeched to a halt and put my car in park. I ran in my house, popped two Xanax and washed them down with a glass of water.

"What the hell is that?" a deep voice said from behind. I dropped my glass on the kitchen floor, which shattered, and spun around. There stood Demarcus.

"Demarcus what the HELL are you doing in my house? How did you get in?" I yelled as urine threatened to leak out and run down my legs.

"I was sitting in front of your house waiting for you to get home. You ran in so fast you didn't see me sitting there. What's up? What's going on? What kind of pills is that?"

"Dude, don't question me," I said seriously with my finger pointed at him. I took a deep breath and calmed myself down. "Look, I just got called in on a case. I gotta go."

"Well, I'll wait until you get back."

"No. You gotta go."

"Listen, we need to talk about what happened at..."

"No! GET OUT! AND DON'T COME BACK!" I screamed, scaring him; scaring myself. I guess because I'd gotten so used to being calm, but this was different because the sound of my voice didn't belong to me. Carolyn Black would have just cussed him out and told him to kiss her beautiful black ass and hell Xan Xan didn't care if the sun came out. So I couldn't place who or where this voice came from, but it sounded like one that belonged to a psychotic banshee. I started to feel embarrassed. My face was hot and tears wanted to fall. I knew I had to get out of there so I left the broken glass on the floor and hurried towards the door. I opened it and looked towards the ground as I waited for him to walk past me, out the door. Once he was outside, I locked the door, turned my back to him and walked off.

"Cee, look, I need to talk to you."

I kept walking and ignored him, but he followed me.

"Cee, Cee! You ain't gotta worry about *her* no more."

My feet stopped me and I stood still. A smile spread across my lips as I turned in his direction. I eased in a little closer to him and slapped the taste out of his mouth. Then, I got in my car and headed to the hospital.

I was so angry that my adrenaline splashed like waves throughout my body. His words "You ain't gotta worry about *her* no more," splashed in the mist of those waves.

"Like I was worried about Foghorn Leghorn anyway," I said out loud to myself. *She* had absolutely nothing on me because it was apparent that *her husband* couldn't leave *me* alone. I had finally started getting over him and I was determined to keep him from messing that up. But I still battled and wrestled in my mind for the entire ride to the hospital and before I knew it, I was pulling back into the hospital parking lot. Xan Xan was kicking in and I was beginning not to care about Demarcus, but I still couldn't stop thinking about him. I tried desperately to think of something else as I got out of the car, but his image had etched itself in my mind.

My heart rate acted like it wanted to speed up as I approached the emergency room doors but Xan Xan slowed it down. I inhaled and smiled because I knew I was ready. Xan Xan had put a bubble around me so I floated carefreely into the hospital to where I saw a super fine police officer sitting in the waiting room. I ducked into the bathroom so I could check myself in the mirror. I wasn't at all pleased by what I saw. I looked decent, but my eyes looked dead. However, Xan Xan wouldn't let me care, so I put on some lip gloss and headed towards the waiting room.

"Officer Petrea?" I asked.

"Yes. I'm Officer Petrea. You must be Ms. Black," he said as he stood and extended his hand.

"That's me," I said accepting it. His grip was so tight he almost broke my hand. Xan Xan couldn't protect me from that nor could it blind me to the fact of how fine Officer Petrea was. My Juicy almost throbbed and then Demarcus popped in my head; pulling the plug. I abruptly pushed him out though because his days of playing with my heart were over.

I involuntarily looked down at Officer Petrea's left hand to see if he was married and of course, he was, but of course, I didn't care. He saw me looking, but I played it off.

"So tell me what's going on Officer Petrea?" I asked as I got my pad and pen out.

"Ms. Black, I just don't know if you're ready for this. We got a call about a bloody 6-year-old boy walking down the street carrying a limp baby. When we responded, the boy had blood all over his clothes and he wasn't wearing shoes. The baby was wrapped in a dirty towel and was so malnourished that we didn't know if he was dead or alive. We asked the child where he lived and he couldn't tell us. He just said the big red house down the street.

We asked where his parents were and he told us that 'mommy and Eddie were sleeping.' We didn't know what the hell was going on so we had one car take the kids to the hospital to have them checked out and then we sent another officer to canvas the area looking for the house. Luckily, there was only one big red house on the street and it wasn't far from where we picked the kids up. But when we got there, none of us were prepared for what we walked into. This Eddie fellow, who is known as a local drug dealer, had been stabbed several times with a large pocketknife and the mother who was high on heroin, was passed out, lying beside him completely oblivious to everything. Luckily, Eddie didn't die but he's barely hanging in there."

Dear Jesus. I thought to myself as he continued.

"And when we finally got the mom coherent enough to talk, she wasn't any help because she barely knew what planet she was on. The little boy can't or won't tell us anything and that poor baby...," he said, his voice trailing off as he shook his head. "It's obvious that the kid saw something but he ain't talking. He asks about his little brother but that's about it. I hope that Eddie will be able to tell us something when he wakes up; otherwise, we're going to be up the creek without a paddle. Come on, follow me and I'll take you to the little boy's room," he said as he walked towards the elevators. I couldn't help but to look at his butt as I followed him. He had a butt like a baseball player, high and plump.

Mmmm! I thought to myself. *I wouldn't mind having you for dinner tonight.* I smiled and kept walking.

He led me onto the children's floor and into a room where a nurse and a female officer were sitting at a table. A cute little boy with big, green eyes and curly red hair, who was dressed in a hospital gown, crawled around on the floor, playing with toy cars. I could see the bruises on his back and legs. I shook my head. *Thank you Xan Xan for serenity*, I thought to myself as I walked over and introduced myself to the nurse and female officer. I took a deep breath and then turned towards the child.

"Hi there young man. My name is Carolyn Black. What's your name?" I asked.

"Peter," he replied as he continued playing without looking up.

"It's nice to meet you Peter. Do you know where you are?" I asked.

"Yes. At the hospital."

"How did you get to the hospital?"

"The policeman."

"How did you like riding in the police car?" I asked.   He stopped for a second, thrown off by my question.

"Uh I can't remember."

"What do you remember?" I asked. He froze for a moment. I saw his hands start shaking and his breathing increased. He squeezed his eyes closed and started singing.

> "Dead leaves, seaweed, rotten eggs, too,
> Stir them in my witch's brew.
> I got magic, Alakazamakazoo."

He then resumed playing with his cars as he hummed and still refused to look up at me or answer my question. I was stunned not because he'd burst incongruently into song, but more so because the children's song, "Witches Brew" by Hap Palmer that he was singing had been *my joint* in elementary school. And I couldn't believe that this child, who was well over 20 years younger than me, knew it. I was so excited that I started singing the second verse.

> "Spider web, moldy bread, mucky mud, too
> Stir them in my witch's brew
> I got magic! Alakazamakazoo."

He stopped playing with his car and immediately turned and looked up at me. The biggest smile I'd seen on a child in a long time crossed his face.

"You know *Witches Brew*?" he asked glowing.

"Of course I do. That was my favorite song in elementary school."

"I bet you don't know the next part." He challenged me. Not one to back down, even to a little kid, I accepted and replied, "I bet you I do."

His eyes locked on mine. "Sing it then."

My eyes locked on his. "Only if you sing it with me." And I said it with a little neck roll.

He smiled. "Ok. On the count of three. One, two, three..."

> "Oooooooo
> My witch's brew
> Ooooooo
> What's it gonna do to you?
> Boo!"

And the next thing I know, he was telling me everything. He told me about the name calling and daily abuse that him and his family sustained at the hands of "the monster" I assumed to be Eddie.

"The monster hit us all the time and he gave my mama shots that made her fall asleep so she couldn't help us or feed us. He makes me sit on the couch and watch scary movies that make me have bad dreams at night. Sometimes he's nice to EJ but most of the time EJ stays in his crib because the monster is always doing this to my mom..." The child walked over to the back of a chair and began humping it, obviously mimicking "the monster" having sex with his mother. I looked at the nurse and the officer out of the side of my eye. They were both sitting there trying their best to plaster and cement on a solid poker face, as was I. But I feared that if the look in my eyes resembled the look in theirs, then we were all failing miserably. Neither of us moved as Peter continued.

"Sometimes they let EJ cry all night until he gets tired. And when they go to sleep, I sneak and feed him."

I wanted to get mad but Xan Xan just wouldn't let me. "Wow" was the best thing I could conjure up in my mind.

"Who's the monster Peter? What's his name?" I asked. He stopped pushing his cars around on the floor and looked up at me.

His eyes darted around the room and his voice dropped to a whisper. "Eddie."

"How did you get those bruises and marks on your back and legs?" I asked.

"Eddie threw a shoe and hit me in my back. I was holding EJ and we fell."

"Peter, I apologize but I need to take pictures of you ok."

"Ok," he said cool as a cucumber. He stood up and the nurse untied his gown. There was a large bruise on his back equivalent to the size of a grown man's shoe. He had scars on his bottom as well as his legs. *Poor kid*. I thought to myself.

"So Peter, how did you get all that blood on your clothes?" I asked cautiously, as I continued snapping pictures. He didn't reply for a while.

"Let's sing *Witches Brew* again," he responded.

I obliged him because it was apparent that "Witches Brew" was to him what Xan Xan was to me. His wasn't budging on anything else pertaining to what happened in that big red house and I decided not to push him. Plus, my gut was telling me that he probably was the one who stabbed Eddie anyway and if that was the situation, then it would be out of our hands.

"Is there anyone else who helps take care of you and EJ?" I asked.

"We stay with Aunt Maggie sometimes. She's really cool and she always makes sure we have a lot of food to eat."

"When was the last time you saw Aunt Maggie?"

"Uh, I don't know. It's been a long time."

"When was the last time you and your brother ate?" I asked gently.

"I ate at school today but I don't know when EJ ate," he replied. "Where is he?"

"He's here at the hospital getting help for his tummy," I answered.

"I want to see my baby brother." He said looking at me desperately.

"Ok. Let me go and check on him and I'll be right back, ok." He looked at me and by the way he searched my eyes, I could tell that he really didn't believe me.

"Peter, I promise that I'll be back as soon as I find out something. It may take a while but I'll be back," I said, looking him straight in his eyes hoping the deadness in *my* eyes from Xan Xan didn't hide the sincerity. He didn't seem to be totally convinced but he relented.

"Ok. But don't forget, ok?"

"I won't I promise." I responded. I turned to the nurse and motioned for her to come outside with me. I got the baby's information and headed in that direction. And even though I really didn't want to, I knew I had to call Val and fill her in on the details.

"Hello?" She answered the phone breathlessly.

"Hello?" I replied.

"Uh, yeah, what's up?" Her words were broken and her breaths were short.

"Hey, I just wanted to let you know that I got called in on a case and I'm at Fosterberg Memorial with a 6 year old boy and a 3 month old baby.

"Why, um, what happened?" she said as her voice fluctuated between normal and a whisper.

"Are you having sex?" I asked as annoyed as Xan Xan would allow me to be. *Why am I annoyed?* I asked myself because under normal circumstances, I would be laughing and trying to imagine what position Maurice had her in.

"No. Um, I'm uh...exercising. Tell me what's going on?" Once I got 6 year old and stabbing, along with malnourished, fighting for his life baby out, the short breaths stopped abruptly and I knew I had her undivided attention. She told me that she would meet me at the hospital as soon as possible. I then made sure that Peter got something to eat and I went to check on the baby. After showing a nurse my badge, I had to wash my hands twice and suit up in a mask and a gown to make sure I didn't spread any germs. I walked into the baby's room and laying there in the hospital crib was something that resembled a baby alien in my mind. The baby's head was the normal size but I could almost see the silhouette of his skeleton poking out around his eye sockets and his cheeks. His skin was ashy gray and the rest of his body resembled his face in that it barely hid his bones. And he was alone, which was the worst part for me. The nurse was in and out but there was no one sitting there with him, talking to him or rubbing his little fingers. I asked the nurse if I could hold him because I knew he needed somebody.

"That would actually be awesome. I know he looks a little scary because he's hooked up to all these machines and IVs, but if you sit down in this rocking chair, I will put him in your arms so that the cords don't get tangled."

"Ok," I replied and sat down in the chair. The nurse put the baby in my arms and instructed me on how to hold him properly. He was light as a feather and his breathing was forced, so I knew this little boy actually was fighting for his life.

"I'll be back shortly to put him back in bed because he can't be out too long."

"Ok," I replied. Once the nurse was gone, I laid my head back and began rocking the baby. "Thank you Xan Xan for your serenity," I whispered out loud. A tear slid down my cheek, but I didn't care because this baby deserved somebody's tears. Then, unbeknownst to myself, I found myself praying over him. I begged God to help me find a safe and loving place for him and Peter. I also prayed for healing over their minds and bodies.

When the nurse returned we discussed the baby's prognosis and I asked how long she thought the baby would be in the hospital. She shook her head and said that because he was so severely malnourished, a lot of damage had occurred in his little body, therefore she didn't know how long he would be in the hospital or if he would even survive for that matter. I thought about Peter. I knew it would break him if his little brother didn't make it, so I made the decision to go get Peter and let him spend some time with his brother. The nurse agreed to let Peter stay in the room with the baby for a while, but he wasn't allowed to hold him; although he could hold the baby's hand and rub his legs.

After that, my next stop was at their mother's room. When I walked in, she was still sleeping. *Thank you Xan Xan for your serenity,* I repeated to myself because otherwise, I would have wanted to flip her out of that bed. Here she was sleeping all peacefully and shit while her baby was fighting for his life and her 6-year-old son was probably on the path to becoming a serial killer because of her.

"Miss Tanner," I said gently and loud enough to hopefully wake her up. But she didn't move.

"Miss Tanner," I said louder and more firmly. She began to stir and eventually opened her eyes. She was beautiful. She was very, very pale and she had bright red hair just like Peter's. As I got closer to her, however, I could see the residue of bruises on her face. She was frail, there were dark circles underneath her light hazel eyes and she had track marks all over her arms. She sat up and looked at me.

"Hello, Miss Tanner. My name is Carolyn Black and I work for Fosterberg County Department of Social Services." She sat up and yawned.

"Uh, yes ma'am. What can I do for you?" she replied groggily.

"Well for starters, you can tell me your name," I said. She scowled.

"Patra Tanner."

"Do you know where you're at?

"Yes. I'm at Fosterberg Memorial," she answered.

"Is it day time or night time?"

She looked out the window. "It's night," she replied, getting a little annoyed and I didn't care.

"Ok Miss Tanner..."

"You can call me Patra."

"Ok, Patra. I'm here to talk with you about your children."

"Ok," She replied casually.

"How old are you?"

"22," she answered.

"What's the last thing you remember?"

"I don't know Ms., what did you say your name is?"

"Carolyn Black," I replied with a little bit of "oomph", which let me know that Xan Xan was about to get off from work.

"Ok. I don't remember anything Ms. Black. All I know is I woke up here in the hospital," she continued.

"Ok, do you know why you're in the hospital?

"Probably because of drugs or maybe my boyfriend Eddie beat me up. Is my face messed up?" she asked, still too casually for me.

"No, your face isn't messed up."

"Well, then who knows?" She answered with a snort.

"Do you remember anything before today at all? I mean anything?" I asked grasping for straws.

"Ms. Black, I'm a heroin addict and my life is like...it's like walking through a museum. I see all these crazy pictures and stuff but none of it makes sense. I don't know if they're from my dreams or from things that have really happened."

"Well, Miss Tanner, the reality of this situation is that the police found your son Peter carrying your three month old baby down the street and they were both covered in blood. When the police arrived at your house, they found you passed out and incoherent lying next to Eddie who'd been stabbed several times right beside you. He's in Intensive Care. Peter, your son, is here in a room and the baby; who is so severely malnourished that they don't know if he's going to make it, is also here being treated," I stated bluntly hoping to jar her up some. She gasped and covered her mouth with her hand.

"Was Peter or the baby stabbed too?" she asked.

"No." I replied.

"Oh my gosh Ms. Black, Peter probably did it then. There's no telling what happened while I was passed out. Eddie's real mean to me and those kids; especially Peter. He beats me, he beats Peter and he's always making Peter watch scary movies. One time I asked him why and he said..." She deepened her voice, mimicking Eddie, "life's scary, he needs to get used to it.' But he's not that bad to EJ though. I guess because he's a baby," she said, nonchalantly with no regard for the kids' wellbeing.

"Miss Tanner, if he does all those things to you and your children what makes you stay with him?" I had to ask because I really needed to hear her answer.

"He pays the bills and he...and he, he gives me my Hattie."

"Your Hattie?"

"My drugs. Heroin."

I chuckled to myself. *Hattie, Xan Xan, Mary Jane, Booz. Everybody has a nickname for their habit*. And then a thought crossed my mind. *Wow, I have three of those habits. Damn.*

"How long have you been using heroin?" I asked.

"I've been doing heroin for uhhhhh, a little over 4 years now," she replied honestly.

"Who takes care of the kids when you're high?" I asked. She swallowed.

"Um, sometimes nobody. Sometimes Eddie or Aunt Maggie. Sometimes I really don't know. Matter of fact, most of the time, I really don't know."

"Ok well, have you ever tried to stop using before?" I asked.

"Uh, kinda but not really. If you want to know the God's honest truth, I've never wanted to stop using because I like the way it makes me feel. But I didn't use drugs during either one of my pregnancies though. I can definitely say that," she said proudly while crossing her arms and laying back in the bed.

Hence, how your ass skated under the CPS radar, I thought to myself.

"Miss Tanner, where is the children's father? Or is Eddie their father?" I asked, praying to God that he wasn't.

"No Eddie's not their father. I haven't been with him but about eight months. I met him when I was still pregnant with EJ. Their real father is married and living in Virginia," she replied and rolled her eyes.

"Well, I will need his name and information please," I said.

"Ok. His name is Edward Tillman but I don't know the exact address. I can get you there in a car, but I don't remember the names of the roads though."

"Ok. Is he involved in the children's life?" I asked.

"Uh no. Didn't you hear me say he's married? He sends the kids some hush money every month and we still have sex every now and then, but he doesn't have anything to do with the kids. They wouldn't even recognize him if they saw him. When me and him meet up, the kids are usually with Aunt Maggie," she stated bluntly but apathetically as well. I couldn't read this broad. I couldn't figure out if she was simply a detached airhead or completely heartless. I appreciated her honesty, but I was alarmed and baffled by her disconnect and indifference. Nevertheless, I continued.

"Ok, well do you have his phone number?" I asked.

"Yes, I have his number," she said and gave it to me as I jotted everything down in my pad.

"Now Miss Tanner, I mean no disrespect by asking this, but for the children's sake, are you sure that he's the kids' father? Are there any other possibilities?"

"No ma'am. I wasn't using when I met Peter's dad, so I remember everything clearly."

"Ok. Well in the meantime, where should we place your kids once they're discharged?" I asked. My question stumped her, so I gave her time to collect her thoughts.

"Uh, well I don't know. I'm adopted and my adopted parents were killed in a plane crash almost 2 years ago, but maybe they can stay with Aunt Maggie," she said, still surprised by my encouraged autonomy, but not my candidness about her children. She was a "keep it real" type of person as was I; therefore, there was no need for modesty. She and I both knew those children were not going home with her

"Who is Aunt Maggie?" I asked.

"Aunt Maggie is my adopted mother's baby sister. She's a school teacher and she practically raised me along with my parents."

"Describe yours and the kids' relationship with her."

"Well, I would say it's pretty good. I moved in with her after me and my parents had this big blow up when they found out that I was pregnant by a married man at 16. We all still raised Peter together though until I turned 18 and moved to Virginia. They told me not to go but I wanted to do things my way. Plus, I was in love with Edward like a dummy and I was really thinking that he was going to leave his wife to be with me and Peter. He put me up in a nice little house and paid all the bills. He bought me a little Honda and opened up a checking account where he deposited money for me and Peter every month. But he hardly ever came over and when he did, Peter was always asleep. He pretty much moved me there to be his concubine. It was ok for a little while because me and Peter didn't want for nothing... except him. I started getting lonely, so I got a part-time job at a call center just to get out of the house and meet people. Shit the job was easy and they let us bring our kids as long as we kept them quiet. Anyways I started hanging out with some people from work and the next thing I know I was hooked on heroin," she said throwing her hands in the air frivolously. I realized that she was a talker, which was cool because I needed to see where she was at, but at the same time, I could feel that Xan Xan was preparing to depart. I looked at the clock, which read 9:36, which meant I had about thirty minutes left.

"I hid it from Edward and my family, but they said I was starting to look bad and so was Peter. I eventually ended up having to tell them because I was in the bathroom shooting up and my mom walked in on me." She paused and began starring off into space as she relived the memory. "I never will forget the look on her face...but anyways, they tried to get me into treatment, but I made it seem like it wasn't a big deal. They really didn't buy into it, but since I had a free house, free car and no financial worries, they didn't want me to lose everything since I refused to come home. Plus, I wasn't giving them Peter because I didn't want him to be like me and not have his real mama...but I didn't keep him from them either. I just had to make sure that we were both clean and spry looking by Friday afternoon when they came to get him. And I had to be decent looking when they brought him back." She got quiet and started contemplating. "You know, that actually kept me on track because I never knew what day they were bringing him back. And since I didn't want them to catch me with my tail between my legs, I was very careful about how much and how often I used. But when my parents died, everything around me started falling apart. I was barely functioning, but Aunt Maggie came to Virginia and stayed with me for her entire summer break and I was happy as hell that she was there. So anyways, one day me, her and Peter went to the grocery store. We go in and there's Edward and his wife standing in the produce section, laughing and flirting around. And he was playing in her hair, all lovey dovey with her and stuff. And I made it a point to walk right past him so I could pester him, but you know that asshole didn't even flinch. Then..." She took a deep breath. "Then to put the icing on the cake, Aunt Maggie walks up to them and says, 'it's beautiful to see two people so in love.' I almost died Ms. Black. I know she didn't know any better but I was so angry at her that I cussed her out and told her to get the hell out of my house. Of course, I regretted it once she was gone, but I wasn't going to bow down and ask her to come back. Mmmph." She grew quiet once again, and then she perked back up. She sucked her teeth and continued. "And do you know that as soon as that bastard got the opportunity, he was calling me, asking me could he come over. I told his ass no, but he came anyway. We ended up having sex, of course, but only because he made me feel like he cared about the fact that I'd lost my parents. Oh and I purposely made Peter stay awake so Edward had to see him. But even though Peter was crawling around on the floor, he pretended like he wasn't even there; the same way he did me at the grocery store. I told him to get his ass the hell out too. After that, I went way downhill, but God sent Peter an angel. Her name was Ronda. Her parents had kicked her out so I let her move in with me in exchange for keeping Peter. Everything was working out fine until Edward's low down dirty ass told me I had to get out because his wife was starting to find a paper trail leading to me. I lost it on his ass and I started to tell his wife everything but the SOB got me the house I live in now with my name on the deed and he still sends me money. So that's how I ended up back in North Carolina." As she gulped in another breath of air and got her "second wind," I discreetly looked at the clock. I wanted her to shut the hell up so I could bounce, but this hussy was a talker and I had no choice but to be a listener under the circumstances.

"Ok anyway, so then I found out I was pregnant with EJ and when I told Edward, all his ass said was how much is *he* gonna cost? I told him I needed three thousand dollars a month and you know his dumb ass agreed. Then, I met Eddie's sorry ass. Wait; hold on, did you realize that their names are Edward and Eddie. Oh my gosh, I just realized that. I should've learned my lesson the first time, huh? Anyways, I never told Eddie anything about Edward or the money he was sending me. I just let him think he's the man of the house." She snickered and rolled her eyes. "He thinks he's doing something because he pays the utilities and supplies my drug habit." She put her hands behind her head proudly. "And I just keep on letting his dumb ass think it too." She laughed in spite of herself. "So while he's paying the bills and supplying my habit, my money's piling up in the bank. Hell a couple beatings is worth it to me," she snickered while looking at her fingernails with a smirk on her face.

I sat there in awe. I concluded that no, this heifa wasn't heartless; she just didn't give a damn. She was a selfish, spoiled, immature, indifferent brat that had no business ever having children. It wouldn't surprise me if she had an undiagnosed attachment disorder, especially with her lack of regard for her kid's safety or wellbeing. And the heifa was sitting here telling me; with a straight face might I add, that she had a bank account full of money yet she chose to stay with a man who terrorized her and her children so that she can stack more money and get high for free. Even though I wanted to be angry with her and shake the shit out of her, I wondered what good it would do. She was completely detached and since she'd been spoon fed for so long, it was apparent that she didn't understand how to be responsible for herself, much less two small children. And to top things off, she still hadn't asked how they were doing. I was starting to get impatient with her because I'd heard enough. My job was to assess her ability *and* desire to protect her children, which was at a zero, so my mission was complete.

"Ok, Miss Tanner. Thank you for your honesty. I don't know how long Peter and EJ will be here in the hospital, but you may want to spend some time with them because once they are discharged, they can't return home with you."

"I know, but you see Ms. Black, I plan on leaving them here in the hospital anyway. I figure y'all will know what to do with them." She shifted around in the bed. "I know I'm a bad mother Ms. Black and I had my tubes tied after EJ so I couldn't have no more. I'm an addict, and I don't plan on quitting and that isn't their fault. I thought having kids would make Edward be with me, but it didn't so ain't no need in me trying to be a mama when I don't have a motherly bone in my body. So if you don't mind, can you tell Peter that I can't be his mother anymore because that's what's best for him? EJ won't know the difference, so he'll be ok."

"Um, no ma'am. That's something you're going to have to tell him yourself. You are his mother and if you're planning to walk away from him, then you're going to tell him and you need to be very clear on why so he doesn't grow up like you; lost and full of questions with no one to answer them."

Her eyes got big and the next thing I know she was crying.

"You're right Ms. Black…" She paused. "I've never tried to find my real parents because I felt like they didn't want me, so why should I care about them? But what if they were addicts like me and knew they would be bad parents? If that's the case then I wouldn't be mad at them anymore. I'd think they were the bravest parents in the world. So yeah, I'll tell Peter the truth. I'm going to spare him from the same heartache I felt when I was a kid."

There was a peck on the door and in walked Val and Officer Petrea. I was relieved because Xan Xan was gone and I was beginning to feel anxious. Then my eyes met Officer Petrea's eyes. I nodded and he nodded back. Without Xan Xan, I could *really* see how fine he was and I could also *feel* how fine he was between my legs.

"Hey Carolyn," Val said walking over to Miss Tanner and me, gladly interrupting my moment with Officer Petrea.

"Hey Val," I said and turned to Miss Tanner. "Miss Tanner, this is my supervisor Valerie Whitman and this is Officer Petrea, one of the investigating officers. Val, Officer Petrea, this is Patra Tanner; EJ and Peter's mom." I introduced them and stepped out into the hallway with Val so I could brief her and get the hell out of there. I really didn't want to talk to her because *she* made me feel anxious, but I had no choice. I briefed her as quickly as I could, almost in one breath. When I finished, Val stood there staring at me. Her eyes were sad.

"Carolyn, are you really being quick and superficial with *me* right now? What did I do to you? Ever since the accident, you just cut me off. Do you blame…"

"Val, here's my notes with the phone number and address for the kids' father and their Aunt Maggie. I didn't do the written assessments so you can handle that and we'll work on placement tomorrow," I said cutting her off and handing her my notepad. Tears welled up in her eyes but she accepted the note pad in silence. I turned away as quickly as I could and damn near ran towards the elevator.

"Hey, Carolyn go ahead and take the day off tomorrow. I'll handle this case," she said. I was confused. I didn't want to take the day off because that meant I would be home alone.

"Why? I'm fine."

"No, you're not, Carolyn."

"Yes I am! I don't want to take the day off. I started this case and the little boy is used to me."

"I'll see you on Wednesday." She turned her back to me and walked away. The walls started to close in around me. I pressed the elevator button impatiently because I had to get out of there. I didn't have Xan Xan or Mary Jane and my thoughts about Demarcus weren't strong enough to sustain me. Once the elevator arrived, the ride down seemed to take forever. When the doors opened, I was back at the emergency room waiting area. I began inhaling and exhaling all the while hauling ass trying to get out of there.

"Sylvia. How are you?" My feet froze and I involuntarily turned around as two women were greeting each other. I shook my head and started trying to catch my breath. Once my breathing normalized and my feet allowed me to move, I almost tripped over a kid in a wheelchair trying to get out of there. As soon as my feet hit the pavement, I broke into a sprint towards my car. However, when I got there, I realized that my briefcase, which had my car keys in it, was still in Miss Tanner's room. The thought of going back into that hospital almost caused my central nervous system to explode. With shaky hands, I pulled out my phone and decided to give in and call Val because there was no way in hell that I was going back into that hospital. Then I heard someone calling my name.

"Ms. Black, Ms. Black!" It was Officer Petrea and he was holding my briefcase. I ran up to him and embraced him like he'd just saved my life.

"Oh my gosh. Thank you so much," I said breathlessly. Then suddenly, I was kissing him...and he kissed me back. In a flash, he was on his Walky Talky requesting to take his lunch break as I drove across the street to a local park. I found the first dark and secluded area that suited my needs and slammed the car in park. By then Officer Petrea's mouth was on my breasts and his hand massaged my Juicy.

I pushed the seat back as far as it would go and reclined it. Officer Petrea pulled my pants down and slowly spread my legs. Thankfully, although I was wearing cotton panties they suctioned my paw print nicely. He took his fingers and continued to massage my suction cup through its cotton barrier causing me to squirm and squeeze my eyes shut.

"Ma'am, I'd like to ask your permission to do with my penis what I'm doing now with my fingers," he said seductively and authoritatively altogether.

"Permission granted," I replied as I gyrated my Juicy around his fingers. That was the end of our conversation. He led me to the front of my car whereby he bent me over the hood and "arrested" me. As he pumped me from behind and slobbered all over my neck, I felt dead. After we finished, I dropped him off outside the parameter of the hospital campus and kept going without a word. He'd knocked the edge off but I still had to get home to Xan Xan. Guilt started crawling up my legs and I started chastising myself. I'd just had sex with a random police officer on my car and the scent of sex was still floating around. I cracked the window and sighed. I blasted music from my radio as I ran yellow lights and cursed at slow drivers delaying me from getting home. I pushed it to the limit with my speed and when I finally reached my street, it was equivalent to driving down a long, dark tunnel with only a glimpse of light at the end.

After getting through the "tunnel", I saw my house. My heart rate increased as I pulled into the driveway just as briskly as I had at the park. I grabbed my purse and jumped out of the car with one goal in mind and that was to get to Xan Xan. For a split second, Miss Tanner crossed my mind and I imagined her plight to get to "Hattie." *Oh my God, I'm an addict,* I thought to myself although my thoughts didn't deter my mission. However, the smell of *his* cologne blowing in the wind did, and I stopped.

"Demarcus, what the FUCK are you doing here? I told you to stay away from me, didn't I?" I glared at him because my patience was wearing thin and I felt dirty from my tryst with Officer Petrea. I needed to get inside my house where Xan Xan and a hot shower were waiting. He stood there silently holding two large brown bags.

"I figured you would be tired and hungry so I brought you something to eat from Giovanni's and I rolled you a fatty so you wouldn't have to."

I was stunned and touched. Then my body began to get into a heated and emotional debate. First, I felt like a whore, as if I'd betrayed him. Then I got angry at myself for feeling that way. Then I got angry at him for hurting me and then I started thinking about all the people that *I'd* hurt. Then I thought about Sylvia. I began feeling nauseated so I ran towards the door. I fumbled around with my keys because my hands were shaking. I desperately needed to get to Xan Xan and that was all that was on my mind. I felt like my body was going to erupt.

"Shit!" I yelled, frustrated with my keys. When I finally got my door open, I dropped my things on the couch and grabbed my bottle of Xan Xan. I quickly popped two in my mouth and swallowed but the freaking things lodged themselves in my throat, so I ran towards the kitchen to get some water. I cut the corner of the island in route to the refrigerator and slid on the glass that I'd left lying there earlier. I almost hit the ground, but I collided with the refrigerator instead, which was fine with me since I was in the process of choking to death and needed water. I used the door handle as leverage while jerking it open all in damn near one movement. I grabbed out a jug of water and gulped it down as if I was returning from a trip to the desert. Once I cleared my airways, I sucked in as much air as I could.

"Damn, Cee. All that for uh aspirin?" Demarcus said, holding the over the counter medicine bottle that I used to house my Xan Xan.

"Put my shit down!" I snapped and snatched it out of his hand.

"Yo, what's going on with you? You acting crazy even for yo' ass."

"I'm acting crazy cause you in my house after I told you not to come back. I'm done with you Demarcus, now get out!"

"Ok. I'll leave but not before I explain some things to you first. Now come over here and light up this blunt so we can talk." I scowled at him as if he must have really lost his mind.

"Uh, I do plan on lighting up that blunt and eating that delicious food that you brought me, but I will be indulging in both only after you are gone. Like you said, I'm tired and I'm hungry. I been working all day and I want to relax. I don't wanna hear shit about you, your ghetto ass wife or anything else that has to do with you. Now, thanks for the food and I'll holla at you."

"A'ight, fuck it then," he responded and proceeded to leave. But he stopped first and swept the glass up off the floor. I put my hand on my hip and watched him. I didn't say a word and I hoped that he didn't expect to get a response out of me because he had to do a whole lot more sweeping than that before he could clean up all the shit he'd done to me.

When he was finished, he looked over at me and then headed towards the door. I wanted to punch him in his face, but at the same time, I didn't want him to go, especially since Xan Xan hadn't kicked in yet and I needed a distraction. But since I'd just cussed him out, I didn't know how to tell him to stay.

Oh yes I do. I thought to myself.

"Demarcus you ain't shit! I haven't seen you or heard from you since you threw me across the floor for your raggedy Ann wife, *Charmanita*..." Her name tasted like rotten lima beans coming out of my mouth. "And you think you can just come up in my house touching my shit like you still have rights over here? Matter of fact punk, I owe you an ass whooping," I said allowing a sudden and mysterious internal rage to guide me as I walked towards him with my fists balled up.

"Don't come over here swinging cuz I'ma put your ass back on the ground again. You already slapped me, plus you and your cousin jumped me at the club so we even. If you coming over here, it better be to talk, otherwise you best be ready to fight," he said and looked at me seriously.

"Word? Is that a threat?" I asked, still walking up on him aggressively.

"Nope, that's a promise," he said straight up.

"What's up then?" I asked and then commenced to swinging. "I'm sick and tired of you walking in and out of my life," I screamed in between blows. He caught one of my strikes with the palm of his hand and twisted my arm behind my back. The next thing I know, I was face down on the floor with pain shooting down my overstretched arm.

"You done?! Huh?! You done?!" He hollered in between breaths.

"Let me go!"

"ARE YOU DONE?"

"Let me go!" I screamed, while trying to break free of his grasp.

"Hell no! Not until you calm your ass down."

I decided to stop struggling and laid flat on the floor completely still. "Ok I'm calm! Now let me go."

"You not gonna be putting your hands on me...unless we making love," he said and slapped my butt with his free hand. Fire shot through my Juicy and the thought of making love to Demarcus softened my spirit some until I remembered that I hadn't washed Officer Petrea off me yet. *Dag I should've waited.* I scolded myself. Not only would the sex have been AWESOME, I for sure would've gotten pleasure out of screwing him and kicking *his* ass out.

"Demarcus, seriously let me go."

"You done?"

"YES! Now get off of me!" My phone started ringing and he let me up. I gave him the meanest look I could conjure up and skedaddled over to my purse to retrieve my phone. Jermaine, I mean Avery's code name, "Xan Xan," flashed across the screen. The devil on my shoulder made me answer it.

"Hello?" My voice was soft and wispy.

"Sup baby?"

"Nothing, um listen, I'm kinda busy right now so can I call you later?" I asked. I could feel Demarcus' eyes burning a hole through my head.

"Yeah. I just wanted to let you know I re-upped on those thangs you like, so when you get free, we'll be waiting on you. And by the way, I'm stroking my cock right now."

I giggled nervously and I'm sure my face turned red. "Ok bye," I said and hung up. I turned around and immediately met Demarcus' stoic gaze. It caught me off guard and I froze for a second. I quickly regained my composure, but I remained silent. I honestly didn't know what to say. The ball was in his court.

"Well, I guess I'ma go. I'll holler at you."

No! Please don't leave me! I screamed in my head knowing the words would never come out of my mouth.

"Alright," I replied with a lump in my throat as I tried my best to be tough and keep from having the stomach virus face. I stood there and watched as the door closed behind him. I felt my chest start to cave in.

"Come on Xan Xan, hurry! I need you," I begged as I felt myself about to crack. I quickly looked around for an outlet and then I thought about Peter and his use of singing as a coping mechanism. I grabbed my phone, connected it to my blue tooth speaker and began playing "Get Into the Groove" by Madonna as loudly as the speaker would go. I squeezed my eyes closed and danced fervently in an attempt to extinguish any thoughts or emotions that threatened to "un-anesthetize" me. I bounced and hopped towards the bathroom so I could get into the shower. I sung to the top of my lungs and twirled in circles as if I were Madonna herself putting on a concert on a hot day in Hawaii. As the hot water rolled down my body, my mind drifted to my sexual escapade with Officer Petrea and I started laughing like a mad woman.

"Oh my GOSH! I can't believe I just slept with some random police officer on the hood of my car in a park!" I said to myself.

I continued with my "mad woman" laugh and then I thought about how erotic it was. "Damn...I just had sex with a fine ass police officer on the hood of my car in a park." I reframed and high fived myself. Hell, I'd needed him when I came out of that hospital and at least he'd made me cum, unlike Mayor Bad Breath Bostain. I reminisced on punching the Mayor in his face and peeing in his car. I really wanted to laugh, but nothing came out with the exception of a light chuckle and a smile.

Xan Xan must be kicking in. I thought to myself. I inhaled and took comfort in "nothing matters" taking my brain captive. My stomach growled and I thought about the food that Demarcus had left. Xan Xan suppressed my pain, but it sure didn't suppress my appetite. I got out the shower and warmed up the baked spaghetti inside the Giovanni's bag. After words, I took a few pulls on the blunt and floated to bed.

Wednesday

I was so happy to be back at work, although Val was really working my nerves. Just as I suspected, Peter wouldn't mumble a word when she went in to talk to him and Miss Tanner's detached frankness didn't coincide well with Val's intolerance. So she wasted a whole day and I ended up having to do everything anyway, which was cool, because it was my case. What pissed me off was that she still kept trying to dictate things. I almost bit a hole in my tongue trying not to cuss her out, but she mistook my mercy for aloofness and started another one of her "Carolyn, why are you acting like this?" conversations. I wasn't trying to hear it so I changed the subject back to Peter as soon as she got started. She took the hint and moved on.

We were able to get Aunt Maggie approved for a temporary placement and luckily we were able to get in contact with Peter's father who agreed to meet us for a Team Decision Making meeting. Aunt Maggie and I sat in the conference room and chatted while we waited for everyone else to arrive. She was a very sweet, soft-spoken woman in her early forties who seemed to be very vibrant and poised.

"Patra's a good girl but she's always been wild and rebellious. I'm just so happy that she allowed Peter to come home with me," Aunt Maggie said. Val had placed Peter in her custody temporarily until we could see what was going to happen with his dad and/or with the police.

"Ms. Blanch, first of all, Miss Tanner at this point has no say so in whether or not she keeps her kids. And secondly, there's a strong possibility that the kids may go with their biological father later on down the road. So you must understand that as of now you will be considered to be a temporary placement unless something happens with dad," I stated. Her face saddened because I could tell that she genuinely loved those kids.

"But, they don't even know him Ms. Black. He's a stranger. Peter will be scared to death."

"I know, but he's their biological parent and we have to consider him first. But in the meantime, thank you for stepping up and being there for those kids."

"I wouldn't have it any other way." She smiled as Val walked in.

"Mr. Tillman is here so he should be arriving with Mario shortly." Val said.

"Ok," I replied.

When Mario walked in with Mr. Tillman, all I could think was *DAMN! Mr. Tillman is one fine ass white man. I heard that Patra.* He was very well put together and wealthy looking. He had dark brown hair and big brown eyes. At first, I thought Peter looked like his mother because of his red hair but Peter actually looked more like his father. I couldn't believe, however, that a man of his caliber would be so distant and disengaged from his children.

"Mr. Tillman, how aware are you of your children's current living conditions?" Val asked.

"With the exception of getting them a nice house to live in, I'm not aware at all," he replied.

"How often do you see the children?" she asked.

"Honestly, I never wanted anything to do with those boys because I've never wanted children. However, they're here and there's nothing I can do about it. I have always supported them financially and made sure they had somewhere nice to live. I made sure Patra didn't have to worry about the bills, insurance or anything else for that matter. She doesn't even have to work for goodness sakes! Her only job is to take care of those kids and she can't even do that! I told Patra to get an abortion both times but she refused. Although I don't understand why, being that she turned out to be such a terrible mother. Leave it to me to knock up the town junkie."

"You watch your mouth when you speak about my niece. You made her into a terrible mother because you enabled her to be one, you sorry piece of trash. You think throwing money at something allows you to close your eyes and open them when you want to? You knew she was on drugs just like the rest of us, but the difference is you had more power over her than we did. She would've listened to you, but you chose not to say anything. You're just as low down as she is when it comes to those kids. *YOUR* six-year-old son Peter almost stabbed a man to death because he felt that that was his only way to protect himself and his family. And *YOUR* three month old son; Edward Jr. is in the hospital fighting for his life and it is just as much your fault as it is hers," Aunt Maggie said eloquently without even raising her voice.

"I know I'm not father of the year, but what kind of mother allows her children to starve and be physically abused when they have a nice home, a bank account full of money and someone like you living right down the street! Sure, I could have come around more but I told you I DIDN'T WANT KIDS and she forced them on me only to get them here and mistreat them for no damn reason. She could've brought them to you at any given time if she wanted to lay around on her sorry ass and get high. Matter of fact Ms. Blanch, since you insist on pointing fingers lets point one back your way. Where were you? Why weren't you checking in on the kids? How could YOU allow them to starve when YOU live right down the street?"

"You son of a bitch. How dare you even try to compare me to the two of you piss poor parents! After Patra's parents died, I've been the only stable person in those children's lives, but she stopped letting me see them because of you!" Aunt Maggie's voice began to elevate and her poised demeanor began to crack.

"What the fuck are you talking about?" Mr. Tillman asked as he slapped the table.

"Excuse me. Ms. Blanch and Mr. Tillman, we're getting off track. We have to focus on the here and now," Val interjected. I sat back and didn't say a word. She wanted so badly to be in control of *my* case; once again, so I was going to let her ass have at it.

"You know exactly what the hell I'm talking about. You saw us that day at the grocery store while you were prancing around with your wife as if you were all in love with her. You stood there in front of my niece, who you were screwing, and your illegitimate son and let me compliment you on how beautiful your relationship seemed to be with your wife. And you've done such a good job of controlling Patra and disregarding your children that you didn't even feel the need to flinch. Nor did she. I had no idea who you were. Nevertheless, she felt like I'd betrayed her and she turned away from me! And when she finally did let me back in her life, it was only sporadically because she was messed up on drugs."

"Ms. Blanch please..."Val interjected again.

"Again, how are her decisions my fault? Yes, I have a wife but I never lied to Patra once. She knew her place. That's why she didn't say anything. I've never tried to control Patra nor have I ever tried to take away her ability to choose. She may not have liked being my mistress, but she sure enjoyed reaping the benefits of it. She's a selfish, spoiled brat and we *all* have to take responsibility for that! But I will not take responsibility for *her* treatment of those children!" Mr. Tillman yelled angrily, ignoring Val.

"That's cause you're an entitled piece of shit," Aunt Maggie responded, resuming her quiet and poise demeanor.

"That's enough," I said calmly. "Mr. Tillman I know in the past that you didn't want anything to do with your children. So let me ask you how you feel now because if you still feel that way then we're wasting our time here."

"Ms. Black, I know it will be a drastic change for me, but they are my sons so they're my responsibility. And seeing as how they're mother can't do the job, then I have no choice but to do it myself," he replied.

"So how do you think your wife will respond?" I asked.

"She's pretty pissed off, so I don't even know how much longer I'll have a wife."

"Serves you right," Aunt Maggie chimed in.

"Ms. Blanch, anymore comments like that from you or Mr. Tillman and you will be asked to step outside. This meeting isn't about a love triangle gone array, it's about a 6 year old boy who will probably have nightmares for the rest of his life and a 3 month old baby who's in the hospital fighting for his life," I said sternly. "Now, let's discuss how to proceed." They knew I was serious, so I didn't have any more problems for the rest of the meeting until Val tried to resume her role as a dictator. She remained quiet throughout everything until we got to the actual decision making part and then she started trying to put in her two cents.

"Ok, the children will stay with Ms. Blanch until a CPS investigation is completed in Virginia on Mr. Tillman. If everything comes back normal, then we will place the children with their father. We will work out visitation for Miss Tanner at a later time if she is deemed fit to do so." My face began burning and I couldn't bite my tongue anymore.

"Val, can I see you outside please?" I asked as I struggled to maintain my composure until we walked outside.

"What's up Carolyn?" she asked as we stepped out into the hallway.

"Look, you're my supervisor so I won't try to undermine you in front of the clients, but this is my case and I'm tired of you trying to step in and govern things once I've cleaned up all the shit that you couldn't. There's no way in hell that those boys; especially Peter, are going to be uprooted and placed with their father without a transitional period. They've been through enough and Peter doesn't even know that man or his wife. So THIS TIME we're going to do things my way and I'm not backing down," I stated candidly and left her there with her mouth hanging open, as I re-entered the conference room. When she came back in, she sat in her seat and remained mum for the rest of the meeting.

"Ok Mr. Tillman and Ms. Blanch, this is how things are going to go. The children will remain with Ms. Blanch pending an investigation in Virginia. If everything goes well we will start setting up day visits then weekend visits with Mr. Tillman to see how the children and you, Mr. Tillman, respond. Once the kids seem to be comfortable with you Mr. Tillman then we will begin transitioning them on a more permanent basis. They will live with you fulltime but they will continue to go with Ms. Blanch every other weekend if that's cool with you, Ms. Blanch."

"Yes ma'am that's fine. I don't mind to keep them every weekend if necessary because I don't want them to forget me," Ms. Blanch replied.

"Well, Ms. Blanch, we will cross that bridge when we get there. Now, so, to wrap things up, Ms. Blanch you will assume guardianship until further notice. You will be responsible for taking the kids to their appointments and making sure that Peter attends school. We will provide you with food stamps and Mr. Tillman you will need to begin compensating Ms. Blanch for the children instead of Miss Tanner." He nodded in agreement. "Also, Peter is going to need therapy, so we are going to have to figure out whether or not to start his services here in NC or in Virginia. That's something we're going to have to brainstorm about. Oh and by the way, Miss Tanner cannot be around those children supervised or unsupervised AT ALL until further notice, do you all understand?"

"Yes." Mr. Tillman and Ms. Blanch said in unison.

"Ms. Blanch I know you have a soft spot for her, but if we find out you've been letting her see the kids without our approval, then we will remove them from your home. We will consider supervised visits later on contingent upon Miss Tanner's compliance with CPS requirements and treatment recommendations, but again you are not to allow her to see them unless we give you the word to do so. Understand?"

"Yes ma'am."

"Alright, that concludes our meeting. We'll work out all the minor details as time progresses and please feel free to contact us if you need anything. Are there any questions?"

"Uh yes, can I see the boys today?" Mr. Tillman asked. I looked at Val because I didn't know how to respond.

"Well, I feel safe with letting you see the baby because he doesn't know any better, but I would like for you to hold off with Peter because he's pretty traumatized right now. And he's not taking too kindly to strangers. I think he needs to be properly prepared before he sees you. Give it about a week or so, ok?" Val chimed in, coming to my rescue, although I loathed having to involve her.

"Ok. I understand," Mr. Tillman replied.

"Alright. Meeting adjourned," Val said.

After Mr. Tillman and Ms. Blanch were gone, Val summoned me to her office. I took a deep breath and shook my head. *Here we go.* I thought to myself.

"Yes," I replied as I stuck my head in the door.

"Come in and close the door please." Val said. I reluctantly followed her orders.

"Carolyn listen. I really appreciate your professionalism today. I'm a supervisor, but I'm not perfect and I don't always do everything right. Please forgive me."

"Val, none of us do everything right. We're humans."

"Well if that's the case then how long are you going to continue punishing me for being a human and making a bad call?" My head immediately started to pound.

"Is this why you called me in your office? Man, I'm outta here," I said and walked out.

Mr. Tillman

Mr. Tillman stood over the hospital crib where EJ, *his son,* laid, looking like a science project. Mr. Tillman took his finger and laid it onto EJ's tiny palm, which automatically closed around Mr. Tillman's finger. Mr. Tillman dropped his head and wept.

Case #: 38587 Sharquita Black

I pulled in at my Aunt Clara's house and parked the car. I laid my head back on the headrest and sighed. Any other time I would be super excited to be attending my cousin Brandon's annual "Before the Cold Comes" cookout, but I felt more anxious than anything. I wanted to scream because I didn't know what was happening to me. I felt like a zombie, although I welcomed the "dead feeling" versus the pain that threatened to rise from the place that I'd compacted it in. I was out of Xan Xan, but I figured Brandon had an ample supply of weed and liquor that would sustain me until later that night when I would be able to meet up with Jermaine, I mean Avery. I checked my makeup and got out of the car.

Brandon had convinced our Aunt Clara to let him use her house because it was in a secluded area with a super large, fenced in back yard and a swimming pool. It was big enough for him and my little brother John to invite as many chicken heads, weed heads and whatever else kind of "heads" that they wanted. The vast amount of hoopties sitting on 22's and other "pimped out" rides assured me that the "heads" inside the party were plentiful. I could hear the DJ pumping "Oh Yeah" by Big Tymers and an unexpected smile crossed my lips as I snapped my fingers, bobbed my head and walked towards the back yard. As I rounded the corner, which led to the entrance of the back yard, the simultaneous glints of gold teeth, short skirts paired with ran over shoes and the fresh smell of gun residue and weed smoke, let me know that I was most definitely at a Brandon and John Black party. I laughed to myself as I scanned the crowd, looking around for them. As to be expected, they were standing by the pool with two "bald head scallywags." I immediately almost pissed my pants, but I held it in because I could see that they were smoking a blunt and I needed some Mary Jane in my life. I quickly rushed over and joined in on the cypher so I wouldn't miss out.

"Ahhhh shit. My God, the dead has arisen," Brandon teased me as we embraced.

"Shut up! I been busy working," I replied. Brandon gave me a, "come on now" look and sucked his teeth.

"Yeah right. You ain't gotta lie to kick it," my little brother John chimed in.

"Don't worry about me. I'm good," I said, embracing him. "So what's been going on?" I asked.

"Shit. You know how we do. Smoke blunts and screw hoes," My little brother John said as he retrieved the blunt from one of his "hoes" and passed it to me. Neither of the girls said a word.

"So, how y'all ladies doing this evening?" I asked, trying to be cordial.

"Fine," they replied and then there was silence. I shrugged my shoulders and hit the blunt. After the blunt was gone, Baldhead Scallywag One and Two promptly walked off without as much as one word. I looked at Brandon and my little brother John and shook my head. Brandon, who knew why I was shaking my head, started cheesing.

"What? They ain't my girls. Those two would belong to this young man right here," Brandon said, looking at my little brother John.

"And? So what? You need to be thanking em'. My hoes took they EBT cards, bought all your food AND cooked it for you ass," my little brother John replied proudly. I dropped my head unable to contain my laughter. "What's them bullet proof hoes you got do for you besides give you sores in your mouth?" He cracked.

"Damn Brandon. It's like that?" I asked laughing. Brandon was laughing too.

"Ok, ok, you got me. You got me," he replied and then licked the side of my little brother John's face. He pushed Brandon away as both of them laughed.

"Nasty bastard. I always knew your ass was gay."

"Shut up and get your hoes to fix me a plate," Brandon replied. We continued laughing and cracking jokes as we walked over to the food table near the pool. As we were fixing our plates a big splash of water gushed across our backs, almost getting the food wet. We all jerked around in unison ready to pounce and saw a little boy playing in the swimming pool.

"Whose kid is that? I thought this was a grown-ups only party!" I hollered, pissed off because my hair and clothes were wet.

"It is. That's Sharquita's youngest son, Liberty. I saw her when she came in, but she must have snuck his little ass in. Where's her ghetto ass at?" my little brother John asked, referring to our trifling cousin Sharquita Black. At 28, one would think the heifa had some sense, but she didn't. It was like her elevator didn't go to the top or something. She had three kids that she barely paid any attention to because she was too busy partying, throwing her twat around like it was a basketball and staying in the middle of some bullshit all the time. I could handle her being naïve or ignorant and making some mistakes along the way, but this heifa flat out didn't give a damn. And if somebody in the family tried to talk to her, she got defensive and refused to take responsibility for what she had done. And she was *so* disrespectful; especially to my aunt and uncle, which really made me want to punch her in her mouth.

We took Liberty in the house and told him to dry off and stay there until somebody came to get him. Then we went looking for Sharquita and found her at the edge of the yard, leaned up against the fence talking to a gold tooth bandit. She was holding a drink in one hand and a blunt in the other.

"Sharquita! Sharquita!" I yelled. She turned around, annoyed.

"What?!"

"Heifa, what you mean 'what'? Why is your child here? This ain't no place for kids," I snapped.

"I ain't got to explain nothing to you!" she said and turned her back to me. My hand involuntarily shot out to grab her by the back of her head, but Brandon intervened.

"Well, you might not have to explain nothing to her but you sure the fuck gonna explain it to me being that this is my damn party," He said, all up in her face. When she saw he was serious, she cowered and started talking.

"Man damn! It's his birthday and I didn't wanna miss the party, so I brought him so he could play in the pool. I figured I could kill two birds with one stone. Plus, he knows better than to touch anything or talk to anybody besides his family," she said. And the fact that she was actually serious blew my mind. We all stood there dumbfounded. None of us knew what to say.

"Sharquita, what kind of sense does that make?" I asked. "Brandon has parties all the time. You could have taken that baby to Water World where kids are supposed to go and play on their birthdays. Not a freaking dark ass party where *grownups* are drinking and smoking and cussing. Do you see any other freaking kids here? And you ain't even watching him."

"Oh hell, here we go Ms. *Social Worker*. So what, am I abusing my kids now?" she asked as she took a deep pull on the blunt and blew the smoke in my face. It took everything in me to keep from socking her ass.

"Sharquita, you gonna make me put you on your back. Straight up. I'm about sick of you and your disrespectful ass. You better thank your lucky stars you're my little cousin or you'd already be on the ground," I said looking her square in her eyes to ensure that she knew I was serious. However, the heifa didn't blink an eye and she sized me up like she was ready to throw down. I guess that was the "Black" in her.

"Whatever," she said snidely.

"So where are the other kids?" my little brother John asked right on time before I pulled her hair out.

"None of your mutherfucking business. Don't question me. I'm grown," she yelled, igniting the "Black" in my little brother John, which resulted in him jerking her up by her shirt.

"What you better do is take your grown ass home before you get your grown ass beat."

"Let go of me John!" She squirmed.

"You get your shit and take that baby home right now! He's in the house in the guest room. Now go before I get a switch and beat your ass like I'm your damn daddy," Brandon yelled. John released his grip and she struggled to get her balance. She gave us all evil looks and staggered towards the house.

"She was about to get the business," my little brother John said, taking deep breaths and sweating.

"Sho was," I agreed. "So, how is her drunk ass getting home?"

"Hell, I don't even know how she got here. She probably got some scrub waiting out there for her," Brandon replied.

"Come on; let's go eat before I lose my appetite." I replied.

So, we all headed back over to the table and retrieved our plates, which my little brother John's "hoes" had kindly wrapped in aluminum foil for us. I dug into my plate and almost bit my tongue because the food was so good, but my instincts kept telling me to go check on Sharquita. I wrapped my plate back up and walked briskly towards where all the cars were parked. Brandon and my little brother John followed me. Of course, there she was, putting her little boy in the backseat of a car that *she* was driving.

"Sharquita, give me the keys so I can take you and that baby home right now!" I demanded.

"No! I don't need you for shit. I'll get us home."

I didn't even listen to her. I snatched the keys out of her hand.

"Bitch, you better give me my fucking keys!" She screamed. I continued ignoring her.

"John, I'll drive her home and you follow us in my car." I tossed him my car keys and got into the driver's seat of Sharquita's or whoever's car.

I was so angry at her that I didn't speak to her for the entire ride to her house. She was my little cousin and I loved her. However, her attitude was terrible and she made it a point to push my social worker buttons regularly, which really pissed me off because if she wasn't my cousin, she would probably be on my caseload.

When we pulled into her apartment complex, my bladder made me engage in a verbal exchange with her.

"I need to use the bathroom real quick before I leave," I said calmly.

"Well, Aunt Clara has a bathroom at her house you can use. Mine is broke," she said sarcastically.

"I can't wait that long and you have two bathrooms," I said as I opened the door and got out. She didn't move for a few seconds but she knew I wasn't going to relent; especially when my little brother John walked over and announced he had to pee as well.

"Your ass can pee anywhere John, what you need to come in my house for?"

"Sharquita, look, ain't nobody got time for this bullshit. Here's my hand to the Lord, if you don't open up that door and let us use the bathroom, you're right...I'm going to pee anywhere and I promise I'ma start by pissing on you," my little brother John said sternly. Sharquita sucked her teeth.

"Come on," she snapped. We walked into her house, which was spotless clean. Even the walls sparkled as if someone was cleaning them regularly. Wall and window washing only occurred at my house when I had the extra money to pay someone to come and do it for me, so I was proud of her for her cleanliness.

"Now, which one of your bathrooms can I use?" I asked.

"The one in the hallway. John you can use the one in my bedroom. And hurry the fuck up so y'all can get out."

I skedaddled to the bathroom because I was less than sixty seconds away from peeing on myself. I pulled up the skirt portion of my beautiful red sundress and squatted over the toilet seat. After I finished using the bathroom, I walked out into the hallway just as a little voice was saying, "Mommy I'm hungry." I assumed it was Liberty talking until another voice chimed in. "Uh mommy, ma'am, Justice and I have to go to the bathroom." I then heard Sharquita's voice whisper too loudly, "Shut up and wait till they're gone!"

No this heifa didn't leave these kids home by themselves, I thought to myself as I headed into the kid's room. When I walked in, she was standing over them, daring them to speak or move. She jerked her head towards me.

"Get the fuck outta here," she snapped. I looked at the kids who were petrified and then my little brother John walked in.

"What's going on? Ah shoot, what's up Percy and Justice?" he said as he walked over to give 10 year old Percy some dap and 5 year old Justice a hug. But neither of them moved until Sharquita gave them a look; giving them permission to speak back.

"Sharquita, please don't tell me you left these two kids here while you were at the party?" I asked, trying to give her the benefit of the doubt.

"Don't come in my house trying to judge me."

"I didn't come in here to judge you. I just asked you a question," I replied frankly.

"And I don't have to answer. This is my house and you need to get the fuck out. What you gonna do? Call DSS on me so I can tell them about how you was smoking weed with me at the party and then drove us home high. Ha, ha, ha. Stupid Bitch. You ain't so hot now are you?" She said, trying to threaten me, which didn't work by the way.

I walked straight up on her and looked her right in her eyes. "Listen Sharquita. Instead of you worrying about trying to throw somebody under the bus, we need to be talking about these kids. Ain't nobody out to get you. We all love you, but you be doing some foul shit. Hell, if you was gonna bring Liberty to the party for *his birthday,* you shoulda went on and brought the other two," I said as calmly as possible, truly flabbergasted at this broad's actions.

"I wanted to go to the party and I couldn't get nobody to babysit. I only took Liberty because I figured I would be able to get by with him being there instead of all three. I miss Brandon's cookout almost every year and I didn't plan on staying no more than 2 or 3 hours. I fed them, gave them their baths and I made those two get in the bed, so I could take Justice with me. My kids are smart," she boasted. "I trained them well. They know what to touch, what not to touch and they damn sure know not to leave this house or let anybody in."

"Ok Sharquita, I understand but what if the house would have caught on fire, what if someone had broken in? Look I'm sorry, it would be different if you were trying to go to work or something like that but Sharquita you were going to a party; getting drunk and high while your kids were unattended."

"Well, what was I supposed to do? I told you I couldn't take all three with me," she asked, serious as a hard attack.

This broad is really crazy. I thought to myself.

"Sharquita, honey, that's when you make the decision to stay home or go somewhere where the kids are welcome. That's what being a parent is all about," my little brother John chimed in. She looked at us both like we were crazy. Like staying home would never be on the list of options.

"Look, I don't need your advice on how to raise my kids. Neither one of y'all have kids so how the fuck would you know?"

"Well, common sense for starters," I snapped getting fed up with her ignorance. "They are little kids Sharquita and you have to keep your eye on them so that you can make sure they're ok. When they get close to their teenage years, if they're mature enough, then you can start leaving them home alone for short periods of time. But not kids under 10," I tried to explain rationally.

"I know what I'm doing and I know how to take care of my kids. I know what they need and how to protect them. They ain't got hurt yet have they?" She argued.

"Sharquita, you really are crazy. I don't know where your ass came from. You ain't no Black acting like that," my little brother John said, shaking his head.

"Fuck y'all and get y'all's *Black* asses the fuck outta my house," she yelled. I shook my head and kissed the kids goodbye. In the car, me and my little brother John couldn't get over how retarded Sharquita was.

"That bitch is crazy Cee. Did you see how scared the kids was when I tried to speak to them?"

"Yeah, I saw it."

"I got a bad feeling about her Cee. The way she thinks is distorted as hell and I don't know where she gets that from."

"I do! Aunt Brenda and Uncle Lee spoiled her to death and gave her whatever she wanted. Now she's ruined."

"Yeah that's true," my little brother John agreed. We returned to the party and I actually found myself having a good time until Brandon; in his high state of mind, started reminiscing about Sylvia.

"Man, can y'all believe Sylvia's gone? She used to love coming to this cookout; her and Olivia."

"I know man. I miss my sister so much," my little brother John replied as a tear slid down his cheek. I began feeling pressure in my chest as the compacted hurt began to rise.

"Um, I gotta go. I'll see y'all later," I replied and jetted out of there without letting them respond. I gulped in the air and took as many deep breaths as I could. I was still holding my red Solo cup, which was half-full of vodka, so I chugged it down and immediately almost hacked my lungs up. I jumped in the car and called Jermaine, I mean Avery, as quickly as my fingers would let me dial his number. I cursed myself because I knew better than to come to any family gathering without Xan Xan.

"What's up baby?"

"Nothing, where you at?" I asked.

"I'm riding around and getting it baby. You wanting some of this thick black cock huh?"

Uh...no not really, I thought to myself but I knew I had to go through him to get to Xan Xan. "Yeah daddy, that's all I could think about all day long," I replied as I almost threw up in my mouth.

"Well, daddy's kinda busy right now so I'ma have to take a rain check. But maybe we can get together tomorrow sometime."

"No! I mean, no daddy. I need that pole now." Which translated into I need that Xan Xan now.

"Well, I'm sorry baby. Zian is in labor and I'm about to head to the hospital so I can meet my baby girl. Plus me and her been talking about getting back together anyway so you and me might have to chill for a while. I'm trying to do the right thing by my kid."

*You mutha...*I thought to myself, but I kept my cool, although my heart was pounding, the pressure was mounting and the emotional pain was rising at a top speed.

"Ok yeah, I understand that. That's cool. Well, do you have any Xan Xan on you this one last time?" I asked, trying to mask my desperation.

"Damn baby. Are you hooked? I might not need to give you no more if you can't handle it," he replied smugly.

"I can handle it. Where can we meet?"

"Damn baby. You need it like that?"

"Yes damnit! Now please, meet me out somewhere or I'll meet you at the store across the street from the hospital," I said swallowing all my pride.

"Word. Well since you fiending like that, I'll meet you. But I'm almost there so if you ain't there in the next ten minutes then I'm sorry."

"I'll be there," I replied and hung up although I didn't know how in the hell I was going to get there in ten minutes; especially since Aunt Clara's house was in the rural part of Fosterberg County. However, my need for Xan Xan got me there in record breaking time, even though I damn near had a few head on collisions in the process. I immediately recognized Jermaine, I mean Avery's car parked discreetly in a dark area on the side of the store and pulled in beside of him. I jumped out and got into his car.

"Damn girl. You acting like a crack head right now."

"Look, just give me the muthafucking Xanax ok," I said impatiently.

"Ok, but what am I going to get in return?"

"Dude, you said you had to get to the hospital and that you were ending things so what do you expect me to do in return?" I asked getting very annoyed.

"Well baby, since this is the end and we are right across from the hospital, I'll give you enough time to suck my dick real quick as a means of payment."

"What? Dude I've never given you head so what makes you think you about to get it now?" I asked, starting to get heated.

"Bitch, you want this Xanax don't you?" he said, shaking a pill bottle full of Xan Xan in my face, enticing me. The fact that he'd just called me a bitch and asked me to give him head was paused for a second at the site of those pills. But, although I was at a very low point in my life, my pride still wouldn't allow me to drop to my knees. However, my mom had an old saying, "there's more than one way to skin a cat" and although, it sounded completely inhumane, it was very fitting for the situation. I pretended like I was getting out of the car and opened the door. But then I "hesitated" and turned and looked back at him and Xan Xan for a second. He looked like a man mixed with a serpent and it scared me shitless. Nevertheless, I carried on with my plan. I hit him with a two-piece and snatched the pills out of his hands. I attempted to jump out of the car but he grabbed me by my hair and violently jerked me back.

"Bitch!" he yelled and backhanded me, just as I heard the sound of glass shattering everywhere. And out of the blue I saw Demarcus punching Jermaine, I mean Avery through the broken, driver's side window.

"Carolyn, get in your car now!" Demarcus yelled. I could hear my adrenaline pumping in my ears but instead of listening to Demarcus, I joined him in beating Jermaine, I mean Avery's ass. But just as I was about to black out and release all my anger and rage on Jermaine, I mean Avery, I felt two strong arms jerk me out of the car, causing the Xan Xan, which I had clutched in my hand as I was swinging, to drop to the ground. It rolled under the car before I could retrieve it.

"No! No! I need those," I screamed as I tried to get the pills.

"Get your ass in this car!" Demarcus yelled as he threw me in the passenger side of my car and ran to get in the driver's seat. I saw Jermaine, I mean Avery, who was starting to recover from the blows reach down under the passenger seat of his car.

"He's got a gun! Hurry Demarcus!" I yelled.

"You fucking junky! You fucking pill head! Yeah that's right; a fucking bad ass social worker who was about to suck my dick for a hit!" I heard Jermaine, I mean Avery yell as he laughed like a hyena. Demarcus jumped in the car and squealed tires getting out of there.

We rode in silence for what seemed like forever, with the exception of a call he made to tell someone to pick up his car for him. Otherwise, he said nothing to me. I was so embarrassed and ashamed. And I could tell that he was furious because he was flexing his jawbone and I saw the veins popping out near his temple. For once in my life, I was actually afraid to speak, so I looked out the window. I noticed that we were going in the complete opposite direction of my house. Buildings turned into empty streets, streets turned into fields and fields turned into woods. For a minute, I started getting nervous.

"Uh, where are we going?" I asked.

He ignored me and kept driving.

"Demarcus, where are we going?" I asked as my heart started beating harder. He still refused to answer. A few minutes later, we finally reached some civilization, although it was minimal. We entered a little town called Vashnite and pulled into a small apartment complex. Demarcus pulled into a parking spot, slammed the car in park, then turned and looked at me. He resembled a raging bull.

"Who the fuck was that dude and what was he serving you?" He asked bluntly with fiery eyes that shook me to the core. I'd never seen him so angry before.

"Uh, uh, uh..." I stammered.

"Answer me, damnit!"

"I'm too tired to fight with you Demarcus. I don't have the energy," I replied in an attempt to keep from answering him.

"Carolyn, I'm not fucking playing with you! Now answer me!"

I lost control. "None of your fucking business!" I screamed so fiercely that it sucked the air out of my body. He grabbed me and began shaking me.

"Tell me! Tell me right now!"

"No!"

"Tell me! I heard him call you a junky and a pill head! And I saw the way you went crazy trying to get to that fucking pill bottle tonight and the last two times I came by your house! Now tell me!"

"Are you more concerned about that or the fact that I was going to suck his dick for them?" I asked vindictively, followed by an involuntary lick of my lips. It was a low blow and it came out before I could stop it. It was as if I didn't have control over my own mouth. He took the blow; however, and he kept going although I could tell I'd wounded him.

"Stop trying to avoid the question and answer me! I swear before the good Lord if you don't tell me, you can be on your way and I'm never fucking with your ass again. I mean that with everything in me!"

"Good mutherfucker! Good! You think that bothers me! Where you been for the last 6 months? Huh? I'll tell you where! You been up another woman's ass, not mine, so what does it matter if your black ass walks out again? Plus, since I'm a junky, I have another blowjob to give so I can get high. Fuck you and get your ass out of my car!" I screamed. He sat there silently as his chest rose and fell indicatively. I'd stumped him. I felt like I'd walked through hell only to step into the valley of the shadow of death. He'd been one of the major things to burn me and leave me hanging yet here he was making demands. I felt myself wanting to mush him in his face, but even I wasn't that crazy, especially sense he was just as angry and irrational as I was. However, I didn't know how long I could restrain myself, so I decided the best thing for me to do was to call his bluff.

"Demarcus, um did you hear what I said? GET THE FUCK OUT OF MY CAR!"

A car pulled in beside us and we both jerked our heads towards the window nervously. We were both relieved to see that it was Demarcus' midnight blue, 1970's Cadillac. Apparently, whomever he called to get his car from the gas station had arrived.

"You sure you wanna do this?" he asked as he turned back towards me.

"You heard me. Bounce."

"Alright then." He opened the door and turned back towards me. "I'ma pray for you and I love you." He got out and slammed the door behind him. I shot him a bird and backed out furiously. I drove to the entrance of the apartment complex and put my address in my smartphone. Once I was on my way home, I thought back over everything. It was as if it happened but it didn't happen, liked I'd dreamed it. One thing that became clear was that I was now going to have to figure out another way to get Xan Xan since Jermaine, I mean Avery was obviously no longer an option. Then, I remembered that I'd dropped a whole bottle of Xan Xan at the store and since it was dark, they were probably still there.

"Yasssss!" I yelled happily. I turned up the radio, grabbed my phone and began searching the address to the hospital since the store was right across the street. As I was typing, I saw bright lights coming in my direction. I looked up and noticed that I was across the yellow line. I panicked and overcorrected which sent my car onto the soft but rocky shoulder. I heard a loud pop and my car began bouncing and rumbling. Once I was finally able to come to a stop and get my nerves together, I got out and assessed the damage. My back passenger tire was completely flat and the rim was bent.

"Of course. Why not? Why wouldn't my tire get flattened out here in the middle of no man's land at night?" I said out loud sarcastically. Luckily, I had AAA so I got back in the car and called them. However, they informed me that it would probably take two to three hours before they could get to me. I shook my head, "of course."

I gave them my location anyway and hung up. I searched for tow companies and began calling them. Most of them were closed or didn't come to Vashnite. When I finally called Vashnite's only towing company, the man's voice was so creepy that I hung up. My phone began beeping, indicating that it was about to die.

"Noooooo!" I welled. I began trying desperately to figure out who else I could call. I definitely wasn't going to call Demarcus and I couldn't call Brandon or my little brother John after I'd ran out on them. I couldn't call Jarrod, I couldn't call Val and I couldn't call my parents. I had no one. My phone beeped again and I knew I had to make a decision fast. A car rode past me and then put on its breaks. My heart began pounding and my hands started shaking. I locked the doors and looked around to see what I could use as a weapon. The car backed up. It was Demarcus. I exhaled a sigh of relief and laid my head back in order to let my heart calm down. He got out and walked towards me.

"You alright?" he asked.

"Yeah, I just ran over something and got a flat tire," I replied telling half of the truth.

"You need a ride?"

"Nah I'm good." *What the?!* I screamed inside my head. I wanted to kick myself because for the second time in less than an hour, I'd put my foot all the way down my throat.

"Alright." He turned and walked away. I watched as he began disappearing in the darkness of night with only his taillights serving as a guide. I gave my pride the middle finger and stuck my head out the window.

"Demarcus! Demarcus! Wait!" I yelled as I grabbed my things. I hung a white towel outside the window, locked the car up and ran to him.

"I uh, do need a ride." I said as I tried to catch my breath.

"Ok. But not until you answer my question."

"Are you freaking kidding me?"

"No, I'm not," He replied earnestly.

"Whatever. You tripping." I said and walked towards his car boldly. He firmly but gently, grabbed me by the back of my shoulders and twirled me back around towards my car.

"You have ten seconds and I'm leaving. One...two...three...four...five...six...seven...eight..."

I glared at him but I knew he was serious therefore I was at his mercy. "Xanax." I said through gritted teeth.

"What?"

"You heard me, now let's go!"

"No, I didn't hear you clearly."

"I said Xanax punk!"

"Alright...let's go."

I slid in the back seat since Demarcus' homeboy was sitting in the front. I didn't mind because I was happy for the distraction.

"You must be Carolyn. I heard a lot about you. My name is Mont," a pecan complexioned young man replied as he stuck his hand out to me. I was happy for the darkness because I'm sure I blushed.

"Nice to meet you Mont," I replied. *Wow, Demarcus told him about me?* I almost squealed to myself as a smile threatened my lips.

"I'ma take Mont home and then I'll drop you off," Demarcus said.

"Alright," I said and let the cushy leather seats embrace me. I laid my head back and closed my eyes.

"Carolyn, wake up. Wake up sissy. Let's go outside and play."

"Ok Sthia."

"Here, give me your hand. We're going to make mud pies."

"Yay! Mud pies!

"Here, help me open the door Carolyn."

"Ok Sthia."

"Push."

"Uuuhhh""

"Ok, there it goes. Come on. Give me your hand."

"Ok Sthia."

"Ooooo. It feels good out here."

"It bright. It bright. Hurt my eyes Sthia."

"Here Carolyn, take your hand and cover your eyes like this."
"Ok Sthia."
"Better?"
"Yep!"
"Ok come on."
"Here's the mud hole Carolyn, but we have to sit right here on the grass so we don't get muddy."
"Tha mud is red!"
"Uh huh and we're going to make cherry mud pies."
"Yay, yay, yay!"
"Oh man!"
"What wong Sthia?"
"I forgot the pan."
"Oh."
"I'm going to get the pan. I'll be right back."
"Oooo, da mud feel cold. Wait! I goin' wich you Sthia."
"Carolyn duck now!"
"...Ahhh! I fall in tha red mud hole."
"Owwww! That hurt! Why'd you do that Olivia?"
"I told you not to play with her Sylvia. I meant to hit her. You shoulda let me hit her.
"Go away Olivia. You're evil.
"Can I get up now Sthia?"
"Yah."
"Huuh! Sthia! Tha red mud cuber ya face!"
"I know Carolyn... I'm ok. Listen Carolyn, Olivia wants to hurt you. Watch her."
"Why Sthia?"
"I don't know why ok!"
"Ok. I love you Sthia."
"I know. And I love you too."
"Sthia, where you going? You disappear! Sthia! Sthia!"

"Carolyn, wake up. Wake up, ma. It's ok." I sat up and looked around as sweat poured down my brow. I was still in the backseat of Demarcus' car. Demarcus was squatted on the pavement leaning over me. I gulped for air and tried to shake the images of my dream.

"Come on. Get out," he said as he helped me out of the car.

"Where are we?" I asked, realizing that we weren't in my driveway, but back at the apartments in no man's land. He sighed.

"Well I wanted it to be a surprise, but since that's shot all to hell because I can't let you go home tonight with that wack ass dude on the loose, welcome to my home."

"Your home?"

"Yeah. I got my own shit," he said as he led me to his apartment door and unlocked it.

"You have to excuse the crib because I just moved in about three weeks ago and I really don't have a lot of furniture yet."

I followed him in cautiously. "Be careful and watch your step. I have shit everywhere." He walked in and flipped on a light switch by the door. I entered very slowly and cautiously behind him. The apartment was very small and it pretty much looked like one big room whereby the living room and kitchen were only divided by the tile and carpet floors and the bedroom, by a wall and the door. The only furniture he had was a flat screen TV, mounted to the wall and a kitchen table with two mix matched chairs. A few boxes and plastic bags with various supplies scattered the floor. And although I could see everything clearly, I still looked around trying to see if Charmanita was going to jump out from somewhere.

"Demarcus, what is this? What's going on? Where are we?" I asked curiously.

"Well, I was going to wait until I had the place together before I brought you here, but since you're so insistent on being a wet dream killer, I decided to go ahead and show it to you. This is my spot. I been working and saving up my loot so I could make my move. I been planning on leaving *her* for a minute so I started getting my shit together. I got my contracting license and I got hired up here in Vashnite as a paid apprentice. I'm working under this white man who is going to show me everything and then eventually promote me or help me start my own contracting business. I make some really good money and they give me full benefits. The cost of living here is cheap as hell so I got this little spot to start me and my son out," he said proudly as he looked around his place like it was a mansion. I stood there quietly, waiting for him to continue because the residue of burnt, over processed red weave still floated around in my mind and unfortunately I wasn't impressed yet. I needed answers. He looked over at me and waited for me to respond, but I said nothing. He sighed.

"Ok. What is it now Carolyn, damn?"

"Where's Charmanita?" I asked bluntly.

"What do you mean? I guess she's home. Where else would she be?"

"Don't play with me dude. You owe me way more than 'I left her,'" I replied.

"Alright. Cool. Come over here and sit down." We sat in the two mixed matched chairs at a small table and he pulled out a half of a blunt. He handed the blunt and a lighter to me as he got up and walked over to the refrigerator. He pulled out two beers and walked back over to me. I lit the blunt and took a few pulls on it. I passed it to Demarcus and remained silent as I waited for him to begin talking.

He took a long pull, held it in for a while and then exhaled slowly. He was really getting on my nerves prolonging things. I was ready to slap the words out of his mouth.

"Demarcus! Any day now dude," I snapped. He looked at me, took another long pull and completely ignored the fact that I was totally annoyed. If I hadn't been in no man's land, with no way to get home, I would have bounced. He passed me the blunt, which I snatched out of his hand. I took a long pull myself so that I could calm down and relax.

"Ok, so, you want the whole story then I'll tell you. Don't interrupt me and don't say shit until I'm done. You got that?" He asked seriously.

"Yeah whatever. Just tell me," I replied.

"Alright. You remember last year when you and me first started back kicking it and we rode to the beach for the night and came back early the next morning? Well, when I got home she..." I cut him off.

"Stop calling Charmanita *she* and *her*! Say her name! She's real Demarcus! She's your fucking wife, say her name!" I said furiously because I was tired of playing games. This was our lives and everything from our past and present was real. I didn't want to dance around the bush no more because the pain had also been real. The pain was still real. I hated hearing her name come out of his mouth, but a punch in my face and him throwing me through the air *for her* had been my confirmation that not only did she exist, *they* existed. Therefore, I had no time or tolerance for sugar coating and avoidance.

"Carolyn, you are really tripping," he replied, but he saw that I wasn't playing so he obliged me. "Ok, like I was saying, so when I got home, Charmanita..." He said her name like it made his breath stink. "Was laying on the bed naked with her legs spread, playing with herself? I knew I was gonna have to bang her or else she woulda suspected something, so I went and got in the shower." I clinched my jaw. "For the first time since I was 10 years old I prayed. I asked God to forgive me for marrying her but I thanked Him for my son. I told Him that I wanted to be with you and as long as I had you, my son, and a way to provide for y'all, I wouldn't need nothing else in this world. I ain't about no bargaining, especially with God, but I welcomed Him into my life and I told Him that I was willing to learn how to let Him be the head of our household if He answered my prayer. So anyway, after I got out of the shower, I banged her brains out, but as soon as I got done, I went straight and signed up for the Contractor's course. I was working, hustling and going to school but I still couldn't figure out a reason to leave her that wouldn't set her off. I definitely couldn't let her find out about you." He stopped, took a drink from his beer and continued.

"Alright, so remember when I came to see you a few months ago and told you that she...I mean, Charmanita got locked up?" I nodded and he continued. "Well, that next week, I was looking for something in the bathroom and I found some condoms...and we ain't never used condoms. So, at first, it really, really pissed me off but then as I calmed down and started really thinking about it, I realized that that was my way out." He started smiling unconsciously, his eyes full of pride. He continued. I remained silent, smiling to myself on the inside, but wearing my poker face on the outside.

"Well, when I went to visit her at the spot, I told her that I was done because she was a liar and she couldn't stay out of jail. She cried and shit, but she knew I was serious and wasn't no changing my mind. She accepted it because deep down she knew that neither of us loved each other anyway. So I stayed at our spot until the night before she got out of jail and then me and my son went to stay at my homeboy's crib. She got out of jail and everything went pretty smooth. We was doing the good co-parenting thang and getting along. She let me come get my son whenever I wanted and since my homeboy has a son too, it worked out. I started putting in applications and kept doing my thang on the low. I stayed away from you because I had to stay focused. Plus, I didn't want to step to you until I had my shit together. But when both of y'all showed up at the club that night it caught me off guard. I just reacted the best way I knew how so I wouldn't blow my cover. It killed me to treat you like that, but I knew that if she..."He rolled his eyes. "If *Charmanita* found out about you then everything I was doing would be over because she woulda never let me go. And I know that if I wouldna grabbed you then y'all woulda fought to the death. Charmanita can fight and your crazy ass can too, so I apologize but I did what I had to do. Plus, your crazy ass cousin about broke my damn jaw." He stopped and looked at me, trying to read my face. He had a kooky smile on his face, but I had no clue what mine looked like because my emotions were like scrambled eggs. I felt wonderful, but at the same time, I felt doubtful. Although I saw the apartment and heard the words that he was saying, I still didn't know if any of it was real. Or if it was going to last. Or how long we would have to walk on eggshells before we could really be together. And I still didn't fully understand what he was saying to me. He kept telling me stories without getting to the actual "moral" of it.

"Ok, so what do you think? What do you have to say?"

"Well Slick Rick, you've definitely sat here and told me a 'Bedtime Story' but you still haven't made it clear what you want and what's going to happen," I replied frankly.

He pounded his fist on the table angrily. "Damn Cee! What don't you understand? I couldn't fake that shit with her! SHIT! I mean with CHARMANITA, another day after me and you got back from the beach. I got a degree, a good job, a place to stay, and my son is going to be coming soon. Cee, you're the final piece of the puzzle and...I gotta have you."

"Well what about Charmanita?"

"What about Charmanita Cee?!" He yelled with fire in his eyes. The poor table endured another punch, but this time it came from me because my level of passion was just as high as his.

"I been through too much for you to beat around the bush and tell me what you think I need to know. I wanna know how long she's gonna have you by your balls. I wanna know how long I'm going to continue having to remain a secret." I then leaned in and locked eyes with him because I wanted to make sure that he had no question about what I needed to hear. "I wanna know when I get to go on an actual date outside of the house with you. I wanna know when I get to walk around in public holding your hand?" My voice began trembling as it elevated. "I want to know when everybody else besides me and you will be able to know how we feel about each other. That's what I want to know!" I yelled as my body shook.

"Cee, she's not going to have me by the balls long. I promise. Just give me some time. I have to be careful about every move I make until the time is right." He paused and moved around in his seat nervously. "I wasn't even going to deal with you until I had everything completely together but...but I can't stay away from your crazy ass that long. It's going to be risky as hell Cee because if she finds out about you then it's going to be war. But if you let me do things the way I have them planned then all the rest will fall into place."

"And when is that going to be?" I asked.

"Look, I've gotta be separated from her for a year and one day before I can divorce her. I only have a couple months left. But in the meantime, if you'll have me, I plan on waking up with you from now on except the days I have my son. And that's only until we have the divorce and custody papers completed."

I didn't respond. It was a lot to digest.

"Oh yeah, I almost forgot. I'll be right back." He ran outside and then returned shortly thereafter carrying a medium size black gift bag and another black, plastic bag with shoes in it. He handed me the gift bag.

"Happy birthday Cee. I got you a little gift. I know you thought I forgot but I didn't. I rode by your house because I was going to drop them off, but I saw you and some other woman getting in the car with a man, so I kept going. You looked beautiful in that gold looking dress you were wearing." My heart melted until my thoughts carried me to my birthday party...and beyond. I blinked and focused back on Demarcus.

"Anyway, I held onto your gift because I knew I would get to give it to you eventually. Open it." I pulled out the tissue paper and inside was a black box with the Jordon label on it. I opened the box and inside was a pair of the hottest Jordon's I'd ever seen. They were custom designed with different splashes of color and graffiti on them.

"They dope ain't they? I bought me a pair too." He smiled. I felt myself getting choked up but for a good reason this time.

"I love them. Thanks Demarcus." I got up and hugged him. We embraced, and it was as if I was a key finally being reunited with my lock, Demarcus. I gripped him with every ounce of strength I had and he reciprocated. He rubbed my hair and planted light kisses on my forehead.

"Cee, I'm sorry I missed your birthday."

"Me too," I replied honestly.

"So um, now that I told you everything, it's your turn," he said. I rolled my eyes.

"Here we go," I said sarcastically.

"I'm not going to judge you Cee. Seriously. Who am I to judge you?"

"I don't want to talk about it Demarcus."

"Well, I didn't want to talk about Charmanita but I did. Now tell me what made you start taking Xanax?"

"I don't wanna talk about it. Let's talk about something else. Tell me about your son," I begged.

"Who's Sthia?"

"What?!"

"You heard me. Who's Sthia? When you were in the car asleep, you kept telling her you loved her, but you also kept asking her where she was going. You seemed pretty distressed, that's why I woke you up."

I shook my head. "You just don't stop do you? I don't want to talk about it. Don't you get it! Take me home please."

"Ok, ok I'm sorry. So since I missed your birthday; tell me what you did," he said. Memories started flooding my mind and I got agitated.

"SHUT UP!" I yelled and covered my ears. Demarcus looked at me like I was crazy. And I agreed with his look because I felt crazy. My phone started ringing and I rammed my hand inside my purse to retrieve it. As I was pulling it out, I saw two Xan Xan smiling up at me. I wanted to do a cartwheel because I forgot that I'd put two emergency Xan Xan in my purse after I'd slept with Officer Petrea to keep myself from getting in that type of situation again.

I looked down at my phone and it read Xan Xan, which meant it was Jermaine, I mean Avery. I sent it straight to voicemail and then a text came through. It read: Bitch, you and your punk ass boyfriend are dead.

I didn't respond and slammed my phone back in my purse. I started trying to figure out how I could ditch Demarcus so I could pop Xan Xan. I stood up and clutched my purse.

"I need to go to the bathroom," I said and began heading in the direction I assumed the bathroom would be. But Demarcus stood up and blocked me.

"I ain't got no bathroom."

"Seriously, I need to go to the bathroom," I said, slightly pushing him aside.

"Hell no, you ain't getting off that easy. You gonna sit your ass right here and talk to me."

"Look, unless you want me to piss on your kitchen floor...and I'm known to piss on people's property, then I suggest you let me go to the bathroom."

"Well piss on the floor then. I have a mop, some hot water and some bleach. Now sit down."

"No! I need to go to the bathroom. Now stop playing with me."

"Fuck it. Go ahead and get yourself together. It's through that door to the right." He stepped aside and I took off. "Your ass is still gonna talk when you get back and ain't no window in there, so don't get no slick ideas," I heard him say behind me. I walked into the bathroom and locked the door. I grabbed Xan Xan out of my purse, waited a few seconds and flushed the toilet. I turned the sink on and breathed a sigh of relief as I prepared to pop Xan Xan in my mouth. Suddenly I heard a loud BANG! I whirled around and saw that Demarcus had kicked the door in. He saw that I had Xan Xan balled up safely in one hand while the other was cupped and holding faucet water. The bull in him returned and he rushed me. He tried to pry my hand open, but I had it clamped so tightly that my fingernails were digging into my skin. He threw me against the wall and started choking me. He pinned my wet hand above my head and he let the one holding Xan Xan go free. I knew what he was doing and I called his bluff. There was no way I was letting go of Xan Xan, so I used that arm to swing. However, due to the position he had me in; my swings were weak as dishwater and useless.

"Let it go! Drop it!" His grip tightened around my neck. I started to feel weak and I couldn't breathe, but I knew he would only go but so far, so I fought it out.

"You really have become a fucking junkie! You would rather let me choke you to death than drop that shit on the floor?" I closed my eyes so I could concentrate on breathing but Sylvia stood behind my eyelids and her face was bloody. I jerked my eyes open and almost had a panic attack. Seeing the fear in my eyes, Demarcus let me go. As I gulped air with Xan Xan still clutched in my hand, I saw Demarcus slide down the wall to the floor out the corner of my eye. As soon as I had enough air in me, I ran back to the sink. I popped Xan Xan in my mouth and bent over to get some water but I caught a glimpse of myself in the mirror. My mouth was partially open and I could see the two pills on my tongue. I also saw Demarcus and he was staring straight at me. I looked away and proceeded with getting water.

"Stop running Cee. Go on and feel whatever it is you dealing with so you can get it over with. Shit's gonna sting for a while, but you'll make it. And I'll be right here beside you."

I paused and contemplated "feeling it." The pills sat on my tongue dissolving. The taste was disgusting...but the pain was too heavy for me to care.

"Feel it damnit! Stop being a pussy and feel it!" Demarcus said as he walked up behind me. I began to pant, but I never let the nasty tasting pills slide from my tongue.

"I'm sorry for calling you a junkie but you're stronger than this Cee. Pain is a part of life that everybody has to walk through sometimes, but you can't ignore it because it's never going to go away until you deal with it. Spit that shit out and fight!"

I felt the pressure in my chest and the hurt began to crawl from the bottom of my feet to the top of my head. I squeezed the sides of the sink and let Xan Xan slide from my tongue into the sink. As I watch my trip to Hawaii go down the drain, a single tear dropped from my eye. The tear that had sat there waiting patiently since my sister had died. The tear that I'd been fighting so ferociously, it'd turned me into a pill-popping whore. Jarrod, Jermaine, I mean Avery, Officer Petrea, the way I'd been treating Val and the way I'd been treating myself flooded my mind. I was so ashamed that I couldn't raise my head, but then I felt Demarcus' hand rubbing my back and I finally felt safe enough to let go. My body began shaking and a waterfall of tears erupted out of me in a scream.

"SYLVIA! AHHHHHHHHHH! SYLVIA! SYLVIA!" Suddenly I began to feel like I was going to suffocate, so I ran outside. I fell to my knees and took in gulps of fresh air in order to replenish my lungs. Demarcus stood right beside me, watching me; protecting me. Once I had the ability to breathe again, he picked me up and carried me back into his apartment. I was so limp and weary that I was unable to bask in the fact that he was carrying me. All I could do was lay my head on his shoulder and rely on his strength. It took everything in me just to inhale and exhale but the tears never ceased.

He carried me into the apartment and sat down in one of the chairs. He repositioned me in his lap so that we were both comfortable and retightened his grip on me. He kissed the top of my head and began rocking me. When I was finally ready to talk, I spilled my guts starting with my childhood issues with my sisters, up until the day I started taking Xan Xan to keep from accepting the death of my sister. I left out my sexual escapades from fear that he would look at me like a whore, but it didn't matter because *I* looked at me like a whore. Once I was done talking, the pain was almost unbearable, but laying on his chest gave me relief. Exhausted, I closed my eyes.

Three weeks later
Sharquita Black

Sharquita walked over to her cd player, took her Queen cd out, wiped it off and put it back into the CD player. She resumed playing "Bohemian Rhapsody" which she'd been playing back to back for the past three days and turned the volume up as loud as it would go. She walked back over to the kitchen table whereby she also proudly resumed her task of snorting her entire name; spelled out in pure Colombian cocaine. So far, over the past three days, she'd only made it to the "q" in Sharquita because although she was no stranger to cocaine or anything else, it was some very strong blow and it was taking her a little longer than she anticipated. She only snorted the curve of the "q" because there was no way that she was ready to handle the tail yet. She then lifted her head and joined in on the song. She swayed and glided her arms through the air. Then she started cleaning and skipping around the house, dancing and singing. "Bohemian Rhapsody" was her "me time" song when all she wanted to do was clean her house, let loose and get as high as she could. And her kids knew that when she was playing that song they weren't allowed to come out of their rooms...for anything. And she blamed that uppity bitch Carolyn because since Carolyn had pulled that CPS shit on her, she had had to stay home with those little bastards instead of being out partying with her friends and kicking it with her new boo.

At five, eight and ten, she personally felt like they were old enough to take care of themselves anyway. They knew not to touch anything electrical and they definitely knew better than to touch any lighters or matches. Percy was the one they had to thank for that lesson because she'd beat the skin off his legs when she saw him playing with a pack of her matches. And being that when she was out, she made sure that they always had food, running water, cable TV and clean clothes, therefore, she didn't understand what the big deal was. As she glided towards the laundry room, she praised herself because she had always chosen to get high outside her home when the kids weren't around or when they were asleep, but now because of that bitch Carolyn, she didn't have a choice anymore. Before they were free to roam throughout the house, go into the refrigerator, take showers and use the bathroom as they pleased as long as they cleaned up their mess and didn't tear up anything. And she had always made sure that they had all types of toys and games so they could keep themselves occupied while she was out doing her thing. Now since Carolyn had forced her to start getting high at home and/or entertain her company at home with the kids there, she had no choice but to confine them all to Percy and Liberty's bedroom because it was the largest. Now the kids didn't have the privilege of roaming freely as they had before hence, causing her to have to take time away from what she was doing in order to cater to them. However, she felt proud that they would at least be in the room together; therefore, they wouldn't be lonely and could play together. And she also felt proud that she continued to do her best to keep from exposing them to her "adult activities."

Her hands wisped through the air as she directed the symphony from "Bohemian Rhapsody" and she finally got the nerve to snort the tail of the white "q". So she floated to the kitchen and bravely took the line in through her nose. It hit her hard and she had to get herself together. The up tempo portion at the end of the song began playing and she started head banging. She jumped and head banged as she danced towards the bathroom so she could clean it...again. As she danced past the kid's door, the devil on her shoulder redirected her attention. She burst into their bedroom in an attempt to not only scare them, but to hopefully catch them in the act of doing something that she could punish them for, especially since it pissed her off that she now had to *serve* kids who she was trying to teach to be self-sufficient. The kids who were sitting on the bed jumped up; startled. The odor in the room from the "bathroom bucket" she'd given them almost took her breath away, which enraged her coke elated mind.

"Why THE FUCK does this muthafucking room smell like this? Didn't I give you little bastards some cleaner and rags and air freshener to keep this shit clean? I let y'all have all the toys and shit that you want and all I ask is for y'all to keep this fucking room clean and you can't even do that! Get this shit cleaned up right now!" The kids looked around the room frantically and despite the fact that it was overcapacity with this and that, everything was neat and in place, therefore, they didn't know what they were supposed to clean.

"Move damnit! Don't just stand there like a deer in headlights."

"Uh, mommy, ma'am what would you like for us to clean?" Percy, the ten year old, asked as politely as he could. He had learned a long time ago that they had to be careful with what, how and when they said things to their mother. And even with the right tone and carefully calculated words, the "when" had always been the tricky part. Their mother could be smiling and striking all at the same time. And then there were times when she looked mad as a bull, yet that would be the time when she showed them love and kindness. He wasn't sure now how she would react, although they'd heeded the warning "not to leave their room when her song was playing," for the past 3 days, which was the cause for the rancid smell in the room.

Percy, being the oldest had always taken on the responsibility of "testing the waters" for himself and his younger siblings in order to protect them. Because his grandparents had raised him for the first five years of his life, he didn't let his mother's irate behavior go beyond his surface because he knew that normal parents didn't treat their kids the way Sharquita treated them. He was also smart enough to know that his little sister and brother; Liberty and Justice weren't built like him therefore they ran the risk of being forced into thinking that chaos and abuse was normal. Liberty was rebellious and full of anger, which made it hard for Percy to keep him from feeling the wrath of Sharquita Black. However, Percy feared something greater than his mother's wrath and that was his little brother's increase in apathy. Justice, on the other hand, was the complete opposite. She was timid and vulnerable. She was always jumpy and she still wet the bed, therefore, he tried to do everything in his power to take the beatings or the brunt of Sharquita's harsh punishments in order to save her. His mother could beat him but she couldn't break him. And as soon as he was old enough, he planned to take his brother and sister and get away from her. He'd started saving couch change or whatever kind of money he could get his hands on since the last time Sharquita had beaten Justice so badly that it had even scared her. After that, Justice's physical punishments almost became nonexistent, but it seemed as if Sharquita resented not being able to beat her, so she upped the ante on mental and emotional torturing.

"Well, for starters Percy the Protector, apparently y'all need to scrub this floor because it stinks in here."

"Well mama, we been peeing and shitting in here for the past three days and we ain't took no bath either. That's why it stinks in here," Liberty said boldly.

"Shut up, Liberty." Percy said, quickly stepping in front of his siblings. "Mommy, ma'am listen, we have been trying to empty the pee bucket outside the window and some of it may have gotten on the floor. And we don't have any more bleach or air freshener. We ran out yesterday morning ma'am," Percy explained and pleaded altogether.

"Percy stop kissing her ass. We ain't ate in three damn days...she left us in here to die."

"To die huh?" Sharquita said quietly and seething. Percy could feel Justice's hands, which were gripping the back of his shirt, begin to shake.

"Mommy, ma'am, you can't mind Liberty. He's always running his mouth. I'll teach him to do better," Percy said, trying his hardest to sound as genuine and humble as possible. Sharquita didn't even hear him. She picked up the thick handled broomstick that she had been carrying and began tapping it up against the wall. Slowly, methodically, tantalizing them. Tap. Tap. Tap. Tap. Tap. Her eyes, which were glassy and extended to the size of fifty-cent pieces, darted from child to child. A snarl slowly spread across her lips. Tap. Tap. Tap. Tap.

"Come here Percy," she said ominously. Tap. Tap. Tap. Tap. His heart pounded but he stepped forward bravely. When he was standing within arms grasp of her, she raised her hand. He stiffened and braced himself for a punch; however, she wrapped her arm around him and kissed him on the top of his head.

"You always want to be the one getting beat for your brother and sister, so I'm going to make you suffer for all three of y'all. Now turn around and face the wall," she said. Percy turned around and "assumed the position;" legs spread, hands above the head and palms and fingers completely flat, almost touching the wall, but not touching the wall.

"I dare you to turn around and I better not see your arms shaking. They damn sure better not touch that wall either or your little brother will suffer the consequences. Understood?"

"Yes mommy; ma'am," he said as he braced himself and waited for the sting of the broomstick handle that she'd resumed tapping against the wall, to strike his back. However, no blows came. His heart dropped because he now realized that his mother was playing one of her games and his little brother and sister were now at her mercy. And depending upon how the wind blew, the range of their mother's mercy was "like a box of chocolates, they never knew what they were going to get."

Tap. Tap. Tap. Tap.

The tapping of the broomstick continued, but within millimeters of the tips of Percy's fingers. Percy didn't need to turn around to see the fear that he could hear floating through the air from his brother and sister. He knew Liberty was standing there with his chest stuck out wearing his "Samuel Jackson" "muthafucka" face, as Liberty liked to call it, because it made him feel tough, as he tried to coat the fact that his insides were simultaneously knotting themselves. Since their mother was a Samuel Jackson fanatic, as was Liberty, she had almost every movie that Samuel Jackson ever played in. And when she came home with one of his movies, she would make popcorn and let Liberty lay on her chest while they all laid in her bed laughing like a normal family. Afterwards, things actually did go back to normal, normal being fear and uncertainty.

Things had been somewhat better for them when their mother was leaving them home alone for weeks at a time because Percy was good at rationing out the food and he was a pro at domestic duties like washing clothes and doing dishes. And at any given time when their mother blew in to repack her suitcase and refill the refrigerator, he made sure that everything was perfect so that she wouldn't have any excuse to flip out on them. Sometimes his hard work paid off, sometimes it didn't, but he usually found comfort in knowing that his mother's itch to get back to wherever she'd come from often curtailed the number of days she remained home. That is until recently when their mother stopped going out and brought the party home. Her cruelty was constant and she'd pretty much confined them to being prisoners in his and Liberty's bedroom. Although Justice had her own room, their mother forced her to sleep in their room because someone was always "crashing" in Justice's bed. Most days their mother made them stay in that room only letting them out in intervals of whatever amount of time she saw fit to give them. Within those timeframes, she expected them to eat, shower and use the bathroom. And because they never knew how much time they had, they scrambled to do all three as quickly as possible. On numerous occasions, Percy and Liberty had peed and ate all while in the shower because Sharquita was known to say, "time's up" within five to ten minutes of them coming out. And failure to adhere to that, "time's up" cue was punishable by pretty much anything.

On a good day, she permitted them to be out of the room all day, cleaning the house from top to bottom. And on those days, she was always kind enough to end the day with a big meal, maybe a Samuel Jackson movie and long, hot showers. The days when she had guests or played her favorite song back to back, over and over, were the most dreaded because they weren't allowed out of the room at all. And sometimes depending on what was going on, their mother didn't bring them food or water. And bathing or relieving themselves outside of their bedroom was definitely out of the question. The first couple of days they'd experienced being in the room all day, they'd all thrown up from the stench of their urine and feces mixed with their body odors. But as things became uniform to them, they adapted to the smell and the hunger...and the boredom...and claustrophobia.

Tap. Tap. Tap. Tap. The slow tapping continued. Percy's arms were getting tired but his ears used the song that he'd began to loath after the first 24 hours of hearing it, as his ally. He concentrated on the words, but he also made sure to pay attention to the rhythm of the taps. He didn't know his mother's plans but he was sure that she would attach some type of pain to it.

"So." Tap. Tap. Tap. Tap. "I left you here to die huh Liberty," Tap. Tap. Tap. Tap. "You have a roof over your head, a bed to sleep in and look at all these fucking toys you dumb ass piece of shit. I cook, I clean and I take care of y'all worthless, cock blocking, I wish y'all was all dead, mutherfuckers, and what do I get in return?" Tap. Tap. Tap. Tap. "Back talk and a stankin' ass room." Tap. Tap. Tap. Tap. "Today Liberty for your ungratefulness and your slick ass mouth, your little sister is going to pay dearly while you stand here and watch. I'm going to break you from running your mouth no matter what it takes to do it." Tap. Tap. Tap. Tap. "Justice hold your hands out. And hold them out until I tell you to drop them." Tap. Tap. Tap. Tap. "And I suggest if you don't want this broom handle busting your knuckles, you better keep em' steady." Tap. Tap. Tap. Tap.

"Ok mama. I'm sorry I talked back to you. Don't punish Justice. Punish me," Liberty begged, finally breaking. Tap. Tap. Tap. Tap. Sharquita returned his pleading with wicked laughter and the tap of her broom. Tap. Tap. Tap. Tap. Justice's arms were already shaking uncontrollably and Liberty knew she wouldn't last long. He jerked his pants down and bent over. Tap. Tap. Tap. Tap.

"Here mama, beat me. Beat me," he begged. The tapping stopped.

"Ok Liberty, you've convinced me. Your ass shall be the one that gets whooped tonight. Trade places with Percy and leave your pants down." Liberty did not waste time getting to the wall and "assuming the position." And since Sharquita hadn't "released" her, Justice remained in her position as well, with her face squeezed; trying her best not to drop her arms.

"Uh, excuse me mommy, ma'am. Can Justice drop her arms now?" Percy asked.

"Open your mouth again Percy and I promise I'ma punch you in it," Sharquita said sharply, silencing him. Justice began crying and her arms began to falter. Noticing her daughter's inevitable defeat, she began walking towards her, raising the broom handle in the air as she prepared to strike.

"Mama! Ma'am, no please!" Percy screamed. Justice's anxiety overcame her and the urine she'd been holding for the past thirty minutes began streaming down her leg. When Sharquita saw the warm liquid running down the child's leg, she stood there and watched until the very last drop leaked out.

"You trifling little bitch. You done went and pissed on my floor. Oh you gonna pay for that." She flew into a fit of rage, grabbed Justice, slammed her face down onto the carpet, and began rubbing the child's face in the urine. "Are you a fucking dog or an animal? Only untrained dogs piss in the floor and since you're acting like an animal, I assume I'm going to have to housebreak you. This is how they train dogs not to piss on floor." Justice tried hard to catch her breath as her heart raced furiously and the pain from the carpet burning her face intensified. Liberty; being his sister's keeper, jumped on Sharquita's back in an attempt to stop her, but she flung him across the room like he was an unwanted booger hanging from her nose. Percy watched helplessly as his little brother's head collided with the side of the dresser; knocking him out cold. And when his eyes rolled back to his mother whose hands were moving back towards Justice's face as if to resume "training" her, he finally lost his cool. He grabbed the broom handle and whacked his mother across the side of her head. Stunned, Sharquita turned and looked at him. Before she could collect her thoughts and strike, he whacked her across the head and face several more times until she tumbled to the floor. She laid there, motionless but Percy was still afraid so he whacked her again.

"Justice go call 911 now!" He screamed in between whacks. Justice, who was sitting on the floor in a trance somehow heard Percy's voice and followed his orders. When she returned to tell him the police was on their way, Percy had bound Sharquita's hands and legs with two cords from video game controllers and was leaned over tending to Liberty.

"Did you call the police like I told you to?" he demanded.

"Yes, I did Percy. And I called grandma too. Is mama dead?"

"I don't know Justice. Don't ask me any questions right now, ok?"

"Ok." She started crying. "Percy?"

"What is it Justice?"

"Is Liberty dead?"

"No!"

Carolyn Black

Ring. Ring. Ring. I opened my eyes and met darkness. I felt a chiseled, rock solid chest beneath my face that slowly rose up and down. A strong arm had itself wrapped around my shoulders tightly. I was confused momentarily because I didn't know where I was or if I was dreaming. However when I inhaled, I knew that I was laying on top of Demarcus because his scent was tailor made to his body. I'd been staying with him at his crib and I still wasn't used to it yet. It had been a few weeks since my breakdown and Demarcus never left my side except for when we both had to go to work. I was healing from the pain of losing Sylvia and I was beginning to fall in love with Demarcus all over again. He hadn't even tried to make love to me and I respected him so much for it because I really didn't have the energy. We were actually working on intimacy and being together like a real couple. Things actually felt different, but *right* this time.

"Hello?" I said groggily into my cell phone.

"Carolyn, where the hell you at? I been calling your house all night!" Brandon screamed into the phone. I sat straight up; my heart started beating into overdrive. *God please no. I can't take no more.* I thought to myself.

"What's wrong?"

"Sharquita. That dumb ass bitch Sharquita. It's too much to explain but you need to get to the hospital right now."

"Is she dead? Are the kids ok?"

"Everybody's alive. Just get here!"

"Ok, I'm on my way," I said and jumped out of bed.

"What's wrong Cee?" Demarcus asked.

"I don't know. Something to do with my crazy ass cousin. Either she's in the hospital or one of her kids is in the hospital. Regardless of what it is, it must be pretty bad for Brandon to be calling me," I said as I began getting dressed. "I just don't know if I'm ready to go back into that hospital yet though Demarcus."

"I'm coming with you," he said as he also got up and began getting dressed.

"No. This is family drama. I..."

"Cee, there's no more I. From now on it's we and I'm going with you."

When we arrived at the hospital, it was like de ja vu. My whole family sat in the waiting room solemnly. My hands began to sweat which made Demarcus squeeze them harder, alerting me that he was there. However, when I walked into the room, instead of receiving a warm greeting, I got attacked.

"Well, well, well. If it ain't the whore of Babylon, coming in dragging yet another man that no one's ever seen before," Olivia said, firing the first shot.

"Shut up before I push your crippled ass over again." I fired back.

"Carolyn don't mind her," Brandon said walking over to me. "Wait, hold up. Ain't this homeboy from the club that slammed you on the ground that night at Buster's?" Brandon asked, eyeing Demarcus.

"Slammed who on the ground!?" my little brother John said and jumped up.

"Chill yo! Y'all called me about Sharquita stay focused!" I snapped as I gripped Demarcus' hand tighter. He remained silent but I could feel his breathing change.

"Well once again, you shouldn't have brought some strange ass man up in our family affairs," Olivia chimed in.

"Say something else Olivia and I'ma make your face look strange. Try me," I said looking her straight in her eyes.

"Hey! This is not the time or place. Now all of y'all sit down and shut the hell up." Uncle Lee, Sharquita's father yelled. Aunt Brenda sat at his side silently shaking her leg. Brandon looked at me with disgust, which cut me to my soul because he'd never looked at me like that before. He was privy to a lot of the dirt I'd done in my life, yet he never judged me. This was new and different for me.

I sighed. "Somebody tell me what's going on."

"Not till' you get that Bama ass fool out of here," Brandon replied nastily. I looked at him completely bewildered. I couldn't believe he was acting like that.

"Homeboy, like your peoples said, this ain't the time or the place. I have no problem talking with you man to man, but at another time," I heard Demarcus say calmly although I could hear the seriousness in his voice.

"Fo' sho'. Oh we gon' talk alright," Brandon replied. "Anyway, let me get at you out in the hallway Cee."

"Alright. I'll be right back Demarcus." I said as Brandon and I walked out into the hallway.

"What the hell is wrong with you? Why you acting like Macho Man Randy Savage right now?" I asked.

"Why you here with this bum ass sucka who put his hands on you? I mean, you been acting crazy as hell since Sylvia died but this right here puts the icing on the cake."

"Brandon, you don't know what you talking about. Stay in your lane, ok. It's way more to this story than meets the eye. I can't explain it all right now, but I need you to trust me, ok. I walked to the brink of hell and he's the one who stopped me from going all the way in. So I need you to chill and tell me what the hell Sharquita's crazy ass did."

"Man, this heifa had the kids locked up in the room for three days straight with no food, no water and a fuckin' piss bucket while she rode the slopes. And then she threw Liberty against a desk or somethin' and he hit his head so hard it knocked him out. Justice has carpet burns all over the side of her face and Percy lost his mind and knocked Sharquita's ass over the head with a broomstick. Everybody's ok, but Liberty has a concussion and so does Sharquita's dumb ass."

"Stupid hussy. That's what she gets. So what now? I mean, you know the hospital is probably gonna call DSS."

"Yeah, I know. And how bout Aunt Brenda's ass been in there taking up for the bitch like it's the kids' fault."

"Well, that doesn't surprise me. If she admits how messed up Sharquita is then she'll finally have to take responsibility for making her that way and you know good and damn well she ain't gonna do that," I replied.

"Yeah you right."

"Carolyn." I heard a voice behind me. I turned around and it was Jenetta's stankin' ass, which really pissed me off. Out of all the Social Workers in Fosterberg County that they could've sent, they sent this bitch. I didn't hide my disgust.

"What?" I asked annoyed.

"What? What you mean what? I'm here to investigate a case and I just happened to see you. But now it all makes sense. I'm assuming that Sharquita Black must be kin to you. Ha ha..." She snickered. "Doesn't surprise me at all."

"What?" I asked as I unconsciously morphed into my fighter's stance.

"Chill Cee. Chill," Brandon said getting in between us. "Look ma, I don't know who you are but if you're here to investigate this case, then you best get to it before you get hurt."

"By who? Carolyn knows she can't touch me and if she does, I'll serve her ass on a platter straight to our supervisor. Ain't that right, Carolyn?" she said smugly.

"She ain't gotta worry about putting her hands on you. It's a whole room full of angry and emotional Blacks in there. And I promise you where one can't get you, another one will. Bet that," Brandon stated bluntly, coming to my defense.

"Whatever," she said and walked off. Soon as she was out of earshot, I called Val.

"Hello," She answered on the first ring.

"Val, this is Carolyn. Listen, I know Jenetta's on call this week, but the case she got called in on happens to be my little cousin. Now, I know I can't take the case because of a conflict in interest, but can't you send somebody else? She already came up in here with that smug ass attitude as soon as she found out it was my family."

"Well Carolyn, like you said, she's on call; so there's really nothing I can do right now."

"Ok. Well I'm telling you right now, it's not a good idea. And technically, because Jenetta knows me, it's still a conflict in interest. And I'm afraid that either the case will be tainted because of our beef or I'm going to end up beating her ass and losing my job."

I heard Val sigh through the phone. "Yeah, you're right. I'll be there shortly."

Brandon and I walked back into the waiting room. I looked around for Demarcus and saw that Olivia had him cornered giving him the third degree. I knew what she was doing and it wasn't trying to get to know him. I was already pissed off because of Jenetta, but seeing Olivia low key throwing herself at Demarcus almost sent me over the edge. I was still in mourning and my emotions were all over the place so I temporarily lost my mind. When I came to, I had a handful of Olivia's hair in my hand and Demarcus was trying to pull me off her. My family was in an uproar and someone called security.

"Carolyn look, you need to go! Right now! Ever since you and Ike Turner came in, it ain't been nothing but trouble. Just go home and I'll call you and tell you about everything later," Brandon demanded, stinging me a second time. I looked at my little brother John for support but he dropped his head and looked away from me.

"Come on Cee. Let's just go ok," Demarcus said, leading me out. I was stunned. All the scars that were finally starting to heal reopened. All the rawness and pain reemerged because once again I felt abandoned and "Black balled" by my family.

"I can't do nothing right. I can't do nothing right. My family doesn't want me around," I cried.

"That's not true Cee. Everybody was tense and in their feelings."

"What about Olivia? What was she saying to you?" I asked.

"She asked me who I was and how long I'd known you."

"What did you tell her?"

"First, I told her I was sorry about your sister. Then I told her that I've known you for years and that you and I had reconnected. I told her you're my girlfriend and that one day I want to make you my wife." I stopped walking and looked at him.

"What?"

"Yeah, that's right. I told her I want to make you my wife when the time is right."

The Next Day

When I arrived at work, I walked straight into Val's office.

"Val, I need to talk to you please." She sighed and braced herself because of how ugly I had been towards her since my sister died.

"Ok, have a seat," she replied.

"First and foremost Val, I want you to know that I'm so sorry for the way I've been treating you. I was angry with you and yes I did blame you for my sister's death, but I also blamed myself. I was hurting so bad, but I refused to feel it and it almost destroyed me." I began getting choked up, but this time I didn't try to suppress it. "Once I finally owned those feelings and actually felt them, it freed me. Knowing that I'll never see my sister again makes my bones ache but I know that eventually I'll wake up one morning and it want hurt so bad. Now, I'm trying to pick up the pieces and I wanted to start with you. Val, you've been one of the few consistent people in my life and I took my pain out on you. That was wrong and I sincerely apologize. Please forgive me."

"Oh Carolyn, you know I forgive you. I just need to know that you forgive me."

"For what?" I asked.

"For being bullheaded and thinking that I know everything. I let my supervisory role go to my head, especially since Maurice and I had worked things out. I was feeling myself but please believe I got knocked off my high horse. So will you forgive me for being an asshole?"

I smiled. "I sure do." We embraced and both of us cried. I cried for my sister and Val cried for me, which was something I desperately needed. Once we finally got ourselves together, we sat down and discussed my cousin Sharquita's case.

"Ok, well Jenetta and I did the preliminary paperwork and assessments but I passed the case on to another team. Carolyn, I'm sorry to say this because it's your family but I doubt if your cousin will get those kids back. After we interviewed those kids, I would have never known that you guys all fall from the same tree. Carolyn your cousin is demonic. She has been torturing those kids for a very long time."

I sighed and shook my head. "I knew she was neglectful, but I didn't think she was abusive."

"Please don't get mad at me for asking but why haven't you guys done anything about this? Especially you." she asked as gently as she could trying not to offend me. But I was done with taking the easy way out so I owned up to my part.

"Well Val, it's different for me because it's my family. I guess I was in denial and I actually thought like most of our clients do, that we could handle it within the family ourselves. Plus, she doesn't come around that much and when she does, the kids are well dressed and well behaved. But I guess I saw the signs and ignored them because I didn't want to admit or believe that my own cousin could possibly be that crazy." Suddenly, I had an epiphany. All the anger and disgust that I'd felt over the years towards the "negligent" family members of the caregivers I'd interacted with in my cases was now laying in *my* lap. I had a total new respect for them because *I* was them. I finally understood that we were equal when it came to loving and protecting our family. The only thing that separated me from them was my notepad and state car. I'd always tried my best to look at them as human beings, but I realized that I unconsciously was looking down at them like I was superior...I was becoming a new woman.

"So what's the plan?" I asked.

"Well, I'm really not sure because again we transferred the case to another team. I do know that your cousin is going to do time. The eight year old has a concussion, the five year old girl has carpet burns so deep on her face that it's going to take years for her skin to come back normal and the ten year old is so parentified that he'll probably never respect authority now that he's free from his mother." I sighed again and dropped my head.

"So, who did they go home with?" I asked.

"The grandparents took the ten year old and the five year old with them. The eight year old is going to be in the hospital for a couple of days for monitoring, but I'm sure he'll go home to the grandparents as well."

"Thanks Val. I gotta make a run real quick and I'll be back ok." I got up and squeezed her one last time. I got in my car and made a phone call.

"Meet me at the hospital in fifteen minutes," I said and hung up. When I arrived at Fosterberg Memorial, Brandon was standing in the lobby waiting for me. As soon as we saw each other, we embraced and I cried. I found a private place for us to talk and we sat down. I didn't have the strength to carry shame on my shoulders anymore so I spilled my entire guts. Unlike Demarcus, I didn't need to sugar coat things because I had no reason to hide anything from Brandon, plus I knew I could trust him to keep my secrets. I told him about my affairs, I told him the whole story about Demarcus and I told him about my battle with Xan Xan after Sylvia died. I told him about Jarrod, Jermaine, I mean Avery, Mayor Bostain, and Officer Petrea and how Demarcus had pretty much saved my life in more ways than one, which was why I was with him. I even told him about the history between me and my sisters and why I'd jumped on Olivia. I needed him to understand because I couldn't bear the thought of him looking at me with the same look that I'd had to endure my entire life from all the people who'd prejudged me.

"Damn Cee. Your ass shoulda been in R Kelly's '*Trapped In the Closet*' Series." He laughed. "That's some serious shit you just told me. No wonder you was on the verge of becoming a pill head. Hell, I would be too. Shit! Please make sure you stop by the crib on your way home so we can smoke a blunt and shake the devil off. Hell, you can even bring your boyfriend." I laughed and it felt so good. Leave it to Brandon to take pain and turn it into laughter.

After we finished talking, we went to see Liberty. We loved on him and of course, Brandon's crazy butt had us all laughing until tears rolled down our cheeks. When it was time to go, we promised him that we would be back.

"Cee, I appreciate you having me come here today. I was really feeling some type of way about you and I'm glad you trusted me enough to tell me what you told me. I love you."

I sucked my teeth. "Stop all that gay shit and bring your ass on." I said looping my arm in his as we walked to the car.

"Well, I guess Aunt Brenda and Uncle Lee are gonna get a second chance to do things right this time," he said.

"Yeah, we all are. Those babies are Black kids and it's going to take all of us to help them get through this."

"You right and we gon' do it too," Brandon replied.

Later that day when I got off from work, I met Demarcus at my house and took him with me to Brandon's house so we could all break bread. They squashed their beef and dapped each other up. After that, they started talking like they'd been homies for years. *Damn I wish it was that easy with girls*, I thought to myself. We sat around and smoked a few blunts as we chit chatted and cracked jokes. In my high state, my eyes kept rolling from Brandon to Demarcus because I never thought I would see the day that Demarcus would actually be hanging with me and my family. My heart began to swell and the love I felt for him became magnified. I finally accepted the fact that it was really going to happen between us. We were actually going to be together like a real couple; something I'd never really experienced in my life.

The doorbell rung and Brandon went to answer it. I expected to see my little brother John but Jarrod walked in instead. *Duh duh dunt...High kill,* I thought to myself. Our eyes met and I shifted around in my seat. He looked from me to Demarcus, but he stayed true to the game and maintained his poker face. Brandon, who was getting a kick of this; the bastard, invited Jarrod to come in and have a seat.

"Nah man, I'm good. I just came by to get a little something, but since you have company, I can come back later."

"Nah, company don't stop me from making money. Come on back and I'll get you right."

When Demarcus and I got back to my house, he asked me about Jarrod.

"So uh, what's up with you and shawty back at Brandon's house? He get at you?"

Damn I thought we played that shit off, I thought to myself, but apparently, we hadn't. I had a choice. I could carry the burden of lying for the rest of our lives or I could fess up and pray that he didn't judge me. I chose the latter.

"Uh, yeah. Needless to say, that was one of the bad choices I made on my walk through hell...and he's not the only one," I admitted candidly. I waited for a response but he said nothing and I couldn't read his face.

"So you uh, must uh, think I'm a whore now, huh?" I asked nervously as I rubbed my hands together. He got up and walked over to me. He cupped my face in his hands.

"Nope. I think you're a survivor. And by the way, be mindful of what you say. That's my girl you talking about," he replied and kissed me on the tip of my nose. I smiled and then I started to cry. He grabbed my hand and pulled me in close. And for the first time ever, we made love, not infatuated sex, but actual love.

CASE#: 38588 BABY MOMMA

Marita Martinez glided her pointer finger across the chocolate icing on top of the small cake that read, "Happy 4th Anniversary Baby" and seductively placed it into the open mouth of her husband of 4 years, Antonio. He took his tongue and licked her finger from the bottom to the top before taking the tip of her finger and sucking the icing off. He then picked his beautiful wife up and sat her on the countertop beside the cake. They began kissing as he slid the strap of her black lace teddy off her shoulder. He then began nibbling on her neck and shoulder as she threw her head back, feeling pleasured. He cupped her breast, teased it with an icing covered finger and gently put it into his mouth so that he could suck on her erect nipple. He laid her down, removed her teddy as well as his boxer shorts, and began making love to her on the counter. They kissed; they caressed and moaned as they pleased each other. And just as they both were about to climax in harmony, the doorbell rang. They both ignored it until the rings became loud knocks.

"Antonio, do not get it. Ignore it baby. It is probably just someone selling something. You know if it was our family they would call first," Marita purred into Antonio's ear as she continued to lick the residues of icing that had somehow made its way onto Antonio's neck.

Bang, Bang, Bang. The knocks became louder.

"Shit!" Antonio spat out as he pulled himself out of his wife, pulled up his boxers and retrieved his sweat pants that were laying across the floor. He almost tripped over their packed suitcases, waiting by the door in anticipation of the trip that they would be taking to France later on that day. Annoyed, he jerked the door open without asking who it was or looking through the peephole. However, once he opened the door and saw who was standing there, his sandy brown skin lost its color and the excitement that he'd just experienced with his wife during their sexual rendezvous turned sour and almost made him throw up. In front of him stood his mistake, his blemish, his infidelity, his brief moment of weakness that he would now have to deal with for the rest of his life. In front of him was Esaña, his 25 year old ex-secretary that had gotten him drunk at last year's Christmas party and seduced him while his wife was away visiting family. In her hand was a car seat that held her daughter, their daughter, a beautiful, bright-eyed baby girl with big curly locks of dark brown hair. Although the baby was beautiful, she was a constant reminder of the mistake he'd made and a humiliating smack in the face to Antonio's wife who although she'd done everything in her power to get pregnant, she could not have kids.

He sighed deeply because he knew that this was getting ready to be a bad situation. He tried to step outside and close the door behind him so that he could get rid of Esaña before his wife came out, but Esaña; being the conniving, vindictive, observant woman that she was, noticed the chocolate icing smeared onto Antonio's shirtless body as well as the suitcases that were sitting in the foyer in front of the door. She quickly pushed passed him and made her way into the house.

"Esaña, what the hell do you want and why are you here this early in the morning?" He asked, following her into the foyer.

"Is that any kind of way to talk to the mother of your child?" She asked deviously in her thick Spanish accent as she sat the child down on the floor. Hearing Esaña's name, Marita quickly threw on her robe and headed to where they were standing.

"Esaña, what do you want?" Marita asked angrily from behind Antonio.

"Aww, why so angry Marita? There is no need because this is none of your concern. This is between me and the father of my child," she said sarcastically and then focused her attention on Antonio.

"I need you to watch Isabella because I have to work today and I cannot afford to lose another job. I will be back to pick her up tomorrow."

"Hell, no you won't. I am not keeping her today. We are going out of town in a few hours so you will have to find someone else," Antonio replied.

"That is not my problem. Take her with you for all I care," she replied as she turned to walk out the door. Antonio began yelling after her, but Marita stood there silently as she absorbed everything she was seeing. The sound of her own breathing overwhelmed her ears, as she looked at her husband, the man she had been with for ten years and married to for four. She thought about him gyrating on top of the trashy little slut that stood in front of her and getting her pregnant. She thought about all the times she'd held her tongue while they discussed parenting and Esaña had taken cheap shots at her. The pain and anguish that she'd sustained at the hands of this woman who cared about nothing but destroying her family began to overwhelm her. She thought about the fact that this woman had given her husband a baby when she knew that she would never be able to do so. And then her eyes roamed from their packed suitcases to the baby girl sitting on the floor and then to the back of Esaña's beautiful, long, brown hair that flowed from to side to side as she arrogantly headed towards the door. As if in a dream, Marita saw herself in slow motion, lunging at Esaña and grabbing her by her beautiful hair.

"You bitch, you are not going anywhere. Now get your fucking child and get the fuck out of my house," Marita yelled as she began pounding Esaña wildly with every ounce of strength that she possessed. The two began fighting and Antonio, who was in shock, froze briefly before his feet would allow him to move. The two women were fighting so ferociously that neither of them was coherent enough to remember the baby girl sitting in the car seat on the floor. In an attempt to pull every strand of Esaña's hair out, Marita jerked Esaña's hair so hard that they both tumbled to the floor, landing on top of the screaming baby. Antonio, whose adrenaline went into over drive because he'd seen them fall onto the baby, grabbed both women and effortlessly threw them to the side. Stunned, Marita and Esaña came to their senses and looked up at Antonio who was leaned over a now silent baby girl.

Carolyn Black

"Fosterberg County DSS, Carolyn Black speaking," I said as I yawned silently.

"Hi, Ms. Black. This is Maryanna Teeters and I'm a nurse at Fosterberg Memorial Hospital. We have a baby here with some broken ribs and a fractured collarbone. Apparently, the biological mother of the child got into a domestic dispute with the baby's father's wife and as they were fighting, they fell on top of the baby. We didn't know what else to do since they didn't physically attack the baby, but we felt that it was in the best interest of the child to contact CPS," the nurse stated through the phone.

"Ok. Thanks so much Ms. Teeters. You did the right thing. I will be by there shortly."

I grabbed my briefcase and headed to the hospital. When I arrived, I met with Nurse Teeters who briefed me on what was going on with the baby.

"Ms. Black, that poor baby is lucky to be alive. They almost crushed the poor thing. Apparently, the husband had an affair and got his young; and very beautiful, might I add, mistress pregnant. The wife stayed with the husband but you and I both know how that goes; especially when there's a child involved." She snorted.

"So I guess I need to start off by talking to the parents. Where are they?"

"They are in the waiting room. Follow me," she said as she led me to where the family was sitting. When I walked in and began sizing everyone up, I was stunned at how beautiful they *all* were; including the man. The woman I assumed to be the wife was seated beside her husband and a very young looking; absolutely breathtakingly beautiful woman with large, perky breasts was seated across from them; scowling. And although the wife was seated closely beside the husband, his cold countenance suggested to me that he didn't want to be around her.

"Hello, my name is Carolyn Black and I'm with Fosterberg County Department of Social Services," I said as I closed the door in order to give us some privacy. The husband sighed, closed his eyes and leaned his head back against the wall.

"Social Services! You see Marita, estúpido! You attacked me, almost killed my baby and now the Social Services is here to take my baby away from me!" The young woman who I assumed to be the baby mama aka mistress, screamed at the wife with a thick Spanish accent.

"Quiete la boca puta! This is your fault! I'm sick and tired of you coming to our home thinking that because you laid down with my husband and got pregnant that you can control my household. This is my husband and today is our anniversary. We are supposed to be in Paris right now; not at the fucking hospital with you and your bastard child," Marita screamed back, her accent just as thick.

"Well, apparently your husband was not satisfied with you or he would not have come to me. You are just jealous that I gave him what you cannot and that is a baby!" The young lady replied while pointing her finger at Marita's face. The husband remained silent.

I rolled my eyes and sighed. *Welp it's going to be a long ass day*, I thought to myself.

"Um, excuse me. Could you all introduce yourselves to me so that I can proceed with my investigation? There is a baby in there with broken ribs and a broken collarbone and right now that's all that we need to be discussing, ok? Now I'll start with you sir. Tell me your name and what's going on here," I said making sure to direct my line of questioning to him because he appeared to be the most rational person present. He sighed again.

"Well Ms. Black, my name is Antonio Martinez. This is my wife Marita and this is the mother of my daughter, Esaña Lopez."

"Your whore," Marita chimed in but he ignored her and continued.

"And as my wife said, we were planning to leave for Paris when Esaña showed up at our house unannounced trying to leave the baby with us. We told her that we were going out of town and could not keep the baby but she did not care and tried to leave the baby there anyway. My wife got angry and grabbed Esaña by her head as she was walking out the door. They started fighting and they fell on top of the baby. The last thing I remember was pulling them off of her."

"It was an accident. I did not mean for the baby to get hurt, but this puta continues to come around disrespecting my home and I just lost it Señora Black," Marita tried to explain.

"Accident! You do not care that my baby is hurt. You would be happy if she died and then you would not have to deal with me anymore. You want to get rid of her!" Esaña yelled.

"No puta! I want you to die! I want to get rid of you!" Marita yelled back passionately.

Starting to lose my patience, I coolly chimed in, "Uh ladies, listen. Both of you are facing felony child endangerment charges and what that means is that if you are both found guilty then neither one of you will be able to be around that baby and that includes you Miss Lopez. Regardless of how you all feel about each other that doesn't matter right now because there is a very hurt baby in there who does not deserve to be in the middle of all this mess. It's apparent that you all's relationship is too volatile to allow this child to return home; therefore, I am going to have to speak with my supervisor about having her placed into foster care."

"Oh my God! No, you cannot take my baby away from me. No! No! You cannot put her into a foster home with some strangers. Please. Please. At least let her stay with my mother. Or maybe she can stay with Antonio's mother, but please do not put her into a foster home with strangers. I have heard about what happens in those places and I do not want my daughter to get hurt," Esaña said as she fell to her knees and pleaded with me.

Feeling no sympathy for her I replied, "Well, she's already hurt Miss Lopez but we will consider a kinship placement for her. In the meantime, I need for you and Mr. Martinez to come up with a list of family members who can provide a safe environment for the baby while I step out and contact my supervisor," I said sternly and walked towards the door. As soon as I stepped into the hallway, they began arguing loudly in Spanish. I didn't even respond. I simply shut the door and called Val. After I finished talking with Val, who agreed to temporary out of home placement, I returned to the family who was still arguing passionately in Spanish. Dismissing the drama, I got straight to the point.

"I need the names, addresses and phone numbers of no more than two family members per side who you feel will be willing to take the child once she is released from the hospital. Otherwise she will be placed into one of our foster homes." I wasn't in the mood to play games with these people. As a woman, I completely understood the wife's actions because I knew that Esaña was doing everything in her power to taunt Marita and make her miserable. I; also knowing the mistress game, understood Esaña's inflated sense of control, but because she was a dangerously beautiful, hotheaded *kid* with peas for brains, she didn't quite understand that her role as the mistress was to be low key and reap the benefits of having a man when and how she wanted him. She was supposed to enjoy the sex; the trips and the money, not get pregnant. But then I had to rethink that because in actuality, Esaña had check mated the Martinez's. She'd knocked out the queen and the king with the birth of that baby. Mr. Martinez was stupid for even getting involved with her, but as I said before, there's something about "the power of the P-U-S-S-Y." Nevertheless, I wasn't there to be their marriage counselor and I had to do my job. Therefore, I opened up my briefcase and took out my notepad; alerting them that I didn't have time for the bullshit. And realizing that I was about business, they began providing me with the information that I needed.

"Ok. You all have until 4:00 p.m. to gather these people that you all have listed and have them at Social Services for a Team Decision Making Meeting. I am going to let the nurses and doctors here know that you, Miss Lopez are not allowed in the room with the baby at the same time as Mr. and Mrs. Martinez. Does everybody understand?" I asked sternly.

"Yes." They replied in unison.

"Good. Miss Lopez, you can sit with the baby for two hours and then Mr. and Mrs. Martinez will have the next two hours. Otherwise, I will see you all at 4:00," I replied and headed back to the office. When I returned, I began the tedious process of running criminal background checks on the people that they'd listed, which in both cases was the grandparents, while Val contacted the police department and formally pressed charges on Esaña and Marita. I really hated that we had to do that because they were otherwise probably fairly decent, law-abiding citizens. However, at the end of the day, we didn't have a choice. We'd have to let the courts decide their fate.

When 3:45 arrived, I sighed and wished that I had a shot of vodka and a blunt. I knew this family was going to act a fool, which meant I was probably going to have to act a fool too. And if they were anything like my dad's side of my family, I knew that this meeting was going to be composed of a bunch of loud Spanish talking, cursing and threats, which I loved by the way. I gathered my notes and went to meet with Val, who would supervise things and Mario, who was going to be the Facilitator. We all went into the conference room and began arranging the seating in an effort to minimize the commotion.

At 4:00 on the dot, the administrative assistant was calling us to let us know that the families had arrived. When I went out into the lobby to greet them, I saw what looked like an entire extended family. Knowing that World War III would break out if I let them all in, I only allowed Mr. Martinez and his parents, along with Esaña and her parents to come into the conference room. I felt so bad for Mrs. Martinez because I knew she felt left out especially since *she* was the wife. Unfortunately, because of the hostility between her and Esaña, there was nothing I could do. She remained in the waiting room alone; seated up against the wall, miserably failing at trying to hide the fact that she was crushed.

The Martinez family sat on one side, while Esaña and her family sat on the other. Val, Mario, and I were seated in the middle and I was so thankful to God that Mario was the facilitator because by the way the families were glaring at each other, I knew that it was about to go down. We introduced ourselves to the family, *thoroughly* discussed the rules of the meeting, and proceeded.

"After meeting with Mr. and Mrs. Martinez as well as Miss Lopez, we have found that due to the volatile nature of the relationship between both families, the baby is not safe in either homes..." Mario began but was cut off by Esaña's mother.

"My daughter is not going to harm her own child. She is not the aggressor here. That piece of trash man and his puta wife are the ones that are the cause of all this. Mi nieta needs to come home with her mother and they should not be allowed to see her," she spat out angrily.

"It was your piece of trash daughter that was sleeping with a married man and is now doing everything within her power to destroy my son and his wife. How dare you call them out of their name! And by the looks of your dress, your daughter learned how to be a piruja from you," Antonio's mother yelled back. And with that, the war began. Both families began screaming at each other and pointing fingers. Poor Mario was doing everything in his power to regain control but they ignored him. Val, who was halfway paying attention because she was too busy doodling hearts with her and Maurice's names inside, was no help. So I politely got up, went to the dry erase board and wrote, "Su nieta irán al hogar de crianza," which roughly translated to, "your granddaughter will be going to a foster home." I then walked over to the phone and pretended to call Zian who was in charge of placement.

"Hi Zian, this is Carolyn. I need a temporary foster care placement arranged for an infant please," I said into the phone loudly enough to ensure that they heard me. The room suddenly fell silent.

"Zian set that up. I'll call you right back," I said and turned to the crowd.

"Listen ladies and gentleman, it's time to get serious here. It doesn't matter who slept with who and blah blah blah. Miss Lopez, like I told you in the hospital, if you all can't get it together, then unfortunately you are going to prolong the length of time that your child is in placement. The child needs to be able to see both parents but it has to be in a safe and nurturing environment. However, it's apparent that there is an enormous amount of hostility within both families even amongst the grandparents, which still poses a threat for the baby. We are really trying to work with you all but your options are limited at this point. Either you come up with a neutral family member or it's a foster home until we can complete our investigation. And we don't want to have to do that," I said honestly.

They looked around at each other silently and then inquisitively.

Esaña looked up and was the first to respond. "What about Aunt Carrie? She is neutral. She is actually cooler with Antonio then she is with me, although she is my aunt."

"Yes, I can agree with that. Aunt Carrie is a really good person. She's a veterinarian and she loves the baby," Antonio agreed. I nodded my head.

"Ok, we will conduct a safety assessment, background check and home visit for your Aunt Carrie. Now let's summarize everything and make sure that everybody is clear about where things will go from here," Mario said, resuming his role as the facilitator. He went over to the dry erase board and began writing.

"Ok, while we're conducting our investigation, the baby will remain in the guardianship of Aunt Carrie if she is deemed appropriate. The other option is foster care until a suitable kinship placement is found. In the meantime, both parents will have to go to mediation and take parenting classes. Parents will have supervised visits but both parents can't be there at the same time. You guys will set a schedule with whomever the baby will be residing with but we can work all that out later," Mario continued. "And until things are resolved, you guys are not to be with the baby alone. None of you..." He said directing his attention towards the grandparents. "Which means that Aunt Carrie and/or a social worker must be present at all times during supervised visits."

"Well, what about that puta wife of his? I do not want her around my baby. This is her fault. If she would not have attacked me then we would not be here," Esaña said snidely. I knew what she was trying to do, but her question stumped Mario. I was trying not to intervene and undermine him as the facilitator but he was drowning. I opened my mouth to respond, but I was beat to the punch.

"What's your name again? Esaña? Let's be very clear about something. You, by no means, are innocent in this situation. In fact, I hold you the most accountable because as the mother, your job is to protect your child not use her as a way to torture and milk the Martinez's. You knew what you were doing when you started messing with that married man, granted Mr. Martinez knew what he was doing when he started messing with you as well. However, you also knew exactly what you were doing when you showed up at their home this morning unannounced with that baby. As a woman, how would you react if you were married and another woman showed up at your door, holding your husband's baby; making demands on your wedding anniversary? Mrs. Martinez may have reacted irrationally, but most women in her situation would have reacted the same way. She is just as much of a victim here as your baby is because she's also caught up in the crossfire of y'all's mess. So as long as she is his wife and poses no threat to the child, then she will continue to be part of your child's life. Your little plans to try and play the trump card with Mrs. Martinez backfired on you because now *you* risk losing custody of your child. And I'm somewhat bothered that the entire time I've been sitting here, you and your family have directed the majority of the blame on Mrs. Martinez and not the two of you. Which furthermore confirms the fact that if we allow you, the mother, to take your child home with you, your focus will remain on trying to hurt the Martinez's instead of being a good parent. So in hindsight, to answer your question, yes Mrs. Martinez has every right to be around your child. In fact, I don't feel that the child would be any more unsafe with her than she would be with you," Val chimed in coolly and calmly, barely looking up from her doodling, which in turn stumped Esaña...and me. I guess the heifa really was listening. But that was Val for you. Just when I thought she was slipping on her pimping, she always showed me otherwise. I also know that she empathized with Mrs. Martinez because of what had happened between her and Maurice. And even though I'd been a mistress myself, so did I.

"So in conclusion, we will be in touch with everyone once we have checked everything out with Aunt Carrie. If the hospital releases the baby before we are done, we will place her with one of our licensed foster parents until further notice. Does everyone understand?" Val asked frankly.

Both families; although they didn't like our plan, accepted it. We told them that we would come back to the table in 30 days to reevaluate and assess how things were progressing. We dismissed the meeting and I began gathering my things.

"Carolyn, can you do the home visit and safety assessment? And Mario can you do the background check for Aunt Carrie?" Val asked. "Shoot I'm ready to go home."

"I bet you are," I giggled, knowing that she wanted to get home to Maurice. She smiled a sneaky little smile because she knew exactly what I was talking about. Although we'd made amends, we still didn't hang out like we did before she got back with Maurice. It was cool though because I spent all my free time with Demarcus. Nevertheless, I still missed having her female companionship. She didn't even know that Demarcus and I were back together because she was always too preoccupied with work and Maurice to have girl talk. Thoughts and regrets about my sister Sylvia popped into my head and my chin began to quiver. But I didn't want to cry anymore so I quickly pushed the thoughts away. On my way back to my office, I stopped to use the bathroom whereby I ran into Marita Martinez who was crying.

"Mrs. Martinez, what's wrong?" I asked although I already knew the answer.

"Ms. Black, all I have ever done was love that man. We have been together since we were in college and we have been married for four years. But as I sit here in the midst of all this, forced to remain silent, it hurts so bad. I am not an ugly woman Ms. Black. I work hard, I listen, I cook, I clean and excuse my language, but I fuck my husband hard almost every night. And I am good at it. I just do not understand why he would do this to me. I am in my own fucking home and I feel like the outsider. That tramp has more power over my husband than I do, only because she opened her legs and popped out a baby. I try so hard not to hate that little girl because I know it is not her fault but it is because of her that I cannot make this all disappear. God knows that I never meant for the baby to get hurt, but it felt so good to finally get to pound her mother's face in." She grabbed a paper towel, wiped her face and shook her head. "I am sorry. I did not mean to bombard you with my troubles. It is just that I do not understand how a woman can knowingly inflict such pain on another woman with such indifference. To me, another woman's man should be off limits. I think that type of woman lacks morals and integrity, but more than anything, I think she lacks respect for herself and for others." She sniffled and walked out the door. I stood there, speechless because I had been that woman. I *was* that woman.

I gathered my things and met with "Aunt Carrie" so that I could conduct the home investigation. She was a very nice woman and she was very verbal about her disgust for her niece's behavior.

"I tell Esaña she wrong but she no listen to me. She was after that marry man from the first day she see him. I tell her mamá but her mamá only care about money," she said using broken English. I smiled at her because she reminded me of my paternal grandmother, feisty with a thick accent.

After I was done, I headed to the car as my phone started ringing. It was my little brother John.

"Wussup bruh?" I said into the phone.

"Hey. Aunt Clara is throwing Aunt Glenda and Uncle Ronnie a surprise party for their 40th wedding anniversary next Saturday, so I was calling to let you know."

"Dag have they been together that long?"

"Yeah, well actually they been together like forty one or forty three years and married for forty."

"Wow, that's what you call love," I replied, thinking about me and Demarcus.

"Yep. Well, you trying to go in on a gift with me and Olivia?"

"Uh, hell no. I'll go in with you but I ain't doing shit with Olivia."

"Come on Cee, don't be like that. She's your sister and she's the only one you have left."

"John, don't try to throw a guilt trip on me. I love her because she's my sister, otherwise I wouldn't piss on her if she was on fire. It's bad enough that I'm going to have to look at her ass during the party." I heard my little brother John sigh through the phone.

"Ok. Well suit yourself."

"Ok," I said indifferently.

"Oh yeah, it's a black tie affair so you have to dress in evening attire."

"Well, I'm cool with that. What about you and Brandon?" I asked because I could only imagine what those two would show up looking like.

"We are going to rent a tux. But I was gonna ask you if you had something Dezenique could wear."

"Dezenique? Who the hell is that?" I asked laughing to myself as the sparkle of gold teeth reflected in my mind.

"What you mean? She's my girl."

"Well, the question is; is she going to be your girl next week?" I laughed. He sucked his teeth.

"Shut up Cee. Bye!" He said and hung up.

One Week Later

"Baby, thanks for coming with me to my aunt and uncle's anniversary party," I said to Demarcus as I stood in the bathroom and put the final touches of my makeup on.

"I wouldn't miss it for anything in the world," he said from the next room, as he got dressed.

I stood in the mirror and admired myself. I wore a black gown with a sweetheart neckline and mermaid bottom along with my grandmother's pearls that she gave me for my birthday.

"You ready baby? The limo will be here to pick us up soon," I asked as I walked into the bedroom. In front of me stood the most handsome man I'd ever laid my eyes on. Demarcus, who had a fresh haircut and shave, was wearing a black formal suit that was slim fit and tapered at the bottom. His shirt, vest and handkerchief were white and his bowtie was black. I was completely in awe of how dapper he looked. All I could do was stare. And apparently, I must have looked just as striking to him because he also was speechless.

"Damn baby. If this car don't come soon, I don't know if we gonna make it to the party," he said smiling.

"I know right," I said as I pecked him lightly on the lips. Shortly thereafter the doorbell rung. I opened the door and there stood Brandon. He actually looked very nice. I couldn't believe it was him until he pulled a blunt out his lapel and waved it in my face. All I could do was laugh.

"Y'all come on so we can smoke this blunt real quick." I grabbed my purse and Demarcus. We got in the limo and there sat my little brother John and two chicken heads. The weave was flowing, the gold teeth were shining and the bullet holes were fresh; however, the chicks actually looked decent enough to be attending a formal event. We greeted each other and Demarcus exchanged dap with Brandon and my little brother John. I was actually nervous because the last time I brought Demarcus around my family, it didn't go so well. I knew that this would be the first time he met my parents and I didn't know how they were going to react. I just prayed that they would accept him and love him as much as I did.

When we arrived, the party was already jumping straight "Black style." My Aunt and Uncle, who thought they were coming to an intimate dinner with my parents, were beyond surprised when they walked in and saw our whole family there. When it came time for us to sit, my hands began to sweat because I was at my parent's table and I knew I had to introduce them to Demarcus. Good thing Mary Jane and a quick shot of tequila had calmed both me and Demarcus' nerves because I knew he was just as nervous as I was.

"Mom, dad this is my boyfriend Demarcus," I said as I finally got the nerve to introduce him. But when the word "boyfriend" came out of my mouth, my pride obliterated my nervousness because it was a word that I hadn't had the privilege of using since I was in college. My mom greeted Demarcus warmly and hugged him. But my dad, being my dad of course had to take another approach.

"Boyfriend? Well hot damn! I was beginning to think my baby girl was a lesbian. It's nice to meet you young man," my dad said as he shook Demarcus' hand while I died silently of embarrassment.

"Now dad, she couldn't possibly be a lesbian; she's been around the block too many times for that. In fact, I can't believe we're seeing the same man again. And a quite tasty one at that," Olivia chimed in smugly as she licked her lips and snickered. I bit the inside of my jaw because I couldn't do or say what I really wanted to because I knew I would ruin the party. Not only had she come for me but she was blatantly coming for Demarcus. Apparently, she didn't learn anything from the last two beat downs I put on her.

"Olivia, shut your mouth right now or I will slap the shit out of you," my mom said.

"Yeah, shut the hell up. Curly don't mind her, she's just jealous because her snobby ass can't get off the doorstep much less around the block," my dad cracked but with a hint of seriousness.

"Come on babe, let's sit down," Demarcus said as he put his hand on the small of my back and led me to my seat.

"Damn, ok Cuz I see what you mean," Brandon whispered in my ear.

"Yeah me too," my little brother John agreed. "Slap that bitch the next time she say something," he whispered.

"It won't do no good. As long as I'm alive she's gonna do everything in her power to try and hurt me. The difference is it doesn't bother me anymore because she looks pathetic," I said as I looked at Olivia and stuck my middle finger up at her. Her mouth curled into a sinister smile as she looked at Demarcus and winked. She'd found a new way to get to me. I could tell Demarcus was uncomfortable with the situation but he knew what she was doing because I'd made him privy to all the bad blood between us.

"Babe, I'll be right back," he said as he got up and walked over to the DJ booth.

"What's he doing?" I asked no one in particular. I saw him say something to the DJ and then he started walking back towards me. I heard the song, "Rock Steady" by the Whispers begin playing. He reached his hand out to me and said, "May I have this dance?"

A smile spread across my face as I accepted his hand. He led me to the dance floor and even though the song was somewhat upbeat, we slow dragged as we sang the words to each other.

"What made you choose this song?" I asked.

"Well because it kinda describes us, plus I knew all these old people would like it too." He laughed. I looked around and sure enough, everybody including my parents had joined us on the dance floor. I started laughing.

"I love you," I said sincerely as I looked in his eyes.

"I love you too, ma," he said and kissed me on my forehead as we picked up the pace and caught up to the rhythm of the song. I was smiling so hard my face hurt...and it felt awesome.

Monday Afternoon

I checked in with the Martinez and Lopez families to ensure that they were following through with our recommendations. Luckily, for them, the judge reduced their felony charges to a misdemeanor since there had been no previous issues. The baby was healing and the parents; including Mrs. Martinez, were seemingly doing a better job of getting along according to Aunt Carrie. Apparently, Val's words had resonated with Esaña because she seemed to have dropped her life's mission of trying to make the Martinez's miserable. However, it was still too early to tell if she was sincere or just acting to get her baby back. At the end of the day, I began gathering my things so I could head home to Demarcus. As I was picking up my purse, my phone began to ring. I started not to answer it because I didn't want to get caught up in a late case. However, since I was on call, I didn't have a choice.

"Fosterberg County Department of Social Services, this is Carolyn Black."

"Carolyn Black. Now why do I have to track you down at work? I've been calling you for weeks and I want to know why you're avoiding me. My company is building some schools for one of the charities that I sponsor in South Africa and we're having a grand opening ball. I need a beautiful, exotic looking woman to be my date and I'm flying out Thursday evening so how about I swing by and pick you up on my way to the airport," he asked nonchalantly as if he already knew that I was going. I laughed.

"Well hello, Brad."

"You're damned right it's Brad," he replied and let out a little chuckle. "Where have you been?"

"I've been busy," I responded, hoping to initiate a game of cat and mouse. I loved torturing Brad and the thought of going to South Africa was enticing in itself. However, I finally had what I needed in my life and that was Demarcus. I was so in love with him that I felt like I wanted to bust, especially since he'd met my family and they'd embraced him. However, although I knew that I wasn't going with Brad, I didn't think a little innocent flirting would hurt anything.

"Seriously Carolyn. I've had to go on two major trips without an escort and you know I don't like doing that. And my fat ass wife just lies around getting fatter. In your absence, I even attempted to work out with her so that she could lose enough weight in time to accompany me on this trip but she was too damned lazy to work out. Carolyn you know I don't beg but I really need you to go with me," he whined.

"So how do you know that I'm not a big fat tub of lard now? It's been quite some time since we've seen each other. What would you do if I arrived at the airport with a spare tire and an extra chin?" I chuckled and then stopped abruptly once I noticed that my belly jiggled in harmony with my laugh. *Damn you Demarcus!* I giggled to myself as I shook my head. I was happy and I'd heard that people got fat when they're happy.

"I'm definitely not worried about that my dear. I remember how gorgeous you looked at the Mayor's Ball, and I highly doubt you've gained an ounce of weight since then. So come on, what's it going to be?"

I loved Brad's spontaneity and a few months ago, I would have jumped at the idea. However, I finally had the man of my dreams and I wasn't going to do anything to risk messing it up.

"I'm sorry Brad but I really do have a lot of things going on here and I just can't leave right now."

"Come on Carolyn. I promise you gorgeous, you want be sorry," he said confidently but seductively all in one. I sighed.

"Brad, I'm really sorry. It's too last minute. I just can't go."

"Damn Carolyn, what's going on with you? Not only have you been dodging my phone calls, but now this? You know you're the only woman I want by my side when I travel. You've never turned down our adventures before. Who is he?"

I was so glad that we were on the phone and not in person because when I thought about Demarcus, I'm sure my face turned red.

"Bye Brad," I said, playfully dismissing him.

"If you change your mind then you know where to find me," he replied and hung up the phone. I rolled my eyes and laughed. He was so cocky...and I loved it. I gathered my things and headed home. When I walked in my front door, I immediately began smiling. There sat Demarcus; looking like a million dollars in his work pants, wife beater and Timberland boots, putting the finishing touches on a nicely rolled blunt. Then the scent of the Giovanni's authentic Italian food that was sitting on the table hit my nose and I wanted to run and jump into his arms because he knew their lasagna was my favorite. It touched me that he knew what I liked and what I needed. I wanted to melt. As I watched him sitting there, it was evident that his gestures were automatic and effortless, not planned or rehearsed. This man really knew me and accommodated me. It made me want to pull his Johnson out and lick it like a lollipop. But I forced myself not to show any emotions and I compelled my nipples to go down. I maintained my composure and walked over to him. I kissed him on his cheek and greeted him.

"Hey baby."

"Wussup?" He replied, still working on the blunt as the faint remnants of his cologne mixed with the smell of his sweat and overly consuming pheromones climbed their way through my nostrils. A shock wave ignited between my legs and had I been fresh and clean; not smelling of my long day's work, I would have raped him right then. But once again, I maintained my composure.

"Nothing much," I replied innocently as I headed to the bathroom. *But I am going to punish you in the bedroom tonight,* I thought to myself. I took a quick shower and ran the razor over my legs just to make sure they were smooth. "Shit, having a boyfriend takes work," I accidentally said out loud. *Oh shit. I hope he didn't hear me.*

I got out of the shower, dried off and slathered on some strawberries and cream lotion that just happened to be edible. I then put on a pair of cheerleading shorts and a tank top and headed back into the living room.

"Baby, you ready to eat?"

"Yep. I sure am, but let's fire up that blunt first so that that Giovanni's will taste extra good."

"Alright, go ahead and spark it while I warm the food up in the stove," he said, as I delightfully obliged. We smoked and talked about our days as the food warmed up. We laughed, giggled and cracked jokes. Joy and happiness overwhelmed me and I just kept looking at him in disbelief.

Demarcus, are you really mine? Was all that was going through my mind as I watched his lips move while hearing nothing that he said. He took my hand and led me to the table. He pulled out my chair for me then began getting the food out of the stove. He set the table and retrieved a freshly made salad from the refrigerator. He grabbed two bottles of water, two wine glasses and a bottle of my favorite wine and sat them down in front of me. I continued trying to hide my smile and the fact that my heart was swelling. But when he sat down, took my hands in his, bowed his head and prayed, I was done. As soon as the prayer was over, I picked up my fork and attempted to take a bite of my food, but I happened to look up at him just as his eyes met mine. We both paused simultaneously.

"Come here," he said with his head tilted to the side. My body, which was temporarily out of my control, gravitated automatically towards his voice; under his command and not mine. He turned his chair around as I stood in front of him waiting at attention.

"Take your shirt off."

I obeyed and pulled my tank top over my head seductively as my breasts slid out one by one. He took his hands, grasped my hips, gently pulled me towards him and captured my nipple in his mouth. He nibbled and licked on it like it was cheese and he was a mouse. He then opened his mouth wider and took my whole breast in. He sucked as he squeezed my hips. He moved over to my other breast, effortlessly with my hips still cupped in his hands. After he was done with my breasts, he nibbled his way down to where my soaking wet Juicy was starting to cusp my shorts. He gave her a French kiss through my shorts and his fingers dug deeper into my hips. My legs got weak. He stood up, picked me up and sat me down in the seat. He got down on his knees, spread my legs and pulled me to the edge of the seat. He peeled my shorts off me, took one finger and began playing inside of my Juicy. I wanted to moan, but I just wasn't quite ready to give in yet. He took his arms, wrapped them around my legs, pulled my Juicy onto his tongue and began French kissing her again. I squeezed my eyes closed and grabbed onto the back of his head; fighting relentlessly not to cum. His tongue stiffened and he began darting it in and out of me. He was sexing me with his tongue.

He made his way back up to my mouth and started kissing me passionately. I was very pleased with the taste of my juices that lingered in his beard and on his tongue. *Thank God, I washed her really really good,* I thought to myself. He stood up and walked me into the bedroom. He laid me down on the bed and took all his clothes off. I began panting in anticipation of what was to come. I couldn't wait for him to get on top of me and pound my brains out. But what he did was very contrary to that. He made love to me again. Slow, sweet and intensely intimate. We kissed and touched and got lost in each other. He told me that he loved me and I cried. We wrapped ourselves up in each other arms and fell asleep.

Ring, ring, ring.

Ring, Ring. Ring.

I jerked my head up off Demarcus' chest and groggily felt around for the phone. I was still high and in a haze so when I found my phone, I put it up to my ear and answered it. However, when I continued to hear a phone ringing, I realized that it wasn't my phone but Demarcus' that was ringing.

"Demarcus, wake up. Your phone's ringing," I said, my voice raspy, as I shook him. I looked at the clock and saw that it read 10:30 p.m. I couldn't believe it because it felt like me and Demarcus had been asleep for what seemed like forever.

Ring, ring, ring.

"Demarcus, your phone is ringing," I said, shaking him a little harder this time.

"So what. Let it ring. I'm sleep," he said a little feistier than I felt was necessary.

"Ok," I snapped, although I reassumed my position back in his arms with my face plastered to his chest.

Ring, ring, ring. His phone started ringing back to back.

"Demarcus answer your phone. It keeps ringing. Something might be wrong," I demanded as I shook him again in an attempt to wake him up.

"Chill! I told you to leave me alone, I'm sleep." He jerked away from me. *Damn, is this the man I just finished making love to? I'm bout to knock his ass out,* I thought to myself as I glared at him. I got up to go to the bathroom and when I came back, the phone started ringing again. Therefore, I took it upon myself to answer it.

"Hello?"

"Who the fuck is this?" I heard a female voice say. *Oh shit!* My heart started pounding. It was Charmanita. I knew I should have hung up, but that night at Buster's and the Carolyn Black in me wouldn't allow me to.

"Who you want it to be?" I snapped back.

"Bitch, who the fuck is this and where is my husband?" That stung because although he was lying beside of me, he was in fact, still her husband.

"Apparently he ain't with you." I laughed arrogantly, digging myself in a deeper hole.

"Oh, for real bitch, we'll see about that," she replied and hung up the phone. Demarcus began to stir and I quickly dropped the phone because I knew I had just made a big mistake.

"What you yelling about?" he asked groggily as he sat up and kissed me on my leg. He then stretched out his arms and reached over to the ashtray to retrieve the blunt. *Shit, should I tell him that it was her or should I lie?* I contemplated to myself. I took a deep breath and elected to tell him the truth.

"Uh, well uh, I...uh answered your phone because it kept ringing," I replied coolly.

"You what?" He turned and looked straight at me.

"I said I answered your phone. It kept ringing and I told you to get it but you wouldn't so I answered it." I saw him begin to morph into the bull. He grabbed me by my shoulders.

"Who was it? Who was it?"

"It was her."

"Her who?" His voice became scary.

"Charmanita!" I yelled. He stared at me as if he was trying to decipher if I was telling the truth, but he knew I was.

"What the fuck did you say to her?"

"I didn't say nothing."

"Don't fucking play with me! What did you say?"

"I didn't say shit. She asked who I was and I didn't say."

"What did she want?"

"What do you mean what did she want? She wanted to join hands and sing Kumbaya with me over margaritas!" I yelled, looking at him as if he was dumb.

"What did she say?" He asked, unfazed by my sarcasm

"She was running her mouth, being disrespectful and then she hung up." He looked at me like he wanted to punch me in my face, but he punched me with his eyes instead. He jumped up and started getting dressed.

"Where you going?"

"Don't fucking worry about it. Your silly ass probably just fucked everything up!"

"Oh yeah, I forgot, I'm still on the down low. Your fucking mistress right?"

"Don't give me that fucking bullshit. I told you that I have to be cool until she signs the divorce papers you fucking idiot!"

"Who the fuck are you talking to like that?" I jumped up. His phone started ringing again and he answered it.

"Charmanita wussup?" He was silent, I guess as she was cursing him out. "Look she's a fucking prostitute, damn. I was in the fucking bathroom taking a shit. I didn't know she was gonna answer my phone." He paused. "Look, skip bullshit and tell me what the fuck you want....Yes I'll be there. Yes, just be ready to go at about 7 a.m. because you know we have to stop and get your grandmother on the way there...Yes, yes, ok. Yeah, whatever. Just have your ass ready to go Friday morning." He concluded the conversation and hung up. I slapped him with every ounce of strength I had.

"A PROSTITUTE? A FUCKIN' PROSTITUTE?" I yelled.

"It's your fucking fault, you shouldna answered my phone. Now I'ma have to kiss her ass and clean this shit up because of you." He yelled back as he held the side of his face.

"Punk, you better be worried about cleaning the shit up with me. And where are you taking her next week?"

"None of your fucking business. That's between me and my wife. It has nothing to do with you."

Once again, I was stunned. I felt like I was back on the floor at Buster's.

"Your wife? Oh word. For real? Ok." My hand tingled, ready to slap him again.

"Look, I didn't mean it like that."

"It's too late now. You already said it!"

"WHAT DO YOU WANT FROM ME? WHAT THE FUCK DO YOU WANT FROM ME? I'm with you every fuckin' day! I'm trying to show you that I'm serious this time. All I ask is for you to trust me. I know what I'm doing and if you would stop being so bullheaded, we could breeze through this shit with no problems! But nothing's ever good enough for your ass!"

I rolled my eyes. "No honey, it's not good enough me. I want all of you! Not just what she'll allow you to give me," I said as tears sprang up in my eyes.

"Look, my son comes first and sometimes that involves me having to do shit with Charmanita..."

"Don't say her name! Don't you ever say her fuckin' name in my house again!" I screamed. He looked at me; stumped, and threw his hands in the air.

"Look, you can hang in there with me and see this through 'til the end or you can go the fuck on somewhere," he replied candidly and walked towards the door.

"Oh, hell nah." I yelled. "At what expense? Being your fuckin' prostitute? Turn your ass around and look at me!" I grabbed him and spun him around. "First of all, don't give me no ultimatum. I been ride or die with your ass since day one. You're the one that keeps taking me on this emotional rollercoaster going back and forth between me and that bitch! Making me feel like you love me and then turning around and leaving me; giving me your ass to kiss. You can save all the extra shit because I understand how much you love your son, but I need to know how much you love me if I'm going to stick around and deal with this shit. I can play number two to your son because he's a child, but I be damn if I'm going to be a prostitute when it comes to your baby mama. All that you've put me through, you at least owe me the respect of telling me what the hell is going on!" I yelled back.

"Damnit Carolyn. It's their annual family reunion and I drive her, her mother, her grandmother and my son to South Carolina every year. They depend on me to bring her mom and grandmother down there because neither of them drive well. Plus...plus I want my son to know his family," he said as his voice and head dropped sullenly.

"Ok fine. If that's the case, I'm going too," I snapped, unmoved by his emotions.

"Ok, yeah sure. Let me know how that works out," he replied, looking at me like I was an idiot.

"Why can't they fly or take the train? I mean there's other ways for them to get there without you taking them. Are you gonna do this shit every year and expect me to stay home?" I inquired.

"Look, you asked me what was going on and I told you. That's the end of the conversation. Now drop it."

Refusing to back down, fueled by my anger, hurt and feelings of betrayal, I pushed him into the door.

"I can't freaking believe I'm here again. Why do I keep letting you do this to me? I ain't taking this shit no more. Get out!" I screamed to the top of my lungs.

"Fuck it! Have it your way then," he said and slammed the door. I remained silent but tears flooded my cheeks. I put a towel over my mouth to silence the sobs that threatened to leap from my throat until I heard his car pulling out of the driveway. Once I was sure that he was gone, I cried as loud as my lungs would allow. He'd done it to me again and I'd let him. Once again, he left me out in the cold while his baby mama reigned supreme and had my man right where she wanted him. I was devastated and then I became enraged. Suddenly the trip to South Africa didn't sound so bad after all.

Case#: 38589 Aged Out

"English! English! Wake up! It's your birthday baby. Wake up." English Terry groggily opened her eyes to see her foster mother, Bertha McClain standing over her smiling. A single candle, the number eighteen, flickered on top of a small birthday cake that she was holding.

"Ms. Bertha, its seven o'clock in the morning," English replied as she rolled back over and pulled the covers up over her head.

"English, I said get up now," Ms. Bertha stated in a more serious tone.

"Why? We can celebrate my birthday later. It's too early."

"Ok," Ms. Bertha replied as English shifted in her bed, enjoying the warmth of her blanket and the softness of her pillow. As she began to doze back off into sandman land, an ice cold splash of water hit her like a pile of bricks causing her to jump up out of her bed. As her eyes opened and she began to register her surroundings, she saw Ms. Berta standing over her holding a bucket.

"Ms. Bertha, what the hell did you do that shit for?" English screamed, as cold water dripped off her face.

"Cause I told your black ass to get up. Today is your eighteenth birthday and you need to pack your shit and get the fuck outta my house. You have given me three years of hell and I'm sick of your ass. You been saying you can't wait until you turn eighteen since you got here and now your ass is eighteen so your wish has come true. Now get up and get your clothes packed."

"But Ms. Bertha, its seven o'clock in the morning and I ain't got nowhere to go. What am I supposed to do? Where am I supposed to go? I ain't got no money."

"Well, that sounds like a personal problem to me. You shoulda thought about all that shit before you burnt all your bridges and walked around here acting like an asshole!" Ms. Bertha said as she put her hands on her hips. She glared at English and waited for her to begin moving.

English couldn't argue with Ms. Bertha because she knew she was right. She had given Ms. Bertha hell as she had all her foster parents before her. It wasn't personal, but she had so much hurt and anger inside that she took it out on everyone around her. And hell it wasn't like Ms. Bertha loved her anyway because she'd only put up with English for the monthly checks she received. Plus, Ms. Bertha got more for her than a regular foster child because English was labeled as "therapeutic" and the state paid more for therapeutic children.

"Well, you little hussy, don't sit there looking like a deer caught in headlights, get your ass up and get to steppin'!" Ms. Bertha said with her eyes blazing. English was scared to death to leave but she'd be damned if she'd let that old witch see her feeling weak.

"Well, fuck you then you fat bitch! And I want that check you got for me yesterday because that paid your ass for this full month and since I'm leaving today I ain't gonna be here for a full month."

"Heffa please! That's reparations for dealing with your ass. I'll be back in here in ten minutes and you betta be packed and on your way outta here!" Ms. Bertha said as she slammed the door.

English sat there in a trance, shaking her leg for a while before she could even move. She was still soaking wet and cold. She got up, pulled out her old raggedy suitcase that she had had since she was 7 years old and began packing it up. She put on dry clothes, put her hair into a ponytail and went to use the bathroom to brush her teeth. After using the bathroom, she looked into the medicine cabinet and grabbed one of Ms. Bertha's bottles of sleeping pills. She closed the cabinet and stared at herself in the mirror for a second. As she looked in her own eyes, she saw all the hurt and pain that she had endured in her life. She wanted to cry so badly, but she refused to let those emotions come out, so she turned around and walked into her bedroom to get her suitcase. When she walked back into her room, she saw that Ms. Bertha had laid a hundred dollar bill on the bed. Her pride made her want to say, "Fuck that bitch and her money," but then her voice of reason made her think otherwise.

"It's my money anyway," she said as she snatched the money off the bed and stuffed it into her pocket. She grabbed her jacket, went slowly down the stairs and walked out the door. She stood on the sidewalk where the sun was barely up and looked around. She didn't even know which way to go...left, right or straight. But one thing she knew was that she couldn't go backwards. She didn't have any friends or family she could go to, so she just started walking.

English walked aimlessly for what seemed like forever. Finally, her stomach started growling and she went to find somewhere to eat. She ordered her food and ate as slowly as she could because she knew that once she finished she would have to leave and face the outside world again. After she ate, she sat there for a while, pretending to read a newspaper in order to kill time. A handsome young man who looked to be in his mid-thirties came up to her table. He had been watching her from the other side of the restaurant. He noticed her suitcase and knew that she would be perfect for his "business" because she looked like she was a runaway with nowhere to go. Those were his favorite. The girl was young and tender with a nice shape. She was a little rough looking, but he figured that she would do once he cleaned her up.

He sat down at her table and began playing on her vulnerabilities. She willingly told him everything about being in foster care and how Ms. Bertha had kicked her out with no place to go. He, of course, didn't care but he played along. He told her that he had also been a foster child and knew what she was going through. Once he had reeled her in, he told her that he could give her a place to stay and a job at his "business" until she got on her feet. She readily agreed. He got up to go to the bathroom and told her he would return shortly. A young pastor, who'd just opened the doors of a new mega church, had also been watching her and her exchange with the young man. When the coast was clear, he went over to her and begged her not to go with the young man because he knew the young man's type. She pretty much told the pastor to fuck off because he didn't know shit about her.

"And he does?" The preacher asked. English thought about it for a few minutes and blew it off because she didn't believe in God and didn't want to be with somebody that was going to try to force God on her. If God loved her so much then why had he forsaken her, her entire eighteen years of life? Defeated, the pastor handed her a card with the name and address of his church just in case she changed her mind. She aimlessly put the card in her jacket pocket and waited for the young man who had introduced himself to her as Arid, to come out of the bathroom. When Arid returned, he paid for her food, picked up her suitcase and led her to his late model Yukon Denali. She hopped in unaware of what she was about to walk into. The preacher, who sat watching out the window, stretched forth his hand and said a prayer for the young girl.

After leaving the diner, Arid took English shopping for "business attire." He brought her clothes, shoes, undergarments and make up. Some of the clothes and shoes seemed a little too provocative for her liking, nevertheless, she felt like a queen because it was her first time ever going on a shopping spree. Little did she know Arid was fattening her up for the kill.

When English arrived with Arid at his house, there were already a few girls inside sitting on the couch. Some of them glared at her, others greeted her with indifference. Bewildered as to whom these girls were and why they were there, English froze as she tried to figure out what was going on. Arid assured her that these girls would become her sisters and were in similar situations as she was. She hesitated, but Arid, knowing he had to be cunning with this one, led her into his room, which was large and fabulous and announced that she was his special girl and could share his room with him. English wasn't sure what to do, but she could smell herself so she asked to take a shower and freshen up. Arid told English that he had an even better idea. He led her into a spectacular bathroom that had a Jacuzzi bathtub and a large walk in shower. He ran her a bubble bath and once she was in, she started to feel so much better. When she walked back into the bedroom, she noticed that Arid was standing at the door waiting for her. He gave her something to wear and told her to come and meet the other girls. He introduced her to them and led her back into his bedroom where he gave her a joint and told her to smoke it. He also gave her a glass of wine to drink. English, who had never done either, was very reluctant to try them, but again Arid convinced her that it was necessary in helping her to relax. And he was right. By the end of the joint, she was laughing so hard that Ms. Bertha and her hard knock life vanished into the smoke.

Taking advantage of the moment, Arid began touching her and kissing her. English tensed up because she was still a virgin and didn't like where things were going. She tried to refuse and push him away but he forced himself on her. However, in order to maintain her dignity and pride, she gave in and reciprocated sex with him because she would rather give it to him then allow him to take it away. Plus, she was afraid of what he would do if she made a big fuss. When he finished, he rolled off her and fell asleep. She laid there staring at the ceiling, realizing that she was now a "hoe" in a "hoe" house. She shook her head sadly, as she tried to figure out how and why she'd ended up at this place in her life. She refused to cry because her pride wouldn't let her. She would die first. She finally drifted off to sleep into a dream world filled with nightmares. She woke up the next morning to Arid climbing on top of her. This time she was sober and thinking clearly, which made things worse. However, once again, she obliged him as a means of self-preservation. Once he was done with her, she took a shower, put on a pair of sweats and waited until he left before she grabbed her things and took off running. She ran until she found a bench in a small park whereby she sat down to catch her breath. A man with a hot dog stand sold her food and drink. As she ate, she began trying to collect her thoughts. She had no clue what to do or where to go. The hundred dollars that Ms. Bertha had given her wouldn't last her throughout the week; therefore, she had to find a way to get money. However, she knew that selling her body wasn't going to be an option. She even considered going back and begging Ms. Bertha for her forgiveness, but she knew the old bat would gloat and send her on her way.

She absentmindedly put her hand into her jacket pocket and found the card that the preacher had given her. A small glimmer of hope peaked inside her mind because she recognized the address on the card and figured what the heck; she didn't have anything else to lose. She picked her suitcase up and asked the hot dog man to call her a cab. When she arrived at the church, which looked to still be under construction, she went and knocked on every door but no one was there. Her little glimmer of hope obliterated into dust and the pressure became too much for her to bear. She sat down on the front steps of the church and broke down. Her pride was of no more value to her because she was tired. Tired of going from place to place, tired of the sadness, tired of being unloved, tired of the anger and more than anything just tired of living the life forced upon her. She didn't really want to die, but she felt that she had no other choice. So she reached into her suitcase, took out Ms. Bertha's sleeping pills, and took as many of them that she could without vomiting.

Pastor Keaton

On the way to the bank to make a deposit, Pastor Ron Keaton realized that he had left one of the moneybags in his office, so he turned around and headed back towards the church. When he arrived, he noticed a young woman lying on the front steps. When he saw the pill bottle lying beside her, he knew he didn't have time to call 911 so he picked her up, grabbed her things; including the pill bottle and rushed her to the emergency room.

Carolyn Black

"Fosterberg County Department of Social Services, Carolyn speaking."

"Hey Carolyn. This Benita Hines from Fosterberg County Memorial Hospital. How are you?"

"Hey Benita, I'm doing great. What can I do for you?" I responded glad to hear from her. We'd been pretty cool in college and she called me from time to time when she had a child in the unit that she suspected was being abused.

"Well, I don't know if you handle situations like this, but we have an 18 year old down here that tried to commit suicide. She turned eighteen yesterday and her foster mother kicked her out. She said she's been out walking the streets because she had nowhere to go. I didn't know who else to call with her being 18 so I figured I'd better call y'all."

"Well Benita, we usually don't handle situations like that, but I can try to help. I'll be there shortly." I said as I let out a sigh and hung up the phone. I really wasn't in the mood to deal with a case, but I sucked it up and grabbed my briefcase. On the way to the hospital, I let a few tears drop because I hadn't heard from Demarcus since our argument and Friday was rapidly approaching. My heart ached so badly because I missed him and I needed him. But I had to get over it and I knew exactly how I was going to do it. Although I didn't want to go with Brad, I knew I had to do something to distract myself. I knew that I would go crazy, sitting at home alone while Demarcus was in South Carolina parading *Clifford The Big Red Dog* around like they were the ideal family.

When I arrived at the hospital, I met with the young woman, English and a very handsome young pastor who apparently had brought her to the hospital. I listened to her story and although her foster mother wasn't committing a crime in asking her to leave, the way she did it pissed me off.

"Where's your family?" I asked.

"Well, my dad murdered my mother when I was seven and her parents were already deceased, so I've been in and out of foster care since then." My heart dropped. No wonder this poor child was so angry and had wreaked havoc in all her foster homes. I needed a moment to think, so I left out to get a bite to eat.

"Excuse me, Ms. Black, do you mind if I join you?" the pastor asked. Baffled by his request I replied, "Uh sure." We went to the cafeteria and ordered our meals. We sat down and of course I was about to dive into my food, but then he took my hands and began praying. I didn't mind praying but I was a little taken aback by him grabbing my hands. Nevertheless, I obliged.

"Amen," he said concluding the blessing.

"Amen," I said and quickly pulled back my hands.

"Ms. Black, my name is Pastor Ron Keaton. I just moved here from Virginia and I am the pastor of The New Light Church of God on Firburn road. Anyway, when I saw English laying on the steps, I recognized her immediately from yesterday. I gave her my card at a diner after I saw a guy that looked like he meant her no good; convince her into going with him. I tried to talk her out of it but she wouldn't listen. I guess she saw for herself that he was a snake in the grass and got away. I just thank God he didn't turn her out."

"Wow. Well I'm glad she came looking for you."

"Well, it's just the grace of God that I forgot something at the church and had to return to get it. Otherwise, I wouldn't have gone back by the church until Friday," he said. I nodded but I didn't respond.

"So, is there anything I can do to help? I mean I'd let her stay with me, but I'm a single man and it would be inappropriate."

"Pastor Keaton you've done enough. That was a really kind thing you did."

"You can call me Ron. Sorry, I'm just so used to talking with my parishioners. God called me to preach about 7 years ago and I haven't looked back since then. But I'm learning that although I'm a pastor, I'm Ron first."

"Ok Ron," I replied with a giggle. We chit chatted a while longer and I actually found him to be a very interesting man. He was cool and not rigid like some pastors could be. I liked him and although I hadn't attended church in like forever, I considered maybe trying his out.

"Well Ron, I guess we'd better get back to English."

"Yeah, you're right. Listen, does Fosterberg County have a transitional living facility here? They have several in Virginia, specifically for children who have aged out of the system with nowhere to go."

"Well, we're kind of a small county; more rural than anything, so to answer your question, no we don't."

"Interesting. I think that might be my next calling. What about a homeless shelter?"

"Nope. Contrary to popular belief, although this is a rural area, most people are hanging in there financially. I've never seen any homeless people around here. Not that they don't exist. I'm just not aware of any."

"Well, you are now," he replied candidly.

"Yeah, you're right. I've been sitting here racking my brain but there's nothing I can do unless I can convince one of our foster parents to take her in. But I don't know how long that will last; plus, we have to keep those homes open for our kids that are under 18, so we may have to look out of the county. She's still in school so that may work in our favor in regards to finding some type of placement."

"Listen, I have an idea. English can stay at the church parsonage for a while. It's a tiny, little cottage that came with the property, but it should be enough for her until we can figure something out. Like you said, she's a student so maybe she can stay there until she graduates and in the meantime save up some money so she can get her own place."

"Well Pastor Ke...I mean Ron," I corrected myself, "being that she's eighteen that will be her decision. I really don't have any jurisdiction over what choices she makes. Sadly, she's really on her own now. However, I can help get her into some different programs and since she's a foster child, we have a program that will pay for her to go to college depending upon her grades and academic record. I also may be able to get her some food stamps and she should already be receiving Medicaid. I'll try to hook her up with a case manager who can help her learn to manage her money and take care of any health needs she has."

"Awesome! Let's go tell her," Pastor Keaton replied.

After we discussed things with English, she was more than happy to accept any help that we offered her. I really liked the pastor because he seemed to genuinely care about her wellbeing. I trusted that he would be good to her and I decided that although she technically wasn't a client, I was going to be there for her as well. As I walked out of the hospital, I actually felt good about what had just transpired.

"Ms. Black, wait a second." I turned around as Pastor Keaton, I mean Ron, caught up to me.

"I meant to give you my card. Our church just opened up a few weeks ago. Well actually the sanctuary just opened up because the contractors are still working on the rest of the church, but I would love for you to come by."

"I'll take that into consideration," I smiled.

"Oh yeah, and one more thing. Um, I hope this doesn't sound too forward but could I take you out for a cup of coffee or lunch one day?" he asked nervously.

"Um, thanks but, I'm going to have to pass on that Pastor," I said putting an emphasis on the word, "Pastor."

"Ms. Black, as I said before, I'm Ron before I'm Pastor Keaton. I'm a man and you're a beautiful and intelligent woman. I'm single and I don't see a ring on your finger so I assume you're single as well. I'm very committed to my walk with God and I'm not trying to solicit anything if that's what you're thinking. I would just like to take you out and get to know you better. Maybe you can help me with this transitional living center."

"Ron, *Pastor*, I'm a heathen. I drink occasionally and I like to cuss and party. And to be frank with you...um I don't know how to say this appropriately, but I also like having sex..." He stepped closer to me. I could smell his cologne.

"So do I Ms. Black. I haven't always been the man that I am today. The only difference is that now I am committed to withholding my inner freak until I get married. Don't let the "pastor" in Pastor Keaton fool you," he said as he handed me his card and walked off.

Well damn. I laughed to myself as I walked to the car. I felt flattered but at the same time, I wanted no one but Demarcus and I was hoping that he'd come to his senses about that whole family trip thing. When I got home, I put on my sweats and decided to give him a call.

"Hello," his deep and sexy voice said through the phone.

"What's up?" I asked, trying to play it cool.

"Shit. What's up with you?"

"Well, I haven't heard from you and I really don't like the way things went down. So I just wanted to call and see if we can try to make amends."

"I mean, you're mad at me because of this trip and it's something that I can't change so it's on you," he replied nonchalantly.

"Wait, soooo, you're still going?" I asked.

"Why wouldn't I be? Because you had a temper tantrum?"

"What?! Nah dude because I'm supposed to be your girlfriend. I took you around my family and I opened myself up..."

"Look ma, I don't have time for this. I holler at you when I get back," he said and hung up in my face. I started to call him back and cuss him out but I had a better idea. I made another phone call instead.

"Hello."

"Brad, is that offer to go with you to South Africa still open?"

"For you Ms. Black, anything is open."

"Alright well I'll see you Thursday evening then."

Laronya Teague

Thursday Evening

As I was gathering the last few items to throw into my suitcase, my doorbell rang. I quickly finished packing and zipped my suitcase up. I dragged my things to the door and answered it. An older white male dressed in a suit was standing there waiting for me. I glanced out and saw a black Mercedes with tented windows parked in front of my house.

"Ms. Black?" he asked.

"Yes, I'm Ms. Black," I replied.

"Good evening. My name is Henry, Mr. Martinelli's driver. I've come to get your bags for you."

"Ok sure," I said as I moved aside to let him get my bags just as the back window of the Mercedes rolled down.

"Carolyn Black. Bring that sweet ass of yours on over here and get in the car," Brad said from the backseat. Usually, I would have had something fly to say back to him but his comment actually kind of offended me. I felt a little bit repulsed, but I refused to back down while Demarcus and the redhead scallywag enjoyed their family time, so I shook it off.

"I will as long as you have a big or sparkling gift worth me walking my sweet ass over there for," I replied dryly. Completely oblivious to my indifference, he chuckled and continued with the "cat and mouse" game.

"Well, besides the fact that I'm taking you to South Africa, I do have something that I feel will make things worth your while. But you have to come see what it is first," he said.

I rolled my eyes and locked my door as Henry carried my bags to the car. I walked over to the other side and got in. Brad's mouth curled into a cocky smile.

"I thought you'd see things my way," he said as he leaned in to kiss me. However, instead of meeting my lips he met my hand mushing his face.

"Back up off me. These kisses ain't free boo," I said without cracking a smile although he still thought I was just playing hard to get.

"That's my girl," he replied and reached up into the front seat and retrieved a large giftwrapped box.

"I think this will be worth your while Ms. Black." He said as he handed me the box.

I opened it and inside was a pair of red leather Gucci knee boots and a small red Gucci clutch to match. Now, normally that would have made my Juicy start leaking, especially coming from Brad; however, I felt nothing but disgust. My mind was elsewhere, mainly in South Carolina where the man of my dreams was going to be with his wife. I felt like a fool because not only had he played me again, but here I was sitting in the backseat of a car with yet another woman's husband. The conversation that I'd had with Marita Martinez ran through my brain and I began feeling guilty. I already had a nauseated stomach because of my broken heart and the guilt was beginning to give me a headache, but I had to do something to appease my feelings of getting played. I had to distract myself from thinking about Demarcus and the only way that *I* knew how to do it was to run into the arms of another man with whom I shared no emotional connection. Looking at Brad made me *sicker* on my stomach and when he put his hand on my thigh while giving me "the look," I almost vomited. However, in order to rebuild my wall I had to play the game and I knew that I would need some added forces so I decided to let the Old Carolyn take control.

"I'd like to see you wearing those tonight, with nothing else," he said as he bit his bottom lip. I rolled my eyes.

"We'll see," I replied.

"You seem a little tense. Is everything ok?" Brad asked finally starting to catch on to my indifference.

"Yep. I'm just stressed from work that's all."

"Well, maybe this will help you calm down," he said and handed me a joint. "I also have some vintage 1965 wine that my father gave to me. It's lovely. I'll pour you a glass," he said as he retrieved two wine glasses. I lit the joint and took a few tokes on it. He handed me a glass of wine and I gulped it down like it was water.

"Damn, would you like another?" he asked.

"Yes, I would," I replied. He poured me another glass as I finished off the rest of the joint. I attempted to be daintier with the second glass but I ended up gulping it down too. However, it did help me to relax. By the time we got to the airport, I was calm, cool and collected. Hell, I was going to South Africa, somewhere I'd never been before and I was actually starting to get excited. That is until we walked into the airport towards the check-in area. Over the speaker system, the song "Rock Steady" by the Whispers floated in the air and I thought about Demarcus. I stopped because I couldn't take another step with Brad.

"Brad I'm sorry but I can't do this. I can't go."

"What? What's wrong? What happened?"

"Love happened. Thanks for everything, but I can't see you anymore," I replied and turned around with my bags, including the Gucci bag, and headed towards the door. Brad stood there looking dumbfounded, but he didn't object. I got into a cab and cried the whole way home, but I was proud of myself. I was a new person. I knew how to heal without hurting myself *and* another man's wife and I owed that to Demarcus.

Sunday Evening

I sat on the couch, drinking some hot chocolate as I watched TV. My weekend had been hell but I made it through. I'd engaged in some retail therapy since I had to find an outfit to go with my new Gucci boots and purse. I also treated myself to a full spa treatment. My hair was flowing and my skin was glowing. My heart was hurting, but I just let it hurt because I knew that the pain would eventually go away. I had learned that although I'd thought I was using men all this time as a coping mechanism, I really wasn't because they actually controlled me to a certain degree. The way I dressed, the way I walked, the way I talked all revolved around getting, keeping or enticing a man. However, as I fingered my silky, straightened hair, I smiled because this time it actually was for me. I wanted to look pretty because *I* wanted to look pretty. Not to impress anyone else.

Knock. Knock. Knock.

I looked at the clock, which read 9:30. *Who the hell is this?* I thought to myself as I got up and headed towards the door.

"Who is it?" I asked as I looked through the peephole, but whoever it was, was covering it with their finger.

"Carolyn, open the door. It's Demarcus." I stood there for a second contemplating what to do. The thump in my heart increased and although I wanted to, I couldn't conjure up any anger. I actually didn't know how I was feeling although the word "immune" popped into my mind. Therefore, I had no problem opening the door. He stood there, holding a large manila folder.

"Can I come in?"

"Sure," I said calmly and moved aside.

"Follow me to the kitchen so we can sit down at the table and talk."

"Ok," I obliged nonchalantly. We sat down at the table and he handed me the folder.

"Read this," he said. I opened the folder and began reading the documents. They were divorce papers with both Demarcus and Charmanita's signatures. My mouth flew open and my heart stopped. I looked up at Demarcus for clarity as well as confirmation.

"That's why I had to go to South Carolina Cee, so we could finalize our divorce. That's where we got married at and it's a long and complicated story about the divorce process but I'm sorry for lying to you and misleading you. I had to play my cards right and I'm sorry you got hurt in the midst of it. But Cee, I'm free and nothing can stop us from being together now." I was speechless.

"Listen, there's just one more thing I need to tell you."

"What's that?" I asked nervously as I waited for him to drop another bomb. He backed up out of his chair, got down on one knee and retrieved a small black box from his coat pocket.

"Carolyn Black, I want you to be my wife. Will you marry me?"

My heart began pounding and my breathing almost ceased. I was in total shock. "Oh my God Demarcus. Are you, are you serious? Like, really?" A tear dropped from my eye.

"Yeah babe. I'm serious. Keeping this secret has been killing me and now I can finally do what I wanted to do since the first day I met you and that's ask you to be mine forever. Cee, you are my nigga and although that may sound crazy, that's the only way I can say it because it sums everything up into one word. I can't live my life without you ma. Straight up. Will you do me the honor, the privilege, of being my wife?'

I nodded my head and smiled. "Yep. I sho' will. Now go on and put that good ring on my finger boy," I said, grinning from ear to ear as he slid the petite, but beautiful diamond on my finger.

"And don't worry, I already asked your dad. I asked him, Brandon and John at the party," he said smiling. I almost tackled him as I jumped out of the chair and squeezed him as hard as I could.

Christmas Eve

"Demarcus are you sure about this? I mean, I don't want to cause any problems."

"Cee, you saw the divorce papers right? And you also saw the ironclad custody agreement too right?"

"Yes."

"Well then, there's nothing Charmanita can say or do. She might not like it but I don't give a damn. You're my fiancée, which means you're going to be around my son. She'll just have to get over it."

"He sure is cute," I said as I turned and looked at Demarcus' four-year-old *twin* sleeping peacefully in the backseat.

"He get it from his daddy. What you expect?" Demarcus boasted playfully. I rolled my eyes.

"Whatever," I replied. He grabbed my hand and kissed it as we drove to meet Charmanita so Demarcus could drop the baby off for Christmas. He'd been with us the past few days and he was a lovely child. I was so happy and I finally accepted being happy. I wasn't afraid or suspicious of it anymore. I'd learned to be happy within myself and the love I shared with Demarcus simply compounded it.

We pulled in at our designated meeting spot and there sat Charmanita. Demarcus got out and walked over towards her car. When she saw me sitting in the passenger's seat, her look went from confusion to rage. She jumped out of the car and came straight at Demarcus.

"That's that white looking bitch from the club ain't it? You bastard. So you really have been messing around with her all this time. That's why you was so adamant about getting a divorce."

"Look, DJ's in the backseat, we ain't gonna do this in front of him. I don't have to explain shit to you."

"I be damn. I don't know her and I be damn if she gonna be around my son." Demarcus came and leaned on my door as a precaution because he knew what I was capable of when it came to her.

"Look Charmanita, it would be different if you were concerned about him being mistreated but you just being a bitch. You know I'll kill you or anybody else if they mistreat my baby so you shouldn't have shit to say."

"Fuck that! I wanna meet the bitch. I have a right to know her if you gonna be bringing her around our baby."

"Look, I'm gonna be marrying her in a few months, so you'll have plenty of time to break bread with her."

"You what?" she yelled. Then I saw Demarcus' body moving around on the window. I knew she was trying to fight him but I couldn't see because he was blocking me. I tried to jump out the driver's side door but movement from the backseat stopped me. DJ was waking up and I didn't want him to see me beating his mama's ass, so I laid my hand on the horn instead, in hopes of getting their attention.

"Demarcus the baby's waking up," I yelled from the window. The commotion stopped and I heard Demarcus yell, "Calm your ass down. You ain't never loved me and I ain't never loved you! Stop being a child and be a fucking woman so we can take care of our son the right way."

"Fuck you, you black bastard! Give me my son."

"I will, but you gonna get your ass in the car and calm down first. I'll get him and bring him to you." I guess she must have listened because Demarcus came and got DJ's things and put them in her trunk. He then came back and got DJ.

"Bye Carolyn," he said sleepily and waved at me. I couldn't help but to smile.

"Bye DJ. Merry Christmas," I replied. I saw the pride swell on Demarcus' face as he kissed DJ and carried him to the car. As I looked over, my eyes met Charmanita's. She looked like she wanted to kill me. I returned her look with a wink and a smile. She gave me an ominous nod. I blew her a kiss as Demarcus got in the car and we pulled off.

"Sorry about that Cee."

"It's all good. Come on let's go eat," I replied as we headed to one of Aunt Glenda and Uncle Ronnie's restaurants for our family Christmas dinner. Demarcus and I walked in holding hands, all smiles. Brandon and my little brother John came over and greeted us, as did my parents. By then, the whole family knew Demarcus and I were engaged which meant that Demarcus had officially been adopted into our family. They'd all grown to love him since I had started bringing him around regularly and when they were with him, I barely saw him. I didn't care though because it made me smile.

After Brandon and my little brother John whisked Demarcus away, I grabbed a drink and sat down with my cousin Sharquita's kids so I could check in on them. After I smothered them with hugs and kisses, I ended up at the chicken head table with Brandon and my little brother John's chicks. I laughed because it made me think about Sylvia's birthday cookout and how back then, I'd *had* to sit with my little brother John's chicken head out of desperation. However, this time I wasn't sitting with them out of loneliness and desperation. I was merely sitting with them because these two were actually cool and had been around for longer than a week.

"Being 'sister save a hoe' again I see."

I sighed and rolled my eyes. "Olivia, dude like why are you sweating me? Jump up off my sack. What do you want? "

"Nothing. I just wanted to give you kudos for always taking care of the charity cases."

"Wait a minute? Who she talkin' bout?" Chicken Head One, which was Brandon's girl asked. I was a bit concerned about her because she'd just gotten out of jail for attempted murder and I knew she had no problem fighting Olivia.

"Nothing. Nothing. She's on pain meds. She's not thinking straight. Don't pay her any attention."

"Awww, leave it to you to take up for the less fortunate instead of your own flesh and blood," Olivia replied condescendingly.

"What the fuck do you want?" I asked annoyed. "Why are you over here? I'm gonna go out on a limb and say it's because...nobody wants to play with you anymore," I said in a childlike voice. "Poor baby, you ain't got nobody to play with since Sylvia ain't here no more huh?" I snickered. "Poor Olivia. Poor pathetic Olivia. Go over there to the kids table, maybe they'll play with you," I said as I turned my back and dismissed her.

"You bitch," she said and spit at me. Luckily, the spit missed me and hit the table but the gesture was enough to set me off.

"You know what, fuck this shit." I pushed my seat back and stood up. "Your ass is completely healed now, so ain't gonna be no excuses for you getting your ass beat. Let's get it," I said and squared up with her.

"Yeah, yeah, I been wanting this for a long time," she hissed.

"What's up?" I said.

"Y'all chill." Chicken Head Two pleaded but I didn't hear her. I swung and hit Olivia in her mouth as hard as I could. Then it was on. I fought her for everything she'd ever done to me. I fought her for Sylvia and I showed her no mercy. The only thing we shared was our bloodline and that was no longer enough to protect her. I fought her as if she was an animal out in the streets. She fought me back in the same manner; however, hate and jealousy shrouded her blows which could have been lethal had I not known what I was up against.

"Oh my gosh! Somebody stop them! Help!"

When I came to myself, my family was pulling me off her. I happened to have a free arm and since I was still within reach of Olivia's face, I tried to smash her face in. However, my little brother John caught my arm.

"Carolyn she's not worth it. She's not worth it."

"Baby please calm down," I heard my mom say.

"No! Let me go! I'm sick of her. Let me finish her! Bitch! I hate you!" I screamed in Olivia's direction. Demarcus and my family surrounded me while no one came to her aide with the exception of her doormat husband. Our eyes met. My look resembled liberation and triumph while hers magnified rage, hate and unwelcomed defeat. Then before my eyes, she morphed back into her fake poised self. A sinister smile spread across her lips as she wiped away a few drops of blood that had trickled down her chin. A chill went down my spine.

New Year's Eve

Demarcus and I walked into my parent's annual New Year's Eve party that they hosted every year at the place where Brandon had held my birthday party. My entire family was there and partied like rock stars. My parents were drinking; my aunts, uncles and cousins were drinking, hell my grandparents were even drinking. Me, Demarcus, Brandon, my little brother John and their same chicken heads from the Christmas Party; believe it or not, were drinking and making our way back to the "secret office" so we could smoke.

"Damn, you remember how tore up we was at your birthday party Cee? Man, we had this room smoked out."

"Hell yeah! That was the party of the century," my little brother John chimed in.

"Yeah, that was the best birthday I've ever had...and the worst all at the same time," I replied sadly.

"Yeah...but I can say this, Sylvia's snobby ass sho' did show me a different side though. Hell, I never knew she was that cool and that heifa had some hoover lungs. She damn near out smoked me!" Brandon laughed. We sat and reminisced about that night. We laughed and shed a few tears but they were tears of joy based off the good memories we shared.

"The only thing missing that night was my Boo," I said as I looked at Demarcus and smiled.

"Awww hell, here you go with that gay shit," Brandon said and rolled his eyes.

"I think it's sweet. Why you don't talk to me like that?" Brandon's Chicken head asked.

"Don't even start it. Matter of fact, come on, it's almost 12:00," Brandon replied, giving me the evil eye. I snickered and winked my eye at him. He shot me the bird. We all laughed and walked back out to the party. A waiter walked around handing out glasses of champagne as we awaited the countdown. At the strike of 12, we gulped down our drinks and kissed our dates.

"Happy New Year's baby," Demarcus said as he squeezed me.

"Happy New Year's," I replied. As we were hugging, the intro to "I Just Want to Be Your Everything" by Andy Gibb began playing. Me, Brandon and my little brother John all looked at each other and sighed. I rolled my eyes.

"Ahhhh hell. Here we go," Brandon said.

"Why, what's up?" Demarcus asked.

"Nothing, this is my parent's favorite song and we had to listen to it almost every day, all day when we were kids." I replied. Demarcus shrugged his shoulders and smiled.

"It's a good song, come on let's dance," he said as he took me in his arms and began serenading me.

"You know this song?" I asked, amazed.

"You'd be surprised at the things I know Ms. Black," he said and twirled me around. I squealed and smiled from ear to ear. As we danced, I looked around at my family. My parents danced slowly and looked into each other's eyes. My dad had his hands on my mom's butt and she had her arms wrapped tightly around his neck. Brandon danced with his Chicken Head cautiously as if he was afraid she'd fall in love if he danced with her otherwise, and my little brother John danced with his Chicken Head as if she was a stripper. I was delightfully entertained and started laughing until my eyes met the eyes of the "Grinch That Stole Christmas" aka Olivia, who was looking at me with the stomach virus face. I looked away from her and held Demarcus tighter.

At the end of the party we half walked, half staggered out. We were all pretty messed up, but Demarcus and the Chicken Heads were in pretty good shape so they were "designated" as the designated drivers.

"Baby, let's stay at my house tonight. My bed misses you." Demarcus said and kissed the top of my head.

"Ok," I replied.

"And we can stop at that gas station across the street from the hospital cause I need to get some blunts."

"Ok baby. Let's get it," I said as we headed to the car.

Dressed In All Black

I watched as the white whore bitch and that black ass "captain save a hoe" walked out of the store. I rubbed my hands together. *Payback is a bitch.* I thought to myself as I popped two pills and pulled out behind them. I owed that whore for what she tried to do to me. My family was ruined and my pride was ruined; therefore, I had nothing more to lose, so I planned to ruin her. Tonight just happened to be my lucky night.

I followed them until we reached Vashnite. Then I sat in the car and waited. I laughed and cocked my gun as I watched them sitting in the car kissing...and giggling and smiling and shit. They had no clue what was coming...me.

Carolyn Black

Demarcus pulled into his apartment complex and parked the car. I looked down at my sparkly new friend, Dia the diamond, and smiled so widely that my jaws began to ache. Demarcus leaned in and we kissed and kept kissing. It was as if our lips were magnets and no matter how hard we tried to pull them apart we just couldn't. My body was on fire. And although me and Demarcus had had sex three times already, I just couldn't get enough of him; especially since this was our first time bringing in the New Year together as a couple. Hell, we'd almost had sex at the party but luckily, we'd been able to restrain ourselves. Just thinking about him and the fact that I was going to be his wife, something I thought would never happen to me, made me climb onto his lap and pull him tighter into me. He was mine, all mine. I didn't have to share him anymore and we no longer had to hide our love.

My kisses deepened as he slid his hand down my back and up my skirt. He squeezed my butt cheek and then took his fingers and trickled them down the crevice of my butt. My Juicy swelled and became sticky wet. This dude then took his pointer finger and started playing with my butthole. It felt good at first until I remembered that I'd taken a dump before we left the party. I'd washed up the best I could but not well enough for his finger to toss my salad. I jerked back clumsily which caused me to fall back and hit my head on the passenger side window.

"What the hell?" He asked laughing, confused.

"Nothing. It just felt funny that's all," I replied coolly. He snorted.

"Yeah right. I know your stankin' ass tore the bathroom up before we left the party. Probably didn't wipe your ass good did you?" he said as he laughed. I shot him a bird.

"Wait, hold on. Let me smell my finger." He put his finger up to his nose and gagged. "Oh God!" he over exaggerated. He then took his finger and shoved it towards my nose. I smacked his arm away and then we began wrestling as he tried his hardest to stick his finger up my nose.

"Demarcus stop! I'm not playing with you!" I screamed playfully as I held his arms in an effort to keep him from touching me.

"What you gonna do? You can't beat me and you're weaker than me."

"That may be true but you're still the one who got shitted on!" I laughed. He took my arms and pressed them down. He leaned down and pecked me lightly on my lips.

"God, I can't wait to marry you Cee."

"Demarcus don't try to distract me so you can rub that poop on me," I joked, although I was mentally floating on a cloud. My phone began ringing.

"What the hell? Who is calling me this late at night?" I asked out loud, as I glanced at the clock, which read 3:00 a.m. Demarcus sat up and I reached down to retrieve my phone, which had fallen on the floor. As I was leaning down I caught a quick glance of the name on the screen and it looked like it said "God." I blinked in bewilderment because I knew I was high and had to be tripping. My hand gripped the phone then I heard a loud BOOM! Glass shattered and the sound and look of what appeared to be red fireworks, blasted through the air. I rolled down onto the floorboard and covered my head.

Once everything was silent, I remained in my position because I was too afraid to move. My entire body was shaking, I was wet with sweat and my high was gone.

"Demarcus," I whispered as quietly as I could.

He didn't answer. I began to panic. My heart began to pound.

"Demarcus," I whispered a little louder and with a hint of desperation.

He still didn't answer me. I waited a few more seconds just to make sure that it was safe for me to move and then I cautiously moved my arms off my head. The light from the full moon shined brightly into the car. I raised up and slowly; reluctantly, began to turn around. When my chin reached my shoulder, my eyes met Demarcus' eyes. They were wide open, looking right at me. Blood was everywhere and half of the top of his head was missing, but he was smiling. Looking straight at me and smiling...

Stay tuned for Social Work: The Carolyn Black Chronicles III Redemption

About the Author

Laronya Teague is the self-published author of Social Work: The Carolyn Black Chronicles. She is a graduate of Winston-Salem State University and NC A&T State University. Social Work: The Carolyn Black Chronicles II is her second book. Ms. Teague also writes screenplays and short stories. She currently works as a Licensed Professional Counselor (LPC), doing group therapy with children and teens residing in residential treatment facilities.

www.ingramcontent.com/pod-product-compliance
Lightning Source LLC
Chambersburg PA
CBHW021459240626
47154CB00002B/442